BOURBON
on the
ROCKS

BOURBON
on the
ROCKS

A. C. Land

Land, A. C.
Bourbon on the Rocks
ISBN: 978-0-9975083-0-7 (print)
ISBN: 978-0-9975083-1-4 (e-book)

Cover Images: © BGI Photography and Scott Crawford
Cover Design: Anita B. Caroll www.race-point.com
Interior Design: Ellie Sipila www.movetothewrite.com

Printed in the United States of America

This book's dedication is divided in two:

In loving memory of Bill "BJ" Conner. Addiction is something I wake up and think about every day because you're no longer here to fight with it.

And to Jeff McGowan—for putting the fear of God into any boy who asked me on a date.

This one is for you, Dads.

BARRY

Her skin tasted like raw sugar. With one hand, I gripped her hip. The fingers of my free hand splayed across the hood of my classic Charger.

My mind was fuzzy. I couldn't remember how much whiskey I'd drunk or if I'd finished off that joint. I knew I'd popped three Percocet, but at this point, I wasn't sure where the tingling buzz was coming from—her or the pills?

She giggled again, and my fingernails dug into the flesh of her side as I pulled her body backward into mine.

Jesus. She was *ah-fucking-mazing*.

"Barry…" She moaned, the sound making every nerve ending in my body fire at once. My head swam in pure ecstasy. I had never felt anything as good as this high, or this girl, or this night.

She froze, her neck speckled with chills like she was cold or scared. I could assist with either problem. My arms snaked around her middle, and I blew warm air across her flesh.

The sound of a deep male voice clearing his throat made blood rush north toward my big boy brain. Forcing my clenched eyes to open, I faced the man in the tan uniform, a golden star affixed to his chest.

The sheriff fisted my discarded bottle of bourbon in one hand. Her fallen pink thong dangled from his other pinky.

She exhaled. "Hi, Daddy."

ONE

BRITTNEY ANN

My brother, Toby, had nicknamed the Plymouth "The Sheep." I never understood why. The car idled at maximum volume with a steady knock under the hood. It had Duct Taped leather seats, which of course, multicolored stuffing stabbed through. The once-white vehicle now had rust spots speckling the bottom of the driver's side door and the hood.

But since Toby was a Marine now, the car was all mine. I didn't care what her name was. When she ran, she transported me away from the farm, where my hair was always tied up and my posture straight.

It was on that farm that I'd spent the first sixteen years of my life, never leaving unless Mom or Daddy or Toby wanted to go. Then one day, I was handed The Sheep's keys. That was the day I first tasted freedom.

Now I was addicted to it.

My hair blew out the open driver's side window as I took a gravel curve a little too close to the edge. The back wheels spun, and the car fishtailed into a skid that I pulled out of with a jerk of the wheel. In another thousand feet, I'd be past the white fence that Toby and Daddy had spent a summer putting up just a year before Toby had left for good.

Pushing my bare toes onto the accelerator, I hit the floor. The Sheep grunted in protest. This car had never been pushed to her full potential. I was reminded why as a violent tremble and that knocking under the hood made my stomach twist into knots.

Tucking my long hair behind my back, I lifted my foot off the accelerator. Good thing, too. Not a second later, Mr. Warman's orange tractor came into sight, and I had to slow down even more.

I cringed, imagining what Mr. Warman would have said to Daddy about me driving like a maniac. Going only a fraction over the speed limit, I made it to the hospital in near-record time.

Lapping twice around the lot, I noticed Ryan's Daddy's pickup parked in the back row, and my heart jolted in excitement.

When Mom had come in to the hospital a few months ago to have her cochlear implants checked out, she'd seen a sign looking for young volunteers for a new summer program. *Yeah, manual, free labor from underqualified, underage kids.*

I popped my neck to the side, working my fingers around the tense spots to loosen up.

If I had to do this, then it was a good thing Ryan was here with me. The thought of his name—just his name—made my tummy tickle with cliché butterflies. I pulled up beside the pickup and let The Sheep idle. Ryan wasn't sitting on the bench seat waiting for me, which made the butterflies all sigh in sadness before curling back into their cocoons. Gathering my over the shoulder purse, I manually locked the doors before heading toward the hospital entrance.

The smell of new carpet and disinfectant made my nose scrunch. Inhaling deeply, I let the scent mutilate my senses. *Better get used to it, sister. You're in for a long summer.*

The woman behind the front desk wore dark purple scrubs. She smiled up and me, and then her focus shifted to the sliding door behind my back. "What the…?" planting her palms flat on the desk for leverage, she leaned forward to get a good look.

It was while I stood there waiting for a Volunteer badge that they burst through the front door like a tornado. There were seven in total. Four of the guys had the fifth one stretched out between them. It looked like he was dead weight in their arms.

Palm cupping over my heart, I sucked in a pained breath. *Not him.*

I could taste my heartbeat on my tongue as I watched blood pour from his arm and puddle on the linoleum. His friends struggled to keep his head supported.

Oh no. This looked bad.

Just when I assumed the worst, Barry opened his mouth and growled out, "I can walk, you fucking idiots."

"Shut up, jackass. We're done letting you make decisions." Bo's palm pressed against the invalid's head, shoving him backward, away from the blood.

Tyler chuckled.

"This is so stupid," Barry groaned, head lolling from side-to-side as the others fought to keep his weight suspended. "All I need is a Band Aid and a couple beers."

Or some Duct Tape, I thought, and then bit into my lip to keep from smiling. The fact he was okay and looking…*amused* shouldn't have relieved me. I shouldn't have cared. I really shouldn't have.

"Beer?" Tyler groaned as he adjusted his stance to support Barry's weight. "Dude, your fat ass is going on a diet. It's tequila or nothing."

Barry smiled. "Fine. I'll take the tequila."

"Really twisted his arm there, didn't ya, Ty?" Gage fought to keep one of Barry's legs from falling.

The two girls who'd come in with them walked over to the counter where I stood. "He jumped off a cliff," Charli said.

A cliff! *Is he suicidal?* My heart raced at the thought. *No.* Not him. Please not him.

"Don't say it like that," Gage snapped. "You make him look crazy."

My thoughts exactly, though I wasn't sure I liked sharing thoughts with Gage Adams.

Charli blew her bangs off her forehead. "Lonna? You talk to them."

Lonna Stuart pushed up to the counter, put her slim hand on my shoulder, holding me in place, and she whispered to the woman on the other side. "We were at the river and the big idiot with the hole in his shoulder jumped off a high cliff. He probably wouldn't have resurfaced if the *other* idiots hadn't dove in after him. So whatever you do, make sure it hurts, and he learns his lesson."

The woman behind the counter smiled. I did not.

Barry was…sure, a little reckless, but that didn't mean he deserved to be in pain any more than anyone else.

"Brittney?" Charli finally saw me, and she beamed. "What're you doing here? Cute dress."

They always said that. I didn't know whether to believe them anymore. "Thank you, my…uh, I like it." Admitting that my mother had picked out the gingham lemon yellow knee-length dress wouldn't look good. Not after all these times. "So what happened?"

Both girls rolled their eyes. I wondered if they knew they did that. Typical best friend stuff—finishing sentences, picking food based on what the other one was hungry for, popping their hip to the same side and putting their hand against it. Like right now.

Lonna grumbled, "The moron jumped. We all screamed and yelled that it was too high, but *nooo.*"

Gasping like she'd just had an idea, Charli gripped Lonna's forearm. "You don't think it's because of what happened with you two, do you?"

"What? No, no way. We hooked up…what? Like, *weeks* ago. Gage is…not over it, but Barry doesn't care about that kind of stuff. It was just sex. Neither of us—"

"Yeah, but your dad really laid into him."

Lonna snorted. "My dad is harmless. Plus, Bare gets into trouble all the time. Hence, why we're here."

"I know, but Lonna—"

"Char, don't worry about him. He's a grown man-child-boy. He'll be fine."

Something ached inside my chest. They were friends with Barry. Best friends, as far as I knew. Lonna never would have dismissed an injury to Charli the way she was dismissing Barry.

"You guys think he'll be okay, right?" I asked.

Both of them nodded. Lonna assuredly—Charli, not so much. Then Lonna patted my arm, complimented my loafers—which were very comfortable—and the two of them left.

I was directed to Human Resources to watch a video on protocol and hospital etiquette.

Ryan was already sitting in a metal folding chair, waiting for me. He lifted his hand in a meek wave of greeting, and then he smiled. He'd gotten white rubber bands put in, so now it was almost hard to tell he even had braces. As we watched the video about different scenarios we were expressly forbidden from engaging in as volunteers, a different video played through my mind.

He grabs my hand, pulling my fingers toward his leg. Squeezing my fingers, he wraps my hand around his thigh, encouraging me to touch him. He whispers something funny-yet-dirty into my ear.

My arms exploded in chills.

We were alone in this room, though that had nothing to do with my overactive imagination. We really were alone.

I couldn't think of something that Ryan might say as he whispered because my mind didn't work that way. I wasn't witty or dirty.

But the thought of him being spontaneous and touching me in any way was a joke. Ryan equaled "safe," and he definitely didn't reach through the distance between us.

That probably wasn't a bad thing. There was something to be said for good guys. Daddy would appreciate the fact that Ryan knew how to keep his hands to himself, even if I found the monotonous pace of this relationship painfully boring.

I leaned back in my metal folding chair and crossed my arms. I was tired of them dangling to the side, waiting for him to get the hint. When the movie was over, we were instructed to find our way back to the front lobby.

"Sorry," I mumbled as my free-swinging arm—*hint-hint* Ryan—brushed against his.

"No problem." He pulled away. We stood in opposite corners inside the elevator. I wondered if he could hear my heart the way I could. Probably not, because he stared at the ceiling whistling what sounded like Frank Sinatra.

Four boys crowded the front lobby. They stood around pulling on T-shirts and smacking each other with towels. "But you do think his mom's coming, right?" Tyler struggled to slide his foot into the leg hole of his suspiciously narrowed pant legs. I hoped he wasn't trying to bring back super-skinny skinny jeans on men.

Knowing Tyler's unfailing persistence, he'd get it done.

"Dude, enough," Gage groaned, shaking his blond curls out of his eyes. "You don't even think she's that hot."

Tyler's head snapped up. His jaw dropped. "Are you shitting me? She's *numero uno* on my mommy-to-do list."

Chase stared at him, tilting his head to the side. "You have a list?"

"Yeah, unlike you, you fat homo, I like moms. I think they're hot. There's something sexy about breasts being used for sustenance."

He cupped his hands in front of his chest and jiggled them like he was actually holding onto something.

I felt pretty sure he was joking. The fact the guys didn't dignify him with a response just confirmed it. Tyler was…Tyler. There was no other way to describe him.

"We're here for assignments," Ryan mumbled to the woman behind the desk. The tops of his ears, his forehead, and his cheeks were a splotchy red color. I wanted to ask him if he was sick, but his eyes kept darting toward the guys across the way.

"They're mostly harmless." I tried to comfort my boyfriend. My teeth nipped into my tongue. I had no reason to defend *them*. And usually, I had no desire to defend those guys either.

"You *know* them?" he gasped…well, as much as one can gasp with rubber bands holding back their overbite.

"They go to my school." *My?* The school belonged to them way more than me. Seniors. Football royalty. Boy wonders. "Bourbon," I corrected. "They go to Bourbon with me."

I might have misinterpreted the meaning when Ryan glanced at Bo and then down at his own arm. Twice more he took Bo in and then shook his head at his own slightly sunken chest. I didn't know what to say to make him feel better. Bo was weird. The guy had muscles in places no person should have muscles. He was ripped in the chest and large across the shoulders—bigger than all the others.

But, admitting objectively, Ryan was smaller than Tyler. The slimmest, leanest of the bunch. And he didn't even have Tyler's sleek blond hair. "They're jerks," I said under my breath.

As far as I could tell they hadn't noticed me, and I wanted to keep it that way. Being a cheerleader, I got my fair share of hazing from football players. That didn't mean I welcomed the attention.

"Yeah, they look like it," Ryan agreed. "Meatheads."

I nodded. Another urge to defend them bubbled to my throat, but I swallowed it down.

TWO

BARRY

B arry! Get down!"
My heart was inside my ears. I could barely hear my friends yelling. "You're going to kill yourself, dude! No one jumps from up there."

Boom.

Boom.

Boom.

My fingernails scrapped into the rocks as I climbed just a little bit higher. "Don't be an idiot. You're gonna fall." That was the plan. The toe of my shoe slipped, and my heart dropped as I thought, *I could die from this height.* Every nerve ending inside my body fired at the same time. This was the kind of high I usually had to purchase.

I liked getting up to get down.

I kicked off the rock and back flipped through the air.

Boom.

Boom.

Boom.

Adrenaline was one of the best fucking drugs in the world. I didn't even feel it when my shoulder clipped the edge of the cliff. "Barry!" one of the girls yelled.

"Fuck!" one of my friends added. Then I splashed face first into the water. My cheek connected with a boulder. I could taste blood as my teeth tore into my lips.

But God, I felt nothing. I felt no pain. Nothing but sheer adrenaline. Then the lights went out.

∾

There was a steady beeping sound.

I was at the hospital. I'd landed myself here a few times before so I knew what it sounded like. I vaguely remembered being dragged out of the river and something about lying across Charli's lap in the backseat of Bo's car. There was something else. It was hazier. Just a picture: Hair. Strawberry blonde hair. With the image came the smell of strawberries, but I was pretty sure it was only because I *thought* that hair should smell that way.

"Am I alive?" I mumbled. It came out, "mlive?"

No one understood.

I could hear them, though, so I knew they hadn't left me. My best friends; my non-blood brothers. Bo said, "Dude, you were supposed to keep an eye on him. You know how he gets."

Tyler snorted. "Did he die?"

"That's always your defense," Gage laughed.

Bo huffed, and I could imagine him scrubbing over his face with his palms, or maybe tearing through his hair with his fingers. He was a worrier. "You're gonna let the idiot kill himself."

"Mlive," I mumbled again.

A hand smacked over my forehead, keeping me flat against the bed. Bo. Had to be. "Shut up, moron. There's a gauze wrap around your face, and we can't understand you. Ty, go get that hot nurse. Tell her he's awake."

Tyler groaned. "Why do I have to? I'm hanging out here for Bare's mom to show up. Make Gage go."

I smiled.

Bo's fingers twitched against my head. "Because you're the fuck-tard that let him climb up there. There's a reason we watch him. He's too stupid to take care of himself."

Ouch. Thanks *brother.*

There was a squeaking sound as a cart was rolled into the room. I opened my eyes just enough to see the tall, slim angel walk through the door. Light beams burst from the ends of her strawberry blonde hair. *Whoa.* A halo glowed around her head. *Holy shit.* She had wings made of pure, unending white light. The wings rose out of her bony shoulders and spread toward the fluorescent bulbs.

I blinked a couple times. Swatting Bo's hand off my face, I leaned up to get a really good look at the beautiful creature who'd come to take me home.

Everything came into sharp focus as a sterile smell stung my nostrils. *I'm. An. Idiot.*

The halo and light beams all dissipated as my vision adjusted. Falling back against the bed, I exhaled my disappointment.

Not-an-angel stood in the doorway. Her mouth hung slack as she stared at my shoulder. Brittney Ann Wilson. The preacher's daughter.

"Goodness, are you alright?"

Goodness. Gage tried to cover his laugh with a cough.

"Fine."

She refilled my water and then fluffed at the blankets at my feet. "Is there anything I can get you, Barry? A warm blanket? Anything?"

The faint smell of strawberries hit my nose as I reached up and caught a piece of her hair between my thumb and forefinger. A part of me was very aware of Tyler and Bo struggling to keep their shit together. Gage and Chase didn't even try. They were laughing to the point of burying their faces in their hands—not to hide their laughter, obviously, but to keep anyone from seeing how red they were turning.

Overly helpful Brittney Ann with her strawberry smelling strawberry hair. Why in the hell would I think about her hair when I was unconscious? Her hazel eyes found me. She was hesitant at first, and then her expression pleaded with me. I wanted to know what she wanted, but at the same time I wanted not to care.

Bo cleared his throat, breaking the trance she'd put me under. "Can I get a warm blanket?" He teased her with a wink.

"Bo!" I hissed. My head fell painfully back against the bed. There was a steady throbbing below my left temple. I barely noticed the way Brittney looked between all of us, her lower lip flapping, as if she were waiting for the punchline to some joke.

Tyler, for once, kept his trap shut. It surprised me, and he rarely did anything to surprise me anymore. Tyler and I had been raising hell together since kindergarten Sunday school.

I got it, though. We'd gotten our asses chewed out the last time we fucked with Brittney because the brat told on us. So I wasn't aching to go through that. Like, my mom probably wouldn't speak to me if I messed with her. *Again.*

"If you'd like," she shot Bo a sugar-sweet smile before she backed the squeaking cart out of the room.

I sighed. "My mom will be pissed if you guys harass her. She looks like a tattletale bitch who'll run to her daddy with anything you say." She more than *looked* it.

They all burst out laughing. Not enough pain killers in the hospital could help me tolerate their good moods right now. Not that I wasn't willing to try a few more opioids, or opiates or, hell, even barbitals.

I tried to find something to throw at them, to make them stop chuckling. My fingers closed around the water she'd just filled. I launched it at Bo and Gage. The water cup smacked into the brick wall behind them with a loud *splat*. My aim had been off since I'd thrown left handed, and I was a righty. The cup was supposed to nail Gage in the temple. Damn.

"Dude!" Gage wiped at the shoulder of his Lacoste Polo. "This is new."

"It looks like all your other ones," Tyler said. Clapping his hands and rubbing them together, his eyebrows wiggled. "I'm more interested to hear about Barry's mom. When she's pissed, do you get spanked? If so, can we trade places?"

I wished I had something to throw at him.

"Aw, don't be a crybaby, Bare." Bo tried to rub my arm and didn't even notice when I flinched. That arm was still bleeding. It wasn't like I was a wuss or nothing. I wasn't.

Bo continued, still oblivious to my agony. "Ty can't help it his mom's a fatass."

"She's not fat!"

"She's fat," Gage agreed.

"At least she doesn't look like a horse." Tyler neighed at Gage.

"My mom's not a horse."

"I said she *looked* like a horse. But now that you mention it—"

"Fuck you, bro." Gage punched Tyler's arm.

Rubbing my forefingers against my throbbing temples, I swallowed the lump in my throat. "Guys, seriously, my head is spinning. Can we play this game of witty bullshit banter later?"

"Yeah sure, dude." Tyler hit my arm playfully. I heard the concern in his voice, but he had to add, "I still wanna tap your mom, though."

I swatted, trying to hit him but closing my fist around air instead.

Brittney Ann returned with a warm blanket for Bo. Fluffing it into the air she held it out to him. "Or would you like me to wrap it around you?" she asked, blinking innocently.

Bo glanced at each of us, his jaw loose. "Uh, no, this is great."

"Good." Then she dropped the blanket on the ground, grinding it beneath her flats. Whipping her hair behind her like a long strawberry lasso, she stomped toward the door. "These walls are thin, just so you know. And I'm not a *bitch*, or a tattletale. I'd appreciate if you watched your mouths. My boyfriend was just in the other room, and the nurse in there heard you as well."

My jaw dropped.

"Dude," Tyler whispered. "Did Brittney Ann Wilson just say 'bitch'?"

Bo cracked first, a deep chuckle echoing off the thin walls. "Oh God, I know you're hurt, Bare, but this is probably the highlight of my summer. We just got that uppity Christian to cuss us out."

"She didn't cuss us out," Chase corrected. He leaned back against the wall with his arms folded. He really didn't like hospitals. I'd almost forgotten he was here. Of all of my friends, I'd have cared the least if *he* wasn't here.

"She wasn't very censored though. It kinda made me hot." Ty palmed and adjusted his crotch because...well, Tyler. "You guys get a look at that cheesedick she called her boyfriend?" He couldn't contain his laughter. As much as I wanted to hear about Brittney's piss-poor taste in dudes, I couldn't make myself give a shit. Oh, wait, I never would have cared about that—injured or not.

"He had a whitehead on his neck." Gage cringed.

"A big one." Ty snorted a laugh into his fisted palm. "That chick doesn't even get how hot she is. If she'd just ask nicely, I'd do her the honors of letting her bounce on my—"

Bo slapped his shoulder. "Honors?"

"Right, yeah, well it would be an *honor*, but she doesn't have to ask all that nicely. What'd'ya think, princess?" Tyler arched his brows at me.

"I really don't give a shit."

"Oh, come on. You know she's banging. You were all about getting with that before big bro beat you down."

I recoiled. This time not because of the pain in my head and arm. Tyler's memory was lacking. Toby had kicked my ass, yes. Twice, actually. But only the second time had it been partially because of her.

Little did she know, I might have actually been serious when I'd asked her out if Toby hadn't broken my nose several weeks before. Brittney had been in the wrong place when I was looking for revenge.

Rubbing my palms in circles over my eyes I tried to scrub away the memory of Toby Wilson's fist flying at my face. When I glanced up at Tyler, he was smiling down at me. Of-fucking-course he was. "Can you, like, not talk for five seconds?"

He shook his head, held up his fingers, and counted off four of them. "Okay, so I'm starving. I could literally eat a skunk's asshole I'm so hungry."

That was it. He said it, and my stomach twisted into angry knots. The ball of vomit hit the back of my throat, and I barely got my fingers around the pink plastic pan fast enough. "Fucker," I snapped a second before I hurled into the basin.

They were all laughing. God, *why are they laughing?* My friends were such dicks. Dammit, I loved them.

In addition to a minor concussion, I needed stitches on my shoulder, and my lip would be fat for a few days. I licked my swollen, strange-feeling mouth. Yeah, I'd probably bite the shit out of that. The doctor gave me a handful of painkillers, which almost made getting stuck with an IV needle worth the trip.

Thankfully, I didn't have to get any other shots, because I was up to date on tetanus and all the good ones. So I was on cloud nine when the doctor said I was good to go.

The guys all waited outside while I slid back into trunks and my Van Morrison T-shirt. It was vintage and one of my favorites. The guys must have known since they'd grabbed it off the riverbank before dragging me into the hospital.

My fingers fumbled over the cotton as I tried to imagine which friend had stopped to pick up my shirt. Tyler, maybe. Except Tyler tended to lose his shit when I was hurt. I could see him pacing back and forth not knowing what the hell to do.

Gage and Chase wouldn't care about my clothes. They'd have left it for sure.

Which left Bo. Of course it was Bo. He was our biggest brother. He kept his head when shit went south. I made a mental note to thank him when no one else was around.

Finding the four of them in the hall outside my room, I noticed what was missing in our posse. "Where're the girls?"

Gage scowled down at his toe as he kicked a scuff off the linoleum. "Lonna took Charli home. Not that it's any of your damn business."

Ouch.

Someone was not letting it go.

I stared at his corkscrew blond hair, waiting for him to say something, or, I don't know, maybe throw another cheap shot at me. "It's been weeks, man. You guys all beat the shit out of me—"

His head snapped up. "You fucked my girl."

I threw my arms out, wincing at the pain that tore through my shoulder. Tyler caught my hands pulling them down. "Dude," he hissed. "Stop overreacting."

"He can't let it go?"

Tyler's eyes widened as he emphasized, "You *did* screw Lonna."

"Weeks ago, and you guys kicked my ass, *and* she's *not* his girlfriend."

"But she's *mine*." Gage pointed sharply at himself, stabbing one of his fingers into his torso. "She's always been *mine*."

"Noted. Not your girlfriend, but *yours*. Whatever the fuck that means."

"Bare…" Bo shook his head. "You know she's off limits."

I threw my hands up again and instantly regretted it. "Ow, dammit, whatever. Dropping it. She's off-limits. She wasn't even that great, anyway." I scowled at the top of Gage's curls, not bothering meeting his gaze. If he wanted to hit me for saying that, I was almost buzzed enough to have that fight.

He shrugged. "I could have told you that." *Yeah, right.* One of the only reasons I'd gone through with it was because of how awesome he said she was. To Gage, the sun shined out of that girl's ass.

Lonna had this sexy, blonde Barbie Doll thing going for her, and I had always wanted a piece of her, even before she'd made it abundantly clear that she *wasn't* drunk and I *was* allowed to peel that pink, lace thong off her.

After a handful of nice words, she'd let me bend her over the hood of my car. It was a fast lay—nothing sweet or adventurous. She went from being the mysterious Lonna Marie Stuart to just Lonna—another girl who blurred in with all the others.

And now I was the dick who'd fucked-over my friend.

Oh, and her dad had busted us together.

I cringed, remembering the sound of her *daddy's* deep voice when he'd yelled at me that night. His fingers had occasionally twitched toward the gun holstered on his hip. My life kept flashing before my eyes. He'd arrested me for the alcohol. I got my first MIP—minor in possession of a fifth of bourbon and his drunk daughter—and almost got slammed with a DWI as an added *screw you.*

Thankfully, the man was so frazzled by the sight of his naked daughter that he didn't do a good job searching my car. Pretty sure having prescription drugs under the seat was worth more than a slap on the wrist.

When the prescription wasn't in my name.

Instead of seriously being in trouble, my dad got to pay a steep fine, and I would be spending the majority of my summer doing community service.

Talk about losing interest in a chick.

The doors to the waiting room opened and the guys walked in front of me like my own personal body guards. "Dude." Tyler nudged Bo in the arm. "There she is."

I hobbled to catch up. They'd already started into the lobby, where both my parents were standing. "Mom?" I pushed past everyone just to get a good look at her.

She glared at the tall blonde lingering beside Dad. "I still can't believe you brought her, Duncan."

"She's my girlfriend, and she's rightfully worried about our son." His arm wrapped around the girl's middle. Ashleigh annoyed me in every possible way. Starting with the obnoxious spelling of her should-be-simple name.

"I take it all back," Tyler said, his eyes raking over the skinny blonde.

My elbow slammed into his ribcage. "Don't."

"What?" he chuckled. "I'm backing off your mom. I'll take your step—"

I punched him in the shoulder, cutting off the crap about to fall out of his mouth. "She's not my *step*-anything." That bitch was not part of my family.

"Barry!" Ashleigh flew across the room and threw her arms around my neck. She smelled like Peachtree. *Is she even old enough to drink?* I figured she probably was, and if there was any alcohol perfect for this young bimbette, it was peach schnapps.

"Get'er off me!"

"Oh, Barry, we were so worried."

I planted both hands on her slim hips and tried to force her backward without her tearing my neck off. "Don't touch me," I growled. Then, because I knew Dad would be pissed about the way I'd spoken to his precious young piece of ass, I bit out, "I'm hurt."

"Oh, oh, Barry, I'm so sorry." Her fingers steepled around her mouth, and tears filled her eyes.

Glaring at her, Mom caught my good shoulder and pulled me away. "Come here, son."

Willingly, I stepped around several of the chairs so we were out of earshot of the others. Tyler, of course, lingered nearby. "Go away," I growled, slapping at the air. He took several side-steps, only just far enough away that he couldn't listen, but still close enough that if I passed out, he'd catch me.

I smiled at the back of my friend's head.

"You okay?" Mom whispered.

Her breath was sweet. Not like any alcohol I recognized, something richer. That was Mom, though; she had class. I caught her cheeks in my hands, pulling her forehead to rest against mine. She must have been at dinner with a glass of sweet red wine when they'd called about me. I imagined her sitting there all alone and a pang of sadness stabbed into my chest.

"I'm fine."

She had a throaty laugh. "Oh, my sweet baby boy."

"I want to go with you," I whispered.

"Not tonight," she answered. Her eyes cut back toward Dad, and her expression deadpanned.

"Want me to say something to him?"

"No, sweetheart," she said, laying her hand against my cheek and taking a step backward. She blinked at me a few times, all emotion leaving her face. My fists clenched reflexively. For some reason, when my parents were in the same room, I had the strangest urge to beat the ever loving shit out of my dad. Mom pleaded, "You're hurt. Go home and get some sleep. I'll see you in a couple weeks."

Weeks?

She must have gotten from my expression how much that bugged me. "They're going on vacation, right? Middle of June?"

"No, they leave *next* week, Mom." I took a step toward her, and she took another one back. "I'm…I could come stay with you."

Once again, she glanced back at Dad and scowled. "We'll talk about it later. Don't want to upset anyone."

What about me? Didn't she want to keep *me* from being upset? I fucking hated living with *him* and that whore.

After Mom let go, Dad clapped hard on my uninjured shoulder. "Second time in two months, Barry. My insurance doesn't like this behavior." *That's* what he had to say to me?

Staring down at my fists, I somehow convinced myself not to hit the man.

THREE

BRITTNEY ANN

H e hasn't even kissed you yet?"

"Shhh!" I hissed at Katy through the phone.

"Oh, get over it. Is your daddy even around?"

I checked the kitchen and, just to be safe, the laundry room. "No, alright. He's gone. That doesn't mean you can ask questions like that, Katy. We're taking things slow. Toby wanted to talk with him over Skype before we got too serious."

"Skype? Oh no, you are not letting your brother *Skype* with your boyfriend. Toby, the baddest ass Marine to ever grace this town with his *fine* butt, will destroy him."

"Katy…"

"I'm serious, Britt. Tell Ryan to run."

"That would be cowardly. I figure, if they become friendly now then maybe they can hang out, maybe play football together, when Toby comes home in November."

A hollow pain ate a hole in my chest as I thought about my only brother not coming home until November. It was June now with muggy Missouri weather in full swing. The morning dew would freeze before I saw my brother's face without the aid of an iPad screen.

Katy was quiet on the other end.

"What?" I finally asked.

"Football?" she sounded amused. "You honestly think Ryan *Freeman* can stand up on the football field beside *Toby* Wilson? Come on, Britt."

"They can be on the same team," I defended. "Toby could teach him some things. I don't know. They don't have to play football. Ryan likes those online video games. Maybe he could get Toby into them."

The kitchen timer went off, and I hurried over to the stove to flip on the light and check inside the oven. The ham was a crisp golden brown, and the pineapples still looked juicy. "I need to get off here. The ham's done."

"Tell me again what you're baking for?"

My eyes rolled.

Oh, eye rolling. *Normal. Teenage. Girl. Stuff.* I wanted to pat myself on the back, but there were already too many priorities lining up. I rushed, "A couple wants to get married at the church. It's tradition. Daddy always invites them over for dinner."

"You don't know them?"

"Katy, I really have to—"

"You could just answer. It's always easier than fighting."

I huffed. She was right. "I'm not sure. I didn't ask Daddy who they were."

"So you're baking a ham for people you don't know?"

"I'm sorry..." I pulled the phone away from my ear and made horrible impressions of crackling sounds. "You're breaking up." *End call.*

But not before she said, "That gets real old, Britt. You're lucky we're still friends."

I knew this. I tried to never look gift friendships in the mouth. Because of the massive amount of guilt brought on by her words, I sent her a text after pulling the ham from the oven. I tried to be very cool and take a picture of my culinary creation. If I were any cooler, I'd have sent the picture with the pound sign. But I'd never fully understood why people did that.

It was burning. Thinking about you. Sorry I hung up.

I waited, wondering if she thought I was as crazy as most everyone else did.

It's fine, Brittney.

Setting out the pasta salad I'd made earlier and the cream corn and mashed potatoes, I did a proud inventory of the kitchen. I popped the rolls into the oven as I ran upstairs to change. "Dinner's almost done," I said, peeking my head inside Daddy's study at the bottom of the steps.

He checked his watch with a slight scowl on his large face. "Thanks darling. If I know Duncan, he'll be twenty minutes late."

"Daddy…" I started to reprimand him. What he held in negativity, Mom always brought out with positive light. When she wasn't around it was my job.

Then it hit me.

That name had caught me off guard, nearly causing me to stumble backward. "Duncan?" I gasped. "Prescott? You're not talking about…oh, *crap*."

"Brittney Ann."

"Sorry Daddy."

"No, now, that's not alright language. I raised you better than that. What's this all about? Barry? You still upset after all that happened with him all those years ago?"

The short answer was *yes*. Not wanting to look like a bitter shrew, I shrugged, trying to appear like I was mature enough to have maintained an objective opinion of Barry *freaking* Prescott.

Daddy stared at me. His eyes had the ability to see straight through a person and read them. My cheeks burned, and I scowled down at my foot as my loafer squished back and forth against the carpet.

It used to freak Toby out the way Daddy knew things just by looking at us, but I'd learned just to avoid eye-contact.

He cleared his throat, and I had to glance up, meeting his gaze. His expression was blank. "Don't be too upset with your old dad. I assume Barry isn't coming. He can't make it into church, so there's a good chance he won't find time to come over here on a Friday night."

That was a valid point. Disappointment pulsed inside my chest, and I was angry with myself for this reaction.

"Brittney?"

"Hmm?"

"I don't want you to worry about him, alright? Even if he is here, it don't got nothing to do with you. I wouldn't let him near you with a ten-foot pole."

"Of course, daddy."

As I walked away, I wasn't quite sure I heard his mumbled words right, but it sounded as if he said, "Unless he wants a couple broken bones. Little shit."

I was smiling as I changed into…into…I stood in front of my pastel closet. This was just ridiculous. Didn't I have anything that stood out? Anything that was…daring, or bold, or…just, different?

My phone went off, and my heart raced in response to the familiar tone—Ryan. After doing a small flip over the mattress to get to the nightstand, I sounded breathless when I answered. "Hello?"

"Hey Brittney Ann, it's Ryan."

I pulled the screen away from my face to glance at it. His name flashed across the front. "Yeah, I know. I have your number programmed in now."

"Oh right, yeah, I always feel the need to introduce myself."

"Oh, well, in that case, it's Brittney Ann." He was quiet. "I was kidding." *Is it too late to bury myself into a hole of embarrassment?* "You said your name—"

"No, no, I got it. Uh, listen, I'm thinking about catching a movie tonight; I was wondering if you wanted to meet me there—I know I can't pick you up at your house yet because I still haven't talked to your brother and honestly your dad scares the sin right out of me, but I'd still like to meet you there—what do you say?" He took a deep breath.

I let his long, run-on sentence sink in. A very girly part of me wanted to squeal with excitement. We'd never officially been on a date before. "Uh, I think that would be fine. I have dinner with my family"—dang, the rolls were probably burning—"and then I could meet you there. Around seven?" I rushed toward my closet and yanked on the strap of a pink dress. I'd worry about the date dress after dinner.

The doorbell rang, and my stomach dropped. Somehow, I just knew *he* was here. My body's reaction to his presence was unsettling. Sure, I'd been worried about him when he'd been injured, but that had been different. I obviously didn't want him dead or anything. But I also didn't want *him* inside my house.

"Yeah, seven sounds great. The show starts at seven-fifteen, so that's perfect."

"What is it?" I asked.

"Uh, *Love Lost*. It's a girly movie I, uh…I figured that'd be something you liked." He sounded really proud of himself for thinking of me.

I swallowed my disgust. "Oh, right. Okay."

Only it wasn't. *I should tell him.* I should just get the words out that I wasn't a big fan of predictable romantic movies—I always wanted to gouge my eyes out before the first half was over. *Love Lost* sounded like the title of the worst sort of eye-gouging misery.

"Is that okay?" Ryan spoke meekly.

I swallowed hard, hating how difficult this was for me. I wanted him to like me, but I didn't want him to think I was weird. Girls should *like* these sorts of movies.

"Great," I exaggerated. After all I hadn't seen it; maybe it would be okay. Maybe it would be the movie of all movies to turn my mind right around about gushy, modern day romance movies. Maybe tonight, Ryan would hold my hand. Maybe he'd kiss me.

A slow heat crept up my neck. "I'll see you there."

"Yup."

Neither of us hung up the phone. I bit into my smile. "Are you going to hang up?" I asked.

"Yeah, are you?"

"If you do—"

"Britt?" Mom called from the stairwell.

"Just a minute, I'm changing." To Ryan I said, "I'll see you there."

I wasn't sure if he was still on the phone when it disconnected. Rushing to pull on the pink dress, I only hesitated for a second to eye my reflection in the mirror. I looked a little frazzled. Excited, maybe. Tonight could be a very big deal as far as my relationship was concerned.

There was a small bag tucked in the back of my closet. If I stood on my tiptoes, I could still barely reach the shelf. Which was the reason the bag was back there. Mom was several inches shorter than me, and the contents were for my eyes only. I pulled it all down, trying not to think of the implications of my actions. The thin, red material slid from the plastic and over my fingers. Shame-coated excitement unfurled inside my gut. "Britt?" Mom called again, her voice closer this time.

My heart raced as I shimmied out of my cotton underwear and into the red, satin thong.

FOUR

BARRY

I dug into my underwear drawer for an old mint can. The blue color on the edges of the tin had faded over the years, but I didn't keep it around because it was pretty. "Functional" was the word I'd use to describe this puppy. Inside were ten pills and a small baggie—all that was left of my reg.

Knocking the tin against my palm, three oblong white pills slid out. I rolled them back and forth with my index finger, checking the writing on the back of each piece of candy before throwing them back, one-by-one, without water. Vicodin ten milligram with three-twenty-five of Tylenol. Anticipation for the oncoming buzz was almost more exciting than the buzz itself. *Aw, who am I kidding?* The high was the reason I got down.

Setting the needle on my record player to the sweet spot, my room was suddenly filled with The Eagles—"Hotel California." Swaying slightly to the mesmerizing sound of the music, I strummed my air guitar, and then I flopped backward onto my unmade bed and let the thrill of being young and wild and crazy fill my veins.

Twenty minutes later, I was stoned out of my mind. A slight tingling in every inch of my body alerted me that shit had just gotten real. If I'd been in pain, it would have been gone. The tip of my nose itched, and my toes were numb. Life was good.

There was a soft knock on my door. "What?" I snapped.

"Barry, we need to talk. It's important."

Everything was important to Duncan Prescott. Everything was serious and business and making good impressions. Rolling my eyes, I wiped a sheen of sweat from my forehead and scratched my nose one last time before sitting up and forcing myself not to look stoned.

Serious, Barry. Look Ser-e-us.

"Come in." The best part about pills was the lack of odor. Dad would have had to be onto me to pop a test on me. Or…I didn't know. He'd have had to give enough of a shit to go through my drawer looking for my stash.

Dad scowled at me. Was he suspicious?

Did I care?

"What's up?" I asked.

He continued with a sigh, his left hand cupping the back of his neck. "I talked to Mitch at St. Augustine. He seemed really hesitant about marrying…" He stepped into the room and closed the door behind him. Afraid of Ashleigh hearing, I assumed. "Look, Barry—you're young, so you don't know how the world works. I'm just going to tell you right now: the way to be happy is to keep your wife happy—"

I broke out laughing, but I stopped when I realized I was the only one doing so. "You didn't keep your first wife happy." They'd only been engaged a week, yet he was calling her his *wife*. I wanted to barf, and not because I was too stoned—I hadn't even taken that much.

He huffed. "There were plenty of problems with my first marriage, Barry. We've already discussed this many times. Ashleigh is a fresh start for me. I want to do right by her. That means having this wedding at St. Augustine. I need your help."

That was a first. "I'm listening." I leaned forward, and a rush of blood flew to my head. *Ah-may-zing.* I scratched my nose again—quite possibly the most annoying side effect in the world.

With narrowed eyes, he stared at my itchy septum. "Mitch has invited us all over for dinner with his wife. Apparently, it's a tradition. They want to meet Ashleigh; they want to know this marriage will work."

"Okay…" *What did I have to do again? Did he say it and I forgot already?*

"You need to come with us."

"No."

"Barry," he growled. "There is not a choice. You're coming with."

I was not going to *Mom's* church so Dad could kiss the pastor's ass and then marry that skank. "It's Friday night. I have plans." I didn't. Not yet, but I could call Madison for a quickie. She was always down for anything. Or I could see what Tyler was doing. Or, hell, I could watch *The Real Housewives*…of Hades. That'd be more fun than going to the pastor's house for *dinner.*

"Not anymore," he snapped, eyes narrowing. "You're coming." He stormed out, slamming the door behind him. *Real mature, Dad.*

I hopped up and grabbed my mint tin. Since this night was sure to suck, I decided to over-indulge. Shaking the container against my palm, two round white ones slid out. I flipped them over, reading the writing on the other side. Oxy fives with enough Tylenol to piss off my liver. I popped them one at a time without water. They kicked in so much faster than the first three. With any luck, they'd last as long as they were supposed to.

ೲ

On protest, I wore my favorite "Back in Black" AC/DC shirt underneath the light blue button down Ashleigh had picked out for me.

Ashleigh beamed. "Barry! Look how great you clean up."

Dad scowled at the letters that were clearly visible beneath the top shirt. I smirked at him, daring him to say anything to contradict his hot, young, mid-life crises.

Ashleigh *was* banging hot. If I didn't hate her mere existence, I'd probably try and screw her brains out. Hell, it took a lot for me to hate a girl too much to opt out of sex. Tyler said it would be good, still. Like to have hate-sex with the dumb blonde. I wasn't so sure I could do it. Not to my satisfaction. She'd probably start crying when I tied her to the bed and gagged her.

Whatever. I didn't really want to find out what she was like anyway.

Dad and Ashleigh talked about wedding plans as we drove out of town toward the Wilson family farm. I'd been an idiot not bringing my headphones. All I could do was lie my head against the back seat headrest and listen to them. Halfway there, I started beating my head against the rest. "Barry, if you don't knock it off, I'm pulling this car over."

"Promises, promises," I grumbled.

"He's just crabby because it's the weekend and he's having to have family time. I used to hate hanging out with my parents too, sweet-heart. It's part of being a teenager." She winked conspiratorially at me in the rearview mirror. The fact she thought we had anything in common only made me long more for that gag.

"Yeah, back when you lived with your parents, huh Ash? When was that? Two years ago?"

"Barry, I am not kidding. I will leave you here and make you walk home."

"Dude, Dad, don't threaten me with a good time."

He swore under his breath.

"Oh, Dunky, we should see if we can get married out here." She pinched his arm, drawing his attention to a farm with Christmas lights on the fence. Christmas lights? It was June.

He let out a slow breath. "I thought the whole reason we went with St. Augustine was because you loved the stained glass windows at the church."

She shrugged. "I do, but what's the point of a summer wedding if it's inside?"

I continued to beat my head against the rest. This time, Dad didn't complain. God, I did not want to be part of this wedding bullshit. For one, I hated the bride. For two, I hated everything.

Outside got darker as the already minimal city lights of Bourbon disappeared behind us. We took another gravel road with barbed wire fences and grazing cattle on every side.

The Wilsons were huggers. Pastor Mitch Wilson was a big, burly guy who liked to give giant bear hugs. He didn't discriminate on who he hugged. He looked like a lumberjack coming after me with a smile on his face. I cringed away from him, but he still wrapped both of his arms around me and squeezed. "Barry," his voice boomed. "How you been, Son?"

"Fine," I grumbled, jerking away from his massive frame. Jesus, he was huge.

Moira Wilson gave little dainty hugs. But it felt like she was putting effort into it. *Full* effort. Arms wide around the shoulders in a tight grip. "Barry," her voice was high pitched and echoed. "Goodness, Barry, it's been so long. How's everything going? How's your mother?" I was sure she'd meant to whisper that, but the woman was practically deaf, and she couldn't whisper.

"Fine." I nodded my head in case she hadn't heard me.

She hugged me again, like she hadn't gotten a tight enough hold the first time.

Ugh, huggers.

Glancing around, I was pleased to see that Toby and his girlfriend, Gwen, weren't here. Their presence might have turned this shit-show into a nightmare. *Might?* No, definitely. Things *definitely* would have been a nightmare.

It was bad enough I would have to endure countless hours of Brittney Ann's optimism. Of course, she wasn't optimistic toward me. She hated me. But to everyone else she was a bright ray of sunshine.

"Mr. Prescott?" Brittney hugged my dad, and then she hugged Ashleigh, who embraced her just as tightly.

"I have heard such wonderful things about you, Brittney Ann. Duncan cannot stop talking about what a wonderful cook you are."

"Oh, well thank you, Ashleigh. I've heard excellent things about you as well."

Breaking their embrace, Brittney blinked at me once, like she didn't exactly know what to do, and then she turned her back.

Glad to see she was the forgiving sort of Christian. One little joke, and I'd been excommunicated.

"Brittney Ann, you know my son, Barry, right?" Dad clapped hard onto my still aching shoulder. It didn't hurt too bad tonight. The stitches had been removed by Doctor Tyler a couple days ago. Plus, two oxy and three vics meant very little pain, but Dad didn't know any of this, so I flinched for his benefit.

Brittney nodded, her shoulders hunched as her little fingers fiddled with a loose string on her ugly dress. "Of course. He's just a year older, Mr. Prescott. We've crossed paths. Plus," she shot me a reproving look over her shoulder, "I saw him at the hospital. You jumped off a cliff, didn't you?"

Narrowing my eyes at her implication, I nodded.

Mitch cleared his throat. "You two were supposed to go to a dance together one time if I'm not mistaken."

Ah, fuck. I hadn't even made it past the foyer and *it* had already been mentioned.

Brittney's bright eyes jumped in surprise. "That was a long time ago," she mumbled.

"I didn't know that," Dad said, fingers digging into my collarbone. I hissed at the sting of his nails against my raw scar.

"Remember?" I seethed between my teeth. "Mom was pissed that I got sick and couldn't go. Stomach flu. I spent the whole night on the bathroom floor."

Judging by the way Dad's jaw flexed, he was starting to remember that not-so-nice little game we'd played on Brittney Ann. "Ah, right."

"That damn stomach flu," Mitch chided. "You missed out on a once in a lifetime opportunity, son. Britt sure looked pretty in her dress."

I took that for what it was: a warning. I'd messed up any chance of ever being with her.

Aw, shucks.

Mitch and Moira showed Dad the new painting one of the ladies at church had done while Brittney went to set the table. Why was she setting the table? Was she their slave? "Son, why don't you go help Brittney?" Dad nodded his chin toward the hall.

No way. He was *not* serious. I forced my jaw to close.

"Now," he murmured under his breath. With the back of his hand, he wiped his perspiring forehead. It was ridiculously hot in this house. Didn't they know about this handy new invention called air conditioning?

"Yeah, whatever."

Brittney walked around the table putting out forks. There were only four seats. "What's this?" I asked, knocking my knuckle against the wood of the table. I wasn't the brightest guy on the planet, but I could count to six.

She stopped, her eyes closed, and she sucked in a slow breath. "I'm afraid our table only seats four. We're going to sit at the bar. I wasn't aware I'd be sitting with anyone, but it's fine. As long as you leave me alone."

"Look, Britt…"

"It's Brittney Ann." No one had ever told me to address them *more* formally before.

My lips twitched in amusement. She busted me mid-smirk and scowled down at her flats. "Fine, Britt*ney Ann*. I'm sorry for all that shit that went down a couple years ago. It wasn't personal."

She stared at me for a second, her lower lip hanging slack. "Your apology is awful." She stomped toward a platter of ham with pine-apples stabbed into it.

She angrily jerked toothpicks from the hog hide sending specks of juice splattering across the room. I caught her wrist, keeping her from flinging pig meat with that last toothpick. "Look, I was a pissed off sophomore who was mad because your brother kicked my ass. So I played a little trick on you. It was harmless. Haven't you ever heard of forgive and forget?"

"Barry," she huffed. Her eyes pinched tight and then flashed open with new vigor burning in their amber depths. "That isn't even the issue. Your apology was lackluster. You barely meant it."

"What? I said *sorry*. What more do you want? Want me to kiss your prissy little ass? Everyone else does it. So why not, huh?"

She jerked on her arm, trying yank free from my grip. Honestly, I'd forgotten her skin was still cuffed under my fingers. Staring down, I swiped my thumb over the delicate fabric of her wrist. She tugged away from me again, and I released her. I could taste my heartbeat in my throat—a reaction I didn't understand at all.

Unblinking, she scrutinized me. She was going to yell at me or rip me a new one or something.

Her chest raised and dropped as she sucked in rapid breaths. The vein in her neck pulsed in quick, throbbing succession.

I reached out my free hand, hesitating in midair before I closed the gap and cupped over her sternum.

I didn't know why I'd done it. I didn't *want* to touch her. I really didn't. But, fuck, that vein in her neck pulsed. My finger brushed her velvet skin.

Boom.

Boom.

Boom.

I had the urge to lay my ear against the rhythm and let it lull me to a peaceful calm. My fingers swiped along the line of her collarbone, and she gasped, bringing me back to reality.

Glancing into her hazel eyes, I froze. *She. Looked. Horrified.*

I pulled away. Clearing my throat, I tried to think of something to say. Some excuse, or some reason as to why the hell I'd just put my hands on her.

"I'm sorry," I said again, really trying to mean it this time. I didn't have a solid excuse for being such a pervert. Her skin just looked fragile and soft, and I was a freaking little kid who couldn't help but touch things I wasn't supposed to.

Except that wasn't a good excuse.

Not even to her.

Letting out a shaky breath, she rolled her eyes and snorted.

CR

"Britt would you mind grabbing some napkins?"

She hopped right up to comply. Why the hell was she running around like their little servant?

I was so busy being pissed off that she hadn't taken my apology that I barely heard Dad say, "He knows Toby. Son, you remember Toby, don't you?"

My head snapped up. "Huh?"

"Toby Wilson? You all played ball together."

"Yeah, I know Toby." *I know how his fist had felt against my nose. I know what a cocksucker he is too.*

"See," Dad said. He loosened his tie. Was he nervous or still hot? I imagined a lot of guys were nervous around Mitch Wilson. The man was built like a brick shithouse, and before he'd become a pastor, he'd been a Navy Seal. So, yeah, sitting in his overly warm kitchen was a little intimidating.

Subconsciously, I scooted further away from Brittney. Another reason guys tended to avoid her, despite how beautiful she was: *Daddy*.

My dad cleared his throat. He stabbed repeatedly at the corn that wouldn't seem to get on his fork. "We were all there the night Toby got hurt. It was a shame. He was real good. Any scouts interested in him back then?"

Similarly, I speared at the cream corn with my fork, causing it to push across the plate. So I tried even harder. Brittney's shoulders bounced as she failed at maintaining her silent laughter. I side-eyed her, challenging her to say one damn thing about my discomfort. She seemed to catch my warning as her lips sandwiched between her teeth.

Mitch sighed. "Just a few. You know, small town and all that. It's hard for the boys to get the attention they need. That Parker kid, though…" Mitch whistled.

"Yeah?" Dad asked, loosening his tie even more. I'd never admit it out loud, but I actually felt a little bad for him. "I've heard some pretty bad things about him," Dad finished.

"Oh no. All talk. Everyone in this town lives in a glass house, Duncan, you know that. Collin Parker's one of the best kids at that school. Comes out here every summer since Toby left to help me with the hay. He volunteers at our youth basketball on the weekends. Collin's a damn fine boy. His brother Luke, now…" Mitch's lips twitched. "Now, he is a riot. Not bad, though. Luke just needs a little more structure in his life. They're damn fine boys."

It was like the parents knew exactly what conversations would piss me off. I hated the Parkers, and most people in this town agreed with me since Warren Parker was the one who'd robbed the Bourbon bank. Yet, Mitch acted like they were saints. And Mitch thought *I* was an asshole? My fingers tightened around my knife.

Beside me, Brittney gasped. "Barry," she whispered. "Your hand."

The sword fell to the plate with a clatter. Like a genius, I'd squeezed the blade, not the handle. There was a sharp slice through three of my fingers. "Shit," I hissed.

"Barry!" Dad snapped.

Oops.

"I meant *shoot*. I, uh…bathroom?"

Mitch jerked his chin toward the hall. "Upstairs, first door on the left."

"Thanks," I mumbled.

Brittney's flats slapped the hardwood as she hurried behind me. "I know where the peroxide is, Daddy. I'm just going to show him."

"Don't take long," Mitch hollered. As I took the first step up the wooden stairs, I heard the conversation in the kitchen shift back to the oh-so-wonderful Parkers. I stomped the rest of the way.

Brittney caught my hand and pulled me into a room that I wouldn't even have guessed was the bathroom—the door was narrower than the others. I'd have pegged it as a closet.

Her expression was severe and serious as she scowled at my injury. "It's not that deep, just a scratch, really. I have some Neosporin, but I'd really like to wash it with peroxide."

"Because you want to see me in pain?"

"That. And your knife had ham on it. I'm not so sure how sanitary it is to leave pineapple juice and meat jammed into a cut."

"When you put it so eloquently…" I wiggled my brows at her.

She fought a smile as she pushed me back against the toilet and straddled one of my legs. I don't think she realized how close our bodies were. If she'd been wearing anything other than this stupid, unflattering dress, she'd have been in serious trouble.

Or, more accurately, I'd have been in serious trouble.

I adjusted the slight strain in my too-tight jeans. Okay, unflattering dress aside, this was sort of a fantasy of mine. Goodie little Christian chick shoving me down and straddling me? Oh yeah, it was unreal. "So you get off on making someone hurt, huh? That make you, like, a sadist or something?"

Her smile vanished. "Please don't do that." She drew my hand toward the light, leaning over my palm as she appraised my wounds.

"Do what?"

"Pretend that you need to be vulgar. You knew it would offend me. It's unnecessary. I'm not going to throw myself at you, so there's no need to make me anymore repulsed by you than I already am."

I did not get that logic. Did she think I was trying to gross her out so that she wouldn't go all football-fan-girl on me? Like I ever cared when that happened.

I slid down the toilet seat, letting my leg harass the hem of her dress further up her thighs as I moved deeper between her. "And you know that I'm not this vulgar all the time because…?"

She didn't answer. There was a bitter tug of a smile on her face as she held my injured fingers over the sink. With her free hand, she untwisted the white cap on the peroxide bottle and dropped it into the ceramic sink basin. She watched my face and not my wounds as she poured way more of the cool liquid over my fingers than was necessary.

Pain hit me and sizzled as it danced through my veins. Reaching out, I threw my free arm around her middle. My head nestled against her stomach as I pulled her body into me.

That slim frame fell on my leg. I braced her, holding on for dear life.

"Fuck," I hissed.

"Sorry," she breathed. Her left hand on the top of my shoulder, she tried to push away from me.

"Not yet," I seethed.

"Why are you holding me d-down?" Her voice broke.

"I don't…I don't know. Instinct, I guess."

"Instinct," she squeaked. "Did…Barry, did you think something was going to hurt me?"

My mind raced as I tried to remember what I'd thought as pain assaulted my palm. Nothing coherent was coming back to me. All I could process now was how damn good she smelled. *Fucking* strawberries. Her bony ass on my thigh, I cupped my hands underneath her shifting her forward just a little. My blood raced south.

Fluttering her eyelids, she leaned into me and inhaled deeply. I wondered if I didn't smell just as good to her as she did to me. That idea thrilled me. *Sweet Brittney liked being close to the bad boy?*

Her amber-hazel eyes stared at my lips, and I almost let out the groan of approval that tickled my throat. Sliding my hand up her back, I eased her forward against me, her mouth was only inches from mine. I knew she could feel the predicament in my jeans.

Which was probably the reason she sucked in a breath of surprise and dropped that industrial sized bottle of peroxide into the sink. Our arms were splattered with the cool liquid and the heat inside my body was doused.

She stared at me, eyes wide. Like she didn't even realize she'd made a mess, or like she wanted me to say something. When I didn't, she whispered, "What're you doing?"

Whatever had been going down between us seconds before was now over. The moment, like the one in the kitchen, had fizzled and ignited into a fiery death, and I'd regained my cool.

"What?" I smiled crookedly, gripping her tighter, more roughly now. "You don't wanna be my nurse?" I winked.

Pink roses stained her cheeks. Without responding, she pushed away at my shoulders. "Band Aids are in the cabinet," she dismissed, flicking her hair off her shoulder, her mouth pencil thin.

There were Band Aids in the cabinet. Normal, tan Band Aids. I didn't bother with them. My fingers throbbed a little, but they weren't bleeding anymore. And, of course, they didn't hurt much.

When I made it back to the kitchen, no one even acknowledged me. Brittney's head was down as she picked the burnt edges off of a dinner roll.

I stared down at my full plate of ham and corn and mashed potatoes. It all looked great, I just wasn't hungry. I really wished I was, though. I wished I could devour the food while it was in front of me. My family was fond of takeout and make-it-from-a-box meals. The next time I'd see something like this would be Thanksgiving.

But the more I ate now, the quicker my high would fade, and the food didn't look *that* good.

Brittney stayed hunched over on herself. She looked defeated, but she never stopped staring at the parents. Like she was waiting for instruction and her body was on autopilot until she received it.

At one point, she pulled her dad aside because she needed to "talk to" him. They hovered just outside the kitchen, so I heard the words *date* and *Ryan* and *tonight*, and then Mitch's obviously deeper voice saying *no* and *too young* and *break bones*.

I smiled down at my own burnt dinner roll, picking it to pieces with my fingers.

Brittney must have been ready for her dad because when she walked back into the kitchen, after a *not a baby*, and *can't control me*, and *it's just a movie*, she looked smug.

I didn't like that for some reason.

After dinner, Brittney cleared the dishes. She put away the leftovers.

Dad kept shooting me wide why-don't-you-help-the-helpless-Christian-chick eyes, but there was no way I was doing that. She hadn't asked for help. Plus, she hadn't even given me a Band Aid.

Then Brittney skipped upstairs, and the parents all chilled in the living room with some wine—red wine. Like Mom would have drunk if she were here. I traced over the logo on the bottle with my thumb nail. A local vineyard. Bringing the neck of the bottle to my nose, I swirled and then sniffed. It was a robust Malbec. "Mom would love this," I commented.

Dad, Ashleigh, Mitch, and Moira all stared at me. I swallowed a pinch in my throat, heat prickling my neck. Obviously, I shouldn't have brought up the divorced other half of my parentage on this night that was meant to be about getting to know Ashleigh.

"Have you seen her lately?" Mitch asked.

"Just at the hospital," I said. Mom had wanted me to come over when Dad and Ashleigh went away on their vacation—the *surprise* engagement vacation that I hadn't been invited to. Instead, Dad had put his foot down and said I had to stay with Tyler (because even at the age of seventeen, I couldn't be trusted alone).

I could have gone to Mom's house. I was practically an adult, and no divorce papers should have kept me the six miles that separated us. But she didn't want to do anything to make him angry. So, no, I hadn't seen Mom. We'd even missed my monthly visit, though I planned to make up for that this summer.

"Oh, right, you fell off that cliff. We've all been praying for you. How've you been feeling?"

"Fine." I couldn't help but feel like Mitch was judging me. His eyes bore into the side of my face, and I couldn't handle the heat of his glare. I stared down at the Malbec.

He caught my shoulder, squeezing my flesh in his powerful grip. I didn't look at him.

"You're going to have to be more careful. Carmine won't stand for too many excuses. Missing camp this summer's bad, and getting hurt…" he whistled. "Hate to be you on opening day of practice."

Groaning internally, I leaned away from him. "Yeah. It's gonna suck."

My buzz was waning, and my tolerance for family shenanigans was almost at its limit.

A few minutes later, after Moira started talking about Gwen's beautiful dog—gag me—Brittney skipped down the stairs in a different cotton dress. An elbow length button-down wool sweater covered nearly all of her.

It wasn't even sixty degrees out there, and she was in wool. Her fingers tugged the ends of the sweater closed in the middle. "I'm leaving, Daddy. I'll be home before eleven." Her eyes flickered to me, and her expression said everything her mouth didn't: *and you're not invited, Barry.*

"Goodnight—"

"You get to leave?" I gasped.

Her lips drew closed and then stiffly opened as she mumbled, "Yes. If you must know, I have a date. With my boyfriend."

I didn't know it was possible for someone to turn purple as quickly as Mitch did right then. "Not your boyfriend," he growled.

She puffed out a breath. "Okay, it's not a date. And he's not my boyfriend. We're just *friends* going to the movies."

Moira laughed. "What her father means is it's nothing serious, *yet*. One of the boys from Zion has had his eye on her for years. They've been talking on the phone for a few weeks. He's volunteering at the hospital with her. Nice boy."

I thought about asking if Zion boy had gotten to second base, but that didn't seem like the right thing to say in front of her *daddy*. Besides, she was already staring down at her shoes, and her cheeks were speckled with pink spots. As great as embarrassing her was, it wouldn't get me out of this house any faster.

"Can I come?"

Britt's eyes nearly bulged out of her head. "No."

"Now, Brittney," Moira started.

"Moira," Mitch warned. "If she doesn't want him to go, then that's her choice."

"That's just plain rude. You said it yourself that she's not going on a real date with Ryan. Why can't Barry tag along?" The woman smiled at me.

"It's fine," my dad said. "He doesn't need—"

"No really," I interrupted, scooting forward so my hands planted on my knees. I was desperate to get out of this overly hot, overly cozy house before I passed into a coma of boredom. "I'll invite my, uh, Madison. It'll be like a double date." I cringed at the word. As long as Madison didn't hear me say it, then it didn't count as a date.

"Madison McNamara?" Moira beamed. "From Brittney's cheerleading squad? Oh, how fun. You like Madison, don't you Britt?"

Brittney kicked her shoe against the floor boards. She grumbled, "Of course, Mother."

"I'm sorry?" Moira tilted the left side of her head toward her daughter.

Brittney exhaled. "Yes, Mother, I like her."

Oooh-hooo, no she didn't. This was going to be so freaking funny. If pissing off Christians was a sport, I'd be an Olympian.

I texted Madison to tell her to wear something hot and meet me at the Multiplex in ten. The great thing about Madison was she was always in something hot and always ready to go. Especially on the weekend. "I'm gonna need a ride." I smirked at Brittney.

The corners of her lips twisted downward. "Of course you do."

"You're not being very Christian today." I bumped her shoulder with mine. She hadn't looked at me the entire time she hugged everyone goodbye.

I did not hug anyone because…just because. Ugh. Hugging.

Tearing off my blue shirt, I threw it into the backseat of Toby's old Plymouth. Brittney's eyes rolled at the "Back in Black" tee, which hugged my pecs just right. Not the reaction I usually got about my chest. It was dark, so she probably didn't get a good look. Madison practically drooled whenever I wore this.

"You'd make anyone question their faith," Brittney mumbled, stomping around the front of the car to the driver's side. I wondered if her faith was in question because of that whole covet thy neighbor nonsense, or if me being a dick really pushed her that far.

"So, who's this boyfriend?" I asked.

She took a left at the end of the driveway, and I rolled down the mechanical window despite the fact we were on a gravel road and the taste of dirt was sure to assault us at any second. Trying to force some of the car's natural musk and dry-rot aroma outside, I waved my hand in the air.

Brittney glared over at me, and then the window, and then me, like the open window was seriously going to mess up her hair. Honestly, it didn't even look like she'd fixed that hair. It hung in long, loose, strawberry loops.

Or, wait, was she pissed because I hadn't asked to roll it down? I mean, it set me off when people touched my stereo, sure, but I didn't really give a damn when they went for the windows. It didn't surprise me that she was such a bitch though.

"None of your business," she growled.

What were we talking about? Ah, it probably wasn't important anyway.

A piece of her silk strawberry hair caught in the wind. Not thinking, I reached out and twirled it around my finger. She froze, and I had to force myself to swallow the lump in my throat. Touching her had seemed…I don't know…instinctive. Then my hand wound into her hair and electricity zoomed through my veins.

I swallowed again, trying to remember what the hell we'd been talking about so I could lighten things back up. Then it hit me. Cheesedick. "Aw, come on—"

"Barry," she huffed. Her eyes squeezed shut, which might have made her a better driver.

I gripped the oh-shit handle as the front tires dropped into yet another deep gravel rut. Jesus fuck, who'd taught her to drive? So far we'd hit six ruts and had slammed on the brakes to avoid hitting an opossum. An *opossum*. I'd have nailed the sucker and counted it as at least ten points in her piece of shit car. I wouldn't have hit anything in my baby.

She let out a slow, steady breath, eyes still pinched tight. "Barry, can we just get this evening over with without you teasing me to death?"

"I don't tease you." I slid my finger from her hair. My heart rate was slowly returning to normal, but I hadn't known it was racing. How long had it been on overdrive? Since before we got in the car?

Using the heel of my hand, I rubbed at the throbbing sensation in my chest. Sometimes the pills did that—made my heart race, I mean. *Yeah, the pills did it…*

She pulled into the parking area in front of the Multiplex and then killed the engine. Her mouth flapped a few times before she inhaled.

"Barry, I know it's your instinct to mess things up and tease people, but I'm begging you not to ruin this for me. He's a very nice boy. He attends church regularly. I'd like to get to know him a little better, and if you run him off, then I can't do that."

"Fine." I shrugged. "I won't say a word. Lips sealed." I zipped my lips with an invisible zipper. I didn't even plan on hanging out with her once I got out of this nasty smelling car, so this would be the easiest promise I'd ever kept.

She scowled over at me. "I can't even tell if you're serious." Her slim body slid between the seats so she could lock the doors in the back. Her ass perked up in the air as she stretched toward the rear passenger door. Jesus, my heart went at it again. *Stupid pills.* I swallowed the pooling saliva in my mouth as that cotton dress inched up her milky thighs. Palm rubbing my chest, I licked my lips. She leaned toward the other door, and I got a whole new view.

Jesus fucking Christ, her daddy never should have let her out of the house with me.

Forcing myself to look away, I yanked at the handle. I ignored her when she called, "Hey, can you lock—"

The sound of her purse and her stomping feet followed me across the parking lot. I tried to tune her out, but I must have failed because when she snapped, "Oooohooo," I turned to look back at her. Her porcelain face pinched up in a scowl. "That little—"

"What's up?"

"Your *Madison*," she growled. I followed her gaze.

On the sidewalk, in front of the Multiplex, Madison had crowd of adoring guys circling around her.

That was about typical. Leave it to her to get dressed up and try to make me jealous. *Try.*

"Babe," I waved her to me with two fingers curling into my palm. Her overly made-up face glowed as she bounced up onto the toes of her spike-heeled shoes. With a light hop she sprang into my arms.

"Barry!" Her boobs threatened to pop out of the shiny, red dress that most girls would have worn as a shirt. She smelled like every content at the perfume counter at Macy's. *Good. Bad. Potent.*

I waved my hand to clear the air. "Damn, Madison, did you bathe in that shit?"

"I wanted to be pretty for you." When she said this her chest pushed out toward me. Given the right angle, I probably could have seen nipple.

"Oh baby, you're pretty." The lack of draw I felt toward this girl relieved me. There was an average rush of blood to my dick, but my heart didn't race at all. I didn't tingle with excitement. Nothing happened when I touched her—no zinging excitement—which made everything in the world feel right again. This was how it was supposed to be.

Brittney made a snorting sound as she stormed past us. I smiled at the sway of her dress brushing against the backs of her knees.

Three fingers grasped my chin, jerking my gaze to the icy eyes before me.

"Brittney?" Madison scowled. "*Brittney?* Come on, Bare. You've pulled some shit off, but not even your dick is magical enough to swing that."

I told her like I'd told my father, "Don't threaten me with a good time, sweetheart."

Her arms wrapped around her stomach as she straightened. She put on a good show, but I'd never met anyone as self-conscious as her. There was a sadness in her that radiated from her every pore. She swallowed it down and smiled.

I didn't care enough about her to want to fix that agony in her eyes, but it was there, so I tended to avoid eye contact.

"You cannot seriously be trying to sleep with her."

"I never said I was."

"Then what's she doing here?" Her arctic glare narrowed on Brittney's back, and I had a sudden urge to step between the girls. I resisted. It wasn't my job to protect the vulnerable little Christian.

"My dad's getting remarried. He was kissing her dad's ass, trying to have the wedding at the church and whatnot. She actually bailed me out by bringing me." It came out like she'd done me a favor when really I'd had to beg for a ride, but I covered for her all the same. *That's what homies do, Britt.* "It wasn't a big thing." I shrugged.

My palm gripped the back of Madison's neck as I forced her to look up at me. "Not that any of it matters to you. I can screw who-ever the hell I want."

Her face crumpled as her hold on her midsection released and her fingers dug into the front pockets of my jeans. "I wasn't trying to make a big deal. I just thought you'd brought another girl on our date."

Eh, that word. "This *isn't* a date."

She smiled. "I know it's not. I didn't mean to say that, Barry. Really. I know we're just hanging out." Madison's eyes darkened again as she glanced down the sidewalk toward Brittney. I wondered if she thought I'd want to keep this not-date platonic because of the other girl. If that was true, then she really didn't know me.

Brittney stood five feet away from a hunch-shouldered kid who was at least three inches shorter than her. The kid had been part of Madison's fan club. This might have been his biggest fault—if not for the visible acne and the pocket boner. He kept trying to hide it by adjusting his pants, but the freak couldn't take his hands out of his pocket or his chub would have been super obvious.

"What'd you do to the poor kid?" I asked, sliding my hand down Madison's back to get a full grip on her luscious ass. She beamed at my PDA.

Keeping her happy and making her feel wanted was the key to getting that overly glossed mouth up close and personal with my phallus. Which, ultimately, was tonight's goal. Getting an insecure girl to blow me was easier than snorting a line of Oxy. I should know.

"Me? Nothing. Lady Gaga came over the loud speaker, and you know I can't resist dancing to Gaga. I went a little crazy. I guess I was grinding against him. It was a total accident. I didn't know he had a date."

"He's her boyfriend." I stared at the kid, remembering the guys joking about him at the hospital. He must have had a stellar personality to snag a ten like Britt, because on the outside, he didn't have much going for him.

Then again, he'd gotten a raging boner for Madison. What did that say for his *astounding* character?

Brittney had said he was a nice boy.

Heat rushed through my veins as I went from curious to annoyed to borderline angry.

"What? He's like…twelve." Madison's high pitched adenoidal voice grated on my ears that were suddenly pumping with blood.

I hazarded a glance back at her. "You think it's okay that you gave a twelve-year-old a boner?"

"Okay, I didn't mean 'twelve.' He looks, like, fifteen."

I continued to stare at the awkward distance between Brittney and the little *skeeve*. What a douchebag. "He didn't say anything to you, did he?"

"Don't worry, Bare. I didn't flirt too much." Her eyes fluttered as her body leaned against mine. The small crease between her boobs blanketed my bicep.

I shrugged her off me. "No, I don't give a damn about that. I'm just thinking about Brittney."

Madison straightened, her glossy lips pouting. "I thought we agreed that you weren't trying to sleep with her."

I arched a brow, waiting for her to realize that I never actually said that.

She slapped my arm and a small sting burned my skin, but I refused to let her know she'd kind of hurt me. "Did he say anything to you?" I repeated slowly this time.

She exhaled, rolling her eyes and refolding her arms. That sadness was back. I stared at my feet. "The creep asked for my number. I shot him down though. I promise. I wouldn't do that to you."

Ah, right. Not that I cared about Madison *ever* giving out her phone number. Something about *him* asking for it struck a nerve, though. I watched Brittney as she smiled at the toe of her shoe, which worked back and forth over a crack in the sidewalk.

That girl over there was a Bourbon cheerleader, just like Madison. She was one of *ours*. It wasn't okay for some outside prick to come up in here and charm her and then hit on Madison. It was one thing when *I* messed with them. This was home turf.

"Wanna help break them up?" I asked. My words ran together. I couldn't tell if I was excited about this new plan, or still angry that little cheesedick had had the nerve to try and pull his shitty game.

She winced. "Do I have a choice?"

Catching her chin with my thumb, I pulled her mouth to mine. I kissed the corner of her lips, causing her to cast me a sly grin.

Nothing happened when I kissed Madison. I mean, nothing ever happened, but this was the first time I ever realized it. I stared at her smile, waiting for my body to react. It didn't. Shaking my head, I accepted that it was probably just me. *Or the pills…*

"Movie time?" Madison asked, more chipper now that her face was inches from mine.

"Fine," I agreed, despite my instinct to rebel out of spite. "But you have to get Chubs to play an arcade game with you."

She frowned. "What? Why?"

Jesus, I swear no one kept her around for her brain. "We're breaking them up," I repeated slowly.

"Why can't I take Brittney?"

My finger slid under the thin strap of her dress, my jagged nail scrapping against her tan skin causing chill bumps to explode down her arms as I skimmed from shoulder to bust. "Because I doubt this little red, fuck-me dress will make Brittney's dick dance. Now do as I say."

"You want me to break them up by flirting with him?"

I arched my brows, daring her to come up with a better solution.

She sighed. "Barry, I don't want to do this. I want to be with you tonight. I was really happy when you called me. I thought one of you guys might because there's supposed to be a party at the House later and I wanted to go with someone, but this is so much better."

All I heard was *I don't want to do this*. Cupping her face in my hands, I forced her to look at me. "Listen, babe, you help me with this, and I'll make sure you don't regret it." Drawing her face to mine I devoured her lips.

When I pulled back, her eyes were shut and jaw slack. I wiped my mouth. That gloss tasted like shit. "Go."

A small scowl tugged on her cheeks. "He's not just going to walk away from her. That's too obvious."

"I know," I said. Pushing her hair aside, I whispered my plan into her ear.

FIVE

BRITTNEY ANN

O h, please Barry. Come play a game with me." Madison yanked on Barry's arm, trying to pull him toward the arcade side. He stayed firm. His expression said he was too cool to be pulled anywhere.

Ryan and I both watched in disgust. "Look at them," I snapped. "Could they be any more vulgar?"

"Do you know her?" He swallowed hard, causing his Adam's apple to bob up and down.

I watched the side of his face, trying to understand that tone in his voice. He sounded, almost, excited. "She's a cheerleader with me."

His eyes widened. "*She's* on your cheer squad. Wow. I can't believe she's still in high school. She looks…"

I didn't know what to make of that. On the car ride here, when I wasn't plotting ways to eject Barry from the passenger seat, I'd planned how I would go about holding Ryan's hand. I didn't have to wait for him to grab my hand. This was a world of gender equality. We were both mature. This step should be easy. *I could do—*

"No," Barry's voice held an edge of finality. "Madison, it isn't happening. Find someone else."

Good gracious! Do they have to be so loud? There were other people in the lobby. Didn't they see that?

I took a deep breath and tried again to talk myself in to reaching for Ryan's hand. At this point, I'd have had to pull his hand from deep inside his pocket. Both of his balled fists were shoved inside the front pockets of his khaki pants. I wondered if he weren't just as nervous as I was.

"Brittney?" Madison said, bouncing over to me. *Bouncing.* My gosh, didn't she realize that her breasts were about to tumble over the top of that very revealing dress? I'd seen that *thing* on the rack at Kohl's. It was meant to be worn as a shirt.

"Hmm?" I couldn't open my mouth or word vomit might escape. I'd be forced to tell her how atrocious I thought her behavior was.

"Arcade game?"

I shook my head. "I'm sorry, Madison. I'm actually on a d—"

"I'll do it." If I hadn't seen the sentence escape his mouth, I wouldn't have believed it had been him. I stared at the side of Ryan's face. His cheeks stained from pink to red to purple.

"Oh, you don't mind, do you Britt?" Madison's face glowed with excitement.

"Can't you play by yourself?" I mumbled.

"Britt," Ryan reprimanded. "We can't leave her out here alone. If her, uh, boyfriend…"

"Not boyfriend," Barry corrected, waving his palms in the air. "Definitely not her boyfriend."

"Oh." Ryan shifted from foot to foot like he was extremely uncomfortable. "Well, if he isn't going to stay out here, then someone else has to stay. It's not safe to leave a girl alone. Especially not such a beautiful girl." He beamed at her.

I stared down at the skirt of my dress, fisting the fabric around my knuckles. Okay, I got that my outfit wasn't as revealing, but surely it went against boyfriend etiquette for him to just announce that he found another girl attractive right in front of my face.

And, hello! If he goes with her, I'll be alone! Very hot, angry tears stung my eyes. *Then again, maybe I'm ugly enough to be left alone.*

"Of course." My voice broke. "Whatever. I'll just wait." Or, I guess it wouldn't have killed me to go play a game with them. The arcade wasn't very large, and I'd never actually been in there. It might be fun.

"Go on in," he dismissed, still smiling at her. "Don't want you to miss the movie because of me."

He hadn't bought my ticket, yet. I hadn't brought enough money. I opened my mouth to tell him, but he'd turned to follow *bouncing* Madison toward the arcade.

Barry's hand caught the top of my shoulder. "Dude," he whispered. I glanced up to realize he'd also grabbed Ryan. His intimidating grip on my boyfriend's elbow had the flesh puckering beneath Barry's fingers. "You're a fucking idiot."

Ryan yanked his arm free. "Language is uncalled for." For a fraction of a second, he glanced back at me, concern flitting across his face. And then he turned toward the arcade with his head held high.

Acid burned inside my throat as *my boyfriend* pulled one of his fisted hands from his pocket and placed his open palm low on her spine. It looked like touching her was the most natural thing in the world. *Because she's prettier? Or because she's showing more skin?*

"He's kind of a dick, huh?" Barry's voice dripped venom. Instinct told me to take a step away, but I remained strong. It wasn't my fault she'd gone with him. In fact, if he'd just played in the arcade with his own date, I could have held my freaking boyfriend's hand. So Barry couldn't be mad at me.

"You promised," I whispered the reminder.

"Huh?"

"You said you wouldn't do anything to mess this night up for me. Your lips were sealed and you weren't doing or saying anything that could ruin this."

He swallowed loudly. His striking green eyes never lifted from my hazel ones. "Right."

I turned toward the register. Maybe if I dug around in the bottom of my purse, I'd find enough change for my ticket. Had Ryan never planned on buying it for me? I guess that had been presumptuous. But he did ask me to the movies. Therefore, this was his idea. So technically, he should have paid for me. Or was that a dated mentality?

How embarrassing. If I'd known I'd need money I'd have asked my parents. Oh, right, that would have been an interesting conversation. Daddy had barely let me out of the house as it was. If I'd told him my boyfriend wouldn't be paying for me, there would have been no chance. He'd have thought that was the most disrespectful thing in the world.

My purse slammed against the counter, rattling the glass case over the candy. The girl with purple hair took a measured step backward. I hissed out a breath. The throaty chuckle from over my shoulder made me growl. Rounding on him with my eyes narrowed, I waited for him to say something.

His lips twitched, but he lifted his hands in surrender.

I huffed. "I need a ticket for that stupid *Love* movie. Just give me a minute to dig for change."

"It'll be eight dollars," Purple Hair said.

I gripped two quarters and three gum wrappers. I was pretty sure there was a five in my wallet, so I only needed three more—

"Make it two tickets," Barry said.

"I do not have money to pay for you," I snapped. My heart did a little flip as he stepped up and handed a debit card to the girl from over my shoulder.

"Any candy?" he whispered, his hot breath ruffling my hair.

Taking a step sideways, obeying the laws of personal space—which he seemed to have forgotten about—I tried to breathe in air that was scented with him.

"Hello? Earth to Britt."

"Huh?" Popcorn basted Barry should have been manufactured as cologne. Girls would murder to wear this fragrance. Good gracious, it was fantastic.

"Any candy?" He repeated, arching his brows and watching me like I was certifiable. "Since you're right, I did fuck up your date. I probably owe it to you."

I knew it. Rubbing my temples to clear my mind, I tried to breathe deeply, ignoring all Barry-scents.

If he expected me to be humble and decline candy, he'd asked the wrong Christian. "I want Red Vines."

"Gimme a Coke," he added.

I didn't believe it was real until the candy and ticket stub was clenched inside my fists. My fingers tightened, on the chance there was still a joke. He'd rip it all out of my hand and laugh in my face.

"What do you say?" he teased, bumping my shoulder with his.

"Why'd you do that?" I exhaled a painful amount of relief.

"No, the answer was *Thank you*. I say, *What do you*—"

"Barry, I'm serious. Why are you suddenly being so nice to me?"

He slurped noisily on his soda and shrugged dismissively. That was all the response he gave. A shrug. Once, though, I thought he looked back over his shoulder toward the arcade. His mouth drew tight, and a muscle in his strong jaw popped.

He was upset, obviously. I wasn't the only one missing a date after all. I had no clue what had him so tense, but I wondered if he was worried about Madison's safety. Ryan had pointed it out—she was a beautiful girl, and she'd been left with a stranger. "He's not going to hurt her or anything. He really is nice."

Barry stared at me, confusion tugging at the corner of his mouth. "Right, yeah. Let's go." He dismissed my concern with a wave of his palm. Opening the theater door for me, he led me into the dark.

"Really, Ryan is very nice. He's never done one thing to make me question his motives, you know? He keeps his hands to himself."

"What's that mean?" Barry asked. He walked toward the back row where there were two empty seats separated from all the others. "That you don't question his motives?"

"It just means that he's good. He's a nice guy."

"And he doesn't touch you? Does he even sneak a boob grab when you're making out?"

My face heated. I was glad we were hidden in the dark so that he couldn't see any blush on my cheeks. "You're doing it again."

"What?"

"That thing where you're vulgar just to repulse me."

He sounded moderately remorseful when he said, "My bad. I'm just trying to figure it out—why you're so into him. I mean, no offense…" His eyes did one long swoop down my body. Even in the dim lights of the theater, Barry's stark emerald eyes were visible raking over the nonexistent curves of my hips.

There was a fluttering sensation inside my belly.

"You're hot," he said matter-of-fact, "and he's, uh, way not. It doesn't fit."

Barry Prescott just called me hot. I swallowed, trying to force myself not to care what he thought of me. I did care though. Only, I just now realized it. My cheeks were on fire, and I was desperate to change the subject. "Thank you," I said. "For the…" I held up the candy, unable to finish with words that weren't accompanied by giddy giggles.

He jerked his head in a nod as if it was no big deal. As if he bought girls things all the time. I imagined that was true. Barry probably went on lots of dates. Not that this was a date. I didn't think that.

I needed Ryan to hurry up. Sitting beside Barry was complicated. My body was at war with my mind, trying to decide whether the dilemma came from the sudden heat coursing through my blood or the hatred my brain insisted I feel toward him.

It was like I couldn't even remember standing in front of the gym my freshman homecoming. I didn't remember seeing his friends take pictures of me and then huddle up as they laughed. I didn't remember the dull ache in the pit of my stomach as I refused to accept that he was standing me up.

Oh, wait, now I remember.

I shuffled, leaning as far away from him as possible. "We're going to have to move once they get in here," I said, gesturing with my chin to all of the rows in front of us with more than two seats.

"That's fine. We'll stay back here until then. That way we'll see them when they walk in." Very sensible; I couldn't argue. "You mind?" he asked, jerking his thumb toward the Red Vines in my lap.

"Oh no, of course not. They're yours after all."

I reached for the package at the same time as he grabbed for it. His wrist rested on my thigh as his fingers dug into the plastic. His warm skin practically *touched* my skin. One thin, cotton dress between us. I shivered.

"You cold?" he asked, finally pulling out the licorice and taking a bite. "Eh, what the hell?"

"They're different than Twizzlers."

"I see that. Not really my thing. You want it?"

I stared at the end, where he'd just taken a bite, and I nodded. Not allowing myself to overthink the situation, I devoured the piece of candy.

"Are you?"

"Hmm?" I chewed, slightly disappointed that this piece didn't taste different than all the others.

"Cold? Are you cold?"

"Oh, no I'm fine right now."

He stared at me, jaw tense, like maybe he didn't believe me. Or maybe he was still mad. "I'm sorry about Madison," I said. For the life of me I couldn't see what guys saw in her. "I know you must be…" I couldn't force nice enough words, and Daddy always said if I didn't have anything nice to say then I just shouldn't say anything.

"Be what?" He waited.

"I don't know. You're into her, and she's, well, *maybe* she's being seduced by Ryan." A familiar pang of agony settled into my stomach. I'd never dreamed Ryan would join the endless line of boys who preferred the Madisons of the world over the Brittneys.

"You think he's the one seducing her, huh?" Those sharp eyes bounced toward the door and then back to me. Relaxing his elbows against his knees, he leaned into my personal space again. "I guess maybe he is. So let me ask again—what is it about that guy, Britt? He doesn't really seem good enough for you."

"He's plenty good enough. I already told you, he goes to—"

"Yeah, I know what church he goes to. But, like, what's he into? What does he do for fun? Who's his best friend, and if they got matching tattoos what would it be of?"

I opened my mouth to answer and then snapped it shut when I realized I had no clue. On any of it. He liked going to the movies, obviously, but was this considered his "fun" hobby? And who was his best friend? My voice was small when I attempted to defend myself. "I already told you that I was still getting to know him."

"Who's my best friend?" he asked.

"Tyler." My hands slapped over my lips as surprise washed through me. I'd known Barry longer. Of course I knew who his best friend was. It helped that he and Tyler had been besties since...I don't know, forever.

His eyebrows wiggled. "Ding ding. What do I do for fun?" Holding up his finger in the air, he shook his head. "On second thought, don't answer that. Too many witnesses."

I giggled. Taking in Barry's appearance, with his classic AC/DC T-shirt and fitted dark jeans, I wondered what sort of tattoos he and Tyler would get.

Maybe something serious as a memento of their friendship. Like a picture of Barry's Charger on their butts. Or maybe they'd get something funnier—like a cartoon character. I imagined them with Homer Simpson on their bare chests, and I couldn't fight a smile.

Barry stared at me, his eyebrows drawn together like he wasn't exactly sure what he was looking at. Then he burst into a smile. "Look, what I'm saying is—"

"I get what you're saying." My amusement dissipated. "I don't understand *why* you're saying it. I'm not sure I understand why you're being so nice to me, either. You think I'm too pretty for him, and I appreciate your opinion, but my boyfriend is the one who's out there with your...Madison. Doesn't that bother you in the least?"

"I wouldn't call her mine." He dismissed her with a shrug.

My jaw dropped. That's what he'd called her at the house. I guess things were different in the cool theater. "What would you call her?"

Another shrug.

"I'm confused. Your tongue was in her mouth."

His smile was sly. "Thought you were watching."

"I wasn't *watching*. You two were attacking each other like one of you needed CPR. It was like a train wreck—you don't want to look, but you can't look away." I bit into my cheek to keep myself from spewing more word vomit. "I'm sorry. That was—"

"Awesome?" he guessed. "You don't gotta worry about offending me, Britt. I'm made of stone." He knocked playfully against his chest.

He met my gaze and stared again. Sharp, defined green to boring hazel. "You know how at school there's gym equipment, like basketballs and baseballs and shit?"

"Are you going to explain something using an analogy?"

"Shush. Don't interrupt unless you're going to say, *Oh, Barry you're a genius.*"

My eyes rolled, and this time I didn't have to make it happen.

When I didn't interrupt, he beamed. "So anyway, there are basketballs and baseballs and every class gets to use them, right? Don't answer, it was rhetorical."

I bit back a laugh.

"Well, there's this one basketball that's worn in all the right spots, and it holds air and bounces perfectly. Everyone uses that one. It's probably touched by fifty hands a day during basketball season, and it just keeps on being the favorite one to play with. But we gotta take care of it, you know? We gotta keep air in it and not bounce it on rocks. Stuff like that. Well, Madison is just like that basketball. We gotta keep her happy, and she'll keep letting us touch her. You understand?"

"Oh." I let that sink in. "I'd be the ball that no one wants to play with."

Barry nodded.

I didn't know why pain stabbed into my chest like I was being skewered. Of course he agreed that I was like the new balls. He didn't even bat an eye.

"No one plays with the balls that are new. They don't bounce as good as the used ones. They're not broken in. We're all afraid we'll hurt them. We just leave them on the rack and stare at them because they're priceless. Then, always, some idiot cheesedick comes along and thinks he can play with that ball. The asshole has to ruin its perfection."

Oh. When he put it like that, I didn't feel so bad about the comparison. "Let me guess, Ryan's the cheese, um…"

"Say it," he enticed. Eyes sparkling in the darkness, he gripped my knee, urging me to break the rules.

With his warm fingers holding onto my bare skin, I felt invincible—the same reaction I'd had at home earlier. My fingers twitched to wrap around his, but I knew better than to give into that reaction. This contact didn't mean to Barry what it meant to me. "No," I squeaked. Clearing my throat, I tried again. "No, I don't want to say it."

"Come on, Britt. I don't have much to live for. It would really make my night to hear you cuss."

I sighed. "Dick."

He burst out laughing. And, okay, it had felt pretty good to say that—there was a rush in being bad.

The tall woman sitting in front of us shifted her weight. "Sorry," I mumbled.

"Don't apologize," Barry snorted, squeezing my knee lightly. "Jeez, Britt, be free. Let loose."

"Shall I start cliff diving?"

He shrugged. "It was fun."

"You wound up in the hospital."

"I'll have stories to tell my grandkids."

"Were you high?" I bit into my tongue, regretting the words the second they passed over my lips.

He startled, eyes narrowed and jaw tight. Even though he'd already insulted my candy, he removed his hand from my knee to grab another piece. The absence of contact made me feel hollow, but I refused to think about it.

Clearing my throat, I tried to change the subject. "So you're into rom-com's?"

"Oh yeah, love this shit. This'll probably be my favorite movie ever. Right up there with *The Notebook*."

"I figured. Your wardrobe fails at hiding that you're a closet Nicholas Sparks fan. It's the Converse. No, the tight jeans. No, the AC/DC shirt really screams romance. You've probably even read *Fifty Shades of Grey*, and not for the sex scenes."

"You know it," he said, nodding. "I'm a big, sappy, hopeless romantic."

"Which is why you brought Madison on this date."

He cringed. "Yeah, okay, I draw the lines of joking at the word *date*."

I didn't get it. "What's wrong with that word?"

When his eyes met mine, there was something different about them. A shield had gone up. The same thing had happened at the house before I'd dropped the peroxide. This time, I was ready for it, and I braced myself for his mood shift. He leaned over the arm rest, so his lips were inches from my ear when he whispered, "I date about as much as you fuck, sweetheart."

I flinched anyway. "Please stop."

"What? Damn girl, I can't just walk around with a sensor. This is me. I'm being honest. I don't take girls to the movies. I take them to my backseat. We roll around for a few minutes, if we're lucky a few hours. Then, maybe, I'll call again when I'm horny."

This time the woman in front of us cleared her throat. "I'm sorry," I said again.

"Fuck this." Barry threw his arms out in front of him. "Let's go find them." He stood up and held out a hand for me. Given everything he'd just said, I shouldn't have wanted to go with him. I definitely shouldn't have wanted to hold his hand.

My fingers slid into his, and that hollow ache inside me filled with numb pleasure. I hated myself for being so happily sated by Barry Prescott.

"How do you do it?" I whispered.

Barry froze, halfway in the theater, halfway out. "Do *it?*"

I hurried to clarify, stumbling over my words, "T-touch people like it's not a big deal? Have sex with them without caring for them? Not-not like *it.* I-I know how that works." *Sort of.*

I didn't look at him, but I could feel the heat of his gaze as he appraised me.

"It's not a big deal because I *don't* care," he said. "If I cared then shit might be weird."

"Do you think that's why I can't do anything with Ryan, because I care too much?"

Barry sucked in a breath. He rubbed over his forehead with his free hand. "Look, Britt. I really don't give a shit about any of this. I don't even know why we started talking about him and you in the first place. I was being a total dick earlier. I told Madison to flirt with him."

I stayed frozen. "Why would you do that?"

"Because if he were any kind of man, or if he deserved your time, he wouldn't have fallen for it. The numb nuts had already asked for her phone number before we got here, and it pissed me off that you thought he was some sort of saint but thought I was an asshole."

"So you were trying to convince me otherwise? Because I have to be honest, Barry, I'm really losing faith in you."

"No, I don't give a damn what you think of me. Just him. He's not good enough for you. I don't want you with him."

"Again," I snapped, "how is this your business?"

I wanted to release his hand but my fingers refused to let go. As long as we were connected, he would have to stay and explain why he'd been such a jerk. If he were free, he might leave me.

A couple in the lobby stepped out of the way so we could storm past them. I heard the woman say to the man, "We were just like them. Remember that?"

My heart raced. I was pretty sure that reaction was because I was upset. The idea that Barry Prescott would ever have *me* as a girlfriend was crazy. I'd have to take an elevator to reach his level of cool.

Plus, I didn't *want* to be his girlfriend.

He jerked open the girls' bathroom door and then pushed me inside. Without waiting for an invite, he stepped in and let the door slap closed. He checked under every stall, and once satisfied Madison and Ryan weren't in here, he eyed the girl applying her gloss in the mirror. He winked at her, and her cheeks flushed as she smiled back at him.

Tucking her hair behind her ear, she fumbled as she tried to shove the tube of makeup into her small purse. She almost walked into the door on her way out. She giggled and said, "Oops," over her shoulder, back at him.

I didn't even think she saw me standing there.

I'd seen her get out of a car when we'd first got here. She was with a guy. I slapped Barry's arm, pulling him from a trance. "Of course you're hitting on people."

"What? The girl I was planning on sleeping with is missing. I need back up options."

My mouth popped open with a suction sound.

He waved at me dismissively. "Don't worry. I know you're not an option. We're not married. You're saving your virtue. Blah, blah, blah, I get it."

"I wasn't worried about *that*. You…you said you were going to sleep with her *tonight*. Is that something that just happens? You don't have to plan or make arrangements? What about birth control? Tell me you use birth control. And, oh my goodness, Barry, you surely——"

His free hand slapped over my mouth as he pinned me back against the cool brick wall. "Chill," he exhaled. "You're overthinking this. I like having sex, so I have condoms on me at all times. Madison's on the pill. She's been on it for as long as I can remember. And we don't have to make plans. We're both consenting, almost-adults. We just agree, and then we do it."

Holy crud. I let that all sink in as his hand slid down my face. "You cool?" he asked, eyebrows arched.

I swallowed hard, thinking. "Do you think you could talk to Ryan?"

Barry leaned back, his wicked eyes evaluating me. "What?"

"About sex. Like what he should and shouldn't do."

"You want to sleep with that guy? Wait…tell me you haven't already."

"No," I cut across before my face actually ignited. "No, of course not. But I'd, well, I'd like to try some things. Kissing, for instance."

Barry's jaw dropped. "He hasn't kissed you. How long you two been together?"

"Um, about a month or so, but we haven't actually seen each other much. And Toby wants to Skype with him before we're 'official.' But we call ourselves——"

Barry's slid his fingers around my face, cupping my jaw. A second later, a warm, moist mouth pressed against mine. The syrupy flavor of his soda made him sweet. I gasped in surprise, and his skillful tongue skated between my lips.

Artistic hands dug upward into my hair, twisting at the roots at the base of my skull.

Big, huge, giant, Mothra sized butterflies took flight inside my gut. Their wings flapped causing a flurry of anxiety and excitement. Heat erupted in my chest. *What if I'm not doing this right?*

I tried to mimic his movements to at least pretend I knew what I was doing.

His eyes were closed, so I closed my eyes. His tongue never stayed in one place too long—moving slowly, methodically, rhythmically. I tried to do the same.

He bit gently on my lower lip, sucking it into his mouth.

My knees buckled.

"What the…?" With lightning reflexes, he released my hair and slipped his arms around my waist to support me. A growl tore through his throat before his features fixed, and he smiled. "Dammit, Britt, you good?"

"You…" I gasped for air. "You kissed me?"

"And you passed out?" He laughed.

Oh goodness. He laughed at me.

Yup, my face *was. On. Fire.*

I shoved at his chest, forcing myself to stand. *Now knees, now is the time to do your job. You can call in sick tomorrow.* I wobbled a little but took several *almost* steady side steps away from him. "You had no right—"

"Oh come on, you liked it." He smirked crookedly, twirling a finger through my hair.

"I did not." *Did too.* I slapped his hand away. "And I didn't *pass* out. I couldn't breathe with your tongue invading my airway. That's all." More like, I couldn't breathe…and think…and kiss all at the same time.

His sinful smile dipped into his jade eyes. "Okay. If that's how you feel."

"And I have a boyfriend. I'd appreciate if you kept your hands and…" I waved my arms gesturing to all of him. "And your other body parts to yourself. Ryan does have a jealous streak."

Barry's eyebrow lifted. He was, dare I say, amused. "I'd be interested to see that," he challenged.

SIX

BARRY

The worst thing about finding Madison jerking Ryan off in the parking lot was that I knew I wouldn't get laid tonight. And Madison was damn good at giving hand jobs. She didn't do it halfway, like some broads. On her knees on the back floorboard of her Neon, with the silk top of her dress pulled just past her nipples, Cheesedick Ry had the full view. The guy had worshiped her before; it was nothing to the way he was looking at her now. Madison fiend for looks like that.

Leaning back with my hands on my head, I let the sting of disappointment eat at my stomach. This was probably my fault, but I was going to blame her.

"I think I'd like to go home." The tiny voice startled me.

Shit.

I hadn't even thought about blocking her. On instinct, I grabbed her hand and threw my free arm around her shoulder. I didn't know much about comforting girls or relationships or anything really, but I knew that Brittney had liked the little skeeve.

Whether she should have or not, she liked him.

Big hazel eyes blinked up at me. "Did you plan this?" she asked, tearing her hand from mine so she could plant her palms against my chest as she, surprisingly, nuzzled deeper into my hold.

"What? No. I was really hoping to get *my* junk played with."

"Ugh." Okay, not surprisingly, she jerked away.

Stomping across the lot, she dug into her noisy, clicking purse. It went against my instinct just to leave Madison with that little douche. I wanted to tear open the door and laugh in her face. Or, I don't know, maybe it would be funnier to Saran Wrap them inside.

But Brittney didn't seem in the mood. She walked away, just like that, with no retaliation and no payback. I threw my hands into the air. "You're not leaving me here."

"It would serve you right," she whisper-yelled.

"What? I didn't do anything."

She gaped. Jumping up and down, she pointed at Madison's Neon. "Oh *puh-lease*! You're not innocent. You *told* her to flirt with him."

Oh, that.

"Right, yeah, I did do that. But I was looking out for you. You're one of *our* cheerleaders, Britt. A Bourbon girl. It's not okay for an outsider—a skeevy little outsider at that—to come in here and play mind games. He had no right hitting on her when you're already too fucking good for him. Don't ask why I care about this, because honestly I don't know. But I do care. You should care, too."

Staring down at her key twisting around her finger, she let out a huff. "Get in if you'd like."

It wasn't that I *wanted* to get into her busted Plymouth. I just preferred it to staying in the Multiplex parking lot. "Want me to drive?" I offered.

"Ha, not on your life."

"*Geesh*, just offering, chick." Honestly, I wished she'd have let me drive. Her methodical driving made me a little crazy. My finger tapped the center column to the rhythm of the Foreigner track that I wished were blaring because it had been stuck in my head for hours.

"Hey, what're you doing now?" I blurted. The words slipped stupidly through my still-stoned mouth.

Brittney's lips flapped a few times before she came up with, "Oh, going home I suppose."

Because I didn't see any way to back out of it, I went ahead and offered. "Wanna go somewhere? Do something? Be a little crazy?"

"No, I don't think so," she answered instantly. Then, after chewing on her lower lip, she sighed. "You know, I really don't have it in me to confess to Daddy that Ryan wasn't the kind of boy I thought. So, okay, where would we go?"

I was surprised. Even though I didn't really know if I wanted to hang out with the snobby little Christian, it surprised me that the feeling was mutual. "Really? You're thinking about it. Hold on, let me call Tyler."

Brittney looked downright horrified as I pulled out my cell and dialed Ty. "He's cool," I whispered.

"I *know* him," she shot back.

I wonder what story of Tyler was running through her mind. When he'd pantsed the janitor, vomited in the mystery meat casserole, or pulled that shit with Annie Malone? Brittney surely knew all the most famous Tyler Newbold stories.

She didn't know the good ones like I did. Like when he'd chugged four Red Bulls in three minutes and spewed all over Gage's new PS4, or when he'd nailed the substitute teacher, or the fact that he seriously regretted pulling that shit with Annie Malone.

I figured it was probably for the best that Brittney didn't know the real Tyler. She'd never agree to hang out if she knew. Not that I really gave a damn if she hung around or whatever.

"'llo?" He answered and burped into the receiver.

I smiled. "Where you at, sugar?"

"With your mom. She said to tell you hi."

"Oh yeah, what a coincidence. I just got done swimming out of your mom's fat ass. She didn't mention you at all."

Brittney made a terrified noise. "Chill," I whispered. "This is normal."

"Ha ha," he chuckled dryly. "There's a party at the House. Get your ass over here, Prescott. Plenty of pussy to go around."

"That's what your mom said," I laughed.

"Oh, fuck you," he laughed and then hung up.

"So…" A twinge of nerves made me shift in the seat. Brittney would not want to go to a party. Least of all at the House. "There's a party."

Her face paled. "A party?" she squeaked. "Will there be alcohol?"

"Nah, they're serving cake and ice cream."

Her face lit up and then fell. "You're not a very easy person to like, Barry."

Chuckling under my breath, I said, "You don't have to drink. Your brother never did."

Her jaw dropped. "Toby went to these parties?"

"A few of them, yeah. I saw him there." I definitely saw Toby there that night I'd called Gwen a cock tease and Toby had taught me some lessons in what not to say to a woman: 1) nothing to Gwen, and 2) not a *fucking* thing to Gwen.

"Oh." Brittney looked torn. "I guess it couldn't hurt anything. I don't have to drink. But Barry?"

"Yeah, what's up?"

"Could we take your car?"

A request I could get behind. "Most definitely. Swing by Dad's place. You know where it is?"

"Yes," she purred.

My car was a classic Charger, black, with custom work done over nearly every inch of the thing. When I was younger, sitting in the garage and watching Dad work on that baby used to be one of my most favorite things to do. I loved her. I'd had no idea he'd bought my girl to fix up and give to me on my sixteenth birthday. Of course, by the time I turned sixteen, I already hated the man who'd rebuilt her, and there was some resentment that transferred into this beautiful car.

I wasn't such an animal that I could ever willingly hurt her. But I'd ripped out the sound system to install a newer one. And I drove like hell on wheels.

Brittney sat in the passenger seat with her hands open, palms up, in her lap. Twice she gulped so loud I could hear her over the rumbling engine. "You're fine," I said, reaching up and massaging the dash. "She's a good girl; she won't hurt you."

Brittney stared at me, wearing an odd sort of smile. "Oh, I know. It's just…well, I've never been in a car like this before."

"Okay? What kinda car do you think this is again?"

Her eyes twinkled. "A dangerous one."

"You think my car is dangerous?"

"With you behind the wheel, Barry? This car is downright deadly."

"I probably shouldn't take that as a compliment."

"You definitely shouldn't take that as a—" She was cut off as I gunned it. Her voice pierced the night in a loud shriek. "Barry!"

Her terrified tenor made my body erupt in cold, agonizing chills.

The same thing had happened when she asked if I was high when I jumped off the cliff. All I could think about was changing the subject. I didn't want to see the inevitable disappointment in her eyes. And now it wasn't disappointment I worried about seeing—it was fear. I didn't want to look over at her and know I'd scared her.

My foot slammed into the brake. I held out my arm to catch her before she crashed into the dash. Her slim fingers caught around my forearm as we braced each other. "Sorry," I mumbled.

"I'm going to regret this night, aren't I?"

"I don't know," I lied because there was a very good chance she would regret it.

ℭℛ

The guys were all sitting out back at the House. They were in mismatching chairs around a makeshift table.

Lonna sat on Gage's lap, and Charli stood duteously behind Bo, but instead of the puppy dog love look she usually wore, Charli's expression was hard, and she glared daggers into the back of his head.

I grabbed two empty milk crates and slammed them into the grass for Britt and me to sit. "Guys, you know Brittney. Brittney, this is the guys." Without sitting, she extended her arm over the center of the table, waiting for someone to shake her hand, which was weird because they did know each other. Formal introductions weren't necessary. She realized this too late and looked seriously embarrassed as she let her hair curtain over her face.

Tyler burst out laughing.

Cheeks flushed, Brittney tucked her dress to her exposed legs before gingerly sitting on the crate.

"What're we playing?" I asked, "And why isn't Charli sitting?"

"It's a free country." Bo waved his hand back at her.

"Really?" Charli sounded annoyed. "I sort of assumed it was invite only?" She stumbled toward the last few crates, grabbed one, and carried it back. Brittney shifted a little—away from me—so Charli could scoot in.

"Circle of death," Gage said. His baby blue eyes shot from Brittney to me, he was trying to ask, without asking, what was going on. I shook my head to say *nothing*.

Because I figured the other guys were thinking the same, I went ahead and said it. "Brittney's parents and my dad were hanging out. We just had to get out of there. Right Britt?" They didn't need to know about that catastrophe at the Multiplex. She was uncomfortable enough without having to relive that in front of my asshole friends.

"Mm-hmm. What's a circle of death?" Her face was pale like all the color had been physically flushed from her usually life-filled cheeks.

Tyler stretched behind the girls to slap my shoulder. His eyebrows arched as if he was expecting me to have more of a story to give to *him* than the *others*. I winked.

Holy hell, was there more of a story? I didn't think so, but that wink was...maybe I was having involuntary eye spasms. Yeah, that worked. I'd tell him that later when we were alone.

Tyler didn't laugh—an oddity for him—as he waited for me to give some other sign that I'd made some headway in the defloration of Bourbon's proudest virgin. I shook my head, and he looked seriously disappointed. More disappointed than a third party observer should look.

"It's fine." Charli patted Brittney's knee. "I'll explain it."

Oh shit. They weren't talking about us, were they? I looked back at Tyler, who looked just as worried.

Charli continued. "It's just a game. You have to take drinks depending on what card you draw."

I heard myself exhale.

Charli's hand still touched Brittney's leg. I stared at the sharp angle of that knee. If I were any better with angles, I could say what degree it was. Sharper than a ninety. Brittney was too tall to be sitting on a milk crate. Just like us guys. We had to bend more than someone like Charli, who almost fit just right.

But Brittney was in a soft dress that slid down her thighs, exposing even more leg than ever before.

Suddenly, I was mad that I'd aided in Charli having a seat at this table. This was my fault. "Want me to switch spots with Charli?" I whispered to Bo.

"It's a free country," he said again. Very subtly he shook his head *no*.

I pretended not to see. "Hey Char, wanna switch crates?"

"Huh?"

"You can still help Britt, you'll just be closer to Bo. It makes sense."

Something hard landed on top of my foot. Bo's heel squished my toes into the grass. He was issuing a nonverbal warning. I bit my tongue to keep from screaming in pain.

I scowled at him. *Now I am definitely switching with her. Dick.*

Charli sprang up, nearly knocking over the table. "Sorry," she squeaked.

Then she fell awkwardly onto my crate, and I took hers. I apologized to Brittney and quickly explained that Charli and Bo had a little something going on. A. *Very. Little.* Something.

Tyler must have heard the whole thing because he burst out laughing. Damn. Now he'd really think that wink had meant something. *Just involuntary eye spasms, Ty, nothing more.* Unless…okay, yeah, fine. I'll admit it. I wanted to bag Brittney.

I wanted to know how her body felt as I slammed into her. I wanted to see those hard angles on every side of me—those elbows beside my head, those knees around my waist. I wanted to feel every inch of her.

It was probably the dumbest, most unattainable thing, I'd ever wanted, but yeah, I did want it. And now that I'd kissed her, I sort of ached for all of her. Usually, like with Lonna, I didn't kiss a girl until the day we hooked up, but Brittney Ann wasn't like that.

Brittney eyed my friends. From overly talkative Tyler, to possessive

Gage, to cranky Bo, to moody Charli, to seductive Lonna, to Chase. Lumpy Chase.

Chase didn't talk much, but he was looking around just like Brittney—like he was waiting for someone to give him some sort of instruction. So I slid the deck of cards across to him and told him to shuffle.

Brittney's bare knee kept rubbing my pant leg. I didn't think it was a big deal to open my palm and grab her exposed flesh, just past the hem of the cotton. The smoothness of her skin sent an electric jolt straight to my crotch. She jumped a little. Eyes wide, she waited for me to say something. She thought I'd touched her to get her attention.

Right. Now what should I say?

"Uh, so this game…" Think Barry, *think, think, think*! All I could think about was the freezing cold shower I'd have to take to maintain the situation in my jeans. "It's a little tough to, uh, pick up on, but you'll do fine."

"I don't want to drink," she whispered. "And you can't drink because you're driving me."

Oh shit. "Uh, well, I'll just drink one. It'll be cool."

She nodded and smiled, almost trustingly. Those golden-speckled eyes twinkled in the sunset light. "Okay. I'll drink one, too."

My jaw flapped open. I had to mentally tell myself to close it. "What? Really?"

"Sure, why not? Drinking isn't bad for you. It's over indulging that's the problem."

I didn't want to argue with her, that drinking probably was bad, because she would know better than me. I yanked two long necks out of Bo's cooler. "You're paying me back," he grumbled.

In the middle of the table—or in our case, industrial sized spool with a block of wood over the hole—the cards were spread into a circle. A can of beer was placed ceremoniously in the middle of all that. "Everyone takes turns drawing cards. Each card means something different…"

I explained it twice to Brittney, but I was pretty sure she got it the first time. Her eyes were wide and excited. She nodded and licked her lips eagerly.

Gage suggested she go first because she was a guest and a lady. I scowled at Chase, who seconded that motion with a little too much enthusiasm. I didn't know what the fat fucker was up to, but for some reason, I didn't like it.

Brittney drew the six of hearts. "It means you give out six drinks. You can split them between people or give them all to one person," I told her.

With wide eyes she looked at Charli, who nodded confirmation.

"Okay." Brittney took a slow breath before saying, "Then I give them to Tyler."

His jaw dropped. "What? Okay, fine, but payback's a bitch."

"Payback?" Brittney's head whipped around and her mouth flapped like a fish's. "I thought it was how the game worked."

"It's cool," I said. "He's being a dick. He has to get a card first."

Brittney's knee rubbed against mine again. She had to know that it was driving me nuts.

Letting out a huff of pent up frustration, I drew a black eight and had to take eight drinks. My beer was almost empty because I never took little sips. When Brittney wasn't looking, I let Bo slip me another bottle. I opened it under the spool top.

Charli grudgingly drew a red two and gave the drinks to Bo, who—at this point—gladly took them.

Bo drew nine, and he used the word "grape" as a rhyming word. "Wait, let me explain. I forgot this one." I grabbed Britt's knee again, ignoring the jolt of excitement that pulsed between us so I could explain. "Nine is nine-nine-bust-a-rhyme. You'll pick up on it."

So Bo said, "Grape."

Lonna, who was on Gage's lap still, said, "Nape."

Tyler snorted. "That's not a word. Take a drink."

"Yes it is," Lonna shot back, flicking her long blonde hair off her shoulder. "You take a drink, idiot. Nape—like the nape of your neck."

Tyler looked unsure, but he took a drink for falsely calling her out. Gage said, "Gape."

Chase had to think about it, which killed the vibe, but then said, "Snape."

"You can't use people," Tyler laughed. "Fucking idiot. Snape isn't even real, anyway."

"Let him have it," I said. "It's just a game."

My hand found Brittney's bouncing knee again, but she was smiling about the game and didn't even seem to notice.

"Fine," Tyler conceded, shrugging. "Rape."

"Oh God." Bo leaned back and rubbed his palms over his face. "Only Tyler would use that word."

Tyler shrugged. "What? It rhymes."

"Just move on," Bo hissed.

Brittney looked flustered as she gnawed on her lower lip. "Um, Crepe."

"What the fuck is a *crepe*?" Gage asked. He shifted a little, causing skinny Lonna to spring forward. She adjusted quickly, tugging her hair into place.

"It's like a pancake," Lonna whispered to him.

"That doesn't rhyme," Gage argued, proving his blood alcohol level was higher than his IQ.

Lonna rolled her eyes. "'Pancake' doesn't rhyme with 'grape,' but 'crepe' definitely does. Barry, it's your turn."

I quickly averted my eyes to show I'd not been looking Lonna's way. "Uh…" Shit, now I couldn't think. *Grape. Gape. Snape. Crepe.* All I could think of were words that weren't real. Like *Alagape.* Or *Fornecrape. Grape?* Uh, *Grape?* Oh damn, I was going to have to drink.

Then came the softest, girlish whisper tickling over my ear. It reminded me of those things I'd always seen on TV—when there's a good angel sitting on one shoulder and a devil on the other. This was definitely the angel, whispering sweetly. "Ape," she said softly. No one heard, but Tyler saw. His lips were half-parted, half-dazed in a swooped smile. He looked frozen in shock. Brittney wanted to help me—it was shocking.

"Ape!" I shouted, feeling a buzz of excitement.

"Oh dangit," Charli groaned. "I was hoping he wouldn't get one. I can't think of anything." She took a drink and the game went on.

SEVEN

BRITTNEY ANN

I was ninety-nine percent positive I was drunk. My vision was fine, but I kept swaying side-to-side just to keep the trees in front of me from dancing too much. If I moved, they tended to stay still.

Since that had never happened before, I decided…okay, yeah, I was drunk.

"One more?" Tyler whispered, tugging the empty bottle from my hand and showing me a full one under the spool top. I wanted to tell him no, but I didn't want to get him in trouble.

After he'd handed me my second beer, he said, "Don't let Bare know I'm helping you out. Deal?"

I didn't want to break our deal now—three beers later.

He pressed this beer against my palm and then curled my fingers around it. He leaned into me and whispered, "Nothing's going to happen to you. I promise. Just let loose a little. I wanna see a drunk Christian chick stripping on this spool."

I gasped. "I'm not *stripping*."

"Whoa, who's stripping?" Barry's deep voice came from my other side. His hand was on my knee again. I wondered if he even realized he'd done that, or if it was completely subconscious. The act probably meant nothing to him anyway.

I was the weirdo that obsessed about touching people.

"I'm not," I said, taking another sip of the beer. I thought I'd been drinking slowly, but Barry was still on his first one. He stared at me out of the corner of his eye. I stared back.

"Seriously you two, stop eye-fucking each other and get a room."

I sputtered into my beer.

A warm hand rubbed my back as I coughed. Yeah, he was definitely not as affected by *touching*. His hands were all over the place, and he didn't seem to mind at all. "What…what is *eye*…you know?" I couldn't say it. My cheeks burned.

Tyler's head fell back as he laughed. Barry just smiled. I was glad all the other guys and Lonna and Charli had disappeared. I felt the most comfortable with Barry and Tyler. Though, that was probably just the beer talking.

"Eye-fucking?" Tyler asked. "You gotta say the word if you wanna know what it means."

Barry reached out in front of me and smacked his friend's arm. "I know, right? I got her to say 'dick'."

The way they talked about me, like I was a child they were corrupting, actually made me feel special. The two of them could have been with anyone doing anything at this party. Yet, they chose to sit out back and watch me sip on a lukewarm beer.

Which tasted awful, by the way. "Fucking," I muttered.

Both of them burst out laughing.

I couldn't tell if they were laughing with me, or at me.

Honestly, I didn't care. That word had tasted vile on my tongue, but at the same time, I felt such a sense of freedom just getting to say it. Daddy would have had a coronary if he'd heard that word come out of my mouth. So would Toby. "Eye-Fucking," I said it again. "What's it mean?"

"Okay, okay. Don't say it too much. I'm already turned on like a motherfucking light switch." Tyler shifted on his crate so he was closer to me.

There was a jolt. I was jerked backward, and suddenly I was only inches away from Barry. "*My* pretentious Christian chick. I saw her first."

"Pretentious?" I snorted.

He smiled.

Tyler cleared his throat. "Right now; what you all are doing— staring deeply into each other's eyes and planning how great it would be to rip off all your clothes and go at it here on the grass—that's eye-fucking, and you guys have been doing it since you got here."

Oh. We had?

Barry laughed. The tops of his ears were a pinkish color. No matter how cool he tried to appear, whispering, "I eye-fuck everything with a pussy," I still sensed his tension.

Or, at least, that was what I told myself.

My phone went off. I recognized the ringtone and my heart dropped. Ryan. Seeing him with Madison had been pretty upsetting, though it probably would have been worse if Barry hadn't been there.

I decided, in that moment, to forgive Barry for standing me up freshman year. It seemed like we'd actually make decent friends. If only I could keep my Mothra butterflies under control in his presence.

"You gonna answer that?" Tyler asked.

"Is it Cheesedick?" Barry asked.

"Yes."

He held out his hand, curling his fingers back on his palm. "Give it to me. I'll put it on speaker."

I didn't even hesitate, which is how I knew we were now friends. I trusted Barry so much more than I should have, all things considered. Placing the phone in his open hand, I exhaled a relieved sigh to be rid of it.

He slid the bar and then pressed the speakerphone button. "Brittney Ann?" Ryan sounded different.

Barry gave me an encouraging head nod.

"Oh, yeah. I'm here."

Tyler had to cover his mouth to keep from laughing out loud.

"Hey, uh, wow this is awkward. I'm really sorry about the movie. I just wanted to call and tell you that things aren't working out for me."

Heat crept up my neck. "*You're* breaking up with *me*?"

"I'm really sorry. I just don't see things working out. And…well, don't take this the wrong way, but we just weren't going anywhere. I sort of met someone. It's…things are——"

"I saw you, you slimy piece of garbage. I saw you in her car."

Barry pulled the phone away before I could grab it and throw it into the river. "Hey, Ry?" Barry's voice was smooth as butter. "Don't worry about Brittney alright? I'm gonna take good care of her. And let Madison know she did a good job, but there's no fucking way I'm touching her after she jerked your nasty ass off."

"She doesn't want you anymore. She wants to be with me."

Tyler couldn't hold it in anymore. "Jesus, Bare! What'd you do?"

He shrugged. "I told Madison to break them up. She couldn't do it without getting her fingers on a dick."

"She likes me," Ryan defended, his voice pitching. "We're going to be together."

"Yeah, good luck with that," Barry said, fighting his twitching grin. "She give you her phone number?"

"Yes, of course." Ryan was victorious.

Barry was unfazed. "You call it yet?"

There was silence on the other end.

"No," he finally admitted.

Tyler doubled over. He was laughing so hard, I was afraid he might vomit. I reached over to rub his back. A hand caught my upper arm, pulling me away from touching Tyler. I glanced at Barry, and he shook his head. Was there a reason I couldn't touch his friend?

"Good luck with that phone number, pal. Like I said, don't worry about Britt. She's in good hands." He brushed my hair off my shoulder and leaned over to kiss my cheek. A giggle burst from my lips, and he chuckled in victory. "Real good hands, man. Don't worry about her at all."

"Wait…"

Barry ended the call and handed the phone back to me. His fingers fisted and fell back to his side. "Can you believe him?" Barry growled. The chuckling, happy-go-lucky version of his personality was gone.

I shook my head. "You didn't have to do that."

"Do what?"

"Pretend like we're…" I didn't know how to say it, so I just waved in the air, hoping I didn't sound, and look, crazy. "You know."

"Fucking?" Tyler guessed.

"Ty, shut up." Barry smiled around the rim of his beer. "No problem," he said quietly before taking a big pull off the bottle.

I decided to find the restroom (despite both of their insistence that it was more sanitary to go outside), and they were going to scout the party. Not wanting to look dependent, I waved goodbye to both of them and walked through the House.

I'd heard about this place. People at school talked about it all the time. It was a river house that had been abandoned years ago.

So-and-so did this at the House. *You-know-who* lost their virginity at the House. *They* did a keg stand at the House.

I didn't even know what a keg stand was. I *saw* the keg and it was *standing* upright. There were people leaning against it, so maybe that was a keg stand. I made a mental note to look it up when I got home.

Most of what I'd heard about this place had come from Toby. *"Don't you dare ever go there, you hear me Brittney Ann?"*

"Fine, yeah, whatever."

"I'm not kidding. This is the most serious thing I will ever say to you. I know Dad thinks that when I tell you something, you do the opposite just to spite me. Well this time, you can't do that. Don't go there. Gwen went there, and she got hurt."

He never would tell me *how* she got hurt. I always assumed it was an urban legend. Like the Hookman who attacked kids who were having sex in their car—a fable meant to warn against the dangers of underage sex.

If Gwen had gotten hurt here, it was probably because she'd tripped on some trash. This place was a complete wreck. I found the bathroom in a little alcove under the stairs. The floor was sopping wet. I was pretty sure I'd made the correct decision when I decided to hold it until I got home.

It was as I was walking back outside that I first saw her. Arms stretched up in the air. She was showing Ann Malone a cheer. It was the cheer we did when the team was on defense. I wasn't surprised Ann looked bored. She'd been a cheerleader as long as Madison.

Then I realized Madison's little show wasn't *for* Ann. Every time her arms lifted into the air, there was a threat of that shirt/dress falling down. A crowd of guys couldn't take their eyes off her. They cheered on her cheering.

Bile rose in my throat. No, wait—it wasn't bile. It was spit. I was so angry, I could spit.

The stars aligned when Madison did a little turn, set her red cup on the table behind her, where no one but me could see, and then she went back to cheering, with her hands high above her head. I acted quickly, not thinking about what I was doing or why I was doing it. I yanked her cup off the table, hawked a big loogie into it, swirled it around once, and then set the cup back down.

I took two steps backward before slamming into a flesh wall. "Sorry," I mumbled to whomever. Turning, I saw that Barry stood in the doorway blocking me.

Heat threatened my neck. Again.

"Barry!"

"Busted," he whispered. That tummy-tickling grin stole over his face. Gripping my elbow, he led me down the hall before actually saying, "Come with me."

EIGHT

BARRY

"Oh, I really don't do things like this…" She stomped ahead of me. I had to run to keep up.

"You kidding? That was badass. Bitch deserved it." I punched excitedly into my open palm. The second she'd picked up that red cup, I'd been pulsing with adrenaline.

She pouted back at me. "It was awfully childish. Something came over me all of a sudden, and all I could think about was getting back at her."

"Why are you defending yourself?" I asked. "I said it was badass."

"Oh, I know, it's just—"

"Britt, stop. It's cool." I massaged the tops of her arms.

She huffed. Biting into her thin lower lip, she held back a stream of words, which seemed to nearly break her. Her face turned red from the exertion. Her hazel eyes begged me to let her ramble.

"Fine." I threw my hands up. "Just spit it out, but I'm not really all that interested. I think you were awesome back there."

Her pinched lips twisted into a soft smile. "Thank you. I'm afraid it was juvenile. I don't know why I do things like this."

Things? Plural? Okay, I was more interested than implied. "Go on..."

"Oh, Barry, it's so silly."

I actually wanted to know what else she'd done, but we'd found the car. It had been boxed in by four other vehicles. "Fucking idiots," I mouthed. I knew I shouldn't have left her on the street. Having anyone parked so close to my girl made me nervous.

"What should we do?" Brittney asked, fumbling through her massive purse like she had a plan. "I'm going to call my father—"

"Wait, whoa." I caught her wrist, stopping her. I had a very terrifying mental image of Mitch Wilson beating my face in because I'd given her a beer. "Do not do that."

"Barry, he expects me home. I'll just explain to him—"

"You cannot let him come here. No adults. It's a rule." It wasn't, there were no rules, but it should have been.

"Fine. I'll call Gwen."

All the blood in my body rushed to my toes. I was working light-headed and empty. "Do not do that," I repeated.

"Why? Gwen isn't an adult. She'll understand this situation perfectly."

I had something called pride. Not much, but just enough that I didn't want Brittney in on what had gone down with Gwen and me all those years ago. Clearing my dry throat, I stammered, "Look, we got a little time before you have to be home. We'll go drink another beer, then come back. One of those cars will surely be gone."

When she didn't respond, I countered with, "We'll go to the bluff. It's only about fifty feet—"

"Is it dangerous?" She asked.

"Uh, not if we don't jump in. We'll just sit. There's enough light from the House that it should be lit up pretty good. Here..."

I entered the code to unlock Bo's Beamer. He'd be pissed, but I would deny any knowledge. I stole the last six pack of Bud Light out of his cooler in the back.

The smell of her sweet strawberry hair enticed me. A buzzing thrill pulsed in my veins. I was beginning to recognize the high I felt just from her presence. Brittney probably was used to guys holding her hand, which was the only reason I moved my fingers to hers this time.

"Toby's so perfect. Everything he ever did was on the mark. Straight A student, beautiful girlfriend, wonderful Christian..." Brittney made two fists and rubbed circles over her eyes.

"For what it's worth, I think your brother's a dick."

She scowled. "I'm allowed to-to-to say th-that y-you're..." She yawned, smacking her lips together as she fell back against the rock and me. I caught her hips, yanking her firmly into me. Fuck me, she smelled amazing. My nose nestled in her hair, and she giggled.

"You smell so fucking good."

"It's shampoo."

"Yeah? Not perfume?"

"No. I don't wear perfume." My finger sliced under the thick strap of her dress, pushing it off the edge of her shoulder. A violent shiver rippled through her body, rocking her forward.

"Whoa." I caught her, hugging her securely against me. "You cold?"

She nodded. I could have told her to put that little jacket back on, but I didn't do that.

"I love Toby," she said.

My teeth ground together. "He's your brother. You're supposed to."

"But he's so perfect. He never does anything wrong. He never did. And-and-and I feel like everyone expects the same from me." Her body twisted so she could bury her face against my shoulder and press her lips into my neck. The cool air of her breath tickled my jaw.

Brittney.

Brittney.

Brittney.

I loved that name. Such a yummy name.

"Ugh," she groaned. Then she went on with her rant. "Even after he enlisted, my parents couldn't stop doting on him. He was supposed to go to college, you know? Play football, maybe. Then he was injured, football went out the window, and my father just accepted Toby's enlistment. Isn't that absurd?"

"Completely," I mumbled, but hell if I could remember the question.

"Spitting in Madison's drink, that was…oh, she just lit me on fire. Ryan was a very nice boy. We could have been like Gwen and Toby. Don't you think?"

Is she drunk? She was talking a helluva lot. "No," I told her. "Gwen and Toby, uh, they're, uh, ate up."

"What? No, they're beautiful together. He loves her more than anything, and he'd do anything for her"—*yeah, I'd noticed*—"and they're going to be married and have two-point-five children and live happily ever after and be perfect, blah, blah, blah…"

Leaning out of my hold, she huffed. Her head rolled on her neck a few times before dropping into her hands.

"What's up?"

Her bottle of beer hovered as she brought it up to her mouth, preparing to take a swig. "I stole panties," she admitted out of nowhere.

My hands froze in midair as I stilled in my quest to reach for her. "Huh?"

She looked me square in the eye when she confessed. "Panties. Sexy panties. From the mall. I was shopping with Mom, and I knew she'd never let me have them. She'd be curious as to why I wanted them. So I stuffed them into my dress and walked out of the store. It was the most exhilarating and awful thing I've ever done." She stilled, staring up at me. "Wait…was spitting in Madison's cup worse?"

"Whoa, whoa, hold on a minute. What color were these panties?"

She turned her beer upside down, pouring what was left onto the ground. Her lips curved downward as she watched the last of it drain out. "Oh Barry, you're not taking me seriously. I think there's something wrong with me. I enjoy doing these things. Isn't that awful?"

I swallowed three heartbeats, trying to decide what she found so *awful* about all of this. "No. So are we talking black…red… purple…?"

Her expression deadpanned. "They're red, Barry, now please focus."

"Hell if I can focus. All I'm thinking about are your panties. You got 'em on now?" My buzz was obliterated. I was one-hundred-percent sober. I just wished my imagination were a little better so I could picture her without that hideous dress. My fingers inched toward the hem, and I imaged sliding that fabric up her thighs—just a little bit.

"Yes." She sounded annoyed as she pushed away from the rock-chair, and me. Without me even having to ask, she fisted the bottom of the dress and hoisted it into the air.

The way a little girl shows a little boy that their parts are different. That's what this reminded me of. One time, probably second grade, a girl had showed me hers, and I had showed her mine. We were not the same. Ever since, I'd always been fascinated by that difference.

I bit into my fist. My teeth tore deliciously into the flesh at my knuckles.

Brittney, however, elicited a different emotion than that

eight-year-old girl had. Brittney awakened desire. My mouth watered at the sight of that red *thong*. Thin straps hugged her slim hips. Milky white thighs, just the perfect fit for my waist. "Are you satisfied?" she asked, cheeks rosy despite her initial burst of courage.

I shook my head. "Not even close."

"Oh, be mature," she groaned, dropping the hem of that dress so it fell over those pearl-smooth legs and then swayed to the rhythm of the wind.

Slamming her fist against her chest, she exaggerated, "I *stole* them! Can you believe me? I feel awful about it. I stole panties thinking my boyfriend would want to touch me...*ever*."

"Honestly?" I forced words through my awed lips as I tried to mentally talk myself down. My heart drummed out an uneven solo, and my mind raced a million miles an hour as I tried to come up with some excuse to make her do that dress move again. I was sure if she did it just one more time, I'd memorize her.

Clearing my dry throat, I stood up and said, "I'm surprised. Not totally upset by this side of you, but definitely surprised."

"What should I do?" she asked innocently. *Kiss me? Suck me? Fuck me?* All of the above.

She gnawed on her lower lip. "I can't return them to the store. Should I tell the police?" Oh, we were still talking about the underwear.

"Whoa, chick, chill. People steal all the time. It's fine. No one got hurt."

Her head hung. "I'm not proud of myself," she admitted. "And I can't even keep them. My mother will see them in the wash and know what happened."

"You can give them to me," I said carelessly. I meant it, but it was careless to say it out loud.

"If you're not going to be helpful, then you should just be quiet."

Was she smiling?

We were both silent for a little bit before she cleared her throat. "I have another confession…"

And I was dying to hear it. My knuckles popped as they pressed into the rock beside me.

She stared down at her flat shoes as her toe worked into the rocky earth. "I sometimes think it might be easier to have sex and get it over with."

That took some processing.

She what?

Then I thought it again.

Kiss me, Brittney. Do me, right here. No one would ever know. Okay, lie. I would definitely tell Ty, and he would tell everyone because he was Tyler, and that was his way. I tossed an empty beer bottle toward the riverbank and Brittney scowled. "You're not leaving that there, are you?"

I arched a brow. "Problem?"

"It's littering," she mumbled.

"I thought we were talking about how you liked living on the wild side."

"Yes," she said cautiously. "But not when a fish could get trapped inside the bottle. Or a duck could get his head stuck." She marched over to the bottle, grabbed it, walked it back to the six pack, and dropped it. She completely missed. "Oops," she giggled.

I tucked the bottle back into the sleeve for her.

Brittney swayed as her fingers tugged into her long, silky hair. She really was beautiful. As her arms lifted overhead, her dress scooted up those creamy legs. "What were we talking about? Oh, right. Katy Lynn did it, you know? With Gage. Now she's free. She doesn't act so uptight anymore. Does that make sense?"

Seeing as how we'd practically thrown sweet, unsuspecting Katy Lynn at Gage, trying to get him over what had happened with me and Lonna, yeah, I knew about them. "Yeah. I heard about that."

Her eyes rolled. "Of course you did. It was so embarrassing for her. You know she really did like him? She talked about him a lot. Then she got over him. It would have been worse if she were in love with him and then realized their sexual relationship wasn't going anywhere. She hadn't invested any time in him. It was done and done." She wiped her hands together like she was brushing dirt off her fingers.

"And what does this have to do with you?"

"Because. If you and I had sex, I would know that you know what you're doing. I would know that you wouldn't hurt me like someone who doesn't have any experience. Then I could move on without having to worry about this stupid, ridiculous hurdle. Does that make sense?"

"Uh, not really." I really, really wished I could read her expression. She had a small smile on her barely parted lips. But what the hell did that mean? "Britt, are you thinking about hooking up?"

Please.

Say.

Yes.

She chewed on her lower lip for a second before releasing it and revealing that smile again. Then, decidedly, she nodded. "I think so."

My heart drummed. I could hear it in my ears. Boom. Boom. Boom. "Now?"

Before I could even think about what to do next, she pulled that cotton dress over her head.

Standing in front of me was one of the most beautiful women I'd ever seen. Red thong and a tank top shirt. She was showing less skin than a swimsuit would reveal, but for some reason, I was more turned on than I had been in a long time.

"Brittney…" I blew out her name with a loud gust of air. My heart was uncontrollable. Slamming my fist against my chest, I tried to still the rapid beating. "What're you thinking right now?"

"I'm not," she admitted, shaking her head. "I don't want to think about anything. You…you have protection right?"

I couldn't tear my eyes away from her flat tummy. She shivered, and I hurried to stand and throw my arms around her. "Don't be cold, babe. I got you." *Don't be cold? Really, Bare? You're some Casanova with that shit.*

She nodded. Her big golden-amber eyes blinked up at me. "I know. Be gentle with me, please."

Holy shit. Had I fallen asleep? Was that what had happened? I had fallen, and I was dreaming. Yeah, that made sense.

My mouth pressed against hers. She tore at my T-shirt, and I wasted no time pulling it over my head. I kissed her softly at first, but the more my mouth touched her skin, the more my body desired hers, the more my need for her intensified.

She didn't just smell like strawberries. She tasted like them, too. It seemed like the most innocent thing in the world. Not perfume. Not some exotic lotion. Just strawberries. Like lip balm and shampoo.

It fit her, and I admitted to myself how disappointing it would have been if she'd tasted like something foreign. Brittney deserved to be natural.

"Just a second." I rubbed over her shoulders a few times, hopefully warming her up enough that I could take a step back. Fluffing her dress in the air, I laid it out flat on the ground. Then I did the same with my shirt.

By the time I reached out for Britt, she had both arms wrapped tightly around herself. "Come here," I laughed.

She shivered in my arms.

Kissing down her neck, I blew hot air against her skin, which only made chills explode all over her. I chuckled. "I can't tell if you're cold or excited."

"Both," she breathed. "I'm-I'm both."

I pushed her, admittedly, a little too roughly. Her body went stiff, and I went on the defensive. "I'm excited, too." And nervous. And anxious to get this over with before she changed her mind.

Gripping tightly to my upper arms, she swallowed hard. "You're not going to hurt me?"

"I'm going to try not to," I corrected. "It always hurts a little."

My hands turned to velvet against her skin. Using my knuckles, I tried to feel for any sharp rocks that might stab her as I lead her onto her back. When I was sure there wasn't anything too uncomfortable, I pushed her flat. Her head lolled to the left.

My mouth explored along her collarbone, sucking her flesh between my lips. Because she seemed unknowing about what to do, I dragged her skinny arm up around the back of my neck where it hung limply. She didn't hold onto me. I wanted to see her tensed up. I wanted to see her excited.

But I didn't *have* to see her like that. I could live with Lethargic -Brittney.

The clasp of her bra sat between the two perfect mounds of her breasts. It had always been a fantasy to undo one of those clasps with my teeth. Yanking the fabric of her tank top just below the subtle lumps of her breasts, I licked down her sternum.

She didn't move. She didn't complain about my teeth on her satin bra. Glancing up, I noticed her eyes were closed.

Is she second guessing this?

Bracing my hands on the ground, I leaned back. Her face was serene. She…she looked asleep. Cupping her face with my palm, I tilted her head up. Her eyes didn't open. "Britt?" Nothing. "Brittney?"

Smiling through sleep, she blinked up at me. "Hi."

Shiiiiit. "Britt, how much have you had to drink?"

"Huh? Oh, those two from that pack. The one you gave me. Then the three Tyler handed me. So four." She giggled. Roses splattered her cheeks with color.

Fuck me. She was drunk. "Tyler gave you beer?" My knuckles fisted into the dirt as I pushed off the ground. Doing the unthinkable, I crawled off of her.

Brittney leaned up on her elbows, still staring at me. Confusion wrinkled a line between her brows. "Yes. Don't worry, it was all sealed."

"I wasn't worried about *that*. Tyler's too stupid to mic a girl. He'd probably end up drugging himself. No, Britt, you're drunk. Put your dress on."

"Hmm? No, I'm fine."

I growled. "Put your dress on. You want me to do this when we're sober, then we'll do it. I'm not doing it tonight."

Hooded eyes stared at me. Her mouth puckered open and closed like a disoriented goldfish. Then she bolted upright, scrambling for her clothes. "That was really stupid of me. Forgive me. Of course you don't want to."

"I want to."

"No, it's fine, Barry. You don't have to say it. I understand. I'm younger. I'm not as popular. I get it."

"No, you don't. I wanna fuck your brains out, but I'm not doing it while you're drunk. You'll regret it. Plus, your brother's already kicked my ass a couple times. I don't really want to deal with that again. Then there's your dad."

The strain inside my jeans insisted that I think about this. Forget Toby and Mitch. Forget the fact that she *might* regret it. I'd always heard that the drunk mind wanted what the sober mind couldn't admit. So maybe…just maybe, she really did want this.

Good. *Then we could do it tomorrow.*

My dick *really* didn't like how sober I was.

Her arms folded over her stomach. It hadn't taken her a few seconds to get her clothes adjusted, and then she twisted and stomped back toward the car. "I'll call my dad," she said. "You don't have to put up with me anymore."

"Dammit, Brittney. You're drunk." And, frankly, she was getting on my nerves. I wanted her to go with someone else, so I could actually enjoy this party.

Then again, the idea of her going anywhere, *with anyone*, made my knuckles curl as dominance unfurled into rage. If she'd taken her clothes off like that for me, then there was no knowing what she'd do for someone else.

She stumbled, and before she could do anything else that would further annoy me, I caught her around the middle and pulled her weight up over my shoulder. That dominance took form as an internal roar inside my chest. I decided right then that I was taking her from this party. And that was that.

"Barry!"

"Just be quiet. I'm taking you to your car at my house. We'll figure out what to do from there." She didn't make another sound as her limp body smacked against me.

I was glad that the car behind mine had left. I dropped Britt to the ground, and she swayed.

"Barry," she said my name slowly. I knew what was going to happen before she held up her index finger and lurched forward. One second she was staring at me, her face pale. The next second she was bent forward, puking all over my shoes.

"Fuck."

This was my own fault, really. This was what I got for sticking my nose in people's business. I didn't even like people much.

My fingers laced through her strawberry hair as I pulled it out of her face. "Try and get some on the grass, sweetheart. My shoes can only hold so much."

She hiccupped a laugh. "Don't make me laugh," she said, gagging again.

She dry heaved several times while I tried to hold on to her silky hair. If she'd let me leave the six pack on the riverbank, I would have had two hands to help her. It was her own fault she'd thrown such a fit about littering. I tucked the empty six pack under my elbow and tried to grab more of her hair. "Okay," I conceded. "We're even."

"Hmm?" She leaned back, wiping her mouth with the back of her hand.

"We're even for that time I stood you up."

She glanced at my shoes and then up at me. "I'd already forgiven you for that. I really appreciate everything you've done for me tonight. I'm sorry I'm so—"

"You're fine," I said, opening the door of the car for her.

"I'm pathetic," she mumbled. I pretended not to hear it because, yeah, she was pathetic. Terrible at drinking. She stole panties for the ugliest guy I'd ever lain eyes on. And she gave me blue balls like I'd never had before. I couldn't wait until she was home, and I was free.

That stupid, empty six pack was on the back floorboard. It was the first thing Mitch saw when he pulled open the passenger door. The fact she'd passed out and was in no condition to drive meant I was directly in the line of fire of her dad's fists. Letting out a very methodical huff, he lifted Brittney easily into his arms. "Won't you come inside, Barry?"

"Honestly, I'm a little afraid to do that."

His dead eyes leveled me. "You should be."

"What?"

"You brought my daughter home after curfew. She reeks of alcohol and cigarette smoke—"

I threw my hands up in surrender. "Hey, she didn't smoke anything."

His eyes narrowed. "How much did she drink?"

"Four beers," I lied. It was close enough. "I didn't know she had so much."

"Come inside," he repeated, and I realized that *this* was not a question or an option.

I followed him through the large oak front door into the overly cozy foyer. "There's vomit on my shoes," I said, not wanting to give him more of a reason to fight me by walking on his floor.

He scowled down at my feet.

"It's not mine." I gestured with my chin to Brittney.

His frown curved back into a smile. "Stay," he said, and I stayed while he carried her up the stairs. If I wasn't mistaken, the man was humming to his near-comatose daughter.

I kicked out of my shoes. If not for the fact they were worn in all the right places and comfortable as hell, I'd trash them. Instead, I'd probably have to figure out how the washing machine worked.

Mitch was not humming on the way back down the stairs. I took a step backward out of defense and realized I was planted flat against the door. Great. Cornered like an injured animal. Hardwood floor boards creaked under the man's weight. "Explain." His large, lumberjack hand caught my hurt shoulder as he pushed me toward the kitchen.

"I think, maybe, Brittney should be—"

"I want to talk to you." He hooked a chair with his foot, kicked it toward me, and then shoved me onto it. "What happened with Ryan

Freeman?" Mitch asked as he opened a cake container and pulled out a half-eaten cherry pie. Then he started to eat it with a fork and no plate. He did not offer me any.

That looked like really good pie. I licked my lips and he still didn't offer me any.

"Explain," he barked.

"Uh, that guy? Okay, he, uh—"

Mitch cleared his throat. "Barry, do not say 'uh' to me again. Finish your story."

Again, not a question.

"Right, so…" I wanted to say uh. "So, Ry, he uh…sorry, he hooked up with another girl."

Gripping tightly to that fork, Mitch glared at me. "This evening?"

"Yeah, at the movies. He let Britt and me go inside, and he went to the parking lot to, uh—"

"Not 'uh.' What happened?"

"He got a hand job." Saying *hand job* in front of the man who'd given me my first communion was single-handedly the most embarrassing thing I'd ever done. I tucked my head, trying not to watch the monstrous way he devoured that delicious-looking pie, one forkful at a time.

If at all possible, Mitch looked even angrier. "So you took advantage of my daughter's delicate state—"

"Hey, I didn't take advantage of shit."

"You will not swear at me." His voice boomed. I shrank against the chair even though I wanted to stay up tall. "This is my house, that's my daughter, you will do as I say."

Not a question.

"Yeah, okay." But not because he said so.

"Barry…" He shook his head. That was a look I recognized. The *you're a lost cause, so why are we having this conversation* look. The *I'm so fed up with your attitude* look. The *I'm done* look. Then Mitch took a breath and his expression softened. Pastor Mitch was back. "Have you spoken to your mother recently? Spent any time with her?"

This again? "No, but I want to." I straightened a little. This wasn't my favorite conversation, but it was better than talking about Brittney.

He pushed a piece of crust around his plate with his fork. *He isn't going to waste that is he*? "You and your father, do you talk much?"

"Not really. I can't stand him for what he did to Mom."

Mitch's brows pinched in confusion. "Meeting Ashleigh, you mean?"

I take it back, this *was* my least favorite topic. Scrubbing my palms over my eyes, I groaned. "Look, can we just talk about Brittney and not my shitty life?"

Mitch glanced up, his face twisted into a smirk. "You think you have a shitty life? Driving a very nice car. Wearing expensive clothes. Living in a large house. Yes, I could see why you'd think that."

"Dude, don't judge me."

He smiled wider. *God, what a prick.* "Then tell me: what's so awful about your life that you felt the need to bring my daughter into your misery?"

"What? I already told you—I didn't take advantage of her. I didn't even touch her." Okay, I touched her. I wanted to touch her some more, but I hadn't *actually* done anything bad to her.

"You didn't have to touch her to take advantage. Just giving her alcohol was too much. My daughter isn't like you, Barry. She's good. She's better than I ever was. She's too good to be out drinking, and you damn well know it. You're lucky I don't kick your ass for bringing her home that way." He fisted his fork, and I had the superb mental image of my limp body flying backward through the sliding glass window behind me.

"This is so stupid. She wasn't even my date."

Mitch bristled, his tight grip made the fork bend backward. "You can rest assured that my daughter will *never* be your date. She deserves to be respected and treated like the angel she is. You, Barry, haven't a clue where to begin deserving my daughter."

My eyes accidentally rolled. If I'd been thinking at all, I'd not have done something so stupid in front of the ex-Navy Seal/currently pissed off father. The fact he was a preacher seemed oddly irrelevant. "You think you deserve her?" he asked, his voice a lethal whisper.

"No," I answered the right way, and then stupidly kept talking. "But you're her dad. You're supposed to think no one deserves her."

That twisted smirk was back. "Exactly. No one on this planet is good enough, but the boy she chooses will know this, and he will spend every day of her life worshiping the ground she walks on, just to guarantee she doesn't find another boy who is just a little more deserving."

I drove with dead silence beating at my eardrums. My overused car stereo implored me to blast some Van Halen or Steve Miller Band or Queen—something just to put the silence out of its misery. I couldn't do it.

My brain was full of thoughts, and I was afraid the music would only make it worse. Never in my life had I thought a melody would hurt a situation. Brittney did this. Acting all mysterious in that stupid cotton dress...she had me thinking she was something different. The way Lonna had had me thinking it. I'd proven Lonna was the same as every other girl. I could do that with Brittney if I wanted. Yeah, that would show Mitch. Show him that his daughter wasn't any more special than any other girl on the planet.

I was the one who needed to be *deserved* a little. He'd said it—I had a nice car, a big house. I was hot, too. He didn't say that, but it was my best quality—good looks. I was going to be a senior, a starting football player.

Brittney would have been so lucky to have my dick.

Yeah, I should have told Mitch that—told him that his perfect little princess, in her stolen panties, wasn't good enough for *me*.

The Charger was roaring a buck-ten down Interstate-44 before I even processed where I was headed. Mom's apartment was in Sullivan. She was probably asleep, but I had a key.

I did not want to see Dad. Not that I thought Mitch would call him and rat about what had happened, but there was always a chance.

I opened the apartment door noiselessly. The TV was set to mute, and Mom was asleep on the couch. An empty bottle of wine lay sideways on the carpet beneath her.

Grabbing the blankets off her bed and her pillow, I tucked her into the couch. Her hair felt weird, like it hadn't been washed in a couple days. Maybe she was sick? That's why she had fallen asleep on the couch.

I kissed her cheek, pulled the afghan around her shoulders, and then tiptoed to my room.

My room in this place was different than my room at home. I only got to spend one weekend a month with Mom, which was total horseshit because she was my mom, and I was old enough to say where I should go. I'd fought with Dad about it plenty of times, but he never budged on this. It was the only thing in the world he cared about—keeping me away from my mom.

She'd moved into the apartment when I was thirteen. I'd been in a big skateboarding faze, so the room was decorated in posters of famous skateboarders that I, now, couldn't name. There was an alarm clock that was shaped like a skateboard wheel, and the dresser had little skateboard handles. So yeah, my friends never came here.

Just like my dresser at home, however, there were goodies hidden inside a tin in it. I kicked off my shoes and stripped down to my boxers before heading for the stash. Buried under a pair of wool socks I'd never worn, the tin felt strange. Lighter than I remembered.

There were just two pills inside. These were small, oval shaped tablets.

I knew for a fact I'd left the muscle relaxers and sleeping pills here. There had been dozens. I couldn't sleep at this house. Not because of Mom or anything. The bed was hard and small and there was an obnoxious dusk-to-dawn light outside the window.

I went through the drawer thinking the candy had escaped the container. What the hell? Had Mom found it all and flushed it? Why would she leave two?

Holy shit. Had someone robbed the place? This wasn't exactly the nicest apartment complex, and this county was notorious for drug-related break-ins. But how could anyone have known the pills were here? Maybe someone knew *I'd* been here.

I looked around the apartment, trying to decide if anything else was missing. The living room TV was obviously still there; so was Mom's TV in her bedroom. Her iPad and phone were on the coffee table. All the kitchen appliances—coffee maker, stand mixer, blender—were accounted for. Her jewelry box looked fine, but I couldn't be sure.

Dammit. I couldn't say anything to her without her knowing I occasionally took recreational pills.

Not knowing what to do, I redressed, downed the two muscle relaxers, then let myself back out the front door, re-locking it with my key, and walked toward the Charger.

Dad was sitting at the kitchen table. I walked right past him on my way to the laundry room. "I just throw shit in here and add soap, right?" I kicked off my still drenched shoes and socks. *Absolutely fucking disgusting.* I dropped it all into the washer. Looking around the room, I couldn't find anything labeled "soap."

"Use the pods," Dad said.

Pods?

"On the back of the dryer." He appeared in the doorway and pointed to an orange tub that was, yeah, on the back of the dryer. I flipped open the container and pulled out three pods—just to be safe. If I'd used too much, Dad didn't notice. "Is there something you'd like to tell me?" he asked, staring down at his bare feet and not me.

Yeah. Instead of getting laid, I got barfed on. Add this to being taunted by a pastor and this night just might have been the worst of my life. I didn't say that, though. "Uh…"

"Why is Brittney Wilson's car outside?"

Shouldering past him, I headed for the fridge. I hoped someone had refilled the bottled water after I'd drank the last one earlier. "Oh, uh, yeah, it's a long story. I don't really want to talk about it."

Someone in this house was more responsible than me—more water. I yanked one off the shelf, twisted the cap, and chugged. Tossing the empty bottle into one of Ashleigh's green recycle bins, I couldn't help but feel like Brittney would have been proud of my eco-friendly move. I turned toward the stairs with a stupid smile on my face. Dad's statuesque frame blocked me.

"I'd like to know why the pastor's daughter's vehicle is in our driveway, Barry. Now answer me."

I weaseled past him. "I went to your stupid dinner. Can't you get off my dick?"

Without undressing, I flopped onto my inviting mattress and fell asleep not thinking about any annoying drunk chicks or ex-Navy Seals.

Muscle relaxers always made me dream about the craziest shit.

Dad was sitting at the kitchen table, not eating the bowl of cereal he'd made himself. I knew he was mad because all the muscles in his forearms strained. It didn't matter how many times I tried to tell him about the skateboard I wanted for my birthday—because it had to be the sick black one with the lime green wheels—he didn't say anything.

His lips were drawn tight like he was angry.

Then the front door opened and closed. "Go to your room," Dad barked.

I didn't go to my room because I didn't take orders. "Barry." Dad exhaled, rubbing his temples with his fingers. "Go now." His voice trembled, and it sank in that something was wrong.

Mom stumbled into the kitchen. High heeled shoes dangled from her fingers. Last night's makeup was smeared across her face. She still looked so pretty.

"Hey Mom." I jumped up to give her a kiss on the cheek. I couldn't ever do that in front of Tyler because he always went on about wanting to kiss her—not on the cheek.

She smelled like cigarettes. I knew the smell because I'd snuck a couple from Bo's grandpa one time, but Mom didn't smoke. She'd never smelled like this before.

"Bare, my sweet, sweet boy." She ruffled my hair and then fell into one of the heavy kitchen chairs, making the thing screech across the linoleum.

"Rebecca, tell your son it's time to go upstairs so we can talk."

"Oh, Duncan…"

"Now! He's still not listening to me."

She let out a small sigh. "I'm sorry, Bare. Just do as your dad says. He wants to yell at me."

"Rebecca…"

"What? That's what you want, isn't it? To yell and get mad. You can't let anything go, can you? It's always a fight, and I'm always the bad guy. I'm the one who has to send him to his room."

My fists balled. If she wanted, I'd fight Dad for her. "Go!" he snapped. "Go to your room, Barry. Do not come out until I tell you it's okay!"

"No!"

"Dammit, Rebecca, do you see this."

She shrugged. From over her shoulder, she winked at me.

"I'm not going to let you hurt Mom."

His jaw dropped. "Hurt her? Her? She's the one...ooh, you've got your hooks in him, don't you woman? Barry, I'm telling you to leave one last time. Leave this room, or I will make you leave."

I believed him. "Mom?" She could come with me. I'd keep her safe. Dad wouldn't hurt her with me around.

She patted my cheek. "Go on, sweetheart. I'm fine."

I sat at the foot of the stairs in protest of actually going to my room.

Their fight started in too low of a murmur to hear, but, like always, it raised in volume. "Yes, yes I stayed all night. Of course I did. It would have woken you both up if I came in drunk. I figured——"

"What? That I'd prefer you staying with him. Dammit, Rebecca, this isn't working."

"Why not? You have your little slut. Why can't I have fun too?"

"Nothing's going on with Ashleigh. How many times do I have to tell you this?"

"Ha! I'm not a fool, Duncan."

He let out a loud groan. "Bex, you do realize you have a problem, right? It's not just the screwing around. You and me, we've always been relaxed about that, we went into this marriage with an open mind, and I'm okay with all of it. But the drinking, the drugs...you're not yourself anymore."

She laughed a cold, hard laugh. "This is the only way I can stand to be part of this family, Duncan."

I barely heard him say, "Then maybe you shouldn't be."

A sheen of sweat coated my forehead. My mouth tasted like I'd been chewing on Brittney's dress...no, that could be a good taste. This was simply dryness. Like cotton.

I stretched the stiffness from my muscles and then shuffled toward the kitchen for a bottle of water. The house was quiet. I decided to go for a run before anyone woke up. Before my tennis shoes were even laced, my stomach let out a nauseated groan. Yeah, running was probably not a good idea after beer and pills, so I kicked off my shoes and flopped back against the mattress.

I must have fallen back asleep. The next thing I knew, my phone rang. Without even opening my eyes, I swiped the bar to answer it. "Hello?"

"Hello? Oh, hello? Hi, Barry?"

Oh god. "Yeah, what's up?"

"It's Brittney."

"I got that. What do you want?" I couldn't even believe I'd wanted to nail her. Skinny little Christian wasn't worth the effort. Sex was too easy to work for it.

There was a small voice inside my head saying *yeah, but if she offered right now, you'd jump at it.* Right, but I knew she wasn't going to offer. That had been a one-time deal. My stupid morals had lost me that victory.

"I left my car at your house, and I was wondering if you wouldn't mind coming and getting me."

Was she serious? I waited, thinking she'd tack on a joke, but it never happened. "You, uh…what?"

"Could you come and get me, please? So that I can get my car."

I pulled the phone away from my face and stared at the screen, expecting this to be some elaborate prank. Who the hell did she think she was talking to? "Isn't there someone else you could call?"

"Oh, well I suppose. I didn't think to call Katy Lynn. She could probably borrow her daddy's truck. And I did talk to Lonna—that's how I got your phone number. I missed my parents; they left before I woke up. Yes, I *could* call someone."

Because having her puke on my shoes was pretty much the extent of my charity. "Okay."

"Okay," she said slowly, her voice soft. "Are you saying you won't come and get me?"

Crap. Crap. Crap. I fisted the sheet beside me. Taking a deep breath, I exhaled heavily. "No, fine, I'll be there in a little bit. Let me take a shower first."

"Wonderful. I'll make breakfast, if you'd like?"

"What? Oh, sure."

I slammed around in the shower. Punching the knob with my fist. She had a lot of nerve to call like that. She didn't think we were, like, boyfriend and girlfriend, did she? Just because we'd made out a little bit. Damn. I was probably going to have to break up with her.

Mitch's words ran through my mind.

Yeah, yeah, she deserved better. Didn't they all?

NINE

BRITTNEY ANN

His flip-flops slapped against the hardwood floor as he followed me down the hall into the kitchen. "I didn't know what you liked, so I made a little bit of everything."

There was a slightly dazed look on his face as he took in the bacon and sausages, pancakes and waffles, orange slices, bananas, pineapple and mango, and three different types of eggs. "Jesus," he said. "You said breakfast. I thought you meant toasting a Pop-Tart."

"Oh, right. No, I figured I owed you after…" I waved my hand in the air. Remembering last night was bad enough. Saying the words out loud would only make my nausea intensify.

Arching one of his thick brows, he said it anyway. "You barfed all over my shoes?"

"Yeah, that."

His long finger moved along the inside of the archway between the hall and kitchen. His lips twitched. "And tried to seduce me?"

"There was that, too."

He smirked. "You spat—"

"I think we get the picture. You remember everything. I remember everything. Maybe we can eat and *not* talk about it."

"It's cool. The first time I got drunk, I woke up with no memory of why I was naked next to a girl or how I got there."

I stared at him, waiting for an explanation. The Barry from last night had been so forthcoming, it was new and welcomed. But this wasn't him.

I wasn't surprised to see him shrug, dismissing the topic altogether. He clapped his hands and rubbed them together. "Let's eat."

"Did you know her?" I asked.

Those dark brows hooded his emerald eyes. "Who?"

"The girl. The one you woke up next to."

He reached up and scratched the back of his neck. "Uh, yeah. Not very well."

"And you had sex with her?" I asked.

"Yeah."

"How do you know if you don't remember?"

He huffed. "What is this, twenty questions? You made me breakfast, then I'll drive you to your car. We don't have to talk. We're not really friends."

I winced. "I was just curious," I mumbled.

Blowing out a heavy breath, his head fell back. His voice was softer when he continued. "I barely knew her. She was a cheerleader. I woke up with a condom still strapped to my dick, and I bailed. Things were real awkward after that. I don't like to get so drunk I don't remember things anymore."

"Well, something good came out of it," I defended.

His lips twisted into a sideways smirk. "Except I don't remember the night I lost my virginity."

Oh. The dreaded *V*-word. "About last night—"

He waved his hand dismissively. Some emotion flashed across his face, but it happened so quickly, I mostly missed it. "Don't worry about it. You were drunk."

"No, I feel the need to apologize. My behavior was—"

"Normal?" he suggested with a quick, harsh laugh. "You were a normal drunk teenager."

I cleared my throat, trying to make my voice work. I blurted, "Are you going to tell anyone?"

He blinked, appearing caught off guard by my question. "Uh, no, probably not."

"Why?"

"Two reasons. One, your dad. Two, your brother."

Though I was glad he'd keep the night a secret, I wished his motives were more personal. "Thank you." My voice squeaked.

"No problem." His sincerity reminded me of last night, and I had the urge to reach up and touch the exposed flesh of his arm. My fingers tingled excitedly, but he stepped past me into the kitchen and the moment, as well as my urge, dissolved.

We ate in silence. I tried, several times to start a conversation but he wasn't very receptive. "Do you feel hung over?" I asked.

"Nope."

"Oh, right. Me either. Daddy left a note saying to drink plenty of water. He'll probably yell at me later. He's not a big fan of drinking. As you probably know."

He nodded.

I pushed scrambled eggs around my plate with my fork. "Did he say anything to you last night?"

With his eyes closed, head shaking back and forth, he took a deep breath—like he needed the air for patience. "Yup."

"Oh. Okay."

I nibbled on a little pineapple, not trusting my stomach enough to eat anything heavy. Once Barry filled his plate for the second time,

I started clearing away dishes. "Do you want to take some home?"

"Nah."

I stored what I could in Mom's blue Tupperware containers and then tossed the rest in the trash. Guilt nipped at my tummy that there were so many eggs to be thrown out. Maybe I'd been showing off my cooking skills a little. I felt indebted to Barry for making sure I'd gotten home last night. Making him a decent breakfast was the least I could do. Pushing the sleeves of my sweater up my arms, I plugged up the sink and filled it with water.

"Why don't you do that when you get back?" he suggested.

"It'll only take a minute." The real reason I lowered dishes into the sink was a subconscious attempt to keep him around longer. Okay, it wasn't all that subconscious.

He let out an aggravated groan, not even trying to hide the exasperated way he rubbed his eyes with his palms.

"Things will go faster if you help," I said.

He made a disgusted, grunting sound. "Excuse me? You want *me* to do *your* dishes?"

"They're your dishes too, silly."

He shook his head down at his white plate. "You should have told me I'd have to clean if I ate. I wouldn't have come."

My chest tightened. "I didn't say you *had* to clean. I just asked." I yanked the dish from his hand and set it gently into the soapy water.

"We have a dishwasher at home," he said, stepping up beside me. He twisted his red ball cap backwards so tiny spikes of black bangs poked out around his forehead. His green eyes were even more astonishing with the morning light filtering through the window behind the sink.

I took a deep breath, tearing my boring hazel gaze from his astonishing green. "I'll wash; you rinse."

"Okay," he agreed.

The silence didn't seem tense. One time he bumped my shoulder. When I glanced over he was smiling down at me. *Oh, be still butterflies.*

❧

He drove way too fast on our way into town. "What're you doing today?" I asked, my fingers fiddling with the hem of my dress.

His grip tightened on the wheel. I pretended not to notice. "Uh, probably hanging out with the guys. I dunno. I sorta owe Madison for last night."

"What?"

He shrugged. "It's complicated."

"Okay." I didn't want to know about it anyway.

"What're you doing?" he asked, peeking over at me from under the hood of his brows.

I hadn't made any plans. My day was wide open. I wasn't willing to admit I'd woken up this morning with the vain hope that Barry would ask to spend the day with me. I guess it wasn't *fine* that I'd released last night's ham all over his shoes. I struggled to think of something. "Probably horseback riding."

"Wow, random."

"Not really. I have a mare in the stables. I take her down to the creek from time to time. Maybe I'll pack a picnic." I wanted to throw in that I'd call a boy to come with me just to make him jealous. But I wasn't sure it would make him jealous. Plus, that wasn't very nice. Also, I didn't have any boys to use as lies. Barry had been sitting there when Ryan had broken up with me. He'd been my first and only boyfriend.

"Alone?" he sounded interested.

Which is probably the reason I put my foot in my mouth. "Probably. Unless you want to tag along."

"No," he spat the word. "No, I don't do horses. I'm going with the guys. And, uh, jeez I don't want to be a dick, but I just have to say it.

You know we're not, like, together, right?"

"We're in a car right now——"

"No, I mean…you know I'm not your boyfriend. Because I don't really do the whole boyfriend thing."

I was probably more offended by the fact he was talking down to me than by the words he was saying. What did I care if he wanted to be my boyfriend? It wasn't like I'd ever wanted that. I might have forgiven him for what had happened two years ago, but that didn't mean I was willing to let it happen again.

"Barry, I was just offering to be nice. I know you're not my boyfriend." For some reason, my voice broke on the word. "What happened last night…I never would have behaved that way sober. I appreciate you having the…" My hands fisted against my thighs. "I just appreciate the fact you stopped me."

"It never happened," he dismissed with a wave of his hand. After pulling onto the bare stretch of grass beside his driveway, he killed the engine of the roaring black Charger. His farewell was a nod of his head and a short, "See ya," and then he was gone. I hadn't even moved from the passenger seat of his car.

I had to pry myself away from the leather and then crawl into the sticky hot Plymouth. Taking my time, I rolled all the windows down by hand. Then I wondered what the heck I was taking my time for. *You don't think he'll come back out here and beg to be your boyfriend, do you?*

Before leaving Barry's driveway, I noticed the music——very loud, a lot of guitar——all coming from the second story. There was only one window that was open with the curtains blowing in the semi-wind.

I couldn't be sure, but as I pulled away, I thought I saw him braced against the sill, watching me.

TEN

BARRY

Thank God she was gone. I was way too sober to put up with her this morning.

That thought in mind, I hopped off my bed, away from the window, and found my goodie stash in the drawer. There were five pure-perc tens left. I knocked them into my hand then dropped them onto the desk. Pressing the flat side of the tin down on each pill, I crushed them one by one. I pulled my driver's license out of my wallet along with a one-dollar bill. I'd once heard that eighty percent of American greenbacks had some form of opioid or cocaine on them. I didn't know if that was true, but I knew why money was the root of all evil.

With the license, I pushed the crushed powder into two straight lines. Rolling the dollar into a straw, I tapped it against the desk once. I snorted one line and then the other up my nose.

The high hit straight to the head.

Flopping back on my bed, I barely heard the Foreigner vinyl. I must have dozed off because next thing I knew, my shoulder was being shaken, and I blinked up at Tyler, Bo, and Gage. "What's up?" I asked. My sandpaper-tongue flicked at the desert-dry roof of my mouth.

"We're going to the river. We tried to call. You didn't answer. You coming?" Tyler asked, concern dripped into his tone

"Yeah, dude, get out of my face." I shoved him backward.

"Someone's crabby," Bo commented.

"He just doesn't know any boundaries." I searched for my shirt. I'd torn it off at some point when I was sleeping. The pills and the still-open window had brought on a sweat storm like none other. I reached up and yanked the window shut.

"Boundaries? Princess, we don't have boundaries." Ty tried to hug me, and I shoved him backward. Pain tore through his eyes as his ass slammed into the corner of my desk. "Jeez, Bare, what's your problem?"

"Nothing. I'm just trying to get dressed. I don't want you to fucking touch me."

"He's high," Gage said.

"I'm not high," I growled.

Without asking permission, Tyler opened my dresser drawer and pulled out my tin. "Hey!" I hurried over and yanked it out of his hand. The small baggie of reg—which was just seeds and stems— fell onto the ground.

"Jesus, you're out already? We got that shit on Thursday."

"Yeah, and I found out my dad got engaged this weekend. Plus, I got to play babysitter to the preacher's daughter. I took a few liberties with my *own* stash. Mind your own fucking business."

He flinched. "I thought things were cool with Brittney."

"Until she barfed on my shoes. Thanks for giving her those extra beers and not telling me. I gave her even more."

They all laughed. Even Tyler snorted a chuckle despite the worried look he shot me.

My phone rang. I thought about ignoring it but then saw Mom's face on the screen, and I scrambled to answer. "Hey Mom."

"Barry?" She sounded upset.

Bracing the back of my neck with my hand, I stepped into the bathroom, away from my friends. "Yeah, what's wrong?"

"Were you here last night?"

"Shit, did I leave the door unlocked? I tried, but the key—"

"No, no the door…it's not the door. Did you take something out of your room?"

Ice filled my veins. "A couple of pills," I mumbled. Had she set me up? She'd left the pills there as a trap. That was why she'd flushed the other ones and left those—to see if I'd take them.

The churning in the pit of my stomach hinted that there was something so much worse going on here. *It hadn't been a trap at all.*

She hissed. "God dammit, Barry. I needed those."

"They were mine."

"Yeah, I'm so sure the pharmacist gave them to you." The phone disconnected with a resounding *click.*

◌

The water was rough, splashing wildly against the rocks. We didn't jump off the low bluff because of that. Instead, we sat on the river bank wolf-whistling at bikinis in passing rafts. We took turns smoking Bo's ganja from Tyler's pipe. All in all, the day was uneventful but worthwhile.

I was exhausted and starving by the time I got home. Bo killed his Beamer in front of my house. His car wasn't the only one in the driveway. "What's going on?" I asked.

"We've been with you all day, genius," Bo said, stepping out and reaching back inside for his shirt.

I wasn't so sure I wanted to get out and face Dad or the police cruiser with the berries and cherries flashing. The sheriff's Expedition wasn't blasting the siren, but that didn't mean I was completely comfortable with that man inside my house.

"Lonna didn't say anything?" I swiped my sweaty palms against my pants. Last time I'd seen Sheriff Stuart was the night he'd busted me on top of his daughter.

"Nope." *God, did Tyler have to look so amused.* "Better go check it out." He nudged at my shoulder.

"You guys are coming with me, right?"

Tyler laughed. Tossing a Popsicle stick into my yard, he stepped out of the car. "Are you kidding? We wouldn't miss this for the world."

Great. I needed new friends—friends who didn't laugh when I was in the middle of flipping the fuck out.

I burst in the house, trying not to look as stoned as I was. Blinking a few times to clear my bleary eyes, I called, "Dad? Dad? What's…?"

Dad and Sheriff Stuart stood in the hall. Both looked relieved to see me. Relieved? Okay, I could live with that.

"Thank God, Barry." Dad caught my hurt shoulder, squeezing tightly. This was as close to a hug as we ever got. "James here is looking for Brittney. You haven't seen her, have you?"

It took me a second. Brittney? Brittney Ann was…she was missing?

"Barry?" Dad repeated. "Have you seen Brittney Wilson?"

Sheriff Stuart's lips pinched as he glared at me. I stared down at my shoes.

"Uh, no, no, not since this morning. What's this about?"

The sheriff flipped open a small notebook and rushed, "This morning? Where? When?"

"She needed a ride to get her car. I picked her up…wait, no, she made me breakfast, then I brought her back here and she left."

She was missing? Seriously? How? Why? Had they checked all

the ditches? There was a lot of farmland out her way. Maybe she'd accidentally driven off the road. Or, and this was just as likely, she'd had car trouble. That piece of shit Plymouth had to be on its last leg. I couldn't believe her dad actually trusted that thing.

Sheriff let out a slow sigh. "Sorry to bother you, Duncan. Her car's at the house, so Mitch figured Barry wouldn't know where she was. It was always a long shot. Besides, the girl's only been gone a couple of hours. Probably getting excited for nothing."

I glanced between the two men, who shook hands like they were saying goodbye.

"So that's it?" I gasped. "You're not going to look for her?"

"Barry," Dad's fingers dug into my flesh as a warning. I cringed.

"Of course we are," Sheriff Stuart snapped. Then he turned away from me, focusing on Dad. "I better get back out to the farm. Moira was calling some people to come and search the grounds."

"We'll come too," I blurted.

What the hell? I couldn't take it back now that I'd said it. But why had I put my foot in my mouth like that? Because I wanted Sheriff Stuart not to think I was a total piece of shit? Maybe. Or because I really wanted to find Brittney. A numb ache set into my stomach at the thought of her missing. I didn't want anything bad to happen to her.

Again, we piled into Bo's black Beamer. This time, we followed Dad and Ashleigh in her little Escape behind the sheriff's Expedition.

"So you're worried about her?" Bo's voice was gruff. He bounced forward in the seat, drumming his fingers on the wheel.

"I don't know," I said. Where the hell could she have gone? That's what had me worried. I'd seen her several hours ago. How many had it been? Three. Four at most. We hadn't stayed at the river very long. It was too hot. We'd mostly gone down there to smoke without getting caught.

Tyler cleared his throat. "Mom will be glad I'm helping look for her. She'll think it will help me get into heaven, which might get her off my ass about getting into college. So, personally, I'm glad we're doing this." He rubbed his hands together excitedly. "Besides, Annie could be there."

Bo sighed, giving him a sideways look. "Of course."

"What? A guy has to think of all his options."

"Ty, she's your *only* option. She is literally the only girl you mention by name. The rest of them are Sugar, Sweetheart, Babe or *Hey, suck my dick, bitch*. Ann is the only one you call by her first name"

Meeting Tyler's gaze in the rearview mirror, I mouthed *suck my dick, bitch?*

A ghost of a smile on his lips, Tyler snapped his fingers. "Good point. It has something to do with her dimples, or the way her red hair—"

Bo threw up his hand in exasperation. "Dude, seriously, I don't care."

"Fine, fine. You don't have to be an ass about it." Tyler let it go, giving me a chance to lean back in the seat and try to think about where Brittney could have disappeared to.

Where, oh where, can Brittney be? I knew there were quite a few acres out there. Hand-me-down land from Moira's father. No way could a pastor afford rent and upkeep.

The big question: was Brittney home?

It seemed pretty unlikely she went anywhere without her car. "Hey, you guys don't think that prick from the movie theater, that Ryan kid, did anything to her, do you?" What if he'd shown up at her house this morning? It probably came out that Madison had played him. Even if he did get jerked-off out of the deal—which was more than he deserved—he hadn't gotten a girl. Something like that could make a guy like him pretty angry.

I rubbed my temples. I couldn't think straight.

"What? No. No, definitely not." Tyler said. "You said that guy was spineless."

I had said that. Ryan was lacking in the vertebrae department, among his other faults.

Our caravan pulled up at the farm behind several recognizable vehicles. Bo moaned, leaning forward on his knuckles on the steering wheel. "What's up?" I asked.

He gestured to Luke and Collin Parker's beat up Ford.

"What're they doing here?" he grumbled.

"Mitch thinks their shit doesn't stink."

"Great." He scrubbed at his face. "Just fucking great."

Tyler's knuckles knocked against the passenger window. "Hey Bare, is that Gwen's car?"

Sure enough, Gwen Mason's green Mustang was parked beside Brittney's vacant white Plymouth. "Shit."

"Didn't think this through, did ya, bud?" Before I could answer, he scrambled for the door handle. "Yes!" Just behind Gwen's car was Ann's blue Cobalt. "She never lets me down. Better go see if she needs some help."

"With what?" Bo groaned. "Man, she's going to slap you again if you don't leave her alone."

But Tyler had practically flown out of the car. Bo pointed after him. "If I ever act like that about a girl, feel free to punch me in the dick."

"No problem." A free hit like that? I wasn't turning it down.

He arched a brow at me. "You're supposed to say *likewise*. I get to dick-punch you if you go all Tyler-Ann lovesick on me."

"Yeah, that too."

Bo smiled. "Yeah, okay, whatever. Let's get this shit over with."

"Okay," Mitch called hoarsely. "We're losing daylight. We're going to split up and search the grounds. Everyone in groups of three or more—we don't need no one getting lost. Keep your cell phones on you. There are some places, down by the creek bed, where you lose service."

A dog bark startled me.

It was a large German shepherd. His body hovered protectively in front of Gwen, and if I wasn't mistaken, his auburn intent-filled eyes were dead focused on me.

It shared its owner's hatred. *Wonderful.*

Everyone grouped off until it was just Bo and me left. Tyler had hooked up with Ann and her little brother—despite Ann's annoyance. "Where should we start?" Bo clapped and rubbed his fingers together.

Out of nowhere, that damn dog bounced up and knocked into me. The thing nearly pushed me over. I got my bearings and thought about kicking the little shit.

"What the hell?" I rubbed the dog paws off my Journey T-shirt. This was my favorite one!

With molten brown eyes, the thing stared at me like I was kibble. Then he licked my face. "Get it down," I yelled, swinging my arms out.

I didn't hate animals or anything—I was cool with them. As long as they weren't in my face or in my house or in my car or touching my clothes.

Gwen caught the *thing*'s collar and pulled him backward. "Down, Dex."

"Thanks so much." My voice was acidic. It had been over a year since she'd graduated, and she still looked like a snobby bitch.

"I know why you're here." Her voice trembled, but she stared me straight in the eyes. Well, as straight as a girl could stare when she was seven inches shorter. Her free hand planted on her hip and she huffed. "And I'm not going to let you get away with it."

Even I didn't know what I was doing here. "Okay…"

"You hurt her," Gwen snapped. "Now you've come to make sure no one ever finds out about it."

"Whoa." Bo chuckled under his breath.

"You're serious?" I said.

"Yes, I'm serious. Pastor Mitch told me what you did to her last night—"

"Wait, what the hell did I *do* to her?"

Gwen stepped up so she was only inches from me. She jabbed a hard pointer finger into my chest. "You got her drunk. We both know what happened."

Except me. I didn't have a clue what Gwen was talking about. "If you think we had sex—"

Gwen snorted. "Look, Barry, I don't want to be around you any more than necessary, but Brittney is my family. I will do anything for her. Knowing you've hurt her infuriates me. I've already called Toby. He's not pleased at all. If you think I'm leaving you alone out here for even one minute, you're crazy."

Bo and I exchanged quick glances. I rolled my eyes at the chick. "Whatever you gotta do, babe."

"I'm not your *babe*," she snapped.

"Great, whatever. So where should we look first?" I wasn't asking her.

She was the one who answered, though. "The barn. Mitch already looked, but he didn't check the stable or the loft. I want to peek in there before heading down toward the hay field."

"Dude?" Bo nudged my shoulder. "Don't you two hate each other?"

Again, Gwen answered. "We do."

I nodded emphatically. "We do." She was the bitch who'd gotten my ass kicked by the quarterback. *Twice.*

Bo's eyebrows arched. "Right. So we're all just hanging out and pretending…"

"We're not hanging out," Gwen clarified, her eyes narrowed on my T-shirt. "I'm not letting him out of my sight. There's a difference." She gave Bo a serious look. "And we're not going anywhere without you."

He glanced at me, like he was waiting for an answer to a question that I did not know. I shrugged, and Bo took that. Hands in his pockets, he stepped between Gwen and me. The dog sniffed him and then marched back to Gwen.

The large hay barn was what I assumed was business as usual. Gwen climbed into the loft and looked pretty disappointed to realize Brittney wasn't hiding topside. So we checked the stable.

One of the horses wasn't in a stall, she stood in the row waiting to be put away. "Dangit," Gwen caught the thing's reins. "Come on, Buttercup. Come inside."

Buttercup was the only saddled horse. She was also stubborn. Her head jerked from side-to-side as she pulled away from Gwen.

I take it back; this animal and I could probably get along.

"Can we ride her?" I asked. I didn't actually *want* to ride the horse, nor did I honestly know how. But I wanted to know if *other* people could ride her. Being on horseback would make searching the fields go a lot faster.

"No," Gwen snapped. "Brittney doesn't let anyone ride her. Well, she does because Brittney doesn't know how to say no, but she doesn't like it. Buttercup's her baby."

Oh my God. *Buttercup's. Her. Baby.*

Those three words stabbed into my chest one at a time like three separate spears.

"She went riding," I exhaled. "She was going horseback riding today. Down by some creek. She was going alone."

Gwen stared at her fingers, clenching on the reigns. "Buttercup's not out of her stall, she came home and tried to get back in."

Dex barked. He ran toward the stable door and then back toward Gwen. Dirt from the ground kicked up so I could taste it. Disgusting ass mutt.

"What is it, Dexter?" Gwen asked.

Bo mouthed *What the hell?* Did Gwen really think the dog could talk?

Once again, the mutt ran toward the door and then back.

"Oh forget this," I snapped, holding out my hand to her. "Gimme the horse."

"What?" Gwen jerked the reins out of reach. "I already told you, she doesn't like—"

"I'm going to ride down to the creek and look for her."

"You don't even know where it is," her voice cracked. "Besides, I already told you, you're not leaving my sight."

I was the reason it had taken this long to remember Brittney. What if she'd fallen off this stupid horse, and she was unconscious in the blistering sun somewhere? Oh shit. I couldn't think like that or I wouldn't be able to get on the horse. *Good horsey. Good ~~boy~~ girl.*

"Fine," I growled between my teeth. "Saddle up another one, buttercup." Because I was doing this with or without Gwen complaining in my ear the whole time.

"I'm not butter—" she huffed.

Gwen, apparently, had ridden enough times that she was comfortable riding bareback. I smiled to myself. I needed jokes like that to keep me going.

She bridled one of the older looking paint horses and then climbed the fence to slide onto his back.

I had a tougher time mounting Buttercup. My tight jeans were not conducive to horse riding. I threw my leg over Buttercup's back, and there was a sharp ripping sound. The feel of cold leather pressed against the outside of my boxers made me cringe.

Gwen couldn't contain her laughter. Neither could Bo. "Don't be a dick," I said. "Stay here and tell them all where we went."

He nodded.

"No!" Gwen's mouth gaped. "I'm not going anywhere *alone* with you. Bo will have to…" She looked around, her head jerking from side to side. "He'll…"

"It's fine," he said, patting Buttercups nose. "I draw the line at horses. It's nothing against Brittney, but I'm just not a fan of being chapped."

Chapped? Would that happen? Bo laughed. "You should see your face right now, Bare. Good luck," he said, winking. "Be nice to Gage's mom." He nudged Buttercup's nose again.

I choked on a violent laugh, and Gwen scowled at me.

She whistled for the dog, who ran up beside her and pranced in a circle. "Keep close, Dex," she whispered, her eyes slid back to me. Did she think that dog would save her from me?

Gwen's horse raced ahead of Buttercup—who seemed more in the habit of leisurely trotting. "Move your ass, Buttercup," I growled. "We look pathetic."

She shook out her long mane and kept pace.

It was no surprise when Gwen and the mutt beat me to the creek. "Brittney!" she called, and without waiting for a response kept calling, "Britt! Are you here, Brittney Ann?"

"Shut up and let her answer."

She flipped me off.

She kept as much distance between our horses as possible while still staying in sight. I was thankful looks couldn't kill. Gwen and that scowl might have pulled it off.

"Help!" Brittney's small voice squeaked.

I dropped off Buttercup, and Gwen fell off her horse, too. We pushed at each other, trying to be the first to see Brittney just on the other side of a clearing. There was a rocky spring, about the size of a large pool, with a loud waterfall. This wasn't what I would call a *creek*.

Brittney stood on a slab of limestone. Just standing there. Like she'd been waiting for someone to put the pieces together and realize she was missing. Her cheeks were a sun-kissed pink, and her entire body trembled. "Don't touch me," she said, holding her hands out in front of her.

An odd request. Gwen had started across the slab and, as soon as Brittney said it, she froze.

I gave Britt another once over. She wore a pair of jean capris and a tank top that made my mind jump to the riverbank last night. Then I saw it. A snake. It's body twisted angrily and swiped at Brittney's shoes.

Probably two feet of the camouflaged serpent lashing wildly out from beneath her foot. Its head was tucked under Brittney's cowboy boot. "I don't know what to do," she admitted. "I'm afraid it's poisonous."

"It's a copperhead," Gwen breathed. I wanted to argue, because how the hell could she tell what kind of snake it was when it's head was hidden under Britt's boot?

But…but if it was a copperhead…then I didn't want to argue.

"Don't move," Gwen whispered.

Brittney tried to smile at me—her dry lips stretched over her white teeth. "Oh, Barry, I had a feeling you'd be the one to find me. I was so silly and didn't even leave a note for Daddy. I just rode down here without thinking. You're the only one I told."

My heart slapped against my chest. "How long have you been here?"

"Just a few hours," she dismissed with a shrug.

So, the whole time.

I wouldn't go so far as to say this was my fault because I *wasn't* responsible for Brittney. Yeah, she should have left a note. Horses killed people, and she'd just ridden off on the thing like it was no big deal.

She was here, and it wasn't my fault. A small mental voice had to say *If I'd remembered a little sooner, she'd already be back at her house with a bottle of water and some food.*

I was going to fix this. If only I could think of something to do to make it all better. "You have service?" I asked Gwen. She pulled out her phone and held it up in the air, because that *always* helped.

"Yeah, just a bar, let me call Pastor Mitch." She crawled up the embankment on the far side.

I scowled after her. "Does she always call him *Pastor*?"

Brittney nodded. "Oh? Yes, mostly. Everyone does, I suppose."

"Except me," I winked.

She exhaled a relieved laugh. "You're quite the rebel, Barry."

Brittney shivered as the snake's body lashed up, hitting her shin. Her crackled lips turned white. "I never realized how difficult it was to stand still."

"Have you tried…I mean, it's kinda gross, but—"

"I can't," she said, clenching her eyes and shaking her head. "I'm too afraid he'll get away."

So she hadn't tried to squish it. "Honestly, Britt, you gotta look at the bright side here—"

"I didn't step on his body. I'm no longer out here alone. This could have happened in full sunlight, not in the shade. Buttercup didn't get hurt. No one was with me, so they didn't get hurt."

"Yeah, I get the point," I said, "You've exhausted the bright side."

"Okay," Gwen called down to us, victoriously punching the air with her cell phone fisted in her hand. "They're calling the conservation. Britt, your mom and dad are coming."

Brittney's shoulders shrank, but to Gwen she squeaked, "Thank you."

I stared between the two girls. "The conservation? How long is that going to take?"

"I don't know, Barry." Gwen struggled back down toward us. I might not have enjoyed the sight of her sliding on her ass through the mud and twigs if she hadn't been such a ginormous bitch.

"It's alright," Brittney said, a hard shudder rippling through her slight body. I stepped forward, rubbing the tops of her crisp apple colored shoulders.

"Dude, it's not—"

"Neither of us are your *dude*," Gwen snapped.

Let me reiterate, GARGANTUAN Bitch.

Not thinking, I slammed my foot over the top of Brittney's. "What're you doing?" she gasped.

"Trust me."

"Don't trust him!" Gwen shoved into me, almost knocking me sideways. I'd never been shoulder-checked by a chick before, and I was definitely positive I didn't like it, but I was sure I would be better braced to never let myself stumble again.

I growled. My fingers slid under Brittney's jaw. "Ignore her; look at me."

Brittney's heavily lidded eyes jumped between us. "What's going on?" she asked.

"She hates me," I said with a shrug. "And I'm going to kill the snake."

Gwen huffed. "You can't kill it. That's why they called the conservation."

Brittney's lack of input enticed me. She didn't want to stand there, holding the snake down, until someone from the state arrived. It could be another hour, maybe longer.

My shoe slipped to the side, so I was standing on top of the squishy one-inch serpent's neck. From what I could tell, his whole body was neck. I swallowed hard, trying not to think about the anatomy of the snake.

Brittney let out another shudder. "What do I do?" she asked, her voice small, like she was seriously relying on me. I was going to protect her, and she trusted that fact.

Fuck. No one had ever relied on me before.

"You're not doing this. She could get hurt." Gwen shoved hard against my shoulder. This time I was ready for it. I barely moved.

My teeth ground together. If Brittney got bit because Gwen was being a cunt, then I was going to hit the whore. Glaring at her, I fisted my fingers into a ball. "You stupid bitch. Don't touch me; I'm trying to help."

Gwen's lower lip trembled. Whatever she wanted to say didn't come through that fly hole. I decided to use a new plan and ignore her in the hopes she'd ignore me back.

Bending forward, I fought to catch the snake's tail as it flailed and struggled to defy me. His body was rigid and strong, but at the same time scaly and pliable.

My heart slammed around inside my ears.

Boom.

Boom.

Boom.

I wrapped my fist around that tail. No matter how hard he jerked, I was stronger. Brittney stared at me in awe. Her fingers slid around my waist, knotting into my sweat-drenched T-shirt as she held on to me. "What're you going to do?" She whispered.

"Kill the snake." I glanced around, looking for anything I could use as a weapon.

"With *what*, Barry?"

Hadn't thought of that. "Okay, what you need to do is run. Get as far away as you can. Gwen get your ass out of here, too."

"In case you fail."

"Screw you."

Brittney's fingers trembled as she gripped the sides of my face and pecked a kiss to my cheek. "You're my hero," she whispered.

This was a bad idea. I shouldn't have gotten involved. I especially shouldn't have wrapped the thing's tail around my hand. I wasn't anyone's hero. Definitely not Brittney's.

Before I could talk myself into changing my mind several things happened all at once. There were car doors and people yelling. Brittney startled, lifting her foot off the angry serpent's head. A pair of fangs dug into my worn Converse—my newer ones were still in the wash. The cool sensation of teeth was flush with the outer layer of my flesh.

My free arm went around Brittney's waist, keeping her out of the way as I tucked her to my side.

Adrenaline fueled my every move. I jerked hard on the snake's tail, lifted it high into the air, swung it around, and then smacked it hard against the limestone.

My secondary plan was to run. I didn't know if I'd drag Brittney with me or save myself. Thankfully, I didn't have to make that decision.

The snake fell limp from my fingers.

With her mouth hanging open and her fingers clawing into the front of my shirt, Brittney stared at the snake. "You broke his neck."

"Yeah. I guess so."

She dug into my torso as she tore at me for support. "Oh my goodness. You did it."

I might have been insulted by her surprise if I weren't equally as shocked. I'd done it. I'd saved her. I *was* her hero.

A victorious sensation pulsed through my veins. I pushed my hands up into her hair, tilting her face toward me with my thumbs on her jaw. Strawberries staining her cheeks, she looked full of life as she burst into a smile that made her so damn beautiful.

She was alive.

Holy shit, she was alive.

The feel of her heart beating as her chest throbbed against my side made me smile. "Thank you," she breathed.

"You're welcome."

"Hands off!" Gwen weaseled her way between us.

My smile ignited into flame and then disintegrated to ash. *Thanks so much, Gwendolyn.* And then everyone hugged. Of course they did.

No one hugged me.

"You killed it?" Moira stared down at the dead snake.

"Yes Mom. Barry saved me." Brittney gave me a hesitant look. I hoped her mom wasn't one of those weird people who actually liked snakes.

Moira frowned. "Oh…oh, right."

"I'm sure it was necessary," Mitch said, his grip tightening on his wife as he pulled Brittney in for a hug also. Never taking his narrowed eyes off me, he hugged Gwen, too.

So, yup, no one hugged me.

I probably had snake guts on me.

Pulling my sticky shirt away from my chest, I looked. Nope. No snake guts.

My pants were ripped. This was extra embarrassing because everyone knew I killed the snake, so they kept looking at me. But not hugging me.

Not like I cared.

I hated huggers. But still, it burned a little that they didn't even try.

Bo and Tyler were painfully surprised I'd been the hero. "No, it's just…" Bo tried, tugging on his hair and not looking at me as he toed a tall blade of grass. "I can't explain it. You never do things like that."

"Like what?" I snapped.

"Step up," Tyler threw in before running off to help Ann into her car.

I glared after him. "I step up all the time."

Bo's brows worked inward. "Really? When was the last time you did something nice for someone because you wanted to, not because you had to?"

I'd driven Brittney to her car this morning. I hadn't had to do that. But it was a little weird I'd stepped up for Brittney twice in one day, and I didn't want Bo to think too much about it, so I didn't mention it. Then I tried to think of the last time I'd done something nice when I didn't have to. I couldn't think of anything. "I don't know man. Just let it go."

Thankfully, he did.

Everyone was invited to stay for barbecue, and despite how weird Brittney's dad was being toward me, I was also invited. Except when I walked up the steps to go inside, Gwen stood in front of me with her arms folded. "Brittney says nothing happened with you guys. I believe her. But I still don't trust you. I never will. It's time to go, Barry."

"What?"

She huffed, blowing her bangs off her forehead. "You had your fun. She hung out with you. You saved her life. Whatever else you were playing at here isn't happening. If this is some sort of bet or some kinda game, it's over. Time to go."

"You're serious?" I asked. Bo and Tyler stood there on the other side—with everyone else who'd been invited to partake in barbecued treats—and *I* had to leave?

"Yes, I'm serious. You come near Brittney again, and Toby's coming home to deal with you. You've been warned."

"I'm not afraid of him."

She laughed.

Okay, I wasn't afraid of Toby *now*. I might have been a long time ago when he was a senior and I was a sophomore. Things were different now. Except, I was a senior and he was a Marine…

No, no I wasn't afraid of him. I stood by that.

"You know what, Gwen? I don't give a fuck about you or Toby."

She probably didn't hear me because she'd turned and walked back inside. I slammed into Bo's backseat. "I didn't want any barbecue anyway."

Tyler and Bo looked at each other, both of them taking their time to get situated. Tyler buckled his damn belt. He never did that.

"Yeah," Bo agreed quietly. "Probably wasn't any good."

Tyler nodded but didn't say anything.

Once Bo dropped me off, I climbed numbly up the stairs toward my room. I put Heart on the record player and then stripped down to my boxers before heading toward my stash.

Which was now empty.

I fisted the container. Usually I was smart enough to refill before shit like this happened. *Stupid fucking Christian distraction.* I threw the tin at the mirror, and with my body aching—even though I had no real reason to feel pain—I crawled into bed.

ELEVEN

BRITTNEY ANN

Gwen knocked on my door. "Britt? I brought you some more water. Can I come in?"

There was music still playing downstairs, meaning the *Brittney's still alive* celebration was still going on. I wouldn't say that I was bummed that Barry hadn't stayed, but, well, I just wasn't in the mood for a party, I guess. "Yeah, sure." My throat was dry. I'd already drunk two bottles of water. Mom warned me not to drink too quickly, so it had been about thirty minutes since I'd had anything.

Gwen flopped onto my bed and smiled widely at me. "How's it going, kid?"

I shrugged. I still remember the first time I met Gwen. She'd taken me under her wing like it was the most natural instinct in the world. I'd still been pretending I was like Katy Lynn back then—outspoken and adventurous. I had no trouble talking to a senior girl who was probably the prettiest girl I'd ever seen.

It actually hadn't been hard making friends with Gwen. I got so used to our friendship, and her relationship with my brother that I

146

didn't bother making any other friends when I got to high school. So when they graduated and Katy Lynn and I stopped talking so much, I didn't really have anyone.

"Daddy said I should have grabbed it by the neck and thrown it."

Gwen shrugged. Gripping my knee, she encouraged, "I don't know if I'd have been brave enough to do that. You did fine, hun. Don't worry about it."

"I'm a little embarrassed," I admitted. "I hate that Barry saw me out there sweating like a pig."

It took half of a second for her demeanor to go from carefree to anxious. Crawling onto her knees on the mattress, she grabbed my shoulders, forcing me to meet her gaze. "Britt, do not give one damn about him. Okay? Barry Prescott is a dog. No, he's worse than a dog. I'd never insult Dexter by lumping them together. Barry's dog shit."

I cringed. "He saved my life."

"Not really. The conservation would have come and taken care of it. Plus, your dad was almost there, he'd have probably killed it himself. Barry just happened to be the first one there. Please, don't hero worship that idiot. That shit goes to his head, and his head can't use anymore air."

"He's not a bad guy," I mumbled.

"How do you know?" she snapped. "I didn't think you hung out with any of the senior boys."

"I don't. Barry goes to our church."

She snorted. "He's been there three times since I started two years ago."

I opened my mouth to defend him. His parents were divorced— that had put a strain on his faith. She slapped her palm over my lips. The hard expression she shot me made me cringe backward. "Brittney Ann, I'm going to say this once. If I find out you're seeing him, or that you're into him, I'm going to have to tell Toby."

The ultimate form of betrayal.

Toby had only asked one thing of me, in addition to avoiding House parties. Stay away from that group of boys. Barry most of all.

Toby would never forgive me for breaking my promise to him.

Gwen's hand fell away, and she rubbed my now sunburnt shoulders. "There are things you don't understand, Brittney. Things people don't like to talk about. You just need to keep in mind that Toby and I would never do anything to hurt you. Can Barry say the same thing?"

I didn't have to think about it. Barry already *had* hurt me. I'd spent hours getting ready for that homecoming dance. I'd spent days looking forward to it. And, honestly, I'd spent the majority of my childhood admiring him from so far away he couldn't see me. It hurt more than I ever told Gwen and Toby that he hadn't shown up that night.

Forgiven; not forgotten.

Staring down at the hem of my dress, I shook my head, and Gwen leaned over to kiss my forehead. She was absolutely the big sister I never had. Toby had asked her to marry him last Christmas, and she wore an engagement ring, but I still found it hard to call her his fiancé. They were so young.

"Your brother wants to see you. He was worried about you. Honestly, I think he packed a bag and was ready to come here and find you himself. He was in the car when I called and told him you were okay, but he won't admit he was on the way to the airport." She winked at me.

I waited until she was gone before digging around for the iPad Toby had given to us last Christmas so we could talk to him.

"Hey sis!" I heard him before I ever saw his face.

He'd gotten a haircut. Again. "I miss you," I said.

He smiled. "I miss you too, little sis. What the hell happened out there? You stepped on a snake's head? Did you think to pinch it by the neck and throw it?"

My eyes rolled. "No, but Dad said the same thing."

He laughed. "Now you know for next time."

"I find it highly unlikely there will be a next time."

"Yeah, you got that step just right, didn't you? So tell me, what's this I hear about Barry Prescott?"

Oh no. "Hmm?" My voice squeaked.

His eyes narrowed. "He was there. He brought you home last night." A faint red flush speckled my brother's cheeks.

"Oh, right, yeah. You remember Ryan? The one I was telling you about?"

Toby listened to everything that had happened in the last twenty-four hours with his jaw tensed and a small vein popping in and out by his temple.

"What an asshole." Toby's mouth had gotten marginally more R-rated since he'd moved to California. "You deserve better than that little shithead, Britt. I knew there was something not right with him. I tried to Skype him, and he kept denying my calls."

"He did?"

"Yeah, and when I talked to him on Facebook, he said he couldn't talk because he was playing some online game. You deserve a guy who wants to date you so bad he's willing to talk to your brother. Man, Britt, you deserve so much more than that."

"Thank you."

He cleared his throat. "And this shit with Barry... You're sure nothing happened?"

"What? Of course I'm sure."

"You said you fell asleep."

"In the car on the way home." And on the riverbank, but I liked my life—and Barry's—too much to tell Toby about my serious lack of finesse. "He didn't want me. He wasn't even drunk. I think I annoyed him, honestly."

While a part of me thought this was mostly true, I only said it out loud because I wanted to protect Barry. I wanted to keep him safe from my brother. There was also a desire to keep what we had together—as minimal as it had been—safe from the outside world.

Toby and I talked until close to ten o'clock. Several times, Gwen brought me water, interrupting my brother-time as she made kissing noises at the screen and told him how much she *hated* him. It was their thing. Reverse psychology and double negatives and whatnot. They were weird but cute.

The next morning, after being checked on by Mom several times and having Gwen call twice, I stood in front of my too-pastel closet. I was going to do something about this. I was going to buy something vibrant. Something hot pink. That's what I was going to do.

Maybe it wouldn't even be a dress.

Mom never said I had to wear dresses, but she did say that I looked like such a little lady in them. Daddy never said much about the way I dressed, but I'd heard him comment on other people's clothes. Even Gwen's. He sometimes thought she looked too *flashy*. He thought Katy Lynn dressed like a *hussy*. I didn't know what he thought about Madison because he'd never met her, but I imagined it wouldn't be good.

I wondered if Barry had gotten a chance to reward her for breaking up my relationship with Ryan.

My fingernail slammed against the door frame as I hastily grabbed the first dress I could get my hands on.

Of course, we were the first ones to the church. I lit all the altar candles. Daddy practiced the gospel. Again. Mom and Gwen sat in the first pew making wedding plans.

I was putting away the candle lighter when Daddy stepped into the vestibule behind me. "We're going to talk about Friday night, Brittney Ann. We never got a chance. I didn't want to yell at you last night, and now that I've had a little time to cool down, I don't think I need to yell. But you've always been my good girl. What's going on with you?"

Perfect. Straight for the guilt trip. "It was one time. It won't—"

"Ah." He held up his hand, cutting me off. "You're talking to a recovering alcoholic, Britt. *It won't happen again* was my mantra for many years."

"I'm sorry, Daddy. I didn't mean to drink so much. I thought I had better control."

He shook his head. "Not smart, Brittney Ann. Anything could have happened to you. You're lucky Barry brought you home."

"I'm lucky he was there at all," I said, more to myself than him. Whether anyone believed it or not, Barry had been a perfect gentleman.

Daddy scowled. "I wouldn't push it."

"Okay, it's true though, he was…" I corrected, "he took care of me."

"Like I said, don't push it. I'm feeling forgiving, but I don't like him. If I think you have a crush on that boy, I might find an excuse *not* to be so forgiving."

"Sorry Daddy." I gave him a hug and then helped him slip into his white robe. He gave Mom, Gwen, and me communion before everyone else arrived. Then it was the waiting game.

I got so distracted talking to Mrs. Turner that I didn't notice them walk in.

"Haven't you got a damn brain, Duncan? This is my church, and you brought that slut—"

"She's my fiancé."

Several people gasped. I found Barry standing in the aisle with his head down. Beside him was Ashleigh. The yelling voices could only have come from his parents. They weren't anywhere that I could see, so I assumed they'd slipped into Daddy's office in back.

There were too many people for me to get to him from the middle, so I walked down the far side, moving against the wall.

"Oh God. You're marrying that bitch?"

Ashleigh's back straightened. She said something to Barry and then turned and marched back toward Daddy's office in the vestibule.

"Oh wonderful. There's the little slut. Yes, Ashleigh? Is there something important…I will not keep my voice down. You two need to leave. Take that little brat with you."

"If you're referring to Barry, he was rather happy to see you this morning." Duncan's tone was bitter

"I don't know why, after the little shit took my pills."

Ashleigh's voice rang out. "I'm sure if he took your pills, there was a good reason. Maybe he wasn't feeling well."

"They were strong muscle relaxers. He brought them into my apartment in a little tin to keep hidden. This isn't the first time, Duncan. Your son has a problem."

"Yes, well, it's hard to see where he got that from."

I was frozen standing behind Barry.

Barry took her pills? No, he took *his* pills that she planned to take from him. How confusing. I wanted to convince myself that this was a one-time thing. He surely didn't take muscle relaxers all the time. There must have been a really good reason. *He needed them.* Yes, that was it. *He needed them because he'd hurt himself killing that snake.* That made sense.

My hand slipped into his. His back stiffened. "I'm going outside for some fresh air. Would you like to join me?" I asked.

He nodded.

I pushed open the door and fresh, honeysuckle air hit me in the face. I breathed in the breeze, needing it to help me relax.

"Now I guess you know, huh?" His voice was strained.

"About?" I bit into my lip. There was no way I wanted to know what he was going to tell me. If he said he took pills when he wasn't sick, then I wouldn't be able to have this burning infatuation with him anymore.

"My family is fucked up," he said, tilting his face to the sun.

Oh, that. "Everyone's family is a mess." I forced a chuckle.

He gave me a sideways look. "Really? Coming from you? Your family is like a Rockwell painting."

"No we're not. My dad used to be an alcoholic."

"Used to be. He's not anymore. He's a preacher. He's in love with your mom. Your brother's a Marine who's in love with his girlfriend. You're smart, pretty, funny. It's not really fair all the shit you guys have going for you."

"My mom's deaf," I said.

"So what? That's not even a big deal."

"I know it's not, but it's not perfect. And I only have pastel clothes. Everything I own has paisleys or gingham. I'm too afraid to tell Mom that I want to wear tight blue jeans and cowboy boots. I only have two pairs of jeans, and they're for horseback riding. Sometimes I feel like a bottle of soda that is all shaken up. No one can tell from the outside, but one wrong move, and I'll explode." My fingers dug into my hair as I scratched at my roots, twisting my strawberry locks around my digits.

"Whoa," Barry said, his eyes devoured me from head to toe. "You're saying you dress like that because you have to?"

"You think I want to look like an old woman?"

He cracked a smile. "You never know."

I groaned, massaging my fingers over my face. "I just don't want to upset my mom. She's the nicest person. I've gone along with these clothes for so long that I'm afraid if I said anything now, it would be offensive."

He nodded.

I didn't know how this conversation had become about me, but he must not have minded. When I said, "I'm sorry, we should talk about you," he shook his head and adamantly refused.

I had to keep biting into my lip to keep from asking him about the pills. Everyone knew that Barry smoked marijuana. All of his friends did, too. Even Lonna.

There was such a big difference between smoking pot and taking pills that weren't prescribed to him, though. I'd never heard of anyone overdosing on marijuana.

I'd worried a layer of skin off my lower lip thinking about drugs and Barry's association to them.

The door of the church opened, and Mrs. Prescott stepped into the sunlight. She froze when she saw us standing there. Her mouth pulled pencil thin, and then she stomped toward us.

"Brittney Ann," she said, her voice curter than I could remember. "I'm sorry about that interruption in there. You know how much I love your father's sermons, but I just can't stay."

Barry shook his head. "Mom…"

"Don't," she snapped.

Barry withdrew. "Mom *please*…"

"I said *don't*." She turned back to me wearing a forced smile. "Brittney Ann, can I have a minute alone with my son, please?"

I nodded. The feel of their eyes on my back followed me all the way to the front door. Despite knowing how wrong it was, I was too curious to close the door all the way. I leaned against the stained glass window listening.

"What's up?" He asked.

"Don't bother. That girl wouldn't ever give you the time of day." Her voice was still short—annoyed sounding.

"Wow, thanks Mom."

"I'm just calling it like I see it. And you shouldn't mess with her head."

There was silence. I wished I could make out their features through the glass.

"Look, Barry, I was taking your pills because I hurt my back. I fell off a stepstool trying to reach the top shelf at the office. You know me and my addiction to creamer. Of course they put it all the way on the top. I tumbled and did a real number on my spine. My prescription ran out. I'm getting it refilled, but the pharmacist said it's going to be a couple days. The insurance is giving me hell."

"Really?" He sounded relieved. Why would he be relieved about her hurting her back? Maybe I was misinterpreting.

"Us old women and these brittle bones." Her voice was throaty now—light.

"What can I do?" he asked.

"Those muscle relaxers you had really helped. If you can get any more of those, I'd really appreciate it."

There was a pause. I wanted his answer to be that he had no way to get anything for her. I crossed my fingers in silent hope that he would answer that way—*he had no connection to anyone who sells prescription drugs other than a pharmacist.* His voice was lower when confessing, "Uh, Brody just gives me whatever he's got. It may not be the same."

"That's fine. Any muscle relaxers, and Valium or Ambien. Any of that really helps."

He sounded skeptical when he said, "How does valium help with your back? And isn't Ambien a sleeping pill?"

"I can't sleep when I'm in pain, baby boy. That's why I need your help. Just promise that you'll get whatever you can. Call me later, once you have it."

"Yeah, okay, uh, sure."

I pulled the door shut. Forcing myself not to look back, I walked down the center aisle, headed for the front pew. *This* was my life. No complications. No drama. No drugs.

TWELVE

BARRY

My probation officer was a staunch cunt who wasn't impressed when I smiled and said, "So, I don't really have to do a hundred hours, do I?" She threatened to give me one hundred more.

All for bagging the sheriff's daughter.

My community service could have been done at the soup kitchen, but since I knew the church did a lot of work there—and I was avoiding Mitch whenever possible—I was stuck at the city library.

My PO filled out the paperwork stating that I would spend three, five-day weeks of eight hour days, which was actually a hundred and *twenty* hours. So I hated her for sure.

Mrs. Kenderson, the aged librarian, hadn't ever transferred the card catalog into the online system though the system had been waiting since Windows 2000 came out with it. So my first summer job was to transfer, by Dewey's messed up system, every card into the computer. Then I was to go to the shelf and make sure the books were in the right places.

Half the books were out of order. For some reason, Mrs. Kenderson had started alphabetizing—by title—in early '05. She gave up that spring with the library in total chaos.

By the end of the first eight-hour day, I wasn't even done cataloging the first hundred books. I hated this place. Why hadn't I just gone to the stupid soup kitchen? Why was I such a masochist?

My phone had four missed calls from Mom and none from anyone else. She'd called every two hours to see if I'd gotten ahold of Brody. And I had. Brody said he could get some Ambien, but he had to steal it from some guy's house.

I wasn't okay with stealing pills. It was one thing when someone sold the extras they weren't going to take and I bought them, but I wasn't about to break into someone's home to raid the stash they needed. Brody assured me he'd have to do it anyway, and since I was the first one to call, I'd get the meds at four bucks a pop—for all his effort.

I hadn't had the stomach to call Mom and give her the *good* news.

After working eight hours, I sat in the library parking lot. My body felt shaky all over. It had been way too long since those Percs on Saturday morning. I hated that I was going to cave. Because if I caved for me, I was caving for Mom, too.

Two hours later, I sat in a different parking lot. Knowing that I had a baggy full of illegal paraphernalia for Mom and a baggy for myself made me tense. I was allowed to get fucked up—it's in the messed-up-teenager handbook. I just wasn't so sure I could help Mom do it.

That hesitation in mind, when I pulled out my phone and scrolled to the *M*s to call "Mom," Madison's name came up first. I thought: *Why not?* After all, hooking up with easy girls was also in the handbook.

She answered on the second ring with, "I knew you'd call eventually."

"Keep your mouth in check, and I'll pick you up in five."

"Aw, Bare, being so charming. What makes you think I'm interested after what you pulled at the movies?"

"Really? You jerked off an acne covered—"

"*Ugh*, don't remind me, okay? That little freak found me on Facebook. He's driven by my house several times. I'm about to call the cops on him."

"Cut the guy some slack, Madison. You give really good hand jobs."

"Yeah, well, I think so." Her voice turned pouty. "I just didn't know you'd be mad at me. You said to break them up."

"And you did. I'm not mad anymore. I just wasn't touching you on Friday. It's done. I'm over it. I'll be there in four."

"You just said five. I don't even have lip gloss on."

"Leave it off. You're pretty enough without it."

"You mean you don't like the way it tastes."

"Something like that." I hung up the phone and dug into *my* baggy for a couple Roxy-15s. Just two of those bad boys should do it. To be safe, I rolled three around in my palm before licking them off and swallowing them.

Madison wore a tiny black dress. Squealing excitedly, she bounced toward the car. "This is so exciting; Barry Prescott wants to hook up. I must have won the lottery."

"Shut up," I laughed.

"No, really," she said. "Ann told me you walked out of church… *church* with Brittney yesterday. Here I thought you'd gone straight on me." Her hand caught my leg, moving intently north. She was daring me to stop her.

I stared into her cool gaze, allowing her free access to touch me wherever she pleased.

"My dad's getting married. He's on this kick about impressing the pastor."

"Oh, so it's not about you bagging the pastor's daughter?" She wiggled her penciled-in brows at me.

Her question made my stomach twist into angry knots. I didn't like Brittney being on Madison's mind. Those two girls were spheres that belonged in different galaxies.

I palmed the back of her neck, squeezing her flesh between my fingers. She gasped, and I asked, "You know what I like about you, Madison?"

"What's that?" She giggled breathily.

I forced her head into my lap. "When you don't talk."

Fumbling with the radio, I looked for my favorite oldies station. Ram Jam's "Black Betty" played.

An oddly fitting melody. My fingers laced through Madison's onyx hair. Whatever her magical mouth was up to, it felt amazing. But before we reached the pull-off for the river, she leaned back and crossed her arms over her pert chest.

Cool air hit my exposed crotch, and I shivered. "You're joking, right?"

"Don't look at me," she huffed jabbing one of her long, pointed nails down at my dick. "You're the one with the issue."

"What? We're almost there, just—"

"Barry! 'Little Barry' doesn't want to play."

Holy shit. I was sporting half-a-wood, and no sooner than I looked down, the whole damn thing went away. "Yes, he does," I snapped. "You just weren't doing it right."

She pouted. "I think I know what I'm doing."

No one could argue with her there.

"Just chill, alright? I can't concentrate because I'm driving." Before she could say that I'd never needed to concentrate before,

I added, "Seriously, don't open your mouth unless you want to go back down there and try again."

"You could be a little nicer. I did try."

I rolled my eyes. "Sorry."

"Yeah, that sounded like an apology."

So I sucked at giving apologies, and my dick wouldn't stand up. *Great.*

I parked by the bushes in case anyone pulled in. We both crawled into the backseat, which Madison always complained about. She slowly took off her clothes, and kept her mouth shut—a vital step— while Little Barry did absolutely nothing. "Something's wrong with me," I gasped. This had seriously never happened before.

"Yeah, I'll say." She started putting her bra back on.

I caught her shoulder in desperation. "No, not yet. Try a little harder."

"Barry, this is pathetic. You're like a walking boner. If it's not working, there's a reason."

"Like what?" I bit out. I needed medical attention, and she was being a bitch. Brittney never would have reacted this way. She'd have been sympathetic. She might even have had a solution.

My teeth ground together as I forced all thoughts of *her* out of my mind.

"I don't know. Maybe your dick only wants snooty Christian bitches." *Aannnd* she was back.

But, really, if she were willing to do the things Madison were willing to do—

The thought didn't even make it through my head before my dick jumped. Just a little. He definitely didn't fire to life, but it was a small reaction.

Shit.

"Be serious," I snapped, refusing to believe this had anything to do with *her*. I could go ahead and die if that was the reason for my impotence.

Madison shrugged. "Maybe it's all the pills, Bare. Did you ever think of that?"

"What?" I gasped. No, I hadn't thought of that. "Could that happen?"

"Uh, yeah, I'd say so. There's a reason you're not supposed to take pain killers when you're not in pain. There are side effects."

I pointed down at my…*absent* erection. "Is this one of them?"

"I don't know," she laughed. "I sure hope so. Let's say it is, okay? I don't want people thinking it's me."

I did up my pants and started the awkward shuffle toward the front seat. She caught my bicep. There was a deep frown on her suddenly unattractive face. "Wait. It doesn't always have to be all about you, you know?" she leaned back, sliding her bra back down her shoulders.

"What?"

Her eyes rolled. "Well, I mean, I'm here. You could—" Her hands slid down her stomach, fingers inching into the band of her lace underwear.

I caught her wrists. "Ha. Not happening."

She huffed. "You know Luke would do it."

Ice rushed through my veins. Luke? *Parker?*

Wow.

Way to be thinking about another guy, bitch.

Yeah, I mean, I was thinking about Brittney, but that was different. She was soft and delicate and kind.

Luke was a *Parker*. Which made him suck right off the bat. And the fact this wasn't the first time I'd heard about his…*desire* to go downtown… Yeah, that annoyed me. What sort of an idiot went out of his way to make *Madison* feel special? She was supposed to feel cheap, or she wouldn't keep being cheap.

"I'm not doing it," I barked.

Madison didn't say a word as she crawled out of the Charger at her house. Not that she could have been heard over the radio. Styx had blared, "Come Sail Away," and then Lynyrd Skynyrd got down to, "Sweet Home Alabama." All of which seemed more important than listening to Madison say anything at all.

When I got home, Dad was sitting in his recliner. He struggled to dig his way out. "Barry? Hey, where ya been?"

"Out." I tried to keep walking, but he called me back. "What?" I snapped. "I'm not in the best mood."

He shuffled awkwardly, staring down at his foot toeing the carpet. "Barry, what're you doing with Brittney?"

Whoa. What the hell? Why was I being bombarded with Brittney all of a sudden? I hadn't even seen her since I skipped out on church yesterday. "Nothing."

"You're not trying to hurt her, are you? Mitch called—"

"Oh fuck."

He scowled at my word choice. Long ago, he stopped trying to fix my mouth. Probably because he figured there were bigger issues to deal with as far as parenting was concerned. That was on the days he wanted to be a parent. Which was today, I guess. "Now listen. He's just worried. Brittney's not like you and your friends."

"As Mitch already made perfectly clear. Got it."

"So why are you spending so much time with her?"

I shrugged. "I don't know. She's cool."

"You're not trying to have sex with her."

"Jesus, Dad."

"Well now, it's a reasonable question. She's a pretty girl."

"Yeah, she's not exactly my type." Again, I tried to get away. This time, he caught my shoulder.

"What *is* your type, Bare?"

"Are we seriously having this conversation?" Did he have to mess with me tonight of all nights? I'd already made plans to go upstairs and stew over whether or not to call Mom and hand over the pills she'd asked for.

Oh, and then I was going to find the trashiest POV porno I could get my hands on and figure out what was wrong with Little Barry.

Dad exhaled heavily, blowing out the air trapped in his cheeks. "You leave here, and I have no clue where you're going. I don't know what you're up to. You show up covered in bruises. You're distant. You don't want to talk. I get that you don't think much of my relationship with Ashleigh, but I'm your father, and if I want to know what you're doing with your life, you need to tell me."

I threw my hands up. "What the fuck do you want to know?"

His posture remained firm, but I saw the hesitation in his eyes. Still, he said, "You're on drugs." It didn't come out as a question, though, because for all his faults, he wasn't stupid.

"You know I am." I met his gaze.

He shook his head, letting out a slow breath. "Pot?" he asked hopefully.

"Yup."

"What else?"

I shrugged. "Little of this, little of that." I could have let him off the hook. *No*, I wasn't addicted to cocaine or anything stupid like that.

I wasn't *addicted* to anything, I didn't think. I just liked catching a buzz.

Another slow breath, like he was trying to keep his temper in check. After all, I was being honest and playing along with his little *communication* nonsense, so there wasn't much reason to lose his cool.

It was inevitable, though, that at any second he'd throw Mom into the mix. He'd say we both had a problem—the apple didn't fall far from the tree. Then I'd be the one to flip. She was still my mom, whether she was going through a hard time right now or not.

"Do you have anything on you right now?" Taking a step back, his eyes widened. "Do you, Bare?"

Oh fuck.

How had I not seen this coming? My fists jammed into the pockets of my jeans. "No."

"Tell me the truth."

"No, I don't have anything." I tried to step past him, but he caught me.

Mouth inches from my ear, he growled, "You were always a shitty liar, son."

"Fine. Yes. But I'm not flushing them."

He glared at me. No, wait, "glare" wasn't a good enough word for what his eyes were doing to me. His finger raised, he pointed straight into my face. "You bet your ass you are. Barry, you're seventeen years old. Do you have any idea how much life you have to live still? College, marriage, babies, a four-oh-one-k, houses, second-houses, grandkids. Can your brain even process the enormity of how big life is? Or are you so hell-bent on killing yourself?"

"What? I'm not trying to kill myself."

"That's what you're doing. There's a reason those pills are given with recommended doses and by prescription only."

My flaccid appendage begged me to make a smart ass comment. I kept it together *because Dad knew.*

Pills.

He knew I was popping painers and muscle relaxers. *How?* Because of what Mom had said at the church?

I wondered if he had suspected sooner. All those times he'd looked at me with disappointment, had there been some underlying doubt inside him? A part of him that knew what I was up to, and Mom had just confirmed it for him? "I just like feeling buzzed. It's the only way I can be part of this family."

Dad flinched, and I remembered the words Mom had said to him in my dream. I couldn't look at him.

"Look, Dad, if I flush them, I'll just go out and buy more tomorrow." This was true. Taking the pills away would piss me off, but I was already planning how I'd get my hands on more. I'd probably have to steal the Ambien this time. No way would Brody sneak back into someone's house so soon after the first time.

"No, you won't," Dad said matter-of-factly. "I'm going to cancel your debit card. You're going to have no money."

My jaw dropped. "You cannot do that."

"Bullshit I can't. It's my money. I don't really feel like paying for your addiction. Now hand them over."

The word *addiction* was a bit harsh. That's what he wasn't understanding. I didn't have an addiction. I just liked to get down. "Fuck you." My fingers fisted inside my pockets and locked over both baggies.

"Barry." He let out another one of those calming-huffs. "Do I have to call the sheriff? I have it on good authority that James wouldn't have any trouble coming over here and searching you."

Low.

Blow.

"You wouldn't…" But I was beginning to think he would.

"Yeah." He nodded. "I'm fed up with your shit. You walk around like a whiny little brat. I made excuses for you after the divorce. I even paid to bail you out of trouble. Well, I'm done. You've got a year left in this house. Let's see if we can learn to stand each other in that time."

Each other?

He couldn't stand me, either? That was horseshit. Everyone loved me. I mean, okay, not *everyone*. I got that Mitch wasn't a fan, and Toby wasn't either, and, okay, Gwen. But most people adored me.

They liked my surly fuck-you behavior. It was endearing, and people dug that.

"Don't look so surprised. You're a miserable son of a bitch to live with."

I was? Pointing toward me, fingers curling back on his palm, he said-without-saying that I wasn't going to get away with keeping my new stash. I rifled through my pockets for both baggies. There was no way I was keeping mine and flushing Mom's or vice versa.

"One isn't mine," I mumbled

He gaped. "What? You're selling now?"

"*No*. I was just holding onto it for someone."

His eyes narrowed. "*They'll* have to find another idiot to do their dirty work. This isn't staying in my house."

Not only was it not staying, but I had the completely humiliating task of flushing it down the toilet. All thirty-five pills. Which may not be much to some people, but it was a helluva few good buzzes to me.

"If you take my debit card, how will I put gas in the car?"

He stared at me for a second, and then a slow, creeping smile spread across his face. "Why would you need gas? You're not going anywhere."

I felt like I'd put that thought inside his head. "You're not serious."

He nodded decidedly. "You bet I am. At least for a couple weeks. Hand over the keys. And the spares."

"Dad, don't be a dick. I need my car. What about community service?"

"You don't need it. Ashleigh can take you to the library. It's about time you spent time together."

THIRTEEN

BRITTNEY ANN

Just like last time, Ryan's truck was in the parking lot. This time, he was sitting inside, waiting for me.

"Hey," he said, and without even giving me a chance to respond, he started in. "Did you know they were planning on doing that to me?"

"Do what?" I asked. Yet again, I felt the need to defend Barry. *Why?* Why would I defend a drug addict who was going to help his *mom* get high? He didn't deserve my defenses.

"At the movies. That guy—the one who was with Maddie. He showed up with you. He was with you afterwards. Did they plan it all along? Was it some kind of joke to see if I'd go through with it? Because I have a really hard time believing she was part of it. I think she's scared of him. She doesn't want—"

I laughed. Oh, man, did I laugh. It was loud and carefree. My cheeks were on fire and I was hiccupping by the time I finally got control of myself. "She"—hiccup—"hates being called Maddie,"—hiccup—"by the way."

He stared at his shoes. "Oh. It was just something I was trying. Why'd you laugh at me?"

"Madison is...how should I say this? She's very promiscuous. Barry told her to break us up by flirting with you. Whatever she did with you was because she takes her job very *literally*."

He shook his head in disbelief.

"Ryan, I don't care if you believe me."

Pointing his finger in my face, he trembled. "You're jealous. She and I had a connection, and you're jealous that I have her and... and...and I bet that guy had sex with you and dumped you. Ha! That's what happened isn't it? Ha! Ha! Ha!" He tried to mimic my laughter. It was fake. But also loud.

Heat trickled up my neck. We'd walked into the lobby of the hospital. I couldn't wait until we were in separate rooms and far away from each other.

"Do you have her phone number?" he asked.

"No," I lied.

"You said you guys were cheerleaders together."

I tried to walk into the emergency room, where my assignment paper said I'd spend the first half of the day, but he caught my wrist. His grip sliced off circulation to my hand.

The most physical contact we'd ever had. His skin was dryer than I'd imagined. I hated it.

"You have her number. Just give it to me. I just want to talk to her. Please, Brittney Ann. It's important."

Feeling sorry for Ryan was not something I expected today. "I'm sorry, but if she didn't...Ow, let go."

"You don't get it, do you? Pretty people never get it. I thought having you like me made me special. I thought things were really turning around. But her? She was so much. She had so much. And it was all a joke." His eyes watered. "I don't want to believe it was a joke, Brittney Ann. I think if I could talk to her, she'd change her mind. We really did connect."

"I'm sorry. I don't have her phone number."

His head dropped in defeat. As he walked away, he tucked his fists into his pockets. I didn't breathe until he rounded the corner, and his shoes stopped squeaking down the hall. I raced to the front desk and slammed down my assignment paper. "I can't work here this summer."

The woman behind the desk gave me a wide-eyed look, like I'd lost my mind. I didn't care. There was no way I was doing that again. Not for volunteer hours I didn't even want to work.

೦೩

"So tell me again; what's this guy look like?"

I let out a small laugh and a sigh. "Gwen, please, let it go. I don't need Toby coming home to kill him just because he grabbed my arm."

"You were scared enough to quit your job," she argued. Lifting a shirt off the rack she held it up to her chest. We both shook our head at the same time. Mint wasn't her color.

"Volunteering at the hospital for the summer wasn't exactly a *job*. Besides, I'm planning on finding some other fun things to do."

"Like read?" she guessed.

Yeah, probably.

We were at the secondhand clothing store on Main Street shopping for some clothes for Gwen. She was going to spend the majority of the summer in California with Toby, and then she was transferring to school there this fall.

I already missed her. "You're going to call a lot, right?" I asked.

"Yes, Britt. I'll call."

Fingering the fabric of a bright pink shirt, I smiled at her. "I know you and Toby will get preoccupied, and you'll forget all about me."

She dug inside the collar of a shirt with her head tucked.

I smacked my forehead. "I didn't mean like that," I said. "I just mean that there's so much more stuff to do out there. Their zoo has the pandas. You have to go see the pandas."

She smirked. "I won't miss the pandas."

It was safe to say I was jealous. Gwen didn't have anything holding her back. She wasn't close to her family. My family had basically adopted her when she'd started dating Toby. All major holidays she spent at our house.

Gwen bought way more clothes than she needed. She was planning on picking Dexter up from the groomers, and my afternoon was wide open. On a whim, I decided to swing by the library. Avoiding the Bourbon Library was a general rule. I loved books, and I liked libraries.

The Bourbon Library had the misfortune of being manned by a somewhat senile woman who couldn't seem to find the right place for anything. It was a crapshoot trying to find any particular book—maybe it was where it's supposed to be, maybe not.

None of Marlowe's books were where they belonged. Again.

I started up and down aisles, scanning for worn spines that looked out of place. Needless to say, I stopped often.

A familiar pair of Converse shoes stuck out in the 900's section. I blew hot air into my palm to check my breath.

Oh yes, very classy Brittney Ann. I'd thought bad things about him all week, and then the second I saw his shoes—*His. Shoes*—I was making sure my breath didn't offend.

Clearing my throat, I tried to make my presence known. His feet didn't move. Was he asleep? Who in their right mind would come into a library in the middle of summer to sleep?

A sheen of sweat covered his green face.

Green? *Oh no.*

"Barry?" I fell down on my knees beside him.

There was wet marks under both of his arm pits. His entire body trembled.

The way he looked reminded me of Daddy that one time. "Barry." I shook his shoulders. Fear trickled down my spine like a cold finger scoring my hot skin.

Daddy hadn't wanted to wake up, either. Toby had screamed for Mommy to come in. She'd made us both go downstairs and leave Daddy alone. But we *had* left him alone. It had been days since he'd come home stumbling all over the place.

Barry's bloodshot eyes blinked open, and I knew.

He wasn't stoned.

Barry was going through withdrawals.

FOURTEEN

BARRY

I'd heard of this place before, but I could honestly say I'd never been here. Lying on the musky library floor, covered in sweat, with a killer stomach ache, thinking about how pissed my mom was—she basically told me never to call her again—and how I hadn't even gotten laid, and my dad hated me, and...the woe-is-me could go on for a long time.

The only good thing was that I'd figured out that the librarian really had no clue when I was working and when I wasn't. I'd pretty much slept all day Tuesday and Wednesday. The shitty sick-all-over withdrawals hadn't hit until this morning.

I must have fallen asleep. The next thing I knew, a cool satin hand brushed my cheek.

How the hell had she found me? It was summer. Bourbon was a small town, sure, but it wasn't *that* small. "What're you doing here, Brittney?" I caught her hand, pushing it away from my face.

"Barry? You have a fever. What's wrong? Are you ill?"

"Don't worry about that. What the hell are you doing here?"

"I'm looking for a book," she said simply. "What's your excuse?"

I blinked up at her, taking in the strawberry cascade of her hair. "Way too complicated. Good luck with that book, by the way; the place is a wreck."

"Yes, I know. I always try to help a little when I come in." She frowned. "What's the matter, Barry? Have you got a summer cold?"

"Sure, we'll go with that."

My blurry eyes blinked a few times, adjusting to the harsh fluorescent lights. Her sharply angled body was leaned over me. "What's really wrong?" she whispered. "You can tell me."

"I just don't feel good," I lied. "You wanna give me a ride home?"

She didn't ask about my car.

Brittney stood there while I explained to Mrs. Kenderson that I wasn't hanging around today, and I'd have to make up my hours. The woman didn't even look like she recognized me. "Okay dear," she said with several feeble head nods.

"You're volunteering at the library?" Brittney beamed. "That's wonderful of you."

I wiped sweat off my forehead with the back of my head. "Yeah, it's not exactly *volunteer* work."

"Oh? They're paying you?"

"More like forced labor."

She looked confused, so I explained. "I got in some trouble, and they slapped me on the wrist with some community service that'll never find its way to my adult record."

She nodded. "When Lonna's dad busted you?"

My stomach rolled, and I braced myself against the brick outside the library. "How'd you know about that?"

"Are you alright?"

"I'm fine." I breathed through my mouth, trying to keep from hurling chunks in front of her. Glancing sideways, I took in her plaid dress and flat shoes. "How'd you know about Lonna?"

Brittney toed a crack in the sidewalk. "I am a cheerleader, Barry. Give me some credit. I get all the good gossip."

Oh shit. My knuckle ground into the rough brick as my gut did a one-eighty. "Uh, Madison didn't say anything about me recently, did she?"

"Hmm?" Brittney's cheeks turned pink.

"That bitch," I groaned. Heat erupted on my skin.

Brittney's cool palm touched my hairline at my neck. "She was worried about you. Really."

"I'm so sure."

"Oh, I shouldn't have said anything. It's just that Madison was under the impression that…well…um…"

"She said it was because of you, didn't she?" I growled.

"Madison seemed to think I could have been a factor. I'm very sorry if I did something to upset you. I'm not sure how all that works, or why, but—"

I punched the brick. Pain sizzled through my knuckles. "Britt, she was trying to get inside your head. She wants to pretend it's everyone's fault but her own." Something foul bubbled in my throat, but I swallowed it back down. "You know…she doesn't want to be the ugly girl a guy couldn't get hard for. Uh, so yeah, It's not about you. It's her."

"Oh? Okay, good. That's…not good, I guess, since you enjoy having sex with her."

"Not anymore." My tone was acidic.

"Right, not anymore. Sorry."

"You don't gotta apologize."

☙

I was still sleeping. The sweat felt like a cold pool of misery, but I was positive I was still sleeping.

And dreaming. Because if this wasn't a dream, I had lost my mind.

"If you're not going to be helpful, you can just go," her angelic voice snapped.

"Hey, whoa. Where the hell do you get off telling *me* to go anywhere, princess? I think if he opened his eyes right now, he'd be more upset about *you* inside his bedroom than *me*." Tyler? Tyler was here.

Brittney huffed. The cool feel of a wet washcloth pressed against my head, and the rolling in my stomach instantly receded.

"He's not going to make it," Bo said. "Ty, just go get the shit."

"No," Brittney snapped. "He's stronger than that." My bed shifted as she planted herself beside me. I blinked through the fog.

"Listen bitch…"

"Dude," Bo warned. "Chill."

"Chill? *Me*? Tell her to fucking chill. He's my *best* friend. He doesn't want to be sober, so he shouldn't have to be. No stuck-up Christian skank—"

"Ty?" Sniffling, I blinked into the brightness of my bedroom. Bad idea. My stomach rolled and I let out a groan.

Brittney's hands cupped over my eyelids. "What can I do?" she whispered.

"Just stay."

I sniffled again, sucking back nothing but trying to clear my sinuses all the same. "Ty?"

"Yeah? I'm here man."

"How'd I get home?" I didn't remember anything after talking to Brittney outside the library.

"Uh, Brittney called us. You were pretty out of it in her car and she didn't know what to do. We dragged you in here, and we've been covering with Ashleigh. It's a good thing she's dumb as a box of rocks. You've been back and forth between gagging up yellow slime and sleeping for the past two hours."

My stomach rolled at his graphic depiction. "Thanks for that."

"Any time. So, uh, yeah, Bo and I were thinking—"

"No," Brittney snapped.

"How long's it been since you took something?" Bo muttered.

I shrugged. "Couple days."

"Dude, you're this—"

"I know," I growled. "I didn't know it was this bad." The word *addiction* played through my mind, and I wondered if I hadn't under-estimated its meaning.

"You're having withdrawals." Tyler's tone was urgent. He tapped his fingers against the edge of my desk. "We have to get you some-thing. I'll call Brody. I'll go get it myself. You can't do this cold turkey. You'll kill yourself, man."

"He's already done it," Brittney seethed. Inching further up the mattress, she laid her flat palm against my chest. "He just has to get the toxins out of him."

Tyler belted a laugh. "Are you living in a fucking fantasy world? The toxins? Do you ever just stop and listen to yourself?"

"Dude," Bo hissed a breath.

"No, I'm serious. She's all rainbows and sunshine. She doesn't understand shit. Bare, I'm going."

"No." I shook my head. Reaching up, I laced my fingers into Brittney's.

"Seriously?" Tyler was awed. I wished I could have properly ap-preciated the view of his face in that state.

"You-you guys are leaving for camp in the morning. You'll be gone for two weeks. Dad took my debit card. Whether I go through this tonight or I do it when the pills you get me run out, I'm going to have to do it. And Brittney's right. I'm already three days in. Might as well do it now."

 ֎

I woke up the next morning with Ashleigh shaking my shoulder.

"Bare? Bare? You okay, sweetie?"

My eyes blinked open to a different light streaming through my blinds—the light of a new day. My stomach didn't feel nearly as risky as it had yesterday, and I was able to sit on the edge of the bed without passing out. "Can I call in sick to community service?" I asked.

"I don't think so." Her brows narrowed. "Besides, if you just get it over with now, you won't have to do it when you feel better. How hard can hanging out in a library be?"

She clearly wouldn't know.

"I'll make you a to-go cup of hot chocolate." She was trying so damn hard to make me like her. She backed out of the room and pulled the door shut quietly behind her.

I had three missed calls and a text message from Tyler:

If you're dead, blame the Christian broad.

I smiled at the screen and typed out a response:

Since I'm alive should I thank you or her?

Him:

Probably her. She stood over you like a protective momma cat all night. Me-Ow.

The image made me smile. Me:

Jealous?

Him:

Fuck yeah. Where can I find one of those that likes to suck dick?

I laughed. Me:

Afraid that's not how it works. They're either prude and perfect. Or cheap and annoying.

Him:

The way I hear it, you don't even like the cheap ones anymore.

I cringed. Me:

What did that bitch say?

Him:

> **Ha. Just a little something about your toy soldier having trouble performing. Tough breaks, sugar nipples.**

Me:

> **I couldn't get it up because you weren't there, babe.**

I threw the phone against the mattress and laid back with my arms under my head. "Barry," Ashleigh called. "We're leaving in a little bit."

"Yeah, okay."

Him:

> **lol. Sorry handsome, I'm using you for your mom. You'll have to settle for fat ass.**

Me:

> **Jeez, Ty, you're calling your mom fat ass now? Didn't she teach you any respect?**

Ty:

> **haha. No, dickweazel, I meant Chase. Bo said to tell you you're a limp dick bastard. I told him you knew. Gotta go, bus is here. Miss you already, sugar nipples.**

I set the phone down. Sadness ate at my chest as I accepted that they were leaving without me. I was going to miss them.

I took a semi-cold shower, not giving a damn about anything but getting the combined smells of sweat and vomit off me. This day was going to suck. My foot twitched against the floorboard of Ashleigh's car.

Mrs. Kenderson, as always, sat behind the large, dust covered desk. "Hello." Her expression was as blank as ever. "Can I help you?"

Good God woman. I rubbed my palms over my face.

"I'm doing community service in here. I'm cataloging all the books into the computer." I didn't have to be such an ass to the geriatric, but so what? Yeah, that's right, *so what?* I was fiending for some fucking pain killers. Bad. Fuck this life. Fuck this town. *Fuckity fuck, fuck.*

"Oh? You're working with that other girl?"

My palms flattened against the desk to keep myself from launching over there and tackling her. "Girl? Bitch, I'm the one who's been in here all week."

"Barry!" Brittney's voice snapped. "That's no way to talk to your elder."

I really wanted to be annoyed that she was here, but that wasn't the emotion I felt. "What're you doing here?" Relief shot through me.

Brittney's arms were loaded down with books. Damn. So she was already leaving. She shifted one of the heavy spines from her left elbow to the right.

"Things didn't work out at the hospital and, as you pointed out yesterday, the library really could use some TLC, so I've decided to help you."

That relief settled into my veins. "You have?"

"Yes. It'll be faster if we work together, won't it?" She labored that lower lip between her teeth.

Maybe she really was an angel. She sure as hell acted like one. It was engrained in me to believe the worst in people, though. "Why're you doing this?"

She shrugged. "Colleges like it when people do volunteer work. Plus, I've been very bored at home by myself."

That was it? She wasn't trying to get into my pants or steal library books or annoy me? She was…*bored?*

Instead of getting stoned and jumping off a cliff, she wanted to volunteer at the library. "Okay, wow, so…thank you."

She grinned, glancing down the strawberry locks that had fanned over her face. "You actually mean that?"

"Yeah, well, uh, look, about last night…"

She waved her palm, dismissing whatever words I would have used to thank her for what she'd done. Not that anything had bubbled to my mouth yet. Cupping the back of my neck, I stared down at my checkered shoes.

Clearing my throat, I mumbled, "No, seriously, I want to thank you. Not a lot of people would have, uh, all that with the wash cloth and whatnot…"

That counted as a sentence, right?

When, after a few seconds went by and she didn't respond, I glanced up and caught her hurrying to look away from me. "What?" I asked.

"Nothing," she rushed. "I just…I find it hard to believe that all the girls you hang out with aren't eager to look out for you."

A smile made its way to my lips. "Yeah, I'm kinda an asshole. And there aren't any permanent girls in my life."

"Oh." She bit into her lip again.

"What's that?" My grin widened.

"Huh?" Her hazel-golden eyes blinked over at me. "What?"

"You were asking if I was single, weren't you?"

"No I wasn't. We were talking about how sick you were." Shuffling the books back to her other elbow, she shifted her weight. "How *are* you feeling, Barry?"

"I don't think I'm going to hurl yellow slime. My vision's a little hazy, but manageable. All thanks to you." If I'd left my fate to my incompetent friends, there I'd be higher then a kite right now.

If Tyler had offered me some candy last night and Brittney hadn't been sitting there telling him no, I knew without a doubt my answer would have been different.

Not that I could blame my friends. I'd heard the stress in Ty's voice. He'd just been looking out for me. I'd probably have done the same for him.

No, on second thought, I wouldn't even have questioned it. If I'd seen him like that, I'd have crushed up some candy, rolled a dollar straw, and held his head in one hand and the bill in the other while he sucked it all back. He wouldn't have even had a chance to say no. That's the kind of friend I was.

"Well, I like to think we're even now."

"Even?" I asked, pinching my fingers against my warm neck.

"You saved my life. I kept you from dying in a pile of vomit." She shrugged like it was no big deal at all. And she didn't mention the pills or my very obvious *addiction*.

A small piece of myself fell in love with her right then, right there in that library.

⍝

I entered the card numbers into the computer, and Brittney checked that the books were in the right place.

It wasn't until she came tottering down the stairs with an art book that was twice as wide as she was that I questioned this system. It was a pretty big dick move to make her do all the walking. I hopped up and yanked the book out of her hand. Her pretty eyes blinked up at me. "You know what? This looks like an insane workout. Why don't you type, and I'll move the books?"

"Oh? Are you sure?"

Catching a piece of her hair that glimmered red in the sunlight, I twirled it around my finger. "Has anyone ever told you, you say *oh* a lot?"

She thought about it, nibbling on her lower lip. "No. I suppose no one's ever pointed it out. Is it bad?"

"I don't know. I can't decide."

She chewed on the inside of her cheek and stared at me, not blinking, like she was waiting for more. When I said nothing, she started to turn away. Her hair flowed from my grip like water sliding over my knuckles.

I didn't want her to go. I grabbed her arm and her eyes focused on where our skin met. She waited. And she waited.

And she waited for me to say something…*anything*.

My eyes were doing the unthinkable. I stared at the way a different, stray piece of strawberry hair had fallen over her face. It danced across her cheekbone and over her jaw, then disappeared into the top of her dress, where milky cleavage would have peeked out if her dress weren't covering everything

"We should count." I licked at the dry roof of my mouth, trying to bring moisture back to the area.

"Huh?"

"How many times you say *oh* in a week. We should count it."

"Why on earth would we do that?" She asked, her breathing was all over the place, and I looked from that lonely lock of hair to her face.

Her hazel gaze now trailed *my* arm, my forearm, my bicep, my shoulder, my chest.

She was checking me out.

"Um, well…" Holy hell, those eyes roved all the way to the floor before closing as she sucked in a slight purr.

When she blinked back up at me, though, there wasn't anything but blankness in her expression, as if she didn't want me to see whatever was hidden inside her thoughts. "Well?" Her voice croaked.

Disappointment rattled my chest. "There could be, like, a punishment. You say *oh* ten times, and you have to do something."

Her nose scrunched up as she chewed on the inside of her cheek. "I'm not so sure."

"C'mon. It'll be fun."

"What sort of punishment are we talking, Barry?"

"I don't know. Let me think about it."

"Oh, alright." Her eyes widened, and her hand slapped over her mouth.

I held up my index finger. "One." I beamed. "Nine to go."

CB

Number two: When she found the library's copy of John Grisham's *The Firm*. Holding it victoriously over her head.

"Oh, look Barry. It's right here."

⁊

Number three: When she was lying on the floor with her shoes kicked off, her ankles crossed, and her hair splayed out behind her like a waterfall. She was reading a thick book without any letters on the front and no pictures on the pages.

She huffed. "Oh alright. I'll get back to work."

CB

Number four: With too many books in her arms, she stepped down the stairs and stumbled top over bottom. With her dress up over the meaty part of her thighs, she blinked up at me, blushing.

"Oh…"

⁊

Number five: When I didn't ask, but she decided to tell me about Gwen and Toby anyway.

"They're what I aspire to, I guess. They have the perfect relationship. He moves, she moves. They tease each other all the time, too. So it's not like they're mushy." Her fingers jammed into her mouth, and she mumbled, "Oh, I'm rambling…"

CB

Number six: When I didn't ask, but she told me about her parents anyway.

"I don't think I understand them, and I'm sure they don't understand me. Oh, am I still rambling?"

&

Number seven, eight, and nine: When I asked about what she was reading right now and why. *Black Beauty*, because it was her favorite, and then, even though I wasn't owed an explanation, she actually told me, anyway.

"Oh, it's all because of Buttercup." Her hand slapped over her mouth and those eyes jumped. "Oh no, I said *Oh*."

&

Number ten: When she was dancing with her headphones on, and I'd caught her, pulled her into me, and pressed a kiss to her cheek.

"Oh Barry," She giggled, and her breath blew out shakily.

&

Her being so damn cute all the time had me thinking about her *all the time*. It was infuriating because I still never knew what *she* was thinking. Yet, she could read me like a book. After the first week in the library, she knew to either bring me a hot cocoa every morning or not even bother talking to me until noon. She knew that rubbing the spot beside my neck in the back—my trap—made me purr like a freaking koala bear.

Also, she knew that going through with her punishment was going to drive me crazy. "I really shouldn't be doing this." We stood at the mall with our arms wrapped around each other, pretending like we were a couple, in case any of the workers asked.

This had been my suggestion. I'd never asked a girl to pretend to be my girlfriend before. I thought I'd regret it instantly; she'd get the wrong idea and think we were something we weren't.

Brittney didn't, though. No matter how many times I said, "This is just for make-believe," she just rolled her eyes and said, "I know Barry. Believe me, I know."

It really shouldn't have bothered me that she was perfectly okay with the platonic state of our relationship. Something hollow in my chest felt itchy and unsure about her easy tone of voice. She was just so *okay* with it. I swallowed hard, forcing that *itchy* feeling to resolve itself.

"Then don't do it, chicken shit." I loved teasing her. My nose fell into her hair.

"I don't say *oh* so much that I need to resort to…" Her voice lowered to a lethal whisper. "Thievery."

I pinched her hip. "Yes, but stealing is *so* sexy."

Her breath trembled. "There's something very wrong with you, Barry Prescott. Very wrong."

I smiled against her shoulder. "In a good way, right?"

She exhaled. "I haven't decided yet. Okay, let's get out of here."

"Wait, you have to—"

She twisted out of my hold, and I quickly yanked her back into me. That hollow feeling didn't like how easily she'd released me. "They're already in my purse," she giggled.

I looked back at the table, and sure enough, the pink underwear that we'd agreed she'd steal were gone. Pressing my lips to the hollow of her neck, I whispered, "There's something wrong with you, Brittney Ann. Something very, very wrong, in a very very good way."

"That's what I was afraid you'd say," she sighed.

FIFTEEN

BRITTNEY ANN

I'd promised myself I wouldn't go back to that library. When I drove home that Thursday after taking care of him, I swore it would be the last time I'd have any contact with Barry. He was clearly bad news. My family didn't want me with him. Plus, the drugs. Too many things were stacked against him, and he hadn't even expressed an interest in me. So, therefore, I would stay far, far away from him.

For some reason, I found myself standing in front of my pastel closet that Friday morning. I cursed it the same as I had for weeks. None of it seemed like *me*. None of it was anything I would have picked out for myself.

Maybe it was the clothes that had decided it for me, or maybe I'd known all along that I wouldn't *actually* be able to stay away. I crept out of the house before Daddy even got back from feeding the chickens. I'd left a note saying that I was planning on volunteering at the library and wouldn't be home until later.

Then I went and sought *him* out.

Being alone in that library with Barry was perfection. He opened up to me about how much he despised his father's relationship with Ashleigh, and how the pain that his mother's absence ate at him.

He joked about his friends, how Tyler was the prankster, Bo the big brother, Chase the loner, Gage the ladies' man. That was all stuff that I already knew, but hearing his love for them made me laugh.

He told me about some of their inside jokes—jokes I was sure he'd never told to anyone. He even mentioned some things about Gage being cruel to Lonna. Then he'd gotten quiet and had walked away from me. He never brought it up again.

He connected with me. Everything I'd ever felt for him, all those years ago, came flooding back like a tidal wave crashing up over the sides of my heart.

My willpower stood no freaking chance.

I'd liked Barry when we were just little kids. He'd stood up for me one time. When we were in Sunday School, Tyler had always made fun of my long arms. He'd called me Stretch Britt-Strong, and Barry had smacked him in the back of the head one time. He told him to lay off. They couldn't have been more than eleven. What did that make me? Ten? Okay, fine. I was ten. I wanted him then.

And, yeah, he'd hurt me when I was fourteen, but that had been forgiven.

I saw a side of Barry in that library that he never showed to anyone else. He was actually really kind. He truly cared about the people in his life. Not animals so much, but that was something I thought we could work around. He'd just never had a pet to love the way I loved Dexter and Buttercup.

Then, on the third week of our library-bliss, it happened.

The doors blew open with a loud bang, and the most obnoxious noise to ever invade a library came by way of four grown boys.

Barry's face paled. "Shit. I told them not to come."

"They're back from camp?" I reached for his hand. We'd gotten comfortable holding hands. I don't know why I wanted to feel his fingers in mine, but when he pulled away, my heart somersaulted to the pit of my stomach.

"Stay here." He dismissed me with a shrug of his shoulder. I had no interest in following because I didn't want to face the other guys. Even if Barry loved them, I'd never shared that respect.

"Sweetheart?" Tyler's voice sounded muffled. I pulled a book off the shelf so I could peek through the bare space and see all of them. Tyler hugged Barry, slapping their fists against each other's backs. Their brotherly embrace made me smile. Okay, getting to know Tyler through Barry's eyes had made him grow on me.

Barry didn't hug the others. They all fell around a table in the center of the room. Bo leaned back with his hands folded beneath his head, and Gage threw his feet up on the tabletop. I scowled. I had to replace the book and move to a different shelf to see them all better now that they were sitting

"What the hell have you been up to, ya limp dick bastard?" Bo laughed.

Barry's head fell back as he hissed. "I'm going to kill Madison."

"Aw come on, man. She was worried about you. I had to cheer her up after you couldn't get the job done." It sounded like a complaint, but Bo was grinning from ear to ear.

Gage snorted. "Dumb slut. She was at my house that night crying about how ugly she was."

"I'm sure you made her feel so much prettier." Barry's voice was deeper and more cautious. I did a double take just to make sure that was actually him.

Gage shrugged. "Nah. She was pissed when she left. Anyone know what the deal is with Parker going down on her all of a sudden? He knows we all put our dicks in that, right?"

They all laughed. Except Bo. His grin retreated. "It's not funny. I ran into Wendy at the grocery store. She wouldn't even give me the time of day because he's apparently the only one who can get her off. If he doesn't quit, we're not going to get laid ever again."

It must have been a sobering thought because they all sat there staring off into space. Barry's chair shifted. I was able to duck as his head swiveled to where I peeked through the books. "What you looking at?" Tyler whispered.

"Nothing," he mumbled.

"Oh yeah? Does *nothing* drive her brother's hand-me-down Plymouth?"

I cringed.

"What?" Barry snapped.

"Toby's car is parked outside. I'm assuming Toby isn't here." I cringed at the amused undertone in Tyler's voice. For Barry's sake, I hated that Tyler was entertained.

"Oh, yeah, Brittney's here somewhere."

"Somewhere?" I didn't recognize that voice—probably Chase's.

"Yeah, she reads a lot. No big deal."

No big deal? *Oh…*

"So you guys just hang out while you're in here working—"

"We don't hang out," Barry dismissed again, he sounded not at all like the boy's I'd come to know. Something sharp stabbed into my chest. I reached up and rubbed at the sensation with my palm. "She comes to read. I put away books. I don't ignore her when she talks to me because I'm not a complete dickhead. That's it."

Sliding the book back onto the shelf, I blocked them all out. The precarious lurching inside my stomach insisted I not continue spying. I hated how surprised I was that he'd gone back to being his usual jerk self so easily. It did surprise me, though.

I truly don't know what else I'd expected.

It wasn't until Bo said my name that my head snapped up.

"Hey Gage, we never got a chance to tell you that Barry rode your mom out at Britt's farm a couple weeks ago."

They laughed. My eyes narrowed, and I fingered the spine of that book, contemplating pulling it away again.

"Don't worry," Barry chuckled deeply. "I saddled up before getting on."

"Fuck you," Gage snapped. "My mom doesn't look like a horse."

Tyler *neigh*'d. They dissolved into more raucous laughter.

"You know what?" Gage's voice was acidic. "Ty, why don't you make a move on Brittney?"

"What the fuck?" Barry gasped. "Seriously?"

"Why not? Tyler's the one who loves virgins."

"I don't love virgins."

"Yeah, you do," Bo and Gage said at the same time.

"Okay, there's a little thrill to it. But I'm not into Brittney."

Wow.

Even Tyler didn't want me. I didn't know any girls that Tyler Newbold didn't want. I must have been some special breed of ugly.

That was fine. I didn't desire his attention anyway.

"Who cares if you're into her? Someone needs to bring that bitch down a few pegs." *Thanks Gage.*

"Dude," Barry breathed. "Don't."

"Don't what?" Gage enticed. "You said there wasn't anything going on with you guys. There's no reason to stay away from her."

Barry said nothing to defend me.

Trying as hard as possible to block them out again, I continued organizing all the nonfiction earth science books. I must have zoned out. When Tyler walked up and knocked on the edge of the shelf, I startled, dropping a large book on my toe.

He hissed his lips behind his teeth as I did a little dance at the shooting pain skating through my foot. "Ow, ow, ow…"

"Sorry." He made a face, and I wanted to smack him just as much today as I had that afternoon in Barry's bedroom.

"I didn't mean to startle you." His sincerity surprised me.

A mental alarm went off inside my brain: *Is Tyler ever sincere?*

He plucked a book off the shelf, flipped it open, and then he did the unthinkable and sat it sideways on top of the *wrong* shelf. "So I was thinking…"

I huffed, grabbed the book, and put it in the right place.

He was smiling when I looked up at him. "Shit like that drives you crazy, huh?"

"I've only been trying to organize this place for the last few weeks. I just finished that shelf."

He nodded. "So you've been helping Barry out?"

Oops. Open mouth. Insert foot. "No," I snapped. Heat grazed the back of my neck. "He told you I haven't."

"Right, right. He did say that."

This time when he lifted a book it was to peek out at the center of the room. "Great view from here. You can hear everything?"

No point lying. "Yes."

"So you know why I'm here?"

"Because you're too much of a coward to tell Gage you don't want to ask me on a date."

He smiled again. "Actually, it's because I think taking you out will thoroughly enrage Barry. I've never seen him so tense. You either *really* pissed him off, or you're *deep* under his skin. Personally, I want to know what it is."

"I'm not under his skin," I mumbled. But I couldn't remember making him angry, either. Maybe it was something I'd missed.

Tyler tossed his blond hair out of his eyes. "Yeah, okay. Whatever you think, little Christian. Look, I wanna take you on a date. But it's not because I'm trying to get into those cotton full-bottom panties."

"How'd you…?" I sucked my words back down with a horrified gasp. I could go ahead and die now.

He laughed. "You look like a brief type of girl," he shrugged. "So what do you say?"

"About my underwear?"

At least they're purple and not white…

Rubbing his stomach, he chuckled to himself. "No, about a movie. Maybe grabbing some grub. I bet we don't get that far. If I know my boy, and I do, he's going to be there before the movie even starts."

I wasn't so sure I was following, but if he had a plan that led me to the Barry I'd come to know, then I wanted to try it. There was a small voice inside my brain reminding me that Barry had dismissed me the same as he had freshman year.

Perhaps I was more like Ryan than I ever planned on being. I hadn't spoken to Ryan since the hospital, but I'd heard through the grapevine that Madison had had Luke Parker set him straight and leave her alone.

Was that what would happen to me? Would Barry have to have another girl tell me that my desire for him wasn't getting me anywhere, and we weren't ever going to happen?

Deep down, I guess I already knew it wasn't going to happen. He was still Barry Prescott. Senior. Football Star. Beautiful. And I was just pastel-Brittney Ann Wilson.

None of that kept my heart from stuttering an uneven rhythm. I *still* wanted to try. "Yes," I said, "I think I'd like that."

Tyler winked at me. "Don't worry, little Christian. This is going to be fun."

There was no way that Tyler Newbold's definition of fun was the same as mine. He swiped his finger along the dusty shelf as he turned to walk away. "Brittney?" he asked softly. "He still sober?"

I nodded and then realized he wasn't looking at me. "Y-yes," I stammered. "I think."

He nodded. "Alright. Cool."

"Is that a good thing?" I croaked, swallowing a handful of frogs to get the words out.

He smiled at me from over his shoulder. Tyler really did have a nice smile. "If you have to ask, you haven't been hanging out with stoned-Barry the past few weeks."

My heart thundered in my chest. I really hoped the Barry I'd gotten to know was a sober Barry.

Later, when I told Daddy about my date with Tyler, he made it perfectly clear that he didn't like it.

"Tyler? You've got to be kidding me." He folded his strong arms, revealing the tattooed sleeve that he'd never had removed though he always talked about doing it.

I toed a line in the floor. "He's a nice boy."

"He's not nice. He's trouble. I thought your brother talked to you about those boys. I thought you learned your lesson after what Barry pulled. Now you want to go gallivanting off to some movie with his friend. You know those two are always in cahoots. They probably have another plan to hurt my little girl. All be damned if I stand by and watch it happen."

"Daddy…"

"No. I'm putting my foot down. Absolutely not."

I stormed up the stairs, swinging my arms and stomping my feet. Why was I upset about this? I didn't want to see Tyler anyway. And, yeah, he'd said Barry would show up, but that could have been a trick. Daddy could be right about that. I flopped diagonally across my mattress.

There was a soft knock on the door. "Come in, Mom." Dad's knocks were anything but *soft*.

She peeked her head inside. "You okay?"

"I'm fine," I mumbled.

"Sorry?" She cupped her ear.

"I'm fine," I said louder.

Some days, I wished she had taught us sign language. Mom spent the majority of her life not hearing a word. She'd gotten cochlear implants when I was little. What sign language I had learned had been long since forgotten.

Dad swore it was Mom who'd saved him from his reckless ways. He said she was an angel who'd swooped in when he was at his darkest.

After getting out of the service, he went into a dark depression. Drinking. Pills. Sex. It wasn't an urban legend, either. Not just something they told us about to scare us straight. Daddy had the proof tattooed all over his arms and back. A girl's name was crossed through and different girls' names were written and crossed out beneath. He'd had Mom's name tattooed on his back the night they met. He'd never had to cross it out.

Toby and I came years later.

My parents weren't young. I sometimes thought about how any children I might have would only know their grandparents for a limited time. I thought my parents' age was the reason Toby and Gwen wanted to get married already.

I laid my head sideways. "I'm fine, Mom," I said it again.

"You want to go on a date with Tyler?"

"No," I said instantly. "That's not it."

Her fingers brushed through my hair—hair that was the same color as hers. "What is it? I'll talk to your father. He needs to understand that keeping you under his thumb isn't the same as protecting you."

Her words brought up the fizzling inside my torso that made that soda-bottle-about-to-explode feeling happen. "Mom." I sat up and pulled my knees up to my chest. I was trying desperately hard not to break down. "I don't like pale colors. I don't even like dresses very much."

Her head fell to the side as she stared, looking confused.

"Please don't be offended. I still want to wear the clothes you made, but I want to wear other things, too. Blue jeans, you know?"

"Y-you have blue jeans."

"Yes, I do. But I only wear them when I'm horseback riding. I don't have any for school. Or, rather, I didn't. I bought a pair when I was out with Gwen a couple weeks ago."

Her voice pitched. "You can wear whatever you like."

"I know, but I don't want your feelings to be hurt."

The way she tucked her head and looked at the floor made me feel like the worst daughter in the world. The hurt had already happened.

"And I like the dresses," I said, hoping to repair what was left of this conversation. "People wear dresses with leggings all the time. You know how cold I get. I wouldn't mind, maybe, a little shorter dresses, so I could wear leggings under them this fall. And then... well, if you don't care, some darker colors. Some brighter colors even."

She smiled softly. "I can do that. Maybe we'll check out some different patterns."

"I'd like that," I emphasized. "Mom..." I cleared my throat. This time she looked me in the eye, prepared. "I want to go with Tyler tonight. It's not a very serious date. We don't have to give him the third degree, and we *definitely* don't have to tell Toby. I just want to catch a movie, and he offered to take me."

She sighed. "You trust him?"

I tried to force myself to be objective. Trusting Tyler Newbold? Wow. *Hmm?* He wasn't exactly the most upstanding guy.

Then again, he was Barry's *bestfriend*, and Tyler was charming. "Yeah, I do."

She nodded and took several steps backward, as if she didn't want to put her back to me as she walked out. Maybe she no longer trusted me. Or maybe I'd blindsided her with my revelation, and she wasn't awarding me the opportunity to do it again.

"Brittney? You know you can talk to me any time. I would have stopped making the dresses a long time ago if I'd known."

"I love that you love to sew. I didn't want to take that from you."

She smiled. "You're a good girl, Brittney. I'll talk to Dad."

Daddy didn't bother covering his tattoos for Tyler. He stood on the front porch in a short-sleeved T-shirt with his arms folded. "Whoa." Tyler hadn't even noticed him until he reached the bottom step, and then he took a measured step back. "Didn't see you there, Mitch."

Dad scowled. "Sir. You can call me *Sir*."

"Right. Sir." Tyler's lips twitched.

If there were an Abort button for this situation, I'd be slamming it with my fist right about now. "Time to go," I said, grabbing ahold of Tyler's shirt. He was an idiot, so of course he checked out my dark jeans. The ones that had made Gwen say, "Wow, those make your butt look great." I hoped Tyler wasn't such a moron that he made a comment like that in front of my dad.

"No later than nine, Brittney Ann," Daddy said, muscled arms twitching.

"Of course."

"Tyler Newbold, I have friends on the police force, I know your parents, and I know where you live. I might be a pastor, but I do own a gun, and if my daughter—"

"Daddy!"

Dad pointed a long, intimidating finger at Tyler. "If there's a hair ruffled on her pretty little head… I would run if I were you."

Tyler gulped loudly. He didn't touch me as he led me to the car. Opening the passenger door for me was smart but seemed out of character. "Thank you."

"He's fucking scary," he mumbled.

"Tell me about it."

Tyler listened to alternative music that made my ears ache. I reached up to turn it down a little, and he scowled. "You're lucky this isn't really a date. Touching my radio is a first strike."

"Strike?"

"Yeah. There's a three strike rule."

"And if a girl strikes out three times you…what, don't sleep with her?"

He sucked his lips behind his teeth. "Now, let's not be hasty. I simply count the strikes. I don't ever deprive my penis of company."

I scowled at him.

"That bother you?" He wiggled his blond brows playfully. "That I said *penis*? Because you thought I was censoring myself?"

He shifted, pulling his phone out of his pocket. Great. He was a text-and-driver. *Strike one, Tyler Newbold.* He smiled at the screen. Probably some girl—someone he'd meet up with to give his *penis* some company after this charade was over.

The phone went off and he laughed.

"So you and Barry, huh?" He asked, sliding the phone into a cup holder in the console.

"There is no *me* and Barry."

Tilting his hand sideways, his long finger slid along my jean at my thigh. "Your mouth says no, but your body says *maybe*."

Other than my bouncing-nervous knee, my body wasn't saying anything. "You're one of those guys at a party who gives off a rape-*y* vibe, aren't you? No means No, Tyler."

He shrugged. "Probably. Anywho, you're nervous. You don't even like me, yet you decided to come. On the off chance I'm right about him showing up—I am, by the way. He'll be there. Probably beat us there."

"I don't think…"

"I'm not done," he said, offended by my interruption. "Your fingers keep twisting around the hem of your shirt. Nice shirt, by the way. You look smoking hot. He's gonna flip his shit."

I think I followed that.

"You can't even sit still you're so anxious. You wouldn't be anxious if you didn't actually want to see him."

"So what if I do?" My voice squeaked. "It doesn't make a difference. He wouldn't even tell you guys that I'd been helping at the library. He's embarrassed by me. Of course he is; I get it. But it doesn't matter what I feel. Stop trying to make it something bigger than it is, please."

"You almost sounded like a bitch. Then you added that *please* on there." Shaking his head like he couldn't figure me out, he chuckled, "Look, Britt. I don't know what you know about Barry, or any of us, but if you hadn't noticed, we don't really do girlfriends. Gage isn't even serious with Lonna. That's why she gave it up to Barry and, yet, she's still with Gage. They're not exclusive." He shivered. "Ugh, sorry. That word…it still gets to me."

I hadn't followed even half of that. "I don't understand."

"Really? Think about it. Have you ever seen Barry with a girl?"

"Yes."

"For more than one night."

"Yes."

His eyes rolled. "I mean for more than one night *in a row*. Not like Madison. She's one night here and there. That's what we're good at. All of us."

"But Gage and Lonna—"

"Nope. They go on dates, and she hangs out with us, so does Charli, but they're not Facebook official, and we all know that's the ultimate ruling. Plus, they go weeks without talking to each other. When we were away at camp, Lonna didn't even answer her phone when Gage called."

I thought about it and came to one ultimate decision. "That sounds *lonely*."

"It is sometimes. Better than being heartbroken, though." Tyler's fingers tightened on the wheel; his teasing expression crumbled.

"Ann?" I asked.

He nodded.

"She broke up with you?" I guessed. I vaguely remembered their break-up. It had been high drama, low resolution. They'd never gotten back together despite Tyler practically getting on his knees and begging.

Another nod, followed by a sigh. "I cheated on her. Biggest mistake of my life so far. She won't even look at me now."

I stared down at my bouncing knee when I asked. "How long were you guys together?"

"Four years."

"*Four years?*" I gasped.

He half-smiled. "I don't know if it counts in the beginning. We didn't really know what *dating* was; we were just kids. We got together in sixth grade. Broke up in tenth grade, but she was the love of my childhood. That girl was…*is* my everything."

"You cheated on her *after* four years?"

"Believe me, nothing you say could hurt me worse than I already feel. After it happened, the guys they …well, they decided being in a relationship wasn't really worth the hell I went through."

I absorbed everything he said, but I still didn't understand. "What does this have to do with Barry not wanting to admit I'd been at the library?"

He smiled crookedly over at me. "He wouldn't admit it to us, Britt, not if he really liked you. It would go against everything we've always hated. If I were you, I'd have been more upset if he did fess up."

SIXTEEN

BARRY

Not until I was home after my shift at the library—with Chicago on the record player—did I remember that my friends were home. Tyler would definitely loan me money for some pain killers. I sat on the edge of my bed with my head in my hands, trying to talk myself out of it.

I didn't *need* them.

That was the important thing. I'd gone this long without the candy, so I didn't *need* it. But I wanted it. My foot bounced against the floor as I remembered the burn of the powder against my septum. Hell, I wouldn't even mind the nausea that accompanied swallowing—or snorting—a few too many.

Tomorrow would be my last day in the library, which meant I had one last day with Brittney, and I wanted to spend that day blitzed out of my mind. Being stoned with her was bound to make the experience that much more astounding.

Except, when I called, Ty didn't answer. Probably at dinner with his family. They had nice, sit-down dinners at his house every night. There was a strict no-cellphone policy at the table.

I shot him a text:

Hey Sugar, call me, it's important.

I waited thirty minutes then texted and called again. Still no answer. Next, I tried Bo, who did not have nice family dinners. Bo usually ate take-out in his very large house—far from his oblivious grandpa

"What's up?" My surprisingly well grounded friend answered.

"Uh, not much." I hesitated. *Just ask*, I told myself. Bo wouldn't say no. He'd be happy to give me the money, too. For some reason, though, I felt more comfortable taking Tyler's money. And, well, I couldn't pillow talk Bo. It was stupid, I knew that, but he'd think I was a powder puff if I called him "sugar." Tyler got the humor. I cleared my throat. "You heard from Ty?"

He munched loudly on something, taking his time to answer. "Nope. He's at the movies with Brittney Ann."

"What?" All the air in my lungs escaped in one loud hiss. "You're not serious."

"Yeah. Dude, you were sitting there—"

"No one said anything about *tonight*."

I thought I'd have time to sabotage the so called date. This couldn't be happening. Not now. I stood up and pulled at my hair. *What drugs? Who gave a flying seagull's fuck about some painers?*

Bo was way too light. "Dude, Bare, come on. Ty could tell you were into her. He's not—"

"Take me there."

I had to go rip Tyler's hands off.

Those hands could not ever know how smooth Brittney's creamy skin was. He couldn't touch her. He couldn't look into those deep, gold speckled eyes.

Oh shit, what if he was better at reading her thoughts than me? What if he knew how to react better than I did?

She'd like that, wouldn't she?

I leaned over on my knees, trying to force my blood to stop rushing through my body so quickly. Dammit, I was going to have to kill my best friend. It would suck, because we'd been friends for a long time. Then I'd have to commission Bo to help me bury a dead body, and I had no clue where I was going to bury him. And then I'd have to kill Bo, because there was no way he'd keep homicide a secret. Fuck, where would I hide Bo's body? He was one big mother fucker.

Sorry Bo, you're getting burned.

He clicked his tongue against his teeth. "Whatever man. I was going to say he's not *you* and wouldn't take a girl his friend is into, but yeah sure, what the hell? I'm bored, anyway. I'll be at your house in a couple minutes."

"Faster than that," I growled.

"Jeezus, fine. You're welcome by the way."

I planned to meet Bo outside so there wouldn't be any nonsense about him getting out of the car and wasting time that Britt didn't have. Dad waylaid me on my sprint down the stairs. He held up his hands, blocking me.

"Whoa, where's the fire?"

How could I tell him that the world as I knew it was coming to an end when I couldn't even reason why I felt that way? "No time to talk." I sidestepped, and he blocked me.

"Hey, Bare." He caught my arm. My body was lurched to a halt despite my insistence that I keep moving. "What's going on?"

"Bo's coming to get me. We're going to the movies." *There* I explained, I tried to jerk free, but he held on that much tighter.

"Are we going to have trouble now that your friends are home? You've been doing fine."

"What? No Dad, no, dammit. Brittney's with Tyler at the movies, and I want to claw my insides out with my bare fingers. It hurts *so* much I can't even take it. Just let me go so I can assassinate my best friend." *Then my other friend.*

Then find somewhere to dispose of their *stupidly* dense bodies.

Then I was going to take Brittney somewhere safe where no one could ever touch her ever, ever, ever again.

"Brittney? Mitch's daughter?"

"Yes," I gasped.

"I thought you said she wasn't your type."

I nodded, not arguing on this point. "I did say that."

His brows narrowed. "So what's the problem?"

"I think it's safe to say my sober-type might be a little straighter lace than my stoned-type."

Dad laughed, but it was not an amused laugh. More like he didn't know what to do, so laughing seemed appropriate. "Can I go?" I asked, jerking my arm again.

He stared at me, deciding, before shaking his head *no*.

I was about to flip out and leave anyway, and then he nodded profusely. "Sorry, sorry. Yeah go. I think. We're probably going to have to talk about this when you get back."

I groaned. "Of course we are."

Bo was rolling to a stop by the time I ran outside and jumped into the passenger side of his Beamer. "Drive," I growled.

"I think you're overreact—"

"Didn't ask for an opinion, just drive."

"So you like her?" he asked.

I rubbed my palms against my jeans just to give myself something to do. "I don't know."

"It seems like you do."

Couldn't disagree there. "I don't want to talk about it."

"I'm just wondering what you're going to say to her...or even him. He did give you several chances—"

"Can we just...I mean...is there any way we can *not* talk?"

Being alone in that library with her had been some of the best days of my life. She was easy to talk to, easy to be around. I could tell her things that I never told other people. I never even thought about it ending. I never planned what would happen when *they* came home.

When they'd called me out for hanging with her, all I could think about was protecting her. Gage would realize I enjoyed someone's company, possibly more than I deserved to, and then he'd strike. He'd never gotten over what I'd done with Lonna.

Then it happened anyway. Gage had gone for her—not personally. He'd sent in Tyler.

Tyler was the most obnoxious of the group. Imagining what my sweet Brittney must have had to do to keep his hands off her...my fists tightened painfully in my lap.

So I could admit it, I guess. Maybe not out loud—not to Bo. But to myself. I *did* like her, and I didn't want Tyler near her.

"Is it bad?" I asked, not recognizing my own voice. "If I do like her?"

"Honestly, man, I have no clue." Of course not. There was a reason he'd pushed Charli away. Bo followed the rules, and he toed the line. We were anti-girlfriend, anti-feelings, and he wouldn't ever break that pact we had.

I'd never understood why anyone would want what Tyler had had with Ann, and I still didn't. My way of having girls and hanging out and not being serious always made sense because no one ever got hurt.

Bo drove slowly. I mean, he drove over the speed limit, but it was a helluva lot slower than I'd have gone. "Can I turn on the radio?"

"As long as it's not that classic shit you usually listen to."

So no radio then.

It wasn't even dusk. The lights of the Multiplex combined with the glare of the sun had the entire street blurred. Somehow, I still saw the two of them. It was like I was drawn to her.

Her long strawberry hair flowed over the top of Tyler's Volvo. His hand was on her shoulder.

They were kissing.

I swallowed past the pinch in the back of my throat. Ache settled into my chest, and I wasn't sure it was possible to be alive and feel this pain. But I guess I was. If I were dead, I wouldn't feel anything. I wished I were dead, though. That would have saved me the burning sensation in my eyes and the sheer agony in my gut.

I fell out of the Beamer, stumbling to keep myself upright. "Barry!" Bo called after me, but I didn't stop. "Wait! I told him you were—"

"Get off her!"

Tyler bowed forward, clutched his knee, and laughed. I'd never been so annoyed by the sound of his idiotic chortle.

Gripping onto his shoulder, I jerked him away from her and the Volvo. Spinning him to face me, his expression froze in shock as I slammed my fist into his nose. My knuckle throbbed from the victorious sting of the assault.

I'd just hit my best friend.

"Barry!" Brittney clawed at my other arm. "Stop it, Barry. Just stop. He was trying to upset you."

And he'd started laughing again, which only made me want to hit him again. "What?" I barked.

"He saw your missed calls. Bo texted him and said you were coming. He saw the car turn onto the street." She pointed to the far end of the road. "He barely kissed me. What's wrong with you?"

"I think I'm losing my fucking mind." I rubbed over my eyes. What was I even doing here? And…was she wearing *pants*? Holy hell, she looked even better than normal. Bending forward, I clutched my knees, trying to catch my breath.

"I'll say." Tyler's voice was distorted. He spat a glob of blood onto the concrete. "Why can't you just say you're into her? I admit I love Annie. No problem."

Even Bo rolled his eyes. "It's a little easier for you, Ty."

"Why?"

"You're an idiot," I retorted.

"And you've been into her since middle school," Bo added, not disagreeing that Tyler was, in fact, an idiot.

"Can I know what's happening here?" Brittney asked.

Sure, except I didn't have an answer.

Why was Tyler still laughing?

"Dude, shut up, or I'm going to hit you," Bo said as he put a thin joint to his lips and started to spark it. He only smoked in public like this when he was either incredibly relaxed, or incredibly nervous.

I hated to take it from him, but at the same time, I didn't want him doing that in front of her. I held my palm up, blocking the sight of the thing. "Don't. I've been clean for a couple weeks. You smoke that, and all hell will break loose. Plus…" I pointed to the preacher's daughter with my other hand. With any luck she'd think it was a cigarette.

"Holy shit. You're still sober?" He glanced back at Tyler, who gave him a hesitant nod. "Dude, I'm sorry." Bo pocketed the thing without another word.

Tyler spat again and then straightened. Pointing at Brittney, he exhaled hard, "I don't know what you're so worried about, brother. She shook the whole way here. Her little legs clenched together every time your name was mentioned."

It pissed me off that he'd noticed that. Like he was watching for any sign that she might be turned on. I didn't want him to see that in her. I didn't want him to see her at all. I jerked back, ready to hit him again. He flinched, throwing his hands up in defense. "Chill. It was a good thing."

Brittney looked mortified. "I did not do that."

"It's okay," I told her. I cupped under her chin with one hand, tilting her face toward me. God, she was so beautiful. Her skin practically glowed in the setting sunlight. My free hand twisted up into her hair.

Kiss her, I told myself. It wouldn't be the first time.

But things were different now. That first kiss hadn't meant anything. That night I'd lain her down on our clothes was a night that had happened to two different people. Fuck. It hurt just thinking about what I'd almost done to her that night. What if she'd been with someone else? What if they'd gone through with it? Ryan probably would have.

My fingers fisted into her hair as I pulled her closer to me.

She's mine. All mine.

For me, women existed in three categories: the women I wanted to sleep with, the women I didn't want to sleep with, and the unicorn. If these categories were to fit into boxes by size, I'd say the first was the largest, the next was second largest, and the last was so small it could hardly be seen.

Because there could only be one unicorn.

Honestly, I held this space inside my head for an imaginary girl who'd never meet expectation. But for the life of me, looking at Brittney Ann, I couldn't remember what those expectations used to be.

Suddenly, my unicorn had to have strawberry blonde hair and hazel eyes. She had to be sweet and innocent. She had to know how to cook. And she had to be the most terrifying driver on the planet.

"What?" She asked, licking her slim lips. Her expression was expectant.

I shook my head. She was *my* unicorn, but I couldn't be any of that shit for her. I was an addict with a friend-pact never to date exclusively. I wasn't saying I wanted to be noble and push her away because she was too good for me, even though she was. I was saying I couldn't do it. I had no clue how to be someone's...*boyfriend*.

The word got caught in my throat. I wouldn't even be able to say it out loud. What about when people asked about us? What would I tell them? That I'd stopped sleeping around to date a virgin?

To be a *boyfriend*.

My fingers untwisted from her hair. I took a deep breath and a step back.

"Barry, is there something you want to say?" Hope shimmered in her amber eyes.

Cupping the back of my own hair, I twisted it, shoving my ball cap up on the top of my head. "This is a bad idea. I, uh, I just came to make sure Tyler didn't hurt you. You're...uh, you're pretty; I've told you that before. And, uh, you're great. You're—"

"A delicate butterfly," Tyler whispered.

"A sweet angel," Bo added.

I swatted my hand back at them. "You assholes. Go away."

Tyler muttered, "What? Watching you fumble this makes up for missing that movie."

"I'm not fumbling. I'm just having trouble saying what I mean." I took a deep breath. *Boyfriend.* The word got caught again.

Yeah, I wasn't ever going to be able to say it. Not today. Not to-morrow. Not to Brittney Ann Wilson. "So, uh, I'm just here to make sure you're okay. Because your dad, you know, he's scary, and I want you to be okay. Ty, uh, he didn't hurt you, right?"

"He didn't hurt me." Her voice was flat.

"You're sure?"

She nodded.

My fingers twitched to nudge her chin upward so she'd look at me. I shoved the meddling digits into my pockets to keep them at bay. "Uh, so, you're good?"

"I suppose. Was there another reason you were here, Barry? Other than to check on me?" Her eyes sparkled with hope again.

I looked away, staring down at the toe of my checkered Converse. "Uh, no, I was just worried. You're, uh, you're too good for Ty. He's a dipshit."

"Is that all?"

Boyfriend. Ugh. I just couldn't.

"You were making sure Tyler kept his hands to himself because I'm too good for him? That's the *only* reason?"

"Uh, yup."

"Thank you," she said, her voice distant. "Have a nice evening, Barry."

Then I did the most god-awful thing I've ever done. I walked her to the passenger side of Tyler's Volvo and watched her disappear behind the illegal tint. Closing the door, I leaned over and tapped the roof with my fist. "Don't. Say. Anything." I growled to the guys.

Tyler exhaled "You're an idiot."

"I said—"

He threw up his hands. "Yeah, yeah, I heard you. What am I supposed to do with her now?"

"You have to take her home." Obviously. "And you still need to keep your hands to yourself. Don't make me—"

"Bare, honestly. You're really losing it brother. I love you and all, but this is pathetic. I'll keep my hands to myself, but some point *someone* is going to come along who wants to touch her. And they will."

No, they wouldn't. She was *my* unicorn.

Besides, that was the best case scenario, because then I'd have Tyler and Bo to help me bury whoever that fucking idiot was. Knowing Tyler, he'd probably have the perfect place to bury a body.

Right next to all the guys who'd messed with Ann over the years.

I waited for Tyler to crawl into the Volvo, and then I got into Bo's BMW.

I needed music, whether it was good music or the shit that Bo listened to. The stereo blared some modern crap. I leaned back against the headrest and blew out a slow breath. I'd done the right thing here. Yeah, I had. This was *not* a mistake. For sure.

Bo opened and closed his mouth a few times before clearing his throat. "So, you're clean. That's...that's real weird."

"Tell me about it."

He hit my leg with his knuckle as a sign of encouragement. I think. "No, man, like weird in a good way."

I stared at him. "If I asked you for drug money, you'd say no?"

I needed something. This was a *need*. After that pathetic display of non-affection, I needed a little something to take the edge off. There was no knowing if she'd even be at the library tomorrow—I ignored the gaping ache inside my chest at that thought. If she wasn't there, then I'd *have* to be blitzed to get through it.

"I thought you were clean?" His heavy brows pinched together.

"Yeah, because Dad took my car and my money, and I've had no way to get anything. I told you guys this."

"And then we offered to help."

"With Britt sitting right there."

"So? You didn't even like her then and, dude, I saw you. You were having some serious withdrawals. If you could turn us down for a chick you weren't even into, then you don't need to go back to that shit."

"I liked her a little," I defended. "And this isn't even about her. I told you then. I'd have had to go cold turkey while you guys were gone. I didn't want to go through that. Now you're back, and you can help me out."

He shook his head a couple times before deciding with a sigh. "No. I'm not helping you."

I slammed my head back against the rest. "You're a dick."

"I know. But Bare, you can't just get down a little. It's do or die with you, and I think you might have a problem. If it'll make you feel better, we'll stop smoking when you're around."

"It would make me feel better if you smoked *with* me, but since you're a jackass, yeah…whatever."

"Oh shit." Bo slammed on the brakes and the Beamer lurched to a stop. The Volvo was pulling out of the parking lot, so Britt was probably okay.

Following Bo's gaze, I saw redheaded Ann Malone walking arm-in-arm, out of the movie theater with some guy I didn't recognize.

"He won't see, right?" I hazarded another glance at the Volvo.

"Surely no—"

There was a violent screeching sound as the Volvo slammed to a stop, red taillights flashing.

"I think we should let him go." Bo shrugged dismissively.

"Yeah right. He almost *actually* killed the last guy. I'm going to check on Brittney."

"Dammit," Bo hissed. "I've got the moron."

Tyler had flown out of the Volvo so quickly I barely saw his blond hair whip out of sight. Right there in the street, he started pushing that guy out of Ann's reach. Cars were stopping, horns blaring.

The passenger door of the Volvo opened, and Brittney's long legs stretched out. Her hand cupped to her nose. She looked startled.

No, wait. Blood poured between her fingers. I raced up to her and dropped to one knee by her side. My heart jumped into my throat. "What the hell happened?"

After swallowing about eight heartbeats, I took a deep breath. Making sure she was safe was more important than killing Tyler. She was so delicate and fragile. Why had her dad even let her out of the house?

I pulled her out of the car. She wobbled, looking dazed. "You weren't buckled in?" I asked, eyeing the blood smear on the dash. That urge to destroy my best friend was back.

Deep breaths. Deep, deep breaths. Take care of her first.

Then kill Tyler. Fucking mutilate his deceased corpse…

Her beautiful eyes watered.

I brushed her hand away to see the mess. It really wasn't that bad. Her nose probably wasn't broken. It was bleeding pretty good, though, and I hated that. Pulling her slight body into me, I wiped at the blood with my thumb.

"Come on. Bo has tissues in his car." Without giving her a choice, I yanked her onto my lap in the back seat. She didn't complain, but her back was stiff.

She'd not sat on my lap while we were together in the library, but there had been plenty of other physical contact. It wasn't a complete day unless my hands had been on her skin more than a dozen times.

Someone on the street told Tyler to move out of the way, and then Tyler told that someone to *go fuck himself.* I ignored it all.

Brittney's head tilted back as I pinched her nose. "I don't even know if I'm doing this right." I tried not to be too rough.

"I'*b* fine."

"Look, Britt…I like you."

Her shoulders straightened.

"It might take me a second to get the words out right, okay? Uh, the deal is that my friends and I, uh, we don't do the whole…serious *boyfriend* thing. Ever. It works out great, and it's probably the reason I'm such a moron when it comes to all this dating bullshit. I have no clue what I'm doing, but Britt, you gotta believe me if I did…you know, like, if I were going to, it'd be with you. That's what I mean when I say I like you. I'm into you."

She still looked confused and maybe a little pissed off. The blood had stopped pouring from her nose. Her skinny fingers brushed at her face. She didn't say anything, so I figured I still hadn't explained right.

"We gotta be realistic. What would happen between us? We'd go on a couple dates, probably have an amazing time together, and then I'd fuck up somehow. It's pretty much inevitable. Then I'd have a broken heart. And I'd get to walk around a miserable son of a bitch like Tyler. It just…I mean…"

"I get it," she whispered.

"Okay, well, can you say something? You think that's right, don't you? You know I'd mess up. And I've seen how pissy Tyler is about Ann. I don't want to be like that."

"Can I go?" She wouldn't look at me at all.

"You're mad at me? I'm actually being honest here. I'm trying not to be a dick, and you're mad."

"I'm not mad," she maintained. "I'm not. I'm hurt."

Hurt? I'd hurt her. Somehow, I wished she were mad at me.

Outside, Ann was screaming, "Tyler, you obnoxious pig! You could have really injured him!"

"Aw, a guy can't take a hit better than that, then he isn't worth your time."

Brittney scooted off my lap and I followed, but I wasn't sure I'd gotten my point across. My palm flattened on her back as I led her. She seemed stiff, and I tried to convince myself it was because of her nose.

Ann slapped Tyler hard in the back of the head, causing him to react by spinning and grabbing her wrist. He pinned her against the Volvo with both of her arms behind her back. "Let me go," she spat.

He leaned into her, grinding his pelvis against her stomach. "Not until you promise to play nice."

She jerked against his hold. "Let go, you jack—"

"Maybe…" Brittney took a step toward them, and I wrapped my hand all the way around her waist to stop her.

"It's fine." Bo shook his head. Shaking his dark hair off is forehead, he looked completely at ease. "Trust me, Tyler's not *that* dangerous. It's Gage you have to look out for." Bo's eyes widened as he realized what he'd just confessed.

Gage…honestly, we didn't talk about it. One time, a neighbor's dog kept barking at night, and Gage had lit the thing's tail on fire. I mean, I didn't really love animals, but that shit had made me sick.

Bo cleared his throat. "Sorry. I didn't mean that." Even though we all knew he did.

Ann groaned. "Let me go, Ty. You already ruined my night."

He rubbed his nose against hers. "What were you doing with that prick? Just answer me that, and I'll let go."

She huffed. "I don't know. Getting a free movie and dinner."

Tyler didn't release her. "He took you out to dinner. Where'd you go?"

"No, he didn't. We were going now. But thanks to you, I get to go home and eat Mom's pot roast. Congrats. You've done it again."

He wore an arrogant smile. "You actually don't sound too pissed."

She couldn't bite into her lips before a grin ripped across her face. "Okay, the guy was kind of a jerk."

"Yeah? Should I go kill him?" he teased.

"If that means you're going to let me go," she teased right back, blinking her big eyes up at him.

"In that case…" With his free hand, he found the front of her thin shirt. The guy was immune to PDA as he lifted the hem and slid his fingers up along her waistline.

A purr of acceptance escaped her throat. "Ty?"

"Yes baby?"

"Let me go."

He growled. "Fine. But I get a kiss first."

"You're a monster; you know that?"

"Hey, I don't have you like this very often. I gotta take what I can get."

Their kiss wasn't, like, a normal kiss either. It was sloppy and passionate, and Ann's whole body molded against Tyler. There were passionate kiss noises.

And Brittney had to mumble, "Yes, I can see why you'd want to avoid being like them."

Except this wasn't a good example. They were never like this. Once in a blue moon maybe, but not all the time. Still, when the kiss broke, Ty looked delirious. His lips trailed Ann's jaw. "Don't make me let go," his voice was off, and I didn't really feel comfortable watching them anymore.

Bo was already by his Beamer, kicking the tires like he was checking the air. I walked over next to him and refused to watch the others. Brittney continued to stare.

I'd have to explain it to her. This was just a bizarre night for everyone, that's all.

"Tyler…" Ann breathed. "Don't do this."

"What am I doing? I just want to be close to you."

"You don't get that anymore."

"Annie, don't."

"I'm not *Annie*. It's just *Ann*."

"I'm sorry. I am—"

"Let me go, Tyler."

"No, wait. I…one more kiss. Please?"

I was glad I'd stopped watching.

"No. Let go, or I'll scream." *Aaannnd* the girl Tyler had turned her into was back.

Bo shot me a look. The question in his expression said: *Should we break them up?* I shook my head. I trusted Ty. He'd never hurt Annie. Not on his life.

"You're killing me," he mumbled.

"Good," she bit back.

Brittney cleared her throat. "Ann, would you mind giving me a ride home?"

What? No, she couldn't leave like this. I hadn't said it right. She was still mad at me. I could still fix this. I had to. We'd become friends, and if she walked away as anything less than that, I…I didn't know what then. "Britt…"

Ann glanced between the two of us. "Sure thing, girl. What're you doing with these guys anyhow?"

As far as I knew, they only knew each other from cheerleading and church. Ann was a year older than Brittney—with us in school. So, were they really *girls*? Was it okay for her to be driving Brittney around? I took a step forward, and Bo caught my arm. He shook his head in warning.

"Nothing," Brittney said. "I got lost. I've found my way again. No big deal."

∾

Pastor Mitch had learned from our family's mistake. Instead of yelling at Tyler—for Brittney's busted nose—in his office, he'd pulled him into the church basement.

Ann and Brittney stood at the top of the stairs laughing their asses off. The insanely good feeling I got from seeing her laugh disappeared when I got a good look at her face. Both of her eyes were black.

"Ann, can we have a minute?" I asked, gesturing between myself and Brittney.

Would it have been so hard to call and check on her? Here I thought she'd avoided the library on Friday because of some misunderstood romance we had, but she actually looked pretty busted up. I bet her dad wouldn't let her go anywhere.

Yeah, that's it. She wasn't avoiding me.

Buuut she still hadn't responded to any of the messages I'd sent.

Ann snorted. "Oh, dude, Tyler is getting an ass-chewing out of this world. No way am I missing this."

Brittney looked hesitant to walk away also. Chewing the inside of her cheek, she said, "Daddy's not very pleased about my face. He wasn't too thrilled that Ann brought me home, either."

"Hazards of dating one of us."

Britt's expression hardened. "Yes, as you've mentioned."

"Come on, come talk to me." I caught her stiff fingers.

"I believe you've exhausted your excuses, Barry. There's not really much else to say. You're not interested in dating me. We'll continue being…are we friends?"

Ann laughed.

"You're sure you can't go away?" I bit out.

"Oh, hell no."

I stared at the pitched ceiling, exhaling heavily. "Of course. Britt, I didn't say I wasn't interested. Just that—"

She cut me off with a huff. One of her arms reached across her body, cuffing her upper arm. Her body arched forward defensively and she pulled her tiny hand out of my grasp. That gesture felt like a permanent goodbye. "You don't want to be Ann. I got it."

Ann pushed against my shoulder. "Whoa, you used me as an excuse? You suck."

"It's not an excuse. Why is the word *excuse* being thrown around? That's not what this is."

Neither one of them were listening to me, though. Ann had turned and pressed her ear to the door, and Brittney gave me a small, unconvincing smile before she too leaned toward the door.

Occasionally they'd giggle, and it was pretty obvious I was being ignored.

Tyler found me in the back pew alone. Dad and Ashleigh were up front, but I was a back row Christian at best.

"Dude." His eyes were wide and unfocused. "Brittney's dad…"

"I know."

"No, man, seriously. I thought I was a goner." Tongue hanging out, he swiped his pointer finger sideways across his throat.

"Yeah, been there."

He flopped down noisily and tossed his straight hair out of his eyes. "Phew. Good luck with that shit."

"I don't think I'm going to need it."

Church started and, because we were both deathly afraid of Mitch, we didn't talk. Except when everyone was singing. Then it seemed okay to pretend-sing and carry on a conversation. "I'm so hungover." Tyler rubbed his eyes with his fingers. Licking the roof of his mouth dramatically, he made a face at me. "It literally tastes like I ate cat litter. I know I didn't because you wouldn't let my drunk ass do that, would you, lover?"

I laughed. This was the part of the Tyler-Ann love fest Brittney hadn't seen. He'd been so drunk last night, he'd tried to fight an oak tree. Then he'd tried to fight me. Then he'd passed out and had almost died in a pile of his own vomit.

"I'm never drinking like that again."

"I think that's what you said last time."

He thought about it then shrugged. "This time I mean it."

My head fell back over the pew as I shrank down in my seat. "Ty, I think I'm losing my mind."

"Again?"

"I'm serious. I can't get off my tongue long enough to explain to Brittney that I like her, but we can't work."

The song ended, and Mitch started preaching again—a clear sign that it was time for us to *stop* talking. Tyler leaned over to sort-of whisper. "Why can't you guys hook up? You're into the broad, right"

I punched his arm.

He gasped and rubbed at the spot on his bicep. "Ow. Fuck dude. I'm just curious."

"A little louder," I hissed. "The deaf broad up front didn't hear you."

Oh dang. I hadn't called her that since I'd been hanging out with Brittney. An instant sensation of guilt twisted my stomach. "I mean, Mrs. Wilson. She…never mind."

Of course, Tyler laughed.

Mitch glared at us.

"Oh shit," Tyler mumbled.

I eyed the back of the pew in front of ours for a good five minutes. The next song started, because apparently they loved to sing here, and Tyler covered his mouth with his hand to speak. "So why can't you guys hook up?"

"Can we please talk later?" I murmured between my teeth.

He stared at the side of my face, burning a hole into my temple with his glare. "You know, sober-you is a pussy."

"What?" I gasped.

He didn't answer other than to press his finger to his lips and say, "*Shh.*"

The worst part was that he was right. I wasn't the adrenaline junkie I'd been when I was a pill junkie. Maybe other things were different, too. Maybe I was different. "You think I could be good?" I asked under my breath.

"What're you talking about?"

"You know, like good. For Britt? Now that I'm sober?"

He glanced around, looking confused. "Man, you're one of the best guys I know when you try at it. So do you want to be good?"

There was a loud, resounding *yes* yelling out inside my mind. It took a full minute for the words to form on my tongue—I wanted them to come out right and not garbled. "Yeah, I think so."

He shrugged, like this was the easiest decision he'd ever helped me make. Which, considering the fact he'd once helped me build a skateboard ramp out of used tires and plywood and then talked me into using it, yeah, this probably was easy for him. "Then what's the question?" He smiled.

I pointed a finger at his chest. "What about you and Ann? You guys hate each other."

"Dude, seriously? I love Ann."

"But you're miserable!" I didn't get it. How could he not see this?

He shrugged. "Because I'm an idiot. You said it yourself. But, Bare, I'd never go back and undo what Ann and I had. Not for all the miserable days in the world. I love that redheaded vixen." He exaggerated, "She *owns* me."

I didn't know if Brittney owned me. I was pretty sure she didn't.

Church ended, and the place emptied around me. I sat there thinking I'd find some sort of sanctuary. Maybe if I sat still long enough, the right answer would fall into my lap.

Mitch pulled off his robes, and then he came down and sat beside me. The pew squeaked under his weight. I didn't move a muscle.

It hit me, like a light bulb flashing on. I didn't want to run away from him. The fear I felt—concern of his fist meeting my face—didn't even register compared to the *feels* I had for his daughter. For the first time in days, my mind was completely at ease, and I knew exactly what I was going to do next.

SEVENTEEN

 BRITTNEY ANN

Katy Lynn was the only person I could talk to about Barry. We'd been texting back and forth for several days. The conversation had started with long explanations of how I'd gotten close to him. She'd replied with excitement. Then I told her how he felt about me and that he didn't want to see me. She'd still replied with excitement.

So when my phone went off after church I rolled my eyes at her message.

Was he there?

Me:

Yes.

Katy:

Omg. How'd he look? Was his hair spiked? Or was he wearing a hat? You know he looks the best in a hat. Actually, he looks the best in a beanie.

I couldn't disagree with that. Me:

I don't know. It didn't really look like he fixed it.

Katy:

Omg. He has the best messy, bedhead.

Couldn't disagree with that, either. Me:

I have to go. Some of the kindergarteners decided to color all over the carpet in the basement.

I made a mental note that if she ever went through a break up, I'd be emotionally supportive and bring her ice cream. I wouldn't talk about how hot her ex was.

It felt like Barry had broken up with me. There was a giant, gaping hole in my chest from where he'd yanked out my heart. No, there hadn't ever been a relationship. He'd never made any promises to me. His lack of commitment didn't change how I felt or what it had been for me.

I was on my knees scrubbing the blue carpet when the door to the Sunday School room opened. "Just a…" Dropping the rag, I flattened my flyaway hair. Not that I cared about what I looked like for him.

Ha! Maybe if you say it again, you'll believe it. "Barry?"

"Hey." Stepping inside, closing the door behind him, he took a deep breath. "I want to be your boyfriend."

Those six words hung in the air. I didn't want to say anything for fear it would erase the meaning of that beautiful sentence.

Then, realizing my jaw hung open, I choked out, "Oh?"

"Yup." He nodded. "I, uh, I don't know if I ever wanted anything so bad in my whole spoiled life. You're beautiful and nice, and all I've been able to think about since you walked into the library to volunteer was how much I like being around you.

"I don't want to *not* be around you, and I have no desire to be around any other girl. I know you said I'm bad at apologizing, but I'm going to give it a try anyway." He took a deep breath. His hand opened, palm pressed flat against his chest. Those emerald eyes seared me.

"I'm really sorry for all that shit I did two years ago. You have no idea how bad I actually felt. I got dressed and sat in my car in my driveway. I know that doesn't make up for it because I still never showed, but if I could go back, I know I'd do it differently. I'm sorry that I'll never be good enough for your brother. He's never going to like me. I know because your dad just told me to watch my back. He was slightly more supportive than anticipated. So that doesn't suck. I figured he'd punch me in the face when I asked permission to date you, and instead he just threatened my manhood if I ever let you come home like Ty did. So you're going to have to wear your seatbelt in the Charger. I like my balls too much to lose them."

He smiled down at his shoe that kicked back and forth on the carpet. "I'm sorry that, despite that threat, I still don't want to walk away. And I'm so fucking sorry that I'm me. I'm all I'll ever be. This is it. If you think I'm enough, then I'd really like you to cut me off because I could spend the rest of the day apologizing for my faults."

"Barry." Muting my smile was impossible. I couldn't keep my face under control and keep my heart from slamming around inside my chest at the same time. *Breathe, Brittney. Breathe.* "That was pretty good. As far as apologies go. I, um, I like you, too. I want you to be my boyfriend."

More than I'd *ever* wanted anyone.

He tugged on his messy, jet black hair a couple times before nodding. "Yeah," he said. "Wow, okay."

"Okay."

Now what?

He answered my thought with action. Taking two quick strides across the room, he gripped the tops of my shoulders to help me stand, and his mouth crashed into mine.

"Hold out your hand," I said.

He stared at the metal brush. "I really don't think I can do this." Still, he let me put the brush in his hand, and then I curled his fingers around the handle.

"Um, I don't want to scare you, but she does nip."

The brush fell to the dusty floor with a *thud*. "Fuck it. No way."

"Barry, please."

"No. No way in hell I'm brushing a venomous, biting horse. What if...Jesus, what if she has herpes, or rabies, or syphilis?"

I bit into my lip to keep from laughing. "Herpes?" I laughed anyway. "Venomous? You know horses aren't poisonous, right?"

His green eyes cut every direction before focusing on the medicine cabinet nailed to the wall at the end of the barn. "Why do you have that thing hanging there? What are those vials for?"

"Penicillin. Medicine for when she has an infection. Vitamins. Her other brushes are in there. Shoes. Nails. What did you think? There was anti-venom in there? Oh, Barry..."

He threw his hands up. "What? How the hell should I know anything about horses? You said the bitch bit. I didn't know what that meant."

"Don't get defensive. It's okay that you're scared."

"I'm not scared."

I cocked my head to the side, admiring his defensive stance with his hands on his hips and his foot tapping the dusty floor.

He took another step backward, bumping against the far stall door. "I'm not," he said adamantly. "I just don't want to do this shit."

"Come on. You rode her before. You can do it. The least you can do is pet her."

He gulped loudly, like he was thinking about it. "Tell me why I have to."

I picked up the brush and then stared down at it. "You don't *have* to."

"Why do you *want* me to?"

I shrugged. "This is what I want to do. I've always loved Buttercup, but I thought it was just because she was my horse. That's not it, though. Ever since Gwen showed up here several years ago with that big, furry dog of hers and I fell in love with him at first sight, I knew. I knew that I loved all animals. During the school year, I volunteer at Dr. Rosen's clinic just to be closer to them. This is what I want to do for the rest of my life, Barry. I want to be around big animals like Buttercup. I want to have big dogs, like Dex, running around my house."

With pinched eyes he sucked in a heavy breath. "Fuck," he sighed. "Do we have anything in common?"

Don't be disappointed, I reminded myself. *Not yet. It's too soon.* A small voice in the back of my head warned that everything I'd ever heard about the beginning of relationships had been about the honeymoon phase. Things should be easy for us because we should agree on everything. "Um, well, you're a football player, and I'm a cheerleader."

He shook his head. "Yeah, but I don't like football all that much."

"I don't like cheerleading, either."

His eyes flashed open, revealing amused emeralds. "No?"

"Not really. I did it because Toby loved football, and I thought it would help me make friends. I always tried to be so vibrant and out-there. Turns out, everyone thinks I'm more chipper than I really am. I have to smile so much my face hurts." I pinched my cheeks between my thumb and forefinger.

His eyes glistened as he watched me. "I like your smile."

"That's because when I smile with you, it's a real smile." I couldn't look at him when admitting this, so I stared down at my shoe working my toe into the dirt.

"You're yourself with me?" He asked. Somehow, despite the distance between stalls, his large hand had found my hip. Thumb swiping back and forth over the band of my underwear, outside my dress. I couldn't fight the heat speckling my cheeks.

"I think I am."

His head leaned toward mine, mouth inches away. "I only play football because at our school you're either a football player or a drop-out. The guys all joined up in middle school, and I just tagged along. Turns out I have the right attitude and stamina for a receiver." His nose brushed against mine. "I'd rather stay home listening to music on vinyl. Or go to a concert. You like concerts?"

"I don't know."

"How do you not know? You either like music that beats so loud you can feel the drum inside your chest,"—his free hand fisted, and he beat his knuckles three times against his sternum—"or you don't."

Listening to Barry Prescott talk about his love for music was single handedly the sexiest thing I'd ever heard. *Exhale, Brittney Ann. Breathe!* "I—I've never been to a concert."

His eyes closed and he shook his head, rubbing his nose against mine. "Your nose is cold," he said, and then added, "I'll take you to a concert. Sometime. Maybe in August. All the good bands come in August."

I pulled on the hem of his gray T-shirt. "Will we be seeing Whitesnake?"

"Is that sarcasm I sense? Whitesnake is actually one of my favorites. They're coming to the Family Arena in August. But I think you'd have more fun at Journey or Foreigner. Start you out more mainstream."

"They're mainstream?" I gasped. "Also, just so you know, you say every band is your favorite, and I'm beginning to think all the shirts are your favorite, too."

He shrugged. "I don't like to discriminate."

"When it comes to music," I clarified.

"When it comes to music," he agreed with a satisfied smile creasing his beautiful face. "So, uh, you think your daddy would mind if we made-out instead of giving Buttercup her Sunday brushin'?"

As much as I loved brushing Buttercup... "I wouldn't mind." I shrugged. "Daddy doesn't get any input."

Barry's lips lightly pressed against my mouth, and then he jerked away. "Fucking bitch!" he screamed.

My heart stuttered. Me? What...? *Oh no.*

He jumped around, cupping his hand to his neck. Pointing back at Buttercup with his middle finger, he scowled. "She bit me. She fucking bit me. *Ohhhooo*, you're dead, horse. You're so dead."

"I'm sorry." My fingers steepled over my mouth. I had the combined horror images of him murdering my baby, and him never kissing me again. Neither of which was okay with me. "I'm so sorry. We should have stepped away from her. She didn't understand."

"Don't defend that future glue stick."

I kicked my foot against the ground, stirring up the dust around us. "Oh Barry, don't talk like that. It wasn't her fault."

He rubbed harder at his neck. "I don't think it's bleeding. What's it look like?" He lifted his hand slightly, and a giggle burst from my mouth. There was a purplish mark about the size of a fist.

My fingers covered my lips again, this time to hide my laughter. "It's...it looks like..."

He found the dusty mirror on the wall. Bracing his knuckles on either side of it, he leaned into his reflection. His head dropped. "A hickey. A giant fucking horse hickey. Just great."

☙

Daddy thought it was funny. "I knew I liked that animal."

Under his breath Barry mumbled, "I'd like her to be glue."

"Now, now. She was just protecting the family."

"From me?" Barry snapped. "She's a horse! Not a dog."

Daddy glared at him. "What have I told you about that attitude?"

"Sorry, Sir." Barry's teeth clenched. My hand slid into his, and our fingers laced together.

Daddy shook his head. "Toby isn't gonna like this none. I can tell you that right now."

"There's no point telling him," I defended. "Really, Daddy, just let me have a chance to get to know Barry. Give us some time before Toby tries to scare him off."

"He's not going to scare me." Barry's eyebrows pinched together. "I'm not going anywhere. I know your brother, and I can take it."

"He's pretty intimidating."

"You think I don't know that?"

"I think…" Daddy cleared his throat. "You should mind how you talk to my daughter. I'm standing right here. I do have a gun. I do know how to…"

I held up my hand cutting Daddy off. "Okay, we're going to leave. I think we'll take a picnic down by the creek." To keep the peace, I tacked on, "If that's okay with you, Daddy."

He deliberated. I think he might have said no if Mom hadn't stepped up at just the right time and placed her small hand on his immense shoulder. "Have a good afternoon, sweetheart. Make sure you pack sunscreen and bug spray. Are you taking the Ranger or the horses?"

"Ranger," I answered instantly. If ever Barry ever went back into the horse barn, it would be a gradual process. He squeezed my hand in agreement.

I went up to my room to lather up with sunscreen and to change. There were three swimming suits inside my drawer. One of them wasn't mine. It was a hot pink tube-top—it was three inches wide of fabric that covered boobs. Just boobs.

My tube-top, black two piece covered my entire stomach. Katy

Lynn, the owner of the pink number, said mine was a tube-kini. All of my swim bottoms were shorts. Hers were skimpy, hot pink, butt-huggers.

Barry and I weren't at *butt-hugger* bikini status, yet. I grabbed the black tube-kini and smiled at my confidence as I shimmied into it. I slipped back into the dress I'd worn to church. As long as Daddy didn't look too closely, he wouldn't notice that I'd dressed down for Barry.

EIGHTEEN

BARRY

The horse bit me. Her horse. She wanted to be a vet.

I adjusted my ball cap to give my shaking fingers something to do.

She didn't want Toby to know about us. Was it really because she thought he'd run me off? Did she really think she didn't know me better than practically everyone else? Didn't she already know that this relationship was *everything*? I wouldn't have jumped in otherwise.

"You ready?" She skipped down the stairs wearing the same dress she'd said she had gone up to change. *Okay then.*

"Uh, yeah."

Brittney packed a beach bag with a couple towels and a large hardback book. Unless we were tearing out the pages for firewood, I didn't know what use that thing would be. I didn't see what she packed for lunch, but everything fit neatly into Tupperware containers that sat perfectly at the bottom of the bag—on top of that book. It was packed perfectly, like this wasn't her first time. "You've done this before."

"Only once."

Ryan. Dammit. I wanted to kill that little punk. Wonder if he'd gotten the honor of Toby-treatment. "So, uh, what'd Toby think about big Ry?"

Brittney's eyes widened. "That's an odd question."

"Just curious."

She shrugged. "He wasn't pleased with him after what happened at the hospital, but Toby—"

"Hospital?" I cut across.

She adjusted the already impeccably packed sack. She wouldn't look at me. "Oh, right. I guess I never told you about that." She pulled the bag over her shoulder and then grabbed my elbow, leading me down the hall. "Let's go outside. We'll talk when we get to the creek."

I didn't like it. Suspense and I weren't friends.

She drove the white, two-seat Polaris. Which was really hot—her driving, that is. Her dress and hair flapped in the wind, despite how she tucked the fabric of her dress between her legs and tried to twist her hair back. I slid my ball cap over her head in an attempt to keep her hair at bay. She looked damn good in my hat.

The smile she gave me was wide and brilliant. I knew this wasn't the fake smile she shot to cheerleaders.

This smile was for me.

Too bad the wind hadn't taken her dress all the way off. Imagining Brittney driving this thing in her bra and panties and my red ball cap...yeah, okay, I was hard. I struggled to adjust myself and keep from falling sideways as she took a sharp turn. "You okay?" she called over the loud engine.

"I'm fucking horny," I admitted.

Her eyes widened. Then she burst out laughing. "How long have you been waiting to admit that?"

"I don't know. How long was your dad around?"

She shook her head. "What am I going to do with you?"

I wiggled my eyebrows. "I have a few suggestions."

When she killed the engine, I was surprised to see she'd taken us to the creek. "We're really at the snake pit? Seriously? I don't want to have a picnic with a copperhead, Britt. Maybe we can find another spot."

"There are snakes all over. And that's the first one I ever saw here. Besides, I'd be more worried about water moccasins."

My jaw dropped. "Well now I am too."

She didn't pause as she unloaded the bag out of the back. The idea to help her didn't hit me until she made a small grunting sound.

"I'm sorry."

She came around the front of the Ranger, struggling to keep the heavy bag on her shoulder. She blinked up at me, confusion lining her face. "For what?"

"I should have carried it. I'm being a bad boyfriend already."

"You are. And just so we're clear, um, despite what happened that night at the House, I'm not having sex with you. Not today."

"I know," I said. "Hey, whoa." I pointed back at the Ranger. "I was joking. I figured, uh, wow I was a complete dick. I didn't mean to make you uncomfortable or anything."

"You didn't." But she wouldn't look at me. "I thought the conversation would come up soon."

"It doesn't have to." I put my hands up in surrender. "Really. I like getting laid, trust me, I do, but I think I like you more. I'm cool waiting."

A part of me wanted to insist she give me a time-line. I needed to know how long I'd actually have to wait and if it was worth it.

The other part of me wanted to punch that jackass in the face.

"You think?" Her voice squeaked. Little strawberries speckled her cheeks.

"I *know*," I rushed. "I *know* I like you more. What I worry about is, like, you're not waiting until you're married, are you?" *Jesus, could I be any more of a dick?* I wanted to take it back. But the words were out there.

She blinked up at me, all expression hidden from her cool, golden-green eyes. "If I am?"

"No, it's cool. It's fine. Just curious."

It was *not* cool. That's what I meant by *think*. I liked her. I did. But I wasn't so sure I could give up sex for the entirety of our relationship. However long it lasted. Plus, I wanted her body so badly, I ached. She drove me crazy.

Little things, like the way she licked her lips, or bent her elbows… her *elbows*, for Pete's sake, drove me insane.

It was those legs, though, those milky, smooth legs that seemed never-ending as they disappeared beneath layers of cotton. Oh, those legs.

"It would bother you," she said matter-of-factly.

"I don't know. I really want to tell you that it wouldn't, but I think that would be a lie. The only thing I can say that's true is that I'm not pressuring you. I promise I won't pressure you. We'll do this at your pace."

"And what if my pace is too slow for you?" she asked, staring down at her finger that tugged at a loose string on her dress.

"I don't know the answer to that, either."

She nodded. "Okay."

Lowering the beach bag to a shaded grassy area, she pulled out two large towels. "Is this okay?" she asked.

I glanced around. "For?"

"I don't know. I thought we could talk. Or read. Or just lay here."

"I'm cool with that. Not the reading part, but the rest is fine."

She laughed. "I could read to you. I have to read to the children at Sunday School who refuse to believe that reading is healthy. I don't see how you're any different."

I shrugged. "Me either."

I flopped onto my stomach, seriously contemplating taking off my shirt. It was really hot, and even though we were in the shade, there was still sun. The last thing I wanted was a farmer's tan from my favorite Whitesnake T-shirt.

Brittney leaned up on her knees at the same time I decided to go for it and take off the shirt. We were both staring at each other as we settled back onto the towels. She wore an all-black swimming suit. Those legs…yeah, *those* legs were fully exposed. Long, skinny arms. Elbows. Collar bone. Cleavage. Holy *fuck*…

Her eyes danced back and forth across my chest. "Barry," she said slowly.

"I was hot," I defended, my hands up in surrender for the second time in minutes. "It's not…I mean, I'm not."

Glancing down at her creamy thigh, her finger traced an invisible pattern, leaving a white trail in her skin with her nail. "It's okay. I was hot, too."

"Yeah, you are," I agreed.

Rolling her eyes, she smiled. "You know just what to say to make a girl feel good about herself, you know that?"

"No, I didn't."

She laid back and I leaned over her, propped up on my elbow. "I make you feel good about yourself? Really?"

"Yes, sometimes. When you look at me. It's like you're…" She shielded her eyes with her palm. "Hold on. Let me get the words right."

I waited.

"It's like you're checking me out, but I never feel like you're comparing me to anyone else."

Well, that one was easy. "That's because there's no comparison."

She grinned. "See. That. That right there. That's what I'm talking about."

"So, you'd say I'm a good boyfriend?"

"The best I've ever had," she said, leaning up on her elbows to press her soft lips to my cheek. Chills raced through my body.

"Really?" I asked

"Yes, really."

That reminded me. "What happened with Cheesedick at the hospital?"

"Cheese…? Oh, Ryan." Her expression was guarded, and my knuckles curled into tight angry knots. For some reason, I had a mental flash of Tyler, Bo, and me holding shovels, standing over a six-foot-deep hole with a distinctly body-shaped figure inside.

"It's silly. He was upset because of what you and Madison pulled."

"Whoa, hold it. I didn't tell her to do that. She got carried away."

"I know. But he was convinced she was this innocent little angel. He thought it was you corrupting her. He even said she was scared of you, that's why she was staying away from him."

Wow. The guy made it kind of hard to *not* feel sorry for how pathetic he was. "What a loser."

"Yeah. He grabbed my wrist a little roughly. I tried to pull away, and he wouldn't let go. He was just upset, that's all. But I didn't want to work there anymore. I didn't want to see him ever again. So I quit my volunteer job and started at the library."

About feeling sorry for him…

The image in my brain shifted. Suddenly that body-shaped figure was alive and we were pouring dirt over the top of him as he begged for a chance, just one more chance, to apologize to my Brittney.

I shook my head, trying to clear that thought. Jesus, I wasn't this violent when I was single. "I'm probably going to break all his bones the next time I see him." That was a PG version to what I was *actually* thinking of doing.

She pushed at my shoulder. "Barry."

I growled. "I'm serious. Is he the one you brought down here before?"

Her brows creased in confusion. "What?"

"You said you'd done this before. You packed that basket like you knew what you were doing. Did you come here with him?"

Her expression was unreadable, but her amber eyes lit. "Jealous?"

"No, I'm not. I just need to know if I should make him suffer when I kill him, or if it should be a merciful death."

Her mouth snapped shut. "Not funny."

Who's joking?

"I went on a picnic with Gwen. We spent a day at the lake last summer."

Bile burned my throat at the mention of that witch. A new response. Probably because eventually I was going to have to tell Brittney what had happened between Gwen and me. "Gwen, huh? You two are close?"

"Yeah. She's the sister I never had."

And the bile threatened to surface. I swallowed hard, forcing it past the lump in my throat. It felt like bad acid reflux burning inside my chest. "Sister. Really? You can't be *that* close. She's away at school, isn't she?"

Brittney leaned back, shifting her face into a sunny spot on the blanket. There was a peaceful smile on her mouth. I knew that I wasn't going to tell her anything that would take that smile away today.

"She went to the community college for a year. I think she wanted to follow Toby to California right away, but she didn't want to be stranded out there if they broke up. They've almost been together two years now, and they're engaged. She's moving in August. She's there right now, so I guess she's already partially moved."

"But she's coming back?" I guessed. "Think you'll tell her about us?" My voice broke, but I was sure she didn't hear it.

"She'll be back. I don't know when exactly. Knowing her and Toby, she'll stretch out her stay as long as she can. I'll definitely tell her, but I'll wait."

"Just like Toby?" Of course. She couldn't tell one and not the other. And why would she tell them she'd committed to me? I didn't exactly have the best track record with making her happy.

"Yes," she said. "It's nothing personal, Barry. I just…okay, it's a little personal. I remember that day he punched you. He just kept hitting you. I screamed for him to stop. We all did. I thought he was going to kill you." Leaning up on her elbows, she stared at me. Horror etched the beauty on her face. I glanced down at the black fabric that covered her stomach.

"I've never seen him so angry. Then, later, when he found out you'd asked me to homecoming, he was irate. Toby hasn't ever told me I couldn't date anyone, Barry. Except you."

NINETEEN

BRITTNEY ANN

We should come up with a code."

I smiled. "That's silly, we'll just say it."

"No, I like this better. Tyler and I have a code. I want a code with you."

I laid my head back against his stomach. I couldn't believe I'd brought *Much Ado About Nothing*, thinking we'd get bored. Talking to Barry made time fly. I didn't know if I'd ever get tired of hearing his voice. His short fingernail slid along the inside of my elbow. "You can touch me more," I told him. My body was so warm, I'd probably ignite into a flame if he took me up on that offer.

Lips crooking into a sideways grin, he shook his head. Whispering softly, he said, "Don't tempt my control." There was humor in those words, but it was very much a warning.

I let the subject drop, opting instead to talk about *signs*.

"Fine. If we're at a party—and I'm not drinking ever again, either—but if we're at a party, and I want to leave I'll…I don't know, I'll wink at you."

He snorted. "Lame. You don't have to drink, babe, but I'm going to want to go to parties, and I know you're not going to want to stay long. We have to come up with something better than a wink."

Babe. *Babe.* Oh my goodness. Be still my overactive butterflies, be still. "How about this?" I held up two fingers in the air and slowly slid them down in the shape of a J. The act reminded me of sign language. This sign wasn't anything from ASL, not that I knew of. Instead, it was mine and Barry's very own language.

He lifted two fingers and slid them through the air mimicking me. "Perfect," he said. "Don't forget it."

"We need one for goodbye."

"Why?"

I shrugged. "Because I want to have our very own goodbye that means 'goodbye for now, but not forever.'"

He grabbed my hand, moved my thumb and pinky finger out of my closed fist. As I watched, he closed the fingers together. He held onto my fist. "Okay?"

"Perfect," I breathed.

"One for hello?" He suggested, his chest rose and fell rapidly under my head.

I opened my thumb and pinky. "It looks like a telephone," I said.

He chuckled. "I know. That's what made me think of the goodbye."

"You're so clever, Barry Prescott."

"Tell me something I don't know."

I twisted to my side, my ear pressed against his ribcage. My hair fell in waves across his stomach. I leaned in, feeling braver than ever, and kissed his pec.

He sucked in a sharp breath. "Is that a sign for something? Or are you actually trying to make me crazy?"

"Does it make you crazy?" I whispered.

"No." His eyes hooded with a desire that I could feel but couldn't put a name to. "I don't want you to worry." He lifted his pointer finger into the air and drew two circles.

"What's that?" I asked.

"It's the universal sign for *be happy*. You don't know that one?"

"Nope. I guess I missed that day of ASL."

"That's right. You actually know sign language, don't you? I probably shouldn't keep lying then."

"It's okay. I'm not well versed. Mom didn't want to teach it to us. I think because it was a reminder of her handicap."

He nodded like he understood. Then his face turned serious. "You need a sign that tells me to slow down."

I held up four of my fingers and slowly closed them over my thumb. "Good?"

He nodded.

"Barry, I trust you." Well, a part of me did.

He brushed my hair behind my ear, our faces only inches apart, I tumbled and fell into his eyes. "I know. For some messed up reason, you actually want me back. But that doesn't change anything. I need to know. Even when you can't say it, or you don't want to say it, there's some other way for you to tell me to back the fuck off."

"Such a charmer."

"It's in my blood." He smirked. Then, again, sobered. "Now I need you to come up with a sign that means goodbye."

"We already did that one, don't you remember?"

"I mean 'goodbye for good.'"

My jaw fell open. "Why would I come up with that?"

"Because I need to know if you use it, you mean it."

I had to really think about it. I wanted to use a sign that I wouldn't ever remember. Something that I'd forget before the day was over. I held up my hand, all five fingers splayed out. Quickly I closed them into a fist and shot my fist into the air.

He nodded. "Good," he said. "That's good."

"How about one for love?" I asked.

His expression was priceless.

"Not because I'm in love with you," I said, pinching his side playfully. I wasn't going to admit it now, anyway. "But, you know, maybe someday. If the time ever comes."

He agreed that the time *could* come for that sign to be important.

We spent the afternoon making up different, meaningless signs that wouldn't mean anything to anyone but us. If ever we wanted to text, or call, or sneak out of class once school started and meet at the janitor's closet in the senior hallway (three guesses who came up with that one), or drive around, or see a movie, or go all the way, or just jog to third base, or talk. We had signs for all of it.

A majority of those signs indicated that he had intentions of keeping me as his girlfriend once the school year started. I wasn't capable of maintaining my goofy smile as I walked into the house after kissing him goodbye. Barry Prescott wanted me to be his girlfriend for a good while. He wanted people to know I was his girlfriend. Oh yeah, I was smiling.

Daddy stood inside the hallway with his large arms folded across his chest. "Well?" he asked.

"Hmm?"

"Wipe the smile off your face, Brittney Ann, and tell me if that boy was a gentleman."

I bit into my lips, trying to force myself not to appear as ridiculously excited as I actually was. It wasn't happening. "He's great."

"Britt…" His thumb and forefinger stretched across his forehead so he could rub his temples. "Don't be charmed so much that you lose sight of who you are."

"I know who I am."

"Good," he said. "At the first sign that boy is a bad influence, I won't hesitate putting my foot in his ass. And I'm not comfortable deliberately keeping this from your brother. You know how he feels about that—"

"Please!" I gasped. "Daddy, Barry isn't the same boy he was all those years ago. Toby will still hold that against him. He won't even give him a chance. But you will. You believe in second chances. That's what you're all about. Please. Let me try this. Let me *have* this."

He let out a heavy sigh. "Playing to my sympathies. You know I can't help but forgive someone who's trying."

I smiled down at my shoes so he wouldn't see my excitement. "Sorry Daddy."

He leaned over and kissed the top of my head. I took it as a sign the conversation was over, but then he whispered, "You know his mom comes to our meetings on Tuesday night."

The hair on the back of my neck prickled. "Aren't those meetings anonymous?"

"They are. I figured you wouldn't tell anyone, so things could remain that way. Bex hasn't been in a few months. Now that she stopped coming to church…" He shrugged to downplay what he was trying to say. Daddy knew only too well the signs of relapse.

"Is she okay?"

"I've called a couple times. She always gives me the run around. Says she won't miss another meeting, and then she does. I tried to talk to her sponsor. She's working on her. I'm more worried about what Bex accused Barry of. Does he do drugs, Brittney Ann?"

"No," I said instantly. "Not…not anymore." *That I knew of.*

"You're sure?"

"Yes."

"Okay. I believe you." He did, too. I never lied to my parents, so he had no reason to doubt me.

TWENTY

BARRY

On Saturday, she crawled into the passenger side of the Charger and said, "I have a surprise for you. I think you'll really like it."

"A new swimming suit?" By my calculations, she had two swimming suits. Both of them covered everything from her tits to the tops of her thighs. Still, I loved them.

Instantly her face reddened. "Oh? Well, yes, I borrowed one from Katy Lynn, but that's not the surprise."

My heart sprinted into over drive. "Whoa, wait. What? What's the different between hers and yours?"

That was a stupid question. Katy Lynn's boobs were about a million times bigger. I never fancied myself a boob-man.

I wasn't just trying to convince myself of this, either. Really. I was completely happy with Brittney's…what were they, a B-cup? *Maybe an A.*

"There's a lot less to hers," she muttered.

"You have my attention." I brought her fingers to my lips and kissed each one in turn.

Brittney twisted, getting comfortable in the seat. "Barry? Can I ask you something important?"

"Yes. Is it about this mysterious swimming attire?"

"No," she laughed. "It's about us. Or, well, you rather."

"Damn. I'd rather talk about what you're wearing."

"Of course you would."

We drove back toward town with our fingers locked together over the shifter. I'd only gotten my car back this week, and having Brittney belted into the passenger seat was fulfilling four out of my five top fantasies.

Having her on the hood would be the final one.

She cleared her throat and shifted, looking uncomfortable.

"What's up?" I glanced her way.

"There's something we have to talk about."

Oh. Shit. She hadn't told Gwen about us, had she?

I swallowed my heart, reminding myself that if she'd talked to Gwen there was no way she'd have gotten into this car so easily. "Okay," I led.

"We never talked about the drugs."

For the first time in my life, this subject had been broached and I hadn't wanted to launch myself out of the car. I relaxed. "What do you want to know?"

"You're not on them, right?"

Was she serious? I stared over at her, waiting for some hint that she was joking. She bit into her lip. Her free hand played with the end of her dress. She was scowling.

Holy fuck, she was serious. "You thought your boyfriend was high, and you got in the car with him?"

"No," she exhaled. "No, but we never talked about it, and you never mention it—"

"Because you were there when I went through the withdrawals. You know I'm sober. I was a fucking prick when I was stoned, Britt. I snapped at everyone, and I lived my life just looking for my next fuck and my next buzz. I haven't been like that with you, have I?"

"No! But I didn't know you, so I didn't know how you acted!" Her lip trembled. "You can't be mad at me for asking. I just…" She wiped under her eyes, and I was pissed at myself for making her cry.

Slamming the brakes, I hit the shoulder of the road and threw the Charger out of gear. Unbuckling my belt and then hers, I pulled her onto my lap. She twisted up against me. "I'm not mad at you," I said, but my voice was a low growl. "Okay, I'm a little mad," I amended, "but just because I thought I was doing really fucking good with you—"

"You are. You're amazing."

"Then why the hell would you think I'm high?"

She shrugged. She looked so damn small. I pulled her tighter against me so I could bury my face in her hair. "I'm not on shit, Brittney. I haven't even smoked a bowl in over a month. This is all me, babe."

"It doesn't make sense," she finally whispered.

"What doesn't?"

"You want to be my boyfriend?"

"Damn right I do. I'm fucking nuts about you, woman."

She giggled softly.

"And don't get into the car with someone when you don't know if they're sober. Seriously."

She shook her head. "I knew you were."

Bo's Beamer was parked next to Tyler's Volvo next to Charli's Mini Cooper. Brittney looked terrified. "You didn't say Charli and Lonna would be here."

"Is that a problem? You don't like them?" I guessed.

"No, no, they're fine. It's just…" Her fingers tightened on her large purse. "Well, my swimming suit is very revealing. I'm not so sure how I'll look next to them."

I stared at her dress, trying to see the lines of the suit through the material. "How revealing?"

"Do you see Lonna's top?"

Lonna had on a black tank top. Unlike the tank top bikini Brittney had worn earlier in the week, Lonna's was a few inches wide and wrapped around her chest and nothing else. "I see it." But I made a point not stare at it.

"Katy Lynn's is a lot like that."

I swallowed a rush of excitement. "Is it wrong of me to be excited? Can I see?"

"I…I have to put it on. My dad…"

"Right, right. You can go into the bathrooms. Look, don't worry about Charli and Lonna. They're really not my type."

She didn't look at me, but I knew she already knew I'd hooked up with Lonna, so I couldn't deny that. As far as Charli was concerned, that middle sized box of girls I'd never have sex with was the one Charli fit into. I had no idea why, but I'd never seen her like that. She was more like a little sister than a hot friend.

Brittney tucked her head as she walked toward the far bathrooms. Lonna whistled at her. "Ready to get your tan on, girl?"

"Um, yes."

I felt an urge to put an arm around Brittney and keep her protected from all of them. She may have been a cheerleader, but she'd never been exposed to Lonna's wrath outside of school.

I gave her a questioning sign for *abort mission*—crossing my two first fingers together and drawing a square. Her eyes narrowed.

Had she forgotten? After we spent the whole week drilling them into our brains, she forgot on the first pass.

She gave me the sign for *no* at the same time she shook her head.

"What the hell are you two doing?" Gage eyed us.

"Long story," I told him. To Brittney I winked. "I love that we have inside secrets already."

She agreed with the fingers of her left hand split like a Vulcan Salute. Hey, there were no rules saying we couldn't use already made-up gestures.

We crawled through prickly brush. I lingered behind the others, staying in eye-distance of the bathrooms. Apparently, the skimpy bikini took a marathon of time to get into.

The guys reached the bank, and Tyler was instantly tense. There was a guy's head poking out of the water. He was closer to the opposite bank, by the main road where homeless people camped out because they couldn't afford a camping spot. Which, yeah, that made sense. Collin Parker.

Then Luke's head broke the surface.

"Retard's at our river," Tyler growled.

"It's a free river," I tried to yell up to him, but Tyler had an easily flipped pissed-off switch, and the Parkers unknowingly hit it.

"He's not going to start anything, is he?" Bo asked, knowing for a fact that Tyler was getting ready to start something big.

I leaned back toward the bushes. The last thing I needed was for Brittney to walk out here and see how juvenile my friends were. Next thing I realized, Bo had knocked Tyler aside to block the idiot, and Luke Parker was parting the water as he stormed our way.

Maybe Brittney wouldn't come out before the guys had finished screwing around. This was just the type of shit she didn't need to see. My friends being…themselves.

Luke walked past Bo and Tyler.

He caught Charli around the middle and he kissed her. *He. Kissed. Charli.*

She wasn't his to kiss. She went limp in his arms, though, like she enjoyed it so much she couldn't use her knees. I expected her to hit him or to respond someway that hinted at how disgusting it was to be kissed by the loser, but Charli practically passed out. When her appendages regained mobility, her fingers knotted into Luke's hair. She pulled him closer to her mouth. She wanted it. What the hell?

Bo's jaw dropped.

I heard Brittney coming through the brush, and I ran to block her. "Just wait a second," I breathed.

She dug into my shoulder as she tried to peer around me. "What's going on, Barry? I heard yelling."

"Yeah, Luke and Collin are here. It's not pretty."

"What? The Parker boys? Why isn't it pretty? They're very nice. They help us put up hay in the summer."

Blood raced through my veins. So they'd hung out before? I wondered if Luke had ever thought about kissing her the way he'd kissed Charli.

Luke's body will look real nice buried beside Cheesedick's.

I gripped Brittney's hip as I pulled her into me. This was mine. If Luke couldn't see that, then I'd tell him. If he didn't get it after that, then I'd kill him "Yeah, well, you don't need them anymore. We can help you with that."

She glanced down at my hold on her. Her eyes narrowed in confusion. "We've already done it this year."

"Yeah, next year. We'll help you. You don't need that prick's help. Or his idiot brother's." I couldn't believe I said all that, especially to her. As if she didn't already realize how pathetically into her I was.

She pushed at my chest. Not hard, just enough that I wanted to beat Luke over the head with the shovel I'd use to bury him. *Was she pushing me away because of him?* "Barry! What's the matter with you?"

"I just don't like them. Not in this town; not around you."

"Oh," she sighed. "Oh." Enlightenment colored her face.

Then her fingers wrapped around my back, knotting against my muscles. Our bodies fit against one another like a hand and a glove.

"You're jealous?" She looked as surprised as I felt.

"No, no. That's not it." I'd never been in a position to feel anything like this, so it was hard to put a name to the poisonous hell-monster roaring inside my chest.

What if Luke had wanted to do that *other* thing his tongue was *supposedly* so good at with my Brittney?

Oh yeah, he was one dead motherfucker…

Her fingers brushed over my hair. "It's okay, Barry. I'd never tell anyone how sweet you can really be. It'll be our little secret, okay?"

Sweet? Yeah, she couldn't hear what I was thinking.

"Forever?" I asked, then realized the implications behind that one simple word. I hadn't really meant it like that.

"For as long as you'd like," she said, her fingers slicing into my hair as she ignored my slip.

Bo was steaming pissed off that Luke had had the nerve to kiss Charli. He kept pacing in front of the water, kicking at rocks. Charli tried, "I'm sorry, I don't know what you want—"

"You didn't have to get so into it, did you?"

She threw rocks into the air and shrugged. "He kissed me. I didn't know what to do." But she had to keep sandwiching her smile between her teeth, which only pissed Bo off more.

"I hate that fucker," Bo seethed.

I knew he was thinking exactly what I'd been thinking about Luke: the guy and his tongue needed to stay away from *our* girls. It was just like Ryan. Even if Luke went to Bourbon, he had no business messing with our turf.

Bo kicked hard into a mound of rocks, causing it to splatter. "And what was with Collin? He needed to make sure Lonna was okay, like we'd ever let anything happen to her."

Collin had pulled Luke away after Bo had punched him. Then

Collin had turned back to Lonna and asked her, only her, if she was okay. Because there weren't two other girls standing there. Because his brother hadn't just assaulted Charli.

Collin probably annoyed me less than Luke, but he still got on my nerves. And I couldn't tell Gage—the second string quarterback—that I didn't hate Collin, the starting quarterback, with a diehard passion like everyone else.

Gage snorted, "What a fucking retard."

Brittney's head snapped up as her eyes narrowed at Gage. Her tiny white knuckles balled around the mass of rocks she'd collected.

I caught her hand, prying her fingers open. "Down girl."

"What? Oh, this?" She dropped them. "I wouldn't throw rocks at your friends, I promise."

I wasn't so sure I believed her. "You sure?" I asked, trying not to laugh at the hard face she was making. "What's up with you?"

"Nothing." She pouted. "Can we get into the water? I'm warm."

"Sure babe."

So I took off my Foreigner T-shirt, and Brittney stripped out of that cotton dress she'd put back on to cover her suit.

Holy fuck...

Words couldn't accurately describe what she had going on beneath that dress. The most delicious sun-kissed skin imaginable, hugged on top with a thin strip of pink fabric. The bottoms were just as revealing, with thin straps that sat high on her bony hips.

"Hot damn." Lonna let out a whistle, which had all the other guys looking this way. A part of me wanted them to look.

See? I thought. *She's mesmerizing.* Then another part of me burned with that aching hell-monster that I now knew was jealousy. *Don't look at her! That creamy skin isn't for general consumption. And I saw her first, assholes.*

Strangely enough, everyone was fairly quiet. A lot of dropped jaws.

I didn't know how I'd have reacted if Tyler, per his usual, made a comment about how her slim legs would look wrapped around his head.

It was bad enough I could imagine his vitriol.

Thankfully, he barely lifted his brows to check her out and then looked away. Unimpressed. Fucking idiot. She was a knockout.

My knockout.

"We're going to float downriver a little way. Leave us alone," I begged.

Other than some laughter, they said nothing. I followed Brittney's swaying hips into the water, the same as I'd follow her anywhere.

TWENTY ONE

BARRY

Fireworks started going off before dusk. The day of holding her in my arms and falling head over heels for her body had gone too quickly.

We had to swim upstream to get back to the guys. I could hear them all laughing. The air smelled like fire-pit burnt hotdogs and… oh no. I stopped swimming and fell back. Brittney stopped with me.

"What is it?" She wouldn't recognize the smell.

"They're getting high."

It was the first time that I really felt a burning need to join them. Out of sight, out of mind had been a nice vacation. Library time was over, and my friends were home. It was time to face reality. A sober life—with not-so-sober friends.

Or I could go smoke a bowl. It wasn't like it would kill anything to smoke reg. Bet Dad wouldn't even care about that. It was the pills that were the real problem.

"We can go back down stream," she said, her angelic voice pulling me from inside my head.

"Huh?"

Her hands gripped tightly to my shoulders, turning me so I could see the seriousness in her hazel irises. "Barry," she demanded. "Either we'll leave, or you can be as strong as I know you are. What's it going to be?"

She really wasn't as tough as she wanted to pretend. It was pretty cute. I kissed the end of her nose. "It's cool," I said. "We're out in the open air, the smell doesn't linger that long. Let's go get some hot dogs."

Tyler saw us crawling out of the water. His eyes widened, and he scrambled on all fours as he tried to grab the pipe away from Gage, who was in the middle of taking a hit. Gage jerked away.

Tyler groaned. "Real cool, dude. What if that was water patrol and not Barry?"

"What? It's medicinal."

"You and I both know medical Mary-Jane still isn't legal here."

Gage shrugged. He was little cooler when he was high. I mean, level-headed cool. Not cool-cool.

Not like I thought it was cool to get high. That's stupid. Who needs that shit?

Oh damn, but it really did smell good.

Brittney pinched my hip. "Ow, what the...?"

"Be strong," she whispered.

"Yeah, Bare. Listen to the little virgin. Getting stoned is bad for you. Side effects include being a dick and fucking my girlfriend, and..." He sucked in his lower lip as he thought. "No, that's about it. Heaven forbid you find your balls and smoke a bowl. Personally, I like you better as Brittney's little bitch."

Apparently, ganja didn't help him tone down being such a dickhead. Sadly, there wasn't even a pill for his condition.

My fingers shook. No matter how tight my fists balled, those digits still trembled. I wasn't mad; I was anxious. It was taking every last ounce of willpower in my body not to fall down in that semi-circle and join them.

"Dude, not cool," Tyler mumbled.

"Yeah, no joke." Lonna stood up and kicked rocks at Gage. "Get over it, you dick. It was weeks ago, and Barry's trying to be sober. You need to put the pipe away and respect that."

Oh shit.

She was trying, for once in her life, to be nice, but the last thing moderately stoned Gage wanted to hear was his girl defending me. "Sit down," he barked at her. "Now!"

Lonna walked a small circle, let out an exaggerated groan and then fell unceremoniously back onto the rocks beside him. Gage handed her the pipe and without question she took a hit.

"So, you gonna hit this or not?" Gage asked, and it took a few rapid heartbeats to realize he was talking to me.

"Huh?" I had to tear my eyes away from the swirl of smoke that slipped from Lonna's mouth.

Yes. Yes, I was going to do it. Dad wasn't here. He'd never even know.

"It'll calm your ass down," Gage said. "You look jumpy."

"Dude," Bo warned. "You're being a dick."

"This is coming from the guy who wanted nothing to do with Charli until Luke kissed her. I'm the dick?"

Charli and Bo were sharing a towel. The tips of their knees touched as they sat side-by-side. Charli squeaked at Gage, "You're not being very supportive."

"Just don't," Bo told her, wrapping his hand around the inside of her thigh to pull her closer to him.

"I'm gonna go," I said, my voice was distant. I'd forced myself to say that. What I really wanted to do was punch Gage in the face and then take that pipe right out of Lonna's skinny fingers, and...*oh God*, I had to get out of here.

Brittney's hands pushed at my back, as she tried to urge me toward the parking lot.

But I couldn't look away from that pipe. This really was stupid. It was one bowl. Not like I was killing anyone. Definitely not myself. I could stop after a couple hits. That wouldn't be hard at all.

Then, damn, I could keep kissing Brittney and maybe put on a little music. We could go to my car and make out. She was down with making out. Stoned kissing was bound to be better than sober kissing.

She kept pushing on my back. "Barry, please."

"I think, uh, yeah, I think I'm just gonna..." I couldn't say it. Gage couldn't have the satisfaction of knowing he'd broken me.

Besides, it wasn't like I was fiending for pills. My toe tapped against the rocks, splattering them under my foot. I could go without painers. But, really, the candy made the experience.

I wouldn't take them like before.

I could just take one a day, and that would keep me lightly buzzed. It'd be perfect because my immunity had probably built back up, so I'd get that much more of a kick from every pill.

"Barry," Brittney whispered, her voice shaking. "I don't care what you do, but if you're doing that, you need to take me home first."

I felt like I'd been doused in ice water as my body went cold. "What?"

She looked me straight in the eye. "I didn't sign on for this. I'm not okay with it."

"This is kinda who I am," I bit back. I knew we'd had that moment in the car earlier, but that was different. *That* was about her knowing I was sober, because I was.

This was about me being who I am, and her telling me I couldn't *do* that. She had no right to keep me from being *myself.* I threw my hand out, gesturing at the perfect swirl of smoke wafting from Lonna's mouth. "And it's just a couple hits. My problem is pills…why are you shaking your head at me?"

"Because I'm not doing it. Your problem is needing something that alters your mind, and you're addicted to that. It's not the marijuana that's the problem, it's you, Barry. You can't just take a few hits and walk away because you have an addiction problem. You and I both know you won't walk away. Either take me home, or I'll call Daddy."

Gage burst out laughing. Rolling over on himself, he slapped his bare knee. "Holy shit, she's going to call her *daddy*. Bare, you better look out."

"Ugh," Brittney grabbed a handful of rocks and flung them at him. While he was stunned, wiping at his shoulders, she dove toward him. Her fingernails dug into his face. "You vile, monstrous, miserable little *child*…"

All I could do was stare at her. She tore into his face with her fingernails, and then his arms as he put them up to cover himself.

"You just have to drag people down. He's so much better than you—so much better than your stupid drug. You can't stand it that your girlfriend wanted him more than you, and you can't stand it that he's capable of saying no and you're not. Oh, and Collin Parker is not *retarded*—you should be ashamed of yourself for using such a word."

Then Gage reacted. He must have just remembered how little Brittney was and how easy stopping her would be.

It took two seconds for him to reach up and smack her hand away. "Gage, don't!" Lonna screamed, and it took that long for me to realize he was actually going to punch Brittney. His fists were clenched. There was a look of determination on his face. He'd drawn back and aimed straight at her beautiful face.

"No!" I yelled.

Brittney tried to reach up and block herself, but Gage knocked her hands away. He had no intention of missing.

Before he could do anything I'd have to kill him for, Lonna's arms went around his shoulders. "Knock it off," she snapped.

Brittney scrambled backward, crab-crawling against the gravel. I caught her, pulling her to her feet. It was easy to plant myself in front of her. "You okay?"

Her arms wrapped around me from behind. "I'm sorry. That was—"

"You're not hurt, are you?" Spinning to face her, I gave her a once over. I couldn't find any scratches or anything; she looked perfect as ever.

I could taste my heartbeat. Staring down at her, I realized how stupid I was. What the hell had I been thinking letting her slap Gage like that? I knew he'd react eventually.

"No, no, I'm…Oh goodness." She blew out a terrified breath and then her fingers fumbled over her mouth. Her gaze fixed over my shoulder.

Lonna bowed forward cupping onto her nose, and Gage stomped toward the parking lot.

"Why didn't you guys stop him?" Charli wrapped her arms around Lonna. "Are you okay? What can I do?"

"Nothing," Lonna mumbled. "I'm fine." She stood up and stormed after Gage. She'd put him in his place. Lonna wasn't the type of girl to let him get away with that.

"That was intense." Tyler exhaled a loud breath. "I thought you had him, Bo."

"Me? You're closer."

"Yeah, but I was watching Barry's six. What's your excuse, you fat fuck?"

Chase's face was bright red. He didn't say anything as he stumbled after the others.

"Let's get out of here," I said, kissing Brittney's forehead.

"Okay," she agreed, her eyes unblinking as she stared up at me. "Are you alright?"

I rubbed at the tops of her shoulders. "I'm fine. I wasn't the one who was almost punched by a chauvinistic asshole. Why do you ask?"

"No reason at all." She folded over herself like she was cold. When I tried to put my arm around her, she shied away, claiming that the path was too narrow for us to walk side-by-side.

Silence wrapped around the car like a cocoon. I'd turned on the radio, but it was quiet, and I wasn't really paying much attention to Kansas because "Carry on My Wayward Son" felt more depressing than my actual situation. "So…uh, you regret what we did, don't you?" I asked, my palms rubbed over the wheel.

What we did.

Those private moments on that river bank were etched inside my mind.

She didn't need to know how much it would bother me if she tried to take this afternoon back. I thought I enjoyed kissing her, but exploring her body was probably the highlight of my life so far.

"What? Oh, no. That's not it."

"But there is something?" I asked.

She chewed on that delicious lower lip. Reaching up, my thumb released her lip from her teeth. I rubbed over her mouth, and she kissed the pad of my digit. "Don't think too hard. I actually want to kiss these again."

Almost inaudibly she whispered, "I won't be with you if you're on drugs. I know earlier I seemed a little unsure about the situation, but I'm sure now. I can't do it. That's just not who I am. It's not something I can sacrifice. I'm sorry."

"You're giving me an ultimatum?" And for the first time, I actually wanted to do something just to defy her. She couldn't control me.

"No," she squeaked. "You're clean right now, and I love you. I've never enjoyed spending time with someone the way I do with you. But if you change… I won't stay around to watch you destroy yourself. It's very simple really." Her shoulders were shaking, and I could tell she didn't like what she was saying, but she meant every word.

"You love me?"

She took a deep breath and held it. Puffing out her cheeks, she exhaled, "Yes. I know it's kind of fast, but it's how I feel. Is that okay?" The last three words came out as a shallow whisper.

"Yeah," I said. "I like it."

"Good." She smiled. "I like it as well." She started digging into her bag. "I feel awful because my surprise for everyone was cookies, and I didn't even think to share." There was a very large Ziploc full of half-melted chocolate chip cookies. "Now they're ruined."

Oh my God, Brittney made the best cookies. She'd sold some at a bake sale last year. Tyler and I had been stoned out of our minds and had eaten every last one.

"I guarantee you Tyler will not give a damn if they're melted. Let me run them back to him real quick."

I already knew that I was going back to get stoned. I had two definitive priorities:

    1. Join them. Smoke quickly but effectively.

    2. Eat those mother-loving cookies.

There were no flaws with my plan. She was staying in the car, she'd never know, and I had to do it. I just couldn't stay away. I did care about Brittney and it tickled the shit out of me that she loved me. I never thought I needed a girl the way I did need her. She'd become part of me.

But I needed this, too.

They must have known. They must have sensed I'd come back. It was just Bo and Tyler, which was perfect. I'd feel no guilt like if the others were still around. "Give it to me," I said, throwing the cookies into Tyler's lap.

"Bare…" Bo hesitated, pulling the pipe further away from me.

"No, don't say a word. Just give it to me."

Tyler's eyes bounced between us. "It's just ganja," he defended. "You're not going to go back to popping pills, right?"

"Of course not." Maybe. That was unclear, too.

The warm glass of the pipe felt at home in my hand. I did need this. My life was so much better with it. Not because getting high was a cure, but because it was a Band-Aid. Being stoned fixed my outlook on the world; it made things better. And I liked *better*.

Except Brittney. I'd never needed to be zonked out to enjoy holding her. I'd never needed to get out of my head to be able to stand her voice. She was the best part of my sober life.

The lighter trembled in my hand. Why the hell was I hesitating? There was no time to back out. I had to do this, eat the cookies, go back to the car.

Smoke the reg.

Eat the cookies.

Go to the car.

But what if…? There was a small voice inside my head warning me to walk away now. Like a little angel sitting on my shoulder. *What if Brittney smells it on me?*

I could say it was in the air; the perfect lie.

What if she didn't believe me? What if she left me? What if all I had was this tie-dye swirled pipe and no Brittney? This small, glass pipe with barely resin left inside.

It's all Tyler had. He lost track of what Annie meant to him, and *poof*, she was gone. Now he smoked and drank and fucked whoever he wanted. But I wasn't sure he felt anything at all.

Oh damn. "I can't."

Bo snatched the thing out of my hand before I could change my mind. "Go," he said, jerking his chin toward the bushes. "It'll get easier and easier to stay away. Just go now."

So I did. I stumbled and ran through the brush, not stopping until I reached the car. My breathing was erratic as I doubled over on myself, bracing my knees. Sucking in several whiffs of air that weren't tinged with the spicy smoke aroma, I regained my bearings. "How'd that go?" Brittney's voice was sweet. There wasn't a hint of suspicion in her tone.

"Fine." I nodded my head to the beat because it felt like the Scorpions were singing right to me.

When Brittney's hand wrapped around mine, her fingers squeezed tightly, like she was holding on indefinitely.

"You're not going to ask if I did it?" I stared at her, breathless from the run and from her beauty.

"No," she said, shaking her head. "I trust you."

Pulling her over the center column, I kissed the top of her head. "Jesus Christ. I don't deserve you."

She smiled. "That feeling's mutual, I assure you."

We sat in the Charger listening to the best music in the world. The sky darkened, and then the world lit up in oranges, blues, greens, purples, and reds. Explosions of colors that made Brittney say *oh*. The magic of fireworks.

She kissed my shoulder. "Happy fourth of July, Barry."

TWENTY TWO

My phone rang. Again. I closed my eyes, waiting for Gwen's ringtone to just stop already.

I slid into a pair of store-bought leggings. Mom had made me two dresses that would look great with them. These dresses were tighter than my old pastel dresses. One of the new ones was burgundy. The other Kelly green. I loved both of them, but especially the green one.

Green might even be my new favorite color.

The tube-top dress hugged my chest. The flair skirt was flattering. I felt confident. But that wasn't new. I'd been feeling all kinds of confidence in the past few weeks. Being the girlfriend of Barry Prescott required a certain amount of self-assurance. Also, backbone was required.

When football practice and cheerleading had picked up in the middle of July, Madison sat me down, gave me a tissue, and *broke* it to me that things weren't going to last for Barry and me.

She said she knew how Barry was and what he needed. "I'm not trying to be a bitch, but if you're not giving it to him, then he's not going to stick around. It's just the facts, Britt."

So far, he'd proven her wrong. Our random bouts of foreplay—when we occasionally got time away from Daddy—were plenty for him. I think. At least, he told me he was okay.

"Guys can't just stop getting laid," Madison had said. "Not once they start. It's like pickles—you can't stop eating them once you start."

I hadn't understood that last part.

I tried not to think about the things she'd said, but sometimes she felt the need to repeat herself.

My phone rang again.

Okay. Okay. I was being a really terrible quasi-sister. The fact that Gwen and Toby still didn't know about Barry had been weighing heavily on me. Barry had even been interested to know when I planned to tell Gwen. I had no status update. Instead, I ignored both her and my brother. Barry and I kept our relationship off Facebook and Instagram. Toby, Gwen, and I didn't have Tumblr or Twitter, so I told Barry to feel free. He'd shown me some of his tweets:

Kissing my girlfriend so effing hard. #gotthefeels.

Yeah, it was best if Toby and Gwen stayed on the outside. They would only bring negativity into my blissful relationship. And I just didn't want that.

The phone stopped.

Good.

I only had a couple hours until Barry picked me up for his dad's wedding rehearsal. We'd gone to the church after practice to decorate. Ashleigh was a big fan of gossamer and tiny little ribbons that big knuckles couldn't tie. Barry was seriously cussing her by the time we left the church.

The front doorbell rang, and my heart reacted. My heart had

a direct link to any connection to Barry. Or maybe it was just the doorbell. If that was him, he was three hours early. I skipped toward the stairs, holding out hope that he was here to surprise me.

I reached the middle step and froze. My heart reacted again. This time the reaction was the organ catapulting toward my toes.

Gwen stood in my foyer. "There you are." She met me on the second step so she could throw her arms around my shoulder and hug me. "I thought you fell off the face of the earth. I know cheerleading practice started, but dang girl, it's still summer. You shouldn't be that busy."

If she expected me to respond, she'd have to back up and let me retrieve my jaw from the floor.

"You okay?" She waved in front of my face. "You look like you've seen a ghost. I didn't scare you, did I? I told Toby you'd be happily surprised. Was I wrong?"

"No," I gasped. Surprised? Definitely. "No, um. You weren't wrong. You…you're here. You're home. Early. Why are you home early?"

Her eyes rolled. "Mom. She met someone. She wants to marry him. So basically she's manic as hell, and I've come to talk her down. She doesn't get off work until five, though, so I have all afternoon."

All afternoon. With Gwen. Lying to her. Not telling her. Keeping a big fat secret.

I swallowed my stomach.

"Um, I…I have plans. I'm leaving at four-thrity. I…" My face was hot. "I just have plans."

Her head tilted to the side. "Plans? Okay. That's cool. We'll hang out until then. Come on. You have to tell me about your summer. Did you go anywhere, do anything? Did you meet any cute boys?" She pinched my side playfully because she thought she was joking.

Oh no. Red alert. *Red. Alert.* The words were on the tip of my tongue. Right there. They were…it was happening. I couldn't stop it. "I'm seeing someone," I said, my mouth suddenly dry.

"What?" she smiled, her back straightened as she leaned into me. Gwen, being of the same gender, understood that I wasn't a fragile porcelain doll that couldn't be touched. She'd always humored me by talking about boys even though my brother insisted I not date until I was at least a day over thirty-five.

I hoped she'd hold on to that smile. "Yeah. We've been together most of the summer."

"Are you kidding me?" She dragged me toward the chaise in the living room. Gwen always sat with her feet tucked under her bottom. Once she was situated, she patted the seat beside her. "Come on. Tell me everything. How did you keep this from me? *Why* did you keep this from me? Oh, wait. I get it. You didn't want Toby to harass him."

"Exactly." I felt more comfortable standing. Pacing, too. "Toby would have made it out to be…he would have…how do I say this?"

"Take your time," Gwen suggested. She bit into her lip to hide her amused grin.

I hoped her amusement would hold out. I took a deep breath and blurted, "I'm happy. I love him so much that I can't even imagine my life without him. He's…he's different. He doesn't care what other people are into. He has his own personal style, and it makes him so dang special. The band T-shirts and the tight jeans… Ugh, I'd hate it on anyone else. His Converses are never tied, and he wears his ball cap to hide the fact his thick hair is always a mess. He's beautiful, of course. And popular. And by some miracle, he actually wants to be with me. He likes me back."

I'd been waiting for Barry to give me the sign that he *loved* me back, but he was holding out.

Gwen's feet kicked off the edge of the couch. She leaned forward, hands braced on her knees like she was preparing for bad news and needed extra support to keep herself upright. She didn't look so tickled anymore.

"Who is it?" she asked, eyes narrowed.

"See, it's funny you should…"

"Brittney." She said my name slowly. "Tell me you're not…tell me you didn't."

"I love him," I repeated. "Barry's not like you think. He's so——"

In one air-rushing move, she stood and smacked me hard across the face. The agony of being hit by someone I loved like a sister burned against my flesh.

Shock colored her features as her fingers cupped around her mouth. "Oh, Britt, I'm so sorry. I am. But you…you cannot be that *stupid*. It's not happening. You're not *dating* him."

"I love him!" If I said it enough, she'd understand. "I love him, Gwen. He's amazing. I know Toby doesn't like him, and I know he stood me up when I was a freshman, but we were just kids. He's apologized for that. He's sorry."

Her eyes narrowed. "Is he now? Has he, by chance, confessed *why* Toby doesn't like him?"

"I…" *Oh.* "It hasn't ever come up."

Her face lined in condescension. "I'm sure it hasn't. He wouldn't want you to know *that* while he was busy manipulating you to fall in love with him." She reached into her back pocket for her cell phone.

"No," I pleaded, catching her wrist. "Please. You're not being reasonable."

"Brittney, there are things you don't understand. You're still young. Barry Prescott is bad news. And, God, Britt…" She shook me off. "He's a druggy."

"No, he's not." The tears had started. The first one spilled over my lashes and burned the hot cheek imprinted with Gwen's palm.

Gwen flicked my tear away. She pointed into my face. "Don't you dare cry for him. He doesn't deserve it."

"I'm not crying *for* him. I love him. I'm-m c-crying because you're…you're going to tell Toby. He's…he's not going to be happy."

"No," she said matter-of-factly. "He's not."

⮜

Toby yelled at me. For forty-five minutes, he yelled at me. The conversation would start to ease off, and then he'd remember something else he forgot to holler about. "Jesus. Tell me you didn't sleep with the fucker. Tell me he didn't already take advantage of you, baby sis."

"Of course not. We're together. We both—"

"You're not *together*," he growled. "I'll be there tomorrow if I have to."

"It's fine," Gwen reassured him. "I'll handle it. Just enjoy your freedom. I'll be there in a few weeks, and you won't be free ever again."

"I look forward to it." He smiled through the screen. And then he remembered he was mad at me, and his face hardened. "Shit, he didn't drag race with you in that car, did he? If he wants to kill himself in that hideous hunk of metal, then…hell, I'm all for that. But he's not taking you down with him."

Since Daddy had already left for the rehearsal, Toby got ahold of Mom and, somehow, convinced her not to let me go anywhere with Barry.

My phone went off not long after Mom came to give me the depressing news. "Hey babe, I'm almost there. You ready?"

My heart actually ached at hearing his voice. "I can't go," I muttered.

There was a pause. "What?"

"I can't go. I'm sorry."

He chuckled because he thought I was joking. "Britt, what're you talking about? We've been planning this for weeks. It's my dad's rehearsal."

"Gwen came home today."

He sucked in a short gasp. *Then. Total. Silence.*

"I see," he said. "So is this it?" He sounded broken and weak, and all I could think about was running my fingers through his hair as I hugged him close.

"No," I gasped. "No, this isn't it. Not for us. We're stronger than this."

"We are?"

"Yes, Barry, we are. If Toby hadn't called Mom and convinced her to keep me under lock and key, then I'd be there with you. It isn't my choice to stay away."

He laughed once, sounding relieved. "Phew. Scared me there for a second. We'll get through this, babe. I'll text you later. I lo…oh shit, I almost said it."

Yes, heart, I can feel you. "I wish you would."

"I will," he promised. "When you dance with me at Dad's wedding."

Perfect. The one place there was no chance I would be tomorrow night.

"Britt?" He whispered

"Yeah?"

"I wanna play with your boobs so bad right now."

I laughed. This was what Toby didn't understand. I wasn't *too* good for Barry. In order for a girl to enjoy dancing with the devil, she had to have a little devil inside her. Cupping my left breast through the fabric of my dress, I teased, "I'm doing it for you."

Growling through the receiver, he whispered, "But I do it better."

I couldn't disagree with that.

CR

I slept uneasily. Nightmares kept making appearances. They were all different. The only common theme seemed to be Madison. She was always laughing at me. Pointing and laughing. Throwing her head back and laughing. In one dream, she had six heads and all of them laughed in different adenoidal pitches.

"I told you so. A little virgin like you never stood a chance."

"But he didn't break up with me because I'm a virgin. My brother broke us up."

"Yeah, that's right. Tell yourself whatever you need. Don't worry, little Christian. I'll take good care of him."

I woke up covered in sweat with tears streaming down my face.

It just wasn't fair. Was it my fault my brother was an obnoxious pig? No. I shouldn't have to give up my love because he couldn't be open minded.

Someone coughed in real time.

I startled awake. My head smacked into the wooden headboard as I jumped backward. "Ow." I rubbed the future knot. "Gwen, what're you doing here?" Clearing my throat, I tried to get rid of that very attractive just-woke-up, cried-myself-to-sleep croaking sound.

"I know you're mad at me."

I was. There was no point denying it. Gwen and I had been friends for a couple years, and I'd never even felt put off by her before. But I *was* mad.

"You're also smart. I know that you *know* I wouldn't keep you from someone you think you care about unless it meant a lot to me. Despite what Toby believes, I think you're plenty old enough to have a boyfriend. Just not Barry. Anyone but Barry."

Since she was being reasonable, I decided to do the same. "You don't know him like I do. He's not the same jerk who sleeps around and does drugs anymore. He's really changed. He's good. He even opens the door of the car for me." Sometimes he did. When he remembered. When he forgot, he became shame faced and embarrassed. The way he punished himself by tugging on his hair and swearing under his breath only made me love him more. His effort was what attracted me more than his chivalry.

She sat down on the bed, wrapped her hands around mine, and looked me straight in the eye. Her lips moved a few times before she finally came up with the words. "For whoever dates him next, I hope you're right. I hope he has changed from the guy I went to high school with. But you are wrong about one thing, Britt. I know Barry Prescott very well. And he knows me."

TWENTY THREE

BARRY

Nothing could improve my mood. I was a ball of pissed-off, pent-up energy. I went for a run before the wedding, and I was perfectly capable of ignoring all the little chores Ashleigh tried to get me to do. No, I wouldn't make breakfast. No, I wouldn't call the band. No, I wouldn't button my top button. And fuck no, I wouldn't take off my favorite Van Halen T-shirt.

Brittney didn't show last night. I could feel her slipping away. It was inevitable at this point. I'd kept this thought at the back of my mind all summer. Whatever we had, had always been doomed... when Gwen got home.

From what I gathered from the brief conversation we had before the rehearsal, Brittney didn't know yet. But she was close to learning the truth.

Try as I might to function like I didn't, I needed Brittney. She was my favorite drug ever, and without her, I was lost.

In a numb haze, I went through the motions of the day. Hello, Grandma and Grandpa. Did I even say anything to them?

Grandpa tugged on my shaggy hair. "You need a haircut, son."

"Oh, leave the boy alone, Vern. He doesn't look like he feels well. Here, I have something in my purse you can have." Then she offered me a Tums that looked like it had been rolling around in the bottom of her purse for at least six years.

Did I say a word before walking away?

Tyler slapped my shoulder. "You look like shit, love."

"I feel like shit, babe."

He straightened my tie. "Can I tell you a secret?"

"Are you going to tell me whether I like it or not?"

He laughed. "Yes. Here it is: Fake it."

I stared at him, and he had the audacity to wink at me. "What?" I gasped.

"Fake it or get the fuck over it."

"Dude, leave me…" I tried to jerk away, but he caught my shoulders so I was forced to look at his serious green scowl. "If you can't get over it, you fake it. No one gives a shit that you're having a bad day or that your chest feels like a landmine went off inside your body. No one cares, so put on that sexy smile I know you got and pretend. Believe me, it works."

So I smiled. And I faked it.

Just before the bells rang, the door of the church opened and she slipped inside. She was here. Holy mother f-word she was here. (She'd been on me to sensor myself, especially in church.)

She wouldn't let me down. She didn't know how to disappoint.

Ashleigh and Dad did their thing. There were rings…oh yeah, the ring. I pulled it out of my jacket and handed the silver band to Dad.

Couldn't stop looking at *her*, though. She was my focal point. Her cheeks were bright red. She stared at something in her lap the entire wedding, and after it was over, I didn't even wait for Dad and Ashleigh to leave before running over and falling down next to her.

The numb ache in my chest receded the second her strawberry scent hit my nostrils. It was better than any line I'd ever snorted. "What happened?"

She shrugged. "Gwen was in my bedroom when I woke up this morning. She was very cryptic and said we'd talk more later. She didn't specify when *later*, so I waited a couple hours. She never came back. I'm sure I'll be in trouble when I get home, but I don't want to think about that now."

Me either. For now, we were still us. I pinched two of my fingers together and swooped them toward my heart. *Are you okay?*

She smiled. Her head nod was accompanied by our sign. *Yes.*

I should do it. Right now. Give her the open hand, flat against my chest. *I love you.* It was now or never.

"Did I miss anything good last night?" she asked.

I'd waited too long. I cleared my throat and blinked. "Uh, no. Not really. Last night sucked. Today's better cuz you're here." I brushed her long hair behind her ear, and she caught my hand, sliding her fingers into mine.

Damn, she felt good.

"Good."

There was a small scowl in the corner of her mouth. I thought about reaching up and rubbing it away with my thumb. No sooner than I thought about it, she half-smiled. "We should make the most of it. I know my brother can be a real pain sometimes, Barry, but he's too old to be sent off for adoption, so we may just have to put up with him. I love you, and I want this to work."

"Me too," I said, kissing the back of her hand.

But I knew I was lying to the both of us.

You're gonna dump me, Britt. The second you find out what I've done, you're gone. Because I was selfish enough to absorb as much time with her as I could before the end, I asked, "Want to prove how much you love me and come dance at a, probably, shitty reception?"

Her nose wrinkled. "That depends. Did you pick out the band?"

"Nope. Dad did."

She started to smile, and I added, "but we have the same taste in music. The lead guitarist has a beer gut and hair-metal hair."

Her eyes rolled.

I thought the music rocked.

Ashleigh, Brittney, and everyone else did not.

There wasn't much slow dancing, but when the music slowed down and the band did a cover of Cyndi Lauper's "Time after Time," everyone flew onto the floor to milk what they could of the moment.

I'd never been one for dancing. Swinging my hips from side to side was about the extent of my *moves*. Brittney was smooth, and even though we barely moved, she had such rhythm that she covered my lack of talent. Holding her so tightly I wasn't sure she could breath normally, I refused to release her. I felt like I was standing at the edge of a cliff, and if I let go of her, I'd fall off.

"Are you okay?" I whispered in her ear.

"I don't know."

Swallowing hard, I forced myself to push it. "What's up?"

"Why doesn't Gwen like you?" she asked with her eyes pinched tight. She didn't want to do this anymore than me.

I was glad to have a second to compose my face.

I could lie about everything and then be the asshole, and a liar, when the truth came out. Because it would—there was no doubt about that now. Or I could tell the truth, and just be an asshole. "She took my virginity. A long, long, long time ago. It happened at a party, beginning of my freshman year. She must have been a junior."

Exhaling sharply, she nodded. "Okay."

Okay. *Okay.* That was it? She couldn't give me any more to work with than *okay*. "You mad?"

She let out another breath. "No, I wish you had told me sooner, but it's okay."

It's okay. "We're okay?"

She nodded.

"Sign it for me."

Her eyes rolled. She gave me our private sign for *yes.* "Really?" I asked. "Jeez, Britt, that was really bugging me. I thought you'd never want to kiss the guy that lost it to your future sister-in-law." A weight lifted off my shoulders, leaving me feeling light as a feather. I was doing the moonwalk off a cliff, and if Britt asked, I was pretty sure I could bench press her right about now.

"It's okay, Barry. I knew you weren't perfect when we got together. I can't hold that against you now."

"You're perfect," I whispered. I opened my mouth to say those three little words, but, of course, the song cut off. I'd been a half of a breath away from being the jackass who yelled over the non-music to tell a girl he loved her.

Kissing the back of her hand as an excuse to touch my mouth to her skin, I held onto her and led her back to the table.

Of my friends, Tyler and Bo and Gage were all here. It was okay because I didn't hardly miss Chase. Except the table had been set for all of us, and there was an empty seat for him and his ambitiously added plus-one. There were a lot of empty seats since the only one of them to bring a plus-one, besides me, was Gage.

Lonna, however, didn't seem in the best of moods. We were all avoiding her, hoping she didn't flip on us. Especially since Tyler asked her if she was ragging and she slapped him.

I held out Brittney's chair, and she slid gracefully into it.

"This blows," Gage mumbled.

"What're you talking about?" Tyler tried, not for the first time. "Free booze."

"Keep your voice down, would you? My dad doesn't know you guys are drinking." Under the table I caught Brittney's knee and pulled her leg toward mine. Her body followed and those long arms wrapped around my arm.

"Holy shit," Bo exhaled. He stood, face frozen in shock, with his palms braced on the table in front of him.

"Oh God," Tyler added. "Bare, run."

They were directly across the table from me and Brittney. She caught on before me, and twisted to see the doorway. "Toby?" she gasped.

Not exactly what I wanted to talk about, but if she insisted... "What about him?"

"Dude, run," Tyler repeated. "We'll create a diversion to buy you some time."

I turned in my chair to see what they were talking about. Sure enough, standing under the paper-flower archway, at my dad's wedding reception, was a very pissed off Toby Wilson. He'd gotten bigger—broader in the shoulders.

He stomped my direction. Gwen followed closely behind him trying to grab his elbow, but he kept shrugging away from her.

I looked around the room at all the oblivious faces. They were about to watch me get my ass handed to me, and they wouldn't even know why.

"Nobody fight him," I said to my friends.

Tyler's jaw worked back and forth. "What, are you serious? Man, I don't think you're seeing things clearly. That's a very pissed off Marine coming this way, and as much as I love you, you're not a fighter. You don't stand a snowball's chance—"

"Nobody," I growled.

I had to prove what she meant to me. I had to make a stand without them jumping in. I could hear that line from *Romeo and Juliet*.

Brittney had read it to me this summer on one of those hot summer days we'd spent down at the creek. Tybalt was trying to get Romeo to fight, and Romeo didn't want to. The day Brittney read it, I remembered it, thinking that this was an imminent future:

"I do protest I never injured thee; but love thee better than thou canst devise.

Till thou shalt know the reason of my love; and so, good Capulet—which name I tender as dearly as my own—be satisfied."

∝

I met him halfway across the dance floor with Brittney on my tail. "Toby what're you—"

"Quiet Brittney," he snapped. His lip curled in disgust as he looked me over.

We probably could have had it out right there if his dad and my dad didn't both join us. We must have looked like a crossroads, the four of us meeting there. Toby's head fell back as he exhaled. "Father, I just want to talk to him."

"What are you doing here? You're supposed—"

"I know; I'll explain. Just let me talk to *him*."

And of course, my dad was giving me that all too familiar *what have you done now* glare.

"You had to crash my dad's wedding to talk to me?"

"Yes," Toby hissed. "Outside. Your friends can come if they'd like, though I'm sure they will without my permission."

He was right. They followed. Even though I told them not to interfere, I worried they would. "Just let me handle this," I repeated.

Tyler nodded, but he had his arms crossed across his chest and his brows narrowed. I mean, in a way it was reassuring. I wouldn't get hurt *too badly* before the guys stopped Toby. In other words, I wouldn't die.

With my head held high, I followed the Marine to meet my fate. There wasn't even a small voice inside my brain that tried to tell me this wasn't worth it. Dealing with Toby was a necessary evil I'd have to deal with to have what I wanted, and I did want her.

More than anything.

"I can explain—"

His knuckles crunched into my nose.

I saw red. Blood blurred in my vision and poured down my throat. "Toby!" Brittney screamed. Her fingers pulled at my hands, as she tried to see the damage. "Why would you do that? He was going to talk to you!"

Then she was gone. Ripped away from me, and I couldn't do a damn thing about it. He pointed right at my face. "You stay the fuck away from my sister."

Holy shit. That had hurt so much worse than I remembered. *Come on, Prescott. Come on, pussy.* I spat out a blood-loogie and wiped the never-ending cascade of liquid falling from my nose.

Brittney was crying. The sound of her broken sobs hurt worse than the pain in my face. "You're being ridiculous. You can't keep me from him. I love him. You have to let it go. So he hooked up with Gwen? So what?"

There was a loud smacking sound—flesh harassing flesh. It took a full second for me to realize he'd backhanded her.

I watched the whole thing happen in real time, but I couldn't process what he'd done to my Brittney because I never dreamed he'd hit her. That's how pissed I could make the perfect Christian. It was a gift, I guess.

Blood boiled inside my veins. "You mother…"

Arms went around my torso, pulling me backward. He *hit* her, and my friends had the nerve to *hold me* back. Fuck that. Like hell I'd stand here and watch that shit. No one would *ever* hurt her. She didn't deserve it. "Let go! Tyler, let me go. Bo, I'm serious. I'm gonna destroy him."

Brittney stood dazed, her cheek in her hand. Toby rubbed over her shoulders. Soothing her. Or, hell, I didn't know. Maybe he was preparing her for the next whack.

"I'm sorry," he whispered. His lips drew into a hard line. "Brittney, I'm sorry. You know I'd never hurt you, but you cannot say that about what he did. They didn't 'hook-up.' He raped her." Grabbing her roughly now, he shook her, like he was knocking sense into her. "What he did to the future mother of my children was *rape*." Dropping Brittney, he pointed a finger back at me.

Wait. He was pointing at *me*.

❧

For a full minute, no one moved. I don't think anyone even breathed. "Wha...me?" I gasped. "You're talking about *me*?"

He was actually standing there lying his ass off to Brittney, and I was too stunned to defend myself.

Gwen snorted in disbelief. Was she seriously in on this, too? I guess she hated me that much.

"Oh," Brittney's small voice trembled.

Oh?

Oh.

   Oh.

      Oh.

         Oh.

            Oh.

               Oh.

How had I never realized the implications of that word? *Oh.* I studied her, still struggling to find my own voice. I watched her as she absorbed those words, and then *believed* them.

"Brittney, tell me you don't buy that horseshit."

She did. She didn't have to say it. Those beautiful hazel eyes pulsed with anger. I'd never seen her like that before. Raw rage flashed across her angelic face. "Britt," I gasped, clawing at Tyler, trying to break free from his grasp. "Please."

Her palm went out. Fingers splayed.

No.

No.

No.

She made a fist.

This could not be happening. Not like this. Not when I didn't even do anything wrong. "Listen to me. This isn't real. They're…"

The fist thrust into the air.

Goodbye. For. Good.

They're lying, Britt, baby. They're lying about me.

My heart shattered into a million tiny pieces. The shards stabbed into my chest and my lungs and suddenly breathing was the hardest thing I'd ever done.

The deal was that I'd let her go. If she gave me the fist, then I'd let her go, no questions asked.

It wasn't fair, though. She didn't know the truth. She didn't even know my side. My girl couldn't just walk away like that. She *wouldn't*. She didn't disappoint people. She didn't disappoint *me*.

"Get out of here," Toby said, kissing the top of her strawberry head. "Go with Gwen. Go home."

And that's exactly what she did.

"Britt…" I tried to follow her. I called after her, but every time I said her name, something pierced the already aching hollow of my ribcage.

"Hey!" Toby pushed me back against my friends. They all cringed away *from me*. All of them. Like they were scared of *me*. "I told you years ago to stay away from her."

"Yeah, you…Jesus, Toby I never took you for such a massive son of a bitch. What, you thought she'd never dump me so you had to lie to her?"

His eyes narrowed. "Lie? It's a lie that Gwen drank too much, woke up with you on top of her, and couldn't get you to stop? I'm sorry, where I grew up, that's rape." His hands went up as he took a step away from me. Nose wrinkling in disgust, he snorted. "Wait, I'm not sorry. I will never be sorry to you."

His shoulders trembled, and I knew he wanted to hit me again. Hell, I *wanted* him to hit me. I wanted to feel something other than this ache in my torso.

He let out a throaty sound, showing his revulsion before spinning on his heel.

I stared after him in awe. Toby wasn't lying.

At least, he didn't *think* it was a lie. That was obvious by his repulsion. He truly believed I'd raped her.

That's not how it happened with Gwen, though. It's not. We…I…it…

I didn't do that. I know I didn't. We were both drunk; we went too far. That's it. End of story.

Tyler's hand clapped my arm, and I startled. "Whoa, whoa bud." His hands went up in surrender. His forced smile didn't convince.

I saw the look in his eyes. He was scared of me. Trying to play it off, he laughed lightly. "That was shit, huh? Bitches, man."

"Don't," I snapped.

"Alright, okay." He took a small step backward.

"Bare," Bo started. "You didn't…"

"Of course he didn't," Tyler defended, even if he didn't believe it himself. "Barry wouldn't do that. Toby's full of shit."

My stomach rolled, and the agony inside my torso rippled outward, gripping every appendage and tearing me to fucking pieces.

"I gotta get outta here. I can't be here." Every step I took away from that spot made it feel so permanent.

She'd left me.

She didn't trust me. One sentence, and her faith was shattered.

Fucking cunt. I didn't know if I was mad at Brittney or that lying whore, Gwen, or the whole world. My fist slammed against the wheel of the Charger. Over and over and over and over, I hit the thing.

I wasn't ever doing this again. It was my fault for letting my guard down. I should have known this would happen. It had happened to Tyler, and he was better than me, so of course it happened.

I drove around, ignoring my phone buzzing in the passenger seat. I'd already gone by Brody's and had snagged a twenty sack and enough Percocet to kill me. I hadn't decided yet if I was going to kill myself. It seemed stupid just to end my otherwise normal life over a girl.

Except, there was a nagging voice in the back of my mind that wouldn't shut the hell up: *I don't remember everything from that night all those years ago. I barely remember anything.*

I tried to ignore the harassing. I tried to pretend it wasn't my voice. Nothing helped. Maybe once I was stoned or once I popped a couple pills…I couldn't do that either because, no matter if she walked away, I knew how disappointed she'd be in me.

I pulled my car down by the river and killed the engine.

My eyes closed, but I didn't sleep. The sky opened up and rain poured down, but I barely heard it.

I couldn't stop thinking about Brittney's face. She'd looked broken. Destroyed. Devastated.

I'd done that to her. I'd caused that. All because I couldn't remember. *Or maybe Gwen was a shit-starting skank.* Okay, okay, I was going to try. Just once. Try and remember what had happened with her.

It was the week of homecoming my freshman year. We'd won the game, and there was a massive party at the House. It was my first

House party. I was stoned, and I'd taken six or seven shots of whatever Logan—the junior fullback—had handed me. I didn't want to look like I couldn't handle it, but my vision blurred.

Everyone was dancing. The music was really shitty, but I danced to it anyway. Then there she was. Not Gwen. It was her friend, Beth. They were juniors too, and Logan told me they were both off limits.

Yeah, because I followed rules. Even *then* I knew nothing about limits. I threw my arm around Beth's neck.

Oh shit, she scowled. Was she mad? "What's the matter, babe?"

Her painted finger jabbed toward the table. Gwen Mason was topless with a lacy purple bra, dancing to no music. "She's totally wasted and won't get her ass down."

"Want me to get her down?" I asked, smiling and winking. The alcohol made both my eyes close. Shit. I didn't want to look like an amateur drunk. I forced them open again.

Beth smiled. "Sure, handsome."

I liked that, being handsome to someone like Beth Hardy. Honestly, I'd probably do whatever she wanted, but if it was simple like dragging another skinny cheerleader off a table, then no problem. Gwen fell into my arms and giggled. Her finger bopped my nose. I gnashed at it. "Watch it, Gwen." Suddenly, I forgot all about Beth. Gwen had crazy honey-brown eyes that made me want to dive into them. Holy shit she was hot.

"It's my birthday!" she yelled over the music.

"Oh yeah?" I teased, leaning in to smell the sickly sweet alcohol and perfume lacing her petite body.

"Yeah! What'd you get me?"

That was it. Everything blurred. I had no clue what had happened after that or how we'd ended up upstairs. The next thing I knew, it was after four in the morning, and we were both naked on a dirty mattress in one of the upstairs bedrooms.

I'd put my pants on and walked home. The only reason I knew

we'd had sex was because I'd still been wearing the condom, and Toby had kicked my ass, and…okay, there were a few bits and pieces of memories from being upstairs. Just little glimpses, nothing definitive.

Still, I tried, again, to remember, focusing this time on the very vague—blurry—image of inside the room.

We'd kissed. She'd kissed me back. My obnoxious hormones had me fumbling over the top of her shirt. Both hands over both of her boobs. She kept giggling, which had killed the mood.

Then nothing. Nada. Zip.

Dammit.

It was almost sunrise when I finally gave up trying to remember and went home. I stashed the drugs in the glove compartment for when I was ready for them. It was inevitable. Without Brittney, I needed something to make me *feel*, but I couldn't admit to myself that I'd lost her yet.

I knew it was true, but sometimes lies were easier to swallow than the truth.

Good thing I didn't take anything, because Dad was waiting with a drug test. My chin dropped against my chest. "Are you serious?"

"Dead serious." He looked it, too, still wearing his tux from the wedding, the bow tie loose and shirt buttons undone.

"You don't have any clue the night I've had," I mumbled.

"I spent my wedding night worried my son was doped up in a ditch somewhere. What did you do, Bare?"

I cringed. "Brittney dumped me."

He had the decency to, at least, look saddened. Letting out a heavy sigh, he said, "Yeah, I figured." Then he shook the piss cup at me. "Which is why you're getting tested."

"Whatever."

I passed the test, surprise, surprise. Then I went up to my room to lie on my bed and not sleep.

TWENTY FOUR

BRITTNEY ANN

My heart had imploded. Watching my family tear into each other in a way they never had before made me feel unbelievably weak. I'd only ever seen Daddy this angry one time; the booze gave him a temper.

This time, it was my stupidity making him pace the floor, clenching and unclenching his fists. The muscles of his arms rippled from his fury. "You knew?" he seethed. "You knew that a *rapist* was going to school…going to *church* with my daughter, and you didn't report him. How could you? Both of you?"

He didn't discriminate against Gwen. She was part of the family, so she was included in Daddy's wrath. Her head tucked in shame. "I told you, Mitch. I came to you for counseling; I told you someone had—"

"Someone," he snapped. "You never said who it was. You never said he was younger than you, and he'd still be there once you left the school. You never warned Brittney that when she was on the away ball bus, for hours at a time, there was a *rapist* on the football team."

Every time he said the word, the cavern inside my chest got bigger.

"I welcomed that boy into our home. I let your sister go places *alone* with him. What if he'd hurt her? Huh? Did either of you even care about that?"

Toby's shoulders straightened defensively. "Of course we care. When Gwen finally told me what happened, I was furious, Father, but she was convinced that he wasn't a run-of-the-mill lunatic, but an idiot who'd taken advantage of a bad situation. We decided not to say anything, mostly because she couldn't bring herself to come forward. He was popular, and his family has money. She didn't want to be the girl who cried rape, and I would never have made her.

"But I asked Brittney…no, I *told* Brittney Ann to stay away from him. It was the only thing I cared about when I left. Keeping her away from those boys, especially *him*—that was my priority. It still is. I told you to keep her away from him."

Daddy bristled. "Don't you put this off on me. You don't tell me what to do. I'm your father. If you'd given me a good enough reason, I sure as hell wouldn't have let her go anywhere with him. I assumed you were holding on to a grudge because of something that happened on the field. How was I supposed to know he violated Gwen? I wouldn't have even guessed that."

Violated. Barry, how could you?

I stood up, my body swaying slightly as my knees questioned whether or not to hold me. Daddy caught my shoulder. "It's okay, princess. Don't be worried. I won't ever let him hurt you."

"I'm not worried."

Toby snorted. "That's the problem, Britt. You don't think. Even if he hadn't attacked Gwen, you should have been a little smarter about yourself. His reputation should have been enough to keep you away."

"I'm sorry," I slurred.

He groaned apologetically. "I know you are. I know you didn't mean to do anything that might have gotten you hurt, and I'm glad he didn't touch you. I don't really feel up to spending the rest of my life in prison, so I guess it's good for me, too. And him. But, Britt, come on. You're not a little kid anymore. The next time I ask you to do something, please remember that I'm not just being a jerk. I'm looking out for you."

"I get it. I made a big mistake. It won't happen again." Because I was never, ever, ever giving my heart away again. I didn't have any heart left to give. "I'm going to my room."

"Britt…" Toby groaned, throwing his head back in exasperation. "Don't be upset for him. He doesn't get that from you."

"Let her go," Gwen suggested. "Sometimes a girl just needs alone time."

I felt their eyes on me as I walked out of the living room. Mom was upstairs nervously re-folding all the linens in the linen closet. She took one look at me, and her calm exterior dissolved. "Oh baby," she cried. Her iron-tight grip wrapped around my arms.

"I'm fine, Mom. Really. He never hurt me."

"I know he didn't," she said.

"You do?"

"Of course I do. Come with me." She grabbed my hand and led me into my own bedroom. Mom situated herself on top of the quilt she'd stitched for me when I was born. I never slept with it, but every morning I threw it over my bed, giving it a place of honor. I sat on top of it feeling unworthy of all this attention. We needed to be talking to Gwen. She was the one who needed sympathy.

What I needed was to curl into a ball and disappear. I was

embarrassed that I'd fallen for his trap, again, and now my family insisted on talking about it.

"Can you imagine the man your father was when I met him? He was vile. He had absolutely no respect for anyone. All he cared about was his next fix and whatever slut he could con into his bed."

My mom just said "slut."

"Oh, close your mouth, Britt. It's not that surprising. I wasn't always a preacher's wife. Dad and I made a commitment to the Lord. It was the only way to save him from himself. When he came to me and promised he'd do whatever it took just to be with me, I never dreamed he meant it. I told him he got one chance. One. If I ever found out he was using, I would leave him. Of course, things change when you're married. You know as well as I do that your father took that one chance, and I still forgave him."

I never even gave that to Barry. He got so much more trust than he deserved. He was probably laughing at me the whole time, knowing that he was getting away with being an addict behind my back.

I wondered if the withdrawals were even real. Had he staged that, too?

The sky outside my window opened up and poured down on the fields. There were bright flashes of lightning and clatters of thunder. Storms used to scare me. Not tonight. My body couldn't afford to feel any more tonight.

"I'm happy it worked out for you, Mom." My voice was as hollow as my body.

"Brittney, sweetheart, don't you understand? Your father was a terrible man. He did terrible things. One time he was so zonked out of it, he didn't even remember going to Uncle Chuck's birthday party. I had to tell him all about it. That had been the final straw for me. That was when I gave him the ultimatum."

"Does this have something to do with Barry?" I asked. "Is there something you're trying to say? I'm not getting it. My head hurts really badly, and I just can't think about this right now, so please, just say it."

She sucked back a sigh as she hid her sympathy. "What do you want to bet that there are nights in Barry's past that he simply doesn't remember?"

My jaw dropped. "You're defending him?"

Her palm flattened on her chest, covering her heart. "Heavens no. I would never defend what happened to Gwen. I think it's awful. But there are always two sides to every story." She brushed my hair behind my ear, giving me a sympathetic look. "I'm sad for you, Brittney Ann. I know how much he meant to you, and even if he doesn't remember what he did to her, it doesn't change the fact he did it. To someone you love, no less."

After pecking my forehead, she stood up. "What do you want to bet there are nights in Gwen's past she doesn't remember, also?"

What the heck was I supposed to make of that?

&

My bed was uncomfortable. I was too cold. The pillow was too hard.

No matter the reason, the result was the same: I could not sleep.

What in the world had I done to make Barry Prescott hate me? So much that he would go to such lengths to hurt me. I didn't think I was a bad person. I hadn't done anything to him personally.

Could his issues all have been about Gwen? He was still mad?

About what? That Toby had beaten him up a couple times. Of course Toby did. Even Barry should have realized something like that would happen.

I rolled over and tried, again, to squeeze my eyes and block out the loud clatter of thunder outside. No dice. The alarm clock, with the neon-green glow, said two-forty-five.

He'd just seemed so sincere with me. He'd held onto me and kissed me with such a gentle touch that...no, no I couldn't do this. It was all a lie. He'd been playing a trick on me, and I'd fallen for it.

Was it all about sex? He was going to take my virginity and then mock me? Or mock Toby for having gotten revenge by hurting his little sister, too. Maybe he'd tell the whole school how easy sleeping with me had been.

But...well, I'm not defending him or anything, but he could have done it. That first night, down at the river. He could have at least *tried* to touch me. Everything would have ended right then.

So, wait. He didn't want to sleep with me. He couldn't have.

Of course he didn't. I was still me, and he was still Barry Prescott. Despite his cruel sense of humor, I wasn't in his league. I was playing T-ball, and he was batting in the majors.

The sun rose and my eyes were still open. Puffy and swollen, but open.

☙

It rained for days. I took it as Mother Nature's way of agreeing that the world sucked.

On Monday, Toby insisted on driving me to cheerleading practice. "Want me to wait outside?"

"No." My voice was still a hollow monotone. I'd been meaning to work on that. Clearing my throat, I forced myself to sound more chipper. "No, I'm fine." I succeeded at sounding fake.

He tugged on the end of my ponytail. "If he tries to talk to you, or if he does anything that upsets you, just call me. You hear?"

I nodded.

A growl tore from his throat. "Come on, Britt. I know you're upset, but don't beat yourself up about this. The guy's an asshole, and you got caught in the middle. I hate seeing you so worked up. You didn't even leave your room yesterday. When was the last time you ate?"

I couldn't remember. Suffering from a broken heart was, apparently, the most miserable ailment known to man—at least, it was the worst thing that had ever happened to me.

"Okay." He scowled. "Just promise you're going to start taking care of yourself. I can't go back to California knowing you're this miserable. It's not right."

Oh great. Way to remind me that in addition to losing Barry, I was about to lose my brother, too. He would only be home for a couple weeks. Then he and Gwen were renting a U-Haul for all of her things since she was leaving, too. For good.

"I'll be back at noon." His voice sounded as concerned as he looked.

I nodded again. My nervous heart beat so hard and fast I wondered if Toby could hear it or if the pounding made the whole car shake the way my chest vibrated.

Because of the rain, both the team and the squad crammed into the gym. I guess I'd been wrong about Mother Nature. Apparently, she was just a meddling brat.

He stood in a crowd of his friends. They huddled around him. Their position looked defensive. I couldn't be sure, because other than Tyler's scowling, none of them looked at me.

Fine. I didn't want him staring at me. I didn't need him. I took a deep, shaky breath. *I don't need him.*

"You okay, girl?" Katy Lynn put an arm over my shoulder.

I shrank beneath her touch. "Fine. I don't want to talk about it."

"I just can't believe it. He's so cute. Why would he *rape* her? It doesn't make any sense. Have you talked to him?"

"No." I forced my voice to stay calm. "I don't want to talk about it."

"Yeah, I understand. We're all just so shocked, you know? Like he could have had anyone—"

"Katy, please."

"Leave her alone."

I cringed. Without a doubt, I'd rather put up with Katy's arduous questioning than face *her*.

Madison's shiny black hair was pulled back in a sleek ponytail. Yet, she apparently felt the need to arch her back—presenting her full, bubbly breasts—as she smoothed non-existent flyways.

"Madison." I nodded, only acknowledging her to be polite. Trying to push past her so I could go stretch wasn't possible. Those *boobs* were everywhere. They brushed my arm.

The worst image flashed through my mind.

He suckled on her nipple, biting it gently between his tongue and upper teeth. Those emerald eyes never left hers. He drank in every moan she made, loving the way she squirmed for him. Her back arched as she tore into his onyx hair, pulling him closer to her chest. Heat flooded between her legs.

Why was I torturing myself with this? Of course Barry had done to Madison the things he'd done with me. *I. Wasn't. Special.* Not to him. Not to Ryan. Not to anyone.

Once I got my first cat, I'd be well on my way to my future as a cat lady. Or a bag lady. Or a librarian. No matter what, I was headed toward spinster-hood.

"Barry didn't rape Gwen," Madison said matter-of-factly. "If you think that, then you really don't deserve him. He's an asshole, and he's selfish a lot of the time. But there's no way he would ever force himself on someone. Pull your head out of your ass. He's not the monster you're making him out to be."

Yeah, well…well… I stared down at my white cheer shoes. "Gwen wouldn't lie," I squeaked.

"I don't give a damn what Gwen would and wouldn't do. She was drunk. She doesn't remember. I'm telling you about Barry. He's the one I know. He's the one you're blaming, and you're wrong."

What if she was right? What if Barry really hadn't done anything wrong? Gwen already admitted she'd been drinking.

No. I wouldn't let his side of the story convince me that he was anything less than what he was. *A. Bad. Guy.* My heart thumped against my sternum. A very hard, painful *thump*. I didn't really believe he was *bad*, did I?

Then, a voice that sounded eerily like my own resonated inside my mind.

No.

◌◌

Toby dropped me off at practice the next morning as well. Because of the rain, I hunched over myself, trying to keep warm. Something soft fell over my shoulders. A jacket. I stiffened before realizing the smell of the jacket was unfamiliar—woodsy.

Wes Thurmond stood beside me. "You good?" he asked, smiling crookedly around his purchased, straight pearls.

I nodded, exhaling in relief. Wes was by no means a nice guy. He was, however, better than some alternatives. At least, I thought he was. *Maybe I should ask Gwen if she knows him personally?*

I rubbed my fingers over my eyes. Where the heck had that thought come from? It almost sounded like I was angry with Gwen, of all people. I wasn't angry with her *at all*. She was the victim in all this.

Glancing back up at Wes, he was still smiling at me.

He shook his head like a dog, trying to get rid of the water in his coifed locks. "Haven't seen you much this summer, Britt. How've things been?"

"Fine," I mumbled.

"Yeah? I heard you and Barry broke up. That sucks. But, honestly, if you want my opinion…" he nudged my shoulder with his own. "I never saw that working out. Barry's easily distracted."

Because I asked for your opinion. I didn't tell him my thoughts because…well, I was me. Too nice, Brittney Ann Wilson. I smiled kindly, and he returned the gesture.

Wes and I were in the same grade. It would be a lie to say he hadn't grown, very nicely, out of that awkward, gangly, middle school faze. Girls loved him. Not me. I still remembered the time he'd peed his pants in first grade.

The doors opened behind us, and I just happened to look back. I swallowed my heart in time to watch all five of them walk in together.

They were so busy stomping their feet on the ground and brushing their wet hair, they didn't even see us. Not right away. When Barry finally looked up, his eyes narrowed.

Wes's hand pressed against my back. He was still touching me.

I shrugged out of his jacket and handed it back to him with a quick, "thanks." There was no reason for me to feel so guilty. I hadn't done anything wrong. I was single. I could touch, and be touched, by whomever I wanted.

Why, then, did I feel so stinking guilty? I wanted to yell at Barry to wipe that hurt look off his face. He had no right. He just…*ugh.*

⌒

Toby stood under the awning. "I could have met you at the car."

"Come on." He caught my upper arm and pulled me.

"Hey, what's…?" Then I saw it.

In the middle of the west parking lot, Tyler and Bo were punching someone. Barry leaned back against Bo's car with his head tilted toward the sky. Rain drizzled onto his beautiful face. I took a step toward him out of instinct, and then my aching chest reminded me that my instincts sucked.

"What on earth? Who…? What're they doing?"

"I don't know. I don't know the kid. It's not my problem. If I go break it up, I'll probably wind up killing Prescott, and Gwen said she wouldn't marry me if I actually killed him, so let's go."

"Kid? They're hitting a kid?"

He shook his head, his expression tight. "No, he was…I don't know, maybe your age."

Toby pulled me toward the east lot. Just before rounding the corner, I caught another look at them. Barry faced me now. His expression blank. Eyes empty.

On the ground, beneath Tyler and Bo, was a very familiar looking jacket. I couldn't see who was wearing it, but I didn't have to. Because I knew exactly how that jacket smelled. Woodsy. And I had a vague flash of the time Wes Thurmond had wet himself in first grade.

TWENTY FIVE

 BARRY

One more day of this, then I'll be rolling a fat fucking joint and swallowing a handful of painers. Maybe two handfuls.

My mantra. I repeated it every day. Somehow, the next day I was strong enough not to succumb. But it wouldn't last. I could feel myself sliding off a very slippery ledge. Dad and Ashleigh were on their honeymoon in Italy. Because of my summer's worth of good behavior, I was home alone. I wondered how long it would take before someone found me passed out, stoned out of my mind, in the middle of the living room. *One more day...*

Wednesday was the fifth day of rainy, gloomy weather. The fifth day since I'd touched her. Five miserably long days since I'd tasted her lips.

She didn't even look at me anymore.

Trust me, I was watching her. My friends all had different suggestions on how to get her back.

Gage: Don't bother. There are hotter, easier girls.

Chase: Well, he didn't have a suggestion because he was gay and didn't know how to handle girls.

Bo: Try and talk to her. Convince her that what had happened couldn't have been as bad as Toby had implied.

Tyler: Kidnap her. Tie her to a chair and do dirty, naughty things to her body until she screamed my name and realized she couldn't live without me.

I was more leaning toward Bo's suggestion, but I hadn't ruled Tyler's out.

There was a loud crash as a branch broke through one of the windows above the bleachers. Glass and water and tree debris rained into the gym. The girls, who'd been under the window, all screamed.

A couple of the guys acted like they wanted to help. I thought about it. I thought, *I should go check on Brittney*. Then remembered that she'd probably yell bloody murder if I went near her. I waited for her to look up at me so I could signal our *okay* sign. She didn't look my way. I stayed back and let people better than me help.

Of course, Collin Parker was one of the good ones. If the gym weren't cast in a grayish darkness, causing everyone to freeze, he probably would have made it all the way across the room to save all the girls and clean up the fucking mess. *Brown nosing douchebag.*

God, I hated everything.

"Alright, alright." Carmine blew into his whistle. "Practice is over."

My head perked up. I didn't hate that.

Then came the low, howling hum of the siren. I threw a look at Tyler, whose brows narrowed. Neither of us knew what to do.

Or maybe we were waiting for someone to announce that the tornado siren was a joke.

Arms wide, Coach swooped in a circular motion—a signal to move our asses. "What the hell you waiting on? Get into the basement."

Tyler moved first, his shoe squeaking against the floor. He took a step toward the girls, hesitated when he saw what he was looking for, and then turned back to the door.

My heart raged inside my ears. The town tornado siren was going off, and we were in the sturdiest building in Bourbon, but we still shouldn't risk it by staying above ground.

Something shoved into my shoulder, and I startled back to reality. I turned to run. "Bare?" Tyler's hand wrapped around my wrist. "I've got him," he yelled back above the crowd of stampeding football players.

"Tyler?" Bo spoke calmly, but it was a forced calm. He didn't have to worry about Chase and Gage because they were already in the basement lifting weights.

Tyler, Bo, and myself were on the fast track to being the first ones in there with them. We'd have our pick of where to sit. We'd all be safe. Gage and Chase and Tyler and Bo and…and…and…no.

No.

No.

No.

I scanned the tops of the heads. She was taller than most of the girls. Her unmistakable hair should have stood out easily. But she didn't. Instead, I saw Annie's red hair and Madison's black hair and even Charli's brown hair.

Fuck.

No.

No.

No.

I broke away from Tyler. Turning on one foot, I spun back toward the gym. I'd had to duck under Coach's arm just to get back down the hall.

The echoing sound of Tyler calling after me, "Barry, what the…?" was the last thing I heard before rounding the hallway toward the gym. Light filtered through the air with a greenish hue. Even the blue lockers were tinged chartreuse.

There was no noise. No thunder. No rain. The silence was so much louder than any storm could ever be.

The quiet whispered: I'm coming for you.

It teased: You can't hide.

It taunted: She's all mine.

I slid into the rain-splattered gym. Scrambling to stand, I darted toward her. She was crouched over, cupping her bloody ankle. A piece of glass had nicked her.

"I fell," she cried, her amber eyes blinking up at me. "I fell and everyone…" her lower lip trembled. "They all left."

I scooped under her knees and pulled her up against me. "I'm not going to hurt you," I whispered into her ear.

"What? Oh, I know." Her eyes widened after she admitted it, and then she blinked up at me. Her body relaxed into mine. *She caved.* "I know, Barry."

We only made it back into the hall when the whole school started shaking. Lowering her to the ground in front of a locker, I wrapped protectively around her—crouched over her on all fours. She didn't scream. She was fearless. But I could feel her heart pounding against my hand.

Boom.

Boom.

Boom.

The noises all stopped, but I didn't let her up. Not for a good, long minute after the building stopped shaking. *Okay?* I signaled.

She nodded. "I'm fine. I…" Her eyes moved back and forth over my face. "Thank you. That was very brave of you."

"You're welcome."

Her ankle was a bloody mess. From the look of it there was no glass in there, but I couldn't be sure. "Let me wrap my shirt around that to stop the bleeding."

"No," she gasped, catching my wrist to stop me. She stared at my arm. "No, don't. Um, it's dirty. I don't want the cut to get infected… or anything. Just…just, don't take your shirt off. Please."

Oh. Right. Yeah, that made sense. My hand wrapped around the blood-covered gash. I had her all alone. Now was the perfect time to tell her. I cleared my throat.

"Don't bother," she whispered.

"Huh?"

"It doesn't really matter what you say. I don't believe you."

Ouch. I rubbed at a hollow ache in my chest. All things considered, this spot really didn't hurt as much as everything else had hurt this week.

"I understand why Gwen never told anyone. I don't think you're dangerous, either, but you did hurt her. You took advantage of a bad situation. So, don't even bother trying to tell me otherwise."

Okay then. Wow. I never took Brittney for a closed-minded bitch, but if the shoe fits…

Internally, I cringed. I was seriously going to kick my own ass for thinking that.

She was not a bitch. She was perfect. I deserved anything she thought of me. Whatever had happened with Gwen—memory aside—I'd had a part in. It *was* my fault I couldn't remember.

But really, I couldn't kick my ass any more than I already was. My whole body already hurt too badly. Nothing I did could make it worse.

"Barry?" Her voice was soft again. "You don't have to keep holding onto my ankle. It doesn't matter. I still won't believe you."

What did keeping her from bleeding to death have to do with her believing me? "You made it pretty clear that you think I'm a dick.

I'm just sorry everything went down the way it did, and if I could go back and undo it all, I sure as hell would. I wouldn't even have let myself get close to you because losing you like this isn't even worth the time I had you."

She flinched.

"I'm sorry," I groaned, smacking my head back against the locker. "Dick, remember?"

"Yeah."

A line of ambulances came to the school. Only three were needed. One for one of the assistant coaches, who'd had a mild heart attack. One for Lonna, who'd put her hand on a piece of glass. One for Britt.

I waited with her while the portly EMT wrapped a bandage around her ankle. Every time she hissed, I imagined what my fist would look like in the fatass's face.

She refused to be taken to the hospital, which resulted in her dad having to come pick her up. Before I realized it, Mitch's large, intimidating hand was on my shoulder. I startled. "I wasn't gonna hurt her," I rushed. "She got hurt, and I waited, and I wanted to make sure she was okay."

Breathing through his nose, eyeing her blood drying on my hands, he asked, "Is she?"

"She doesn't need stitches or anything. It's just a cut."

When his arm came back up to pat between my shoulders, I rightfully flinched. "I'll take it from here, Barry. Good work."

"That's it?" I swallowed hard. Walking away would be nice. Why couldn't I be normal and do that?

"That's it," he said with a decisive nod.

"Did, uh, did Toby…?"

His eyes darkened a shade. "He told me his theories."

"Theories?"

"Are they true?" Mitch asked.

"I don't know," I said. "I can't remember." We were having this conversation in front of Brittney, and I was glad she would know my side, but at the same time, it didn't really change anything. Besides, I was pretty sure she was deliberately not listening. *Stubborn little...*

"Lot of things in this life I can't remember," Mitch said, grabbing my shoulder and twisting me away from his daughter. "My wife reminded me of that the other night. Hell of a thing, that is..."

He nudged me on, and then he turned back toward his daughter. His voice was different, more chipper, when he addressed her. "Can you walk, Brittney Ann, or do you need my help?"

"I can walk," she squeaked.

"Wait," I caught his arm. "Wait a goddamn minute—"

"Now."

I threw my hands up in surrender. "Sorry, uh, just...do you think I *didn't* do it?"

"Don't know. Seems to Gwen you did. That's what matters. Sometimes, Barry, there are two people inside of us. The man we are when we're sober, and the man we are when we're not. We can go on pretending they're the same and that they deserve the same treatment, but it just isn't so."

Did that help me? In any way, would his idiotic self-help bullshit help me get Brittney back and figure this shit out and stop beating myself up wondering if I had raped Gwen? I cringed. That word bothered me.

There weren't many words that made me cringe, but that one did.

Rape and *Retard* and *Faggot* were three words that should have been written on magic pieces of paper then lit on fire and forgotten forever. But if those words were gone, we'd have just found different words that meant the same thing. It wasn't the word but the power behind it that broke our bones.

Still, it didn't seem likely that I could follow through with something when the word itself sent chills right to my spine.

☙

Practice was canceled for the rest of the week, and the start of school was postponed for several weeks. I was left alone in my empty house with too many pain killers and way too much reg. Sitting at my desk for hours, I spun one of the Percocet around and around and around until it skidded off the edge.

Then I took another one out of the baggie and spun it around and around and around. A swirling top of never ending anything.

My addiction was infinite. A nonstop chaotic circle that wasn't going anywhere. I couldn't chase the adrenaline away with the drugs, or the drugs away with the unicorn, or the unicorn away…my palm slammed down hard on the pill.

Why the hell wouldn't she just leave my mind already? She was haunting me. No one had ever disturbed me like this.

Walking away, I knew I wasn't leaving the pill behind forever. Eventually, I'd lose the battle of willpower, and the pills would consume me.

☙

I didn't know what day it was, but the phone rang in the middle of the night, and I shuffled out of bed toward my desk. My phone was plugged in, and the cord didn't reach the bed. I had to sit down in the chair and wipe my eyes before answering Dad's call, "Hello."

"Barry?" If he hadn't sounded alarmed, I'd have given him hell about not trusting me or not learning international time differences.

"Barry, son, are you there?"

"Yeah, Dad, I'm fine. No drugs, I promise. Just sleep."

"No, no, I'm not worried about that. Look…" There was a hissing sound. The call muffled.

"Dad?"

Another hissing sound.

"Dammit! Barry, can…?"

The call disconnected.

I unplugged the phone and carried it downstairs to the kitchen. I yanked a bottle of water from the fridge and had just untwisted the cap when the phone shrieked again. In hindsight, having a Duran Duran song as a ringtone probably wasn't the smartest move. "Yeah?" I answered, killing the bottle of water.

"Barry?" he said in a rush. "It's your mom."

One time I fell backward in the pool; water ran up my nose. It was the same sensation when it flew backward through my septum, too. "What?" I gasped, choking. "What the hell happened?"

"I'm sorry, if I were any closer…yes, sweetheart, it's over there… Barry? She's at the hospital. She overdosed. We're not on a flight un—"

"Is she okay?"

Overdosed? How…what? This was all my fault. I'd not told anyone she'd asked me for those pills. I'd not told anyone how bad her struggle had gotten. I did this. I let this get out of hand.

"She's fine. They're going to send her to a rehab facility, but I'm still her emergency contact. They called the emergency line. The fees are probably going to be through the roof, and…"

"Are you fucking kidding me?" I screamed. My body was shaking as I took the stairs two at a time to get back to my room. I couldn't deal with his shit and focus on *real life problems.*

I had to get dressed. Socks. Shoes. No, no, I needed pants. I needed to get off the phone. "She'll have to pay you back when she's out of rehab, so sorry there are fees."

"Barry, wait, no…"

The phone disconnected as it shattered against the wall.

Now where was I? Pants. Shirt. Shoes. Okay. Keys? The Charger let out an exceptionally evil growl, which I would forever remember.

TWENTY SIX

BRITTNEY ANN

It didn't feel like a dream. Except everything hued in a sickly olive color. The sky, the ground, the Barry—his eyes, his (once) black AC/DC T-shirt, his skinny blue jeans, checkered Converse. It was all green.

And so was my vomit. "I'm so sorry." I tried to speak between heaves.

His fingers twisted into my hair, pulling it out of my face. "You're fine, babe, don't worry about it. You're just a normal teenager."

"Normal?" *Hiccup.* "It's normal to barf on someone's shoes?"

Oh, did he have to smile? Those sparkling emerald eyes obviously stood out against the jade backdrop. *Obviously.* "I don't know. I'm not very good with what's normal," he said. "At least you didn't get drunk and forget losing your virginity."

"I tried to *seduce* you." *Hiccup.*

"That's okay, baby. I won't ever tell a soul."

"Did you know her?" I asked.

"Who?"

"*The girl. The one you woke up next to.*"

"*Uh, yeah. Not very well.*"

"*And you had sex with her?*"

His eyes narrowed. "*Yeah.*"

"*How do you know if you don't remember?*"

"I barely knew her. She was a cheerleader. I woke up with a condom still strapped to my dick, and I bailed. Things were real awkward after that, so I don't like to get so drunk I don't remember anymore."

"Well something good came out of it."

"Except I don't remember the night I lost my virginity."

Everything was green. The dance floor, the flowers, the DJ, the Barry—green eyes, green tux, green Converse. This couldn't be a dream, though. It couldn't. It was all so familiar.

The backs of his fingers brushed along my jaw, pushing back my natural waves. His mouth pressed against my ear. "*Are you okay?*"

No. "*I don't know.*" *Maybe. What the heck was wrong with me? Why couldn't I just get the words out? This was Barry. We were honest with each other. Always.*

His body stiffened. He knew what I couldn't say. "*What's up?*"

My eyes pinched tight. I couldn't look at him when I asked it. "*Why doesn't Gwen like you?*"

"*She took my virginity. A long, long time ago. Beginning of my freshman year, she must have been a junior.*"

Oh. Oh. That was...she took his virginity. Why did it feel like I should have already known this? Maybe because it had been obvious. Not the virginity part. The fact that Barry and Gwen had history.

Everything made so much more sense now.

I refused to allow myself to feel jealous. That was surely what had happened with Toby. He was jealous. That's why he attacked Barry. When did it happen?

His freshman year? So three years ago. A full year before Toby and Gwen even started dating.

I knew it was the wrong emotion to feel, but I was relieved.

Everything filled with color. Rich blues and reds. Flowers—a pastel pink. My dress and Barry's eyes were the only green in the entire room.

"Okay," I said, lying my head against his chest.

All the air in my body was sucked out, like someone had shoved a vacuum down my throat. *No. No. No. No.* How had I forgotten? He told me weeks ago about the night he lost his virginity—the night he was with Gwen. "*I don't remember.*"

Before he ever had a reason to lie to me.

Throwing the sheet off, I pushed to the edge of the bed. I was burning up and freezing at the same time. Somewhere in the back of my mind, I was aware of the house phone ringing.

"Gwen!" I yelled her name. She was staying downstairs in the guest bedroom. "Gwen!"

My family was moving around, so maybe it wasn't as late as I thought. I stormed down the stairs. Blood surged in my veins.

Gwen had just pulled a robe over her shoulders. She rubbed at her eyes with her knuckles.

I pushed her back against the door of the guest room. Her head smacked the frame. "Ow, Brittney Ann, what's the—"

"You said he raped you. That's what you said, right?"

She froze. "No, I didn't say that. I never said that."

My fingers knotted into tight balls. I'd never wanted to hit anyone so badly in all my life.

"Brittney…" her eyes widened in alarm. "I've said it all along that I didn't remember what happened that night. I hated him because he took advantage of the circumstance, but I never called it *rape.*"

"Why was that word used? Why was it even mentioned?"

Very subtly she glanced over my shoulder at my brother.

My soon to be *dead* brother.

I pounced at him, throwing my hands around his neck, trying to bring him to the ground. "You liar!" I screamed. "You lied to me!"

"Britt. Ow, dammit, Britt." With very little effort, he pulled both of my arms above my head and forced me to submit. *Ooohhho*, if that was supposed to make me feel better, it did not. I kicked and kicked…and kicked.

He growled. "What's the matter with you, screaming your head off at two in the morning."

"I just remembered!" I tried to kick between his legs.

He easily deflected. "Hey, if you want nieces or nephews, you won't do that again."

Ew. I pulled against his arms. *Useless.*

Stupid, overgrown Marine.

"Let me go!" I snapped. "You lied to me. You made me think he was bad. You made me turn against him. I love him, and you made me…"

Oh goodness, what must he think?

"Let me go! I have to call him. I have to go find him."

"That won't be necessary." Daddy's voice, even and controlled. Too controlled.

"I didn't lie," Toby seethed, pointing over me toward his fiancé. "I know Gwen. I know she wouldn't have given herself to him."

She groaned, rubbing her fingers against her eyes. "Toby, I was drunk. It was a long time ago."

His jaw flexed. "It doesn't matter; I know you. I know you better than anyone. The fact he didn't walk away when you were that intoxicated is proof enough. He shouldn't have done anything but take you home and tuck you into bed."

"That's what he did to me!" I gasped, slamming my fist against my chest. "That's what he did. He doesn't even remember what happened with Gwen. He was just as out of it as she was. You can't blame him. It happened. It wasn't either of their fault." This time my foot connected with his shin. He released me as he stumbled backward. Dad was given a full preview of Toby's foul mouth.

"Enough," Dad said. "That's enough. Everyone go get dressed. We're going to the hospital."

What? I hadn't even hit him that hard. He was already standing straight. He didn't even limp. "What's going on, Father?" He feigned a proper attitude now that his mouth had outed him. *Snot.*

"That was Duncan Prescott on the phone. From Italy." Daddy deliberately avoided looking at me. "Bex was taken to the hospital late last night. They called him, looking for an emergency contact. I guess she's been pretty out of it."

Oh no. I had to find Barry. I had to tell him. He'd need me with him when the news came in. "We have to go by his house."

Daddy shook his head. "I'm afraid Duncan called Barry first."

"What?" I gasped, rubbing at a numb spot on my chest. "He knows?"

And I wasn't even there to hold his hand.

"Barry didn't take it too well. Duncan tried calling him back, but his phone's going straight to voicemail...Brittney Ann!" Daddy called after me as I raced up the stairs. I had to get my phone. I had to call him. He'd answer for me.

My phone was buried under a layer of sheets. Untwisting it all, I sent the device flying in the air to land, unceremoniously, on the hardwood. Flopping off the mattress, I tumbled after it. Ringing twice, the call went to Barry's voicemail. I called four more times before Daddy stepped into my room. "Get dressed," he said.

I didn't argue.

We rode in silence.

Flashing lights could be seen a half mile before we reached the interstate—probably because of the luminescent glow off the wet pavement. "What's going on?" I gasped. "Daddy, what is it?"

He didn't have an answer. Daddy always had an answer.

An officer in a slicker stopped us from pulling onto the highway.

My stomach gurgled with anxiety. If they didn't let us onto the on-ramp, I would take off running. No way would they keep me from him tonight.

"Sir, the interstate's just closed down. Big pile-up. You'll have to go around."

Around? Oh, right. Yeah, that would be faster. I smacked Daddy's shoulder. "Ask about Barry. Ask if he's been here."

"Ow, Britt. You heard the man. The highway is closed."

"But there's traffic on there, right? What if he got on there before they stopped traffic? We have to go get him!"

The officer had already backed up and started waving his hand giving Daddy the go-ahead to turn around.

Toby whispered in my ear, "You really think some road block is going to stop him or that car?"

Fair point.

Barry would drive through the ditch, get off the interstate, and then he'd—in his words—*haul balls* to get to his mother. He'd never let a roadblock keep him from her.

Route-66 ran parallel to I-44. We had a perfect view of all the vehicles backed up, trying to get past the collision. It looked like two tractor trailers had fallen sideways onto each other and several—now unrecognizable vehicles—had ran straight up over the top of the trailers.

"I didn't see his car waiting in the traffic." My voice trembled.

Toby rubbed my shoulder. "He probably got turned around, just like us."

I folded forward on myself, tucking my head between my knees.

This whole time I was so worried about what would happen if he hurt me. I never even entertained the idea of being the one to hurt him. But I had. I had done the unthinkable.

That black Charger wasn't in the parking lot of the hospital. I know because I checked, and then I ran twice around the nearly empty area. "Brittney," Toby chased after me. "Brittney, stop this."

"He's not here," I mumbled, accepting the truth and then folding over myself so I could catch my breath and try to still the throb in my side.

"I know that." Sliding his arm around my waist, Toby led me back to the minivan, where both of my parents stared at me. Daddy clapped onto my shoulder and glanced over the top of my head. "Stay with her," he said to my brother, who nodded.

"Of course."

"It's okay," Toby assured me with a whisper out of the corner of his mouth. "He's stuck in traffic. He'll be here. It's fine."

Now he was contradicting himself. If Barry had gone through the median, then he would have beaten us here.

I was numb.

The Emergency Room was exactly as I remembered it the day I'd seen Barry carried in by his friends. The aroma of new carpet and sterile packaging brought on a sting of memories. Hugging my arms around my middle, I tried to keep myself together.

There were no restrictions on the amount of people they allowed into Bex's room because the Emergency Room wasn't even busy tonight.

Yet.

It wasn't three minutes after we walked into her room—she was asleep—that a nurse came in asking us all to stay put. "There was a bad pileup on the interstate. We're bringing in some of the survivors."

"Is there anything we can do?" Daddy asked, leaning forward in his seat. "I'm a pastor."

His words resonated. The nurse nodded and smiled just a little. "Just stay put," she repeated. "And pray."

Gwen, shuffling uncomfortably, excused herself. "I think I shouldn't be back here," she whispered. Toby agreed. And, honestly, so did I.

We tried to make our way into the waiting room before the doors opened and the stretchers came through.

We weren't fast enough.

Toby pushed me back against the wall. His body blocked my view, but he still demanded, "Close your eyes."

What? Clawing at his shoulder, I tried to see around him.

"Brittney Ann!" His voice was severe. "Do as I say."

There was only one stretcher. Only one ambulance. Despite all that had crowded at the highway. "Toby?" I gasped, already knowing the answer to the worst question I would ever ask. "Toby, who is that? Toby, tell me it's not…" My voice croaked. My fingers clawed at my brother's arm. "Tell me it's not him."

Before he could answer, I caught a glimpse of the patient's torn Don McLean T-shirt.

TWENTY SEVEN

BARRY

Seventy.

Seventy-five.

Eighty.

Eighty-six.

The accelerator lurched beneath my foot. I knew the Charger was giving me all she had, but it wasn't enough.

Ninety.

Ninety-four.

The hospital was in Sullivan, only six miles down the interstate. I should have been in Sullivan, too. The plan, all along, was that I'd stay with Mom when Dad was gone. I was supposed to crash at her apartment eating old take-out and Oreos for breakfast. She'd never cared about that stuff. She cared more about seeing me smile than seeing me eat a piece of fruit.

So what? That was my mom, and she was beautiful in her own way, and I loved her, and she couldn't die, because if she died, I'd be out of reasons *not* to kill myself.

That thought hit hard. Feeling entirely out of reasons to stay alive was the most numbing thought in the world. There's no pain, because pain comes with needing, or wanting, to live. Numbness precedes imminent death.

I was raw, from the tippy top of my head to the points of my biggest toes.

Ninety-nine.

One-hundred.

One-hundred and one.

She would make it, right? Overdoses didn't have long-term effects. They either killed you or they didn't, and if they didn't, you were okay. Right? *Right?* Why couldn't someone just answer that I was right? Why was I alone and pissed off at the world? Had I been such a bad person in my seventeen years that I deserved this sort of solitude?

Had I really screwed everything this perfectly?

One-oh-four.

Something flashed up ahead.

I let off the gas.

One-oh-one.

There was a screeching sound. More flashing. *Oh shit.*

I slammed on the brakes.

Eighty-four.

The back tires fishtailed.

I worked the wheel, regaining control of my girl.

Sixty-seven.

There were two tractor trailers stacked on top of each other. Behind them, cars had started a pileup. The pavement was still slick from days of rain and storm. I could feel the Charger's tires slipping and hydroplaning.

Fifty-two.

Forty—

⤳

Silence was the loudest noise ever.

Louder than the sirens and the crunching metal and the screaming and the pain…and even the numbness. Silence trumped it all. In
the seconds before my car smacked into the twisted-up piece of red
metal, my ears buzzed with the noisiest quiet there ever was.

Nothingness.

My eyes closed; my mind blanked. And I pictured the most beautiful girl in the world. A perfect girl. So perfect she, by all rights,
shouldn't exist.

I imagined the unicorn.

My body flung forward over the steering wheel. I wanted to close
my eyes and go back to that happy place with the perfect girl, but I
couldn't. I couldn't see her anymore, and I couldn't hear her voice,
and I couldn't remember how her lips felt.

Because everything was silent. Everything was blank.

And I knew I was dead.

I knew because there was a crushing pain on top of my thigh.
Someone was screaming blood-curdling yelps of pain, and it terrified me to think that that *someone* could be me.

I was going to the other place—the place she would never go. The
place where my friends would someday find me—for all the shit we'd
done, we were exiled there. But Brittney wouldn't ever come here.
She couldn't ever feel this pain.

Her thigh wouldn't be ripped in half, and she wouldn't have to
listen to the screaming or the silence. The never-ending, unrelenting
silence that Brittney wouldn't ever know because she was too good
to ever be exiled. *Good.*

There was a split second of apprehension when I took in everything. My eyes blinked open.

Straight in my line of sight was the red, crunched metal of that other car. An arm hung out the windshield. A bloody arm that could have been male or female, I couldn't tell. There was no body attached.

Then everything went black.

TWENTY-EIGHT

BRITTNEY ANN

It took a lot longer than it should have for me to calm down. I did the only thing I could think to do. I called the only person I could think of.

Tyler.

He stood in front of me, tossing his weight from foot-to-foot. He was angry. I didn't know why he was angry. He hadn't even asked about Barry yet. Not that I knew anything. No one would tell me squat.

After Toby physically hauled me into the waiting room and handed me a hot chocolate—that was now cold—I sat perfectly still. I'd only gotten up once, to retrieve my purse to call Tyler. That had been twenty minutes ago.

Now here he was.

"You don't know anything?" he spat.

Blinking up at him, I swallowed hard. "I'm not family. They won't even talk to me about him."

"Fucking bullshit," he hissed.

"Watch how you talk to my sister," Toby seethed.

"Fuck off," Tyler shot back.

"Please." I threw my arm out between the two of them. "Tyler, they let you go back there with him last time."

His eyes narrowed. "Last time?"

"When he fell off the cliff. Or when he jumped. Or whatever. You boys were all back there. So they'll let you. I can't even get into the emergency room now."

There may have been an episode of hysteria that I wasn't exactly proud of. I was okay now. My fingers tightened around the styrofoam cup. Yeah, I was okay. As long as I didn't move, or think about whatever pain he was in. My heart pulsed, and I forced an image of Barry's bloody face out of my mind.

Speaking between his teeth, Tyler's eyes shifted from me to Toby as he asked, "Can I talk to you for a minute…alone?"

I could tell my brother was going to protest, but if it would get Tyler back to Barry quicker, then I had to do it. I sat down my cup and stood on shaking knees as I walked around the matching brown pleather waiting room chairs.

My arms folded over my stomach as I met the semi-cool air outside. Glancing around, I noticed the parking lot had almost filled.

Tyler stepped past a shrub and I followed him, not paying attention to where we were walking.

A gasp of pine scented air froze in my throat as my back slammed into the brick wall. "Ah!"

My hair twisted several times around his tight fist. With a tug, my neck jerked backward so I was forced to look into the cold eyes that had never before terrified me like they did now.

Shoving my palm into his chest, I tried to push him away. He planted his body flat against mine, driving my back into the jagged bricks. "Here's how this is going to go…" His voice dripped venom.

A jolt of true fear raced through me.

"Don't fight me. Just listen. You messed up. You were a bitch when he needed you to be on his side. So you don't get to tell me what to do. You know why? Because he's my brother. And you're a dumb cunt who broke his heart. Don't ask about him. Don't come near him." With the index and middle fingers of his other hand, he hit against my temple. Tap. Tap. Tap. Tears froze in my eyes as I gasped at the pain.

Tyler's pelvis ground against my stomach. "You don't even get how special he'd have made you, doll face. You'd have been his fucking princess, but not now. Not anymore. So don't come around. Don't even let his name fly through your judgmental little head. Do you understand?"

I couldn't nod. His hold was too tight locked on the roots of my hair. "Yes," I gasped. But I wanted to argue. I wanted to tell him how wrong I had been.

I knew it *now*.

I needed Tyler not to be angry with me because I needed to get to Barry.

"Good." His fingers unknotted, and I fell to my knees, scraping my flesh on a hard pebble.

I breathed in a quick gasp, trying to find the words to tell Tyler he was wrong about me.

Kneeling down in front of me, he hissed, "Wipe your eyes and fix your pretty little dress. You tell your brother about this…" His tongue clicked against his teeth and then he shrugged. "Well, I don't really give a shit."

He walked back through the sliding doors ahead of me. I wasn't positive, but I thought he was whistling.

TWENTY-NINE

 BARRY

Beep.
     Beep.
          Beep.

There was an awful taste in my mouth, almost sulfuric. My nose itched. I knew, despite the idiotic amount of pain in my left leg, I was on pain killers.

My eyes flew open. "Fuck."

"Whoa, whoa, brother." Tyler caught my arm and pushed it back to the bed.

"What…" I started to sit up, and pain stabbed into every inch of me. "Uh." I fell back down.

"Just chill, alright. Relax. You're banged up pretty good."

"What?"

"You wrecked her." He shook his head. "There was a bad pileup. Couple people are dead. Looks like you caught the ass end of it, but they had to cut you out of our girl. Your leg…"

Then I felt it again. My leg was on fire. "Oh shit."

"Yeah, yeah, just stay still." He moved over me so he could hit a button on the wall.

A woman's voice crackled through a speaker. "Can I help you?"

"Yeah, my brother's up. He needs something more for pain."

"Be right in."

I had to lean up to look down at my leg. It was covered in plaster from the bottom of my toes all the way to my crotch. "What the fuck, Ty?"

"It's broken." He tapped the top part, above the knee. "Apparently, this is the most stubborn bone in the body, but your sweet little steering wheel showed it zero mercy. The doctors think it's not a bad thing. If you hadn't been pinned, you'd have flown out... Oh, and one other thing; I had to tell them we were brothers. They weren't going—"

The door slid open, and someone shuffled in.

I knew the drill.

The nurse carried a syringe full of clear liquid. The machine behind my head beeped excitedly as I watched her. "Do not stick me with that," I growled.

Tyler's eyes danced back and forth between the two of us. He forced a smile. "Bare, you already got an IV. She doesn't have to stick you, man."

I knew that. Even before the witch untwisted the needle and started for the clear cord, but that wasn't what I meant. "No," I said, letting out a pained breath. "I don't want it."

"Bare, man, you're really banged up. You—"

"I don't want it. Something non-narcotic. You bring anything in here with opiates in it, and I'm shoving it down your throat."

The lady blanched, pulling the needle-less syringe back toward her chest.

"He doesn't mean that," Tyler micromanaged, holding his palms up in the air. "He's just in a lot of pain, that's all."

The woman all but ran out of the room. I flopped back against the stretcher only to realize more than my leg ached. I hissed, and Tyler laughed at my idiocy. "Yeah, well, she won't come back now, sugar nipples. You'll be lucky not to get handcuffed after that little show."

"I don't want it."

"You're being stupid." He shook his head.

"My mom…"

"Yeah, no one can get ahold of her or your dad."

"No, she's here somewhere. She OD'd. This is where I was coming. Go find my mom."

"What? Holy shit." He marched to the door and threw it open. There was a lot of noise for a few seconds as he disappeared, and then there was nothing. I was alone in the brightest room in the history of hospitals.

Beep.

Wait. If Mom hadn't called Tyler…

Beep. Beep.

And Dad hadn't called him…

Beep. Beep. Beep.

The door slid open again. I didn't have it in me to sit up and look at him. Plus, I was saving all my energy for whatever he'd say about Mom. She was fine. Yeah, she was fine.

The last thing I expected was for Toby Wilson to pull a chair beside the bed and fall down into it.

"Will you die?" he asked around half-a-smile.

I groaned, only to realize even that action made me hurt. I winced and—news flash—it hurt. "You'd like that, wouldn't you?"

"I don't know." He sobered.

"Don't lie. Just because…" I twisted wrong, and a sharp pain stabbed through my side. Toby slid to the end of his chair and held out his hands like he was going to heal me with his touch.

"I don't wish you dead." He frowned. "Not anymore."

I waited. He'd not given me much of a reason to say anything, and I was still saving my energy for when Ty had any news on Mom.

Toby cleared his throat. Using his thumb and forefinger, he massaged his ear lobe for a few seconds. "Do you remember what happened with Gwen?"

I shook my head. An act which, yeah, hurt.

"Yes. I assumed as much from your reaction the other night. I…" He cleared his throat again like there was a massive frog in there trying to work its way out. "I suppose I overreacted. Gwen told me all along that she didn't remember, and I took that to mean the worst. I think I could have even been the one to convince her it had been something it might not have been. What I don't get is why you didn't simply tell me. You know, when I first hit you all those years ago, why didn't you just say that you hadn't done it, or that you didn't remember? It would have saved everyone a lot of heartache here."

"Seriously?"

I waited for him to nod one short, dignified nod.

"I thought you were pissed I hooked up with your girlfriend. I didn't know you thought I…" I couldn't say the word that was written on the magic paper and ignited—not to Saint Toby.

"Oh." His eyes widened. I hated that he had his sister's golden-green, almond-shaped eyes, and I hated that he sounded like her, too.

Once more, his throat cleared. This room was almost bursting with awkward. And that was before the door slid open and Tyler walked in, followed closely by the nurse with the needle. I leaned up ready to fight her if it came to it. "I said no—"

"Chill." Tyler held up his hands, his eyes danced back and forth between me and Toby, and the lines of his jaw flexed. "Chill brother," he said to me.

"It's non-narcotic," the nurse huffed. "'Fraid it won't help as much."

"Fine," I breathed. "That's fine."

The medicine went in slowly, but my vein still sizzled in relief. "Thank you," I mumbled.

"Mm-hmm," she mouthed. "Only supposed to be one visitor at a time."

Toby stood. The nurse left, but Toby lingered, eyeing his feet. "I hope you get to feeling better, Barry."

"I'm sure you do," Tyler spat.

"Dude." I shook my head at him.

He looked confused but, thankfully, sat back and kept his trap shut.

"Why are you here?" I asked Toby.

Palm cupping the back of his neck, he sighed. "Honestly? I have no clue. I know I'm going to regret telling you this, but Brittney... she doesn't believe it. Not anymore. I'm not sure she ever really did. She said you could never hurt anyone, and now Gwen believes her, and I'm the bad guy."

My heart raced, and to my embarrassment, the machine alerted the two of them to my reaction. I cleared my throat, trying to downplay it. "I mean, why are you *here*?"

Toby's eyes shot to Tyler, who answered for him. "They're with your mom."

"What?" I gasped

"They're in the other room with your mom." He squeezed my shoulder. "She's fine, by the way."

A breath of relief escaped my lungs. It felt like I'd been holding that in for hours. Or maybe weeks. "Fine?"

"Yeah. She took too many muscle relaxers and passed out at work," Toby said. "She's been asleep for a few hours. The hospital called your dad, who called us. He said you were pretty freaked out and was worried you'd do something stupid. You gotta give the man some credit—"

"He knows me."

CR

Tyler stayed the entire day in the hospital with me. Annoyingly, his foot tapped across the floor, and every time the nurse came in with the little cup of pills, rolling her cart and intently heading toward me, he jumped up and intervened. "He doesn't want pain killers," he said.

The woman rolled her eyes. "Say it again, boy. I heard you the first ten times."

Then she'd hand me the cup, scan the tag on my ID bracelet, and she'd hum some old song I didn't recognize. "They're not narcotic, I promise." She didn't sound very interested either way.

I tossed my head back and took the pills, knowing for a fact they weren't narcotic. I knew the shape and numb high caused by those pills. These were different.

Most importantly, I had no desire for them; they made me feel good, not high.

Tyler continued to tap his foot against the floor despite my begging for him to get lost. Nothing worked to get him out of my room. My knack for landing in the hospital always made him a little crazy, but his tapping toes was over-the-top. "You okay?" I finally asked.

He nodded, his head jerking up and down. "Yeah man, I'm fine."

A little later, after trying and failing to get her out of my head, I flopped against the bed and swore at the pain slicing through my thigh. "*Shit*. Where the hell is she? If she believed I didn't do it, then she should have come."

Tyler stared at me for a minute—a full goddamned minute—with his lips twitching like he had something he wanted to say. Then he tugged on that idiotic ultra-straight blond hair of his. "Don't know man. Maybe something came up. She'll come around. You'll see."

That was his story. I wasn't so sure I bought it, but I didn't have it in me to argue.

Tyler hung around until Dad and Ashleigh showed up and told him to go get some sleep. They took me home from the hospital that afternoon. Dad never apologized about what he'd said about Mom, though he kept going out of his way to make me feel comfortable.

He'd fluff my pillow under the cast—a monstrosity which I'd come to love and hate, mostly hate—and I'd knock the pillows down. Without complaint, he'd fluff them again. Only to have them knocked back down.

The final straw of my overly mature behavior, came when I insulted Ashleigh. She'd burnt frozen lasagna (a nearly impossible task, but somehow she'd managed), and I had to say something. Mostly because I was cranky and in pain and sad, so I took it out on her. "I know Dad didn't marry you cuz you can cook. Must be your fat ass that drew him in."

Her eyes welled, and Dad smacked me upside the head. "That's enough. Dammit, Barry. I'm done coddling you. I'm sick of it. You're hurt. You'll heal. Your mom is going to be fine. Now get the hell over yourself. I didn't mean anything by what I said on the phone, but still…" He took a deep breath. "I'm sorry. I shouldn't have said it."

I wanted to tell him he sucked at apologizing, but he didn't. He really didn't. "Okay."

"Okay?" He asked slowly, taking a step back like I was a wild animal ready to attack him, and he didn't want to get too close.

I shrugged. Toying with a loose string on my oversized shorts, I didn't look at him. "Yeah, okay, it's fine. You didn't make her take the pills, you didn't make me wreck. You're right. I'm being a baby."

After that, I wallowed around on my bed, barely getting up to hobble toward the bathroom. The week passed.

Until Tyler showed up on Friday afternoon. Tearing the covers off the top of me, his nose wrinkled. "Sugar, you stink. Get your ass up and shower."

"I can't. I have a—"

"Then take a fucking sponge bath, cuz you're coming to the game."

"Am not.

"Are too. I have reinforcements ready if it comes to dragging you out of this house."

"You're an asshole," I grumbled.

He grinned. "You still love me."

"I don't think I do."

"Yes, you do. We're BFFs for life."

"You're an idiot," I groaned, sitting up and stretching. My body hurt so freaking bad. Lying unmoving for so long with bruises wasn't smart. "You can't be best-friends-forever for life. That's just dumb."

He smiled wider. "Come on, babe. You know you love me."

I didn't. I hated him. I hated everything.

I washed my hair using the detachable showerhead and leaned over the tub to take the coldest, half-shower in history.

Mostly, I'd spent the week in my boxers. They were easy to get out of, but to slide back into a clean pair, I usually needed help. Let's just say Ashleigh and I were a lot closer than I'd ever dreamed. I didn't want to be that close to Tyler, so I MacGyver'd myself into a clean pair using the toes of my right foot to pull them up the cast.

In hindsight, I should have been doing this all along. Ashleigh hadn't been able to look me in the eye since Monday.

Tyler was leaned over the back of my desk chair. "Here," he said, when I hobbled back into the room. He tossed me a plain white

T-shirt and my jersey. Leaning on my crutch, I caught it all against my chest.

"I'm not—"

"Man, do not make me dress you. Just put it on. Thanks to your pretty ass taking so long, I'm running late."

I got dressed, but not because he'd told me to. The jersey fit loose around my shoulder without padding. "Am I not wearing pants?" I said. The idea of wearing a pair of oversized sweats—the only thing that would fit over the cast—to the game made me cringe. I did not want to do that. In fact, I wouldn't. That would be the final straw.

Tyler turned, holding a pair of cut jeans in his hands. One of the legs was completely obliterated. "Tell me those aren't mine," I snapped and attempted to lunge at him.

He sidestepped easily. "Ah ah ah. Don't hurt yourself, sugar tits. Of course they're yours. Your fatass couldn't fit into mine, and Bo didn't want his pants cut. There was no other choice. Sorry Bare. Sacrifices had to be made." He threw them at me, and they landed on the ends of my fingers.

Oh man, these were my favorites. My lucky jeans. The ones I'd been wearing when Arnel Pineda signed one of my favorite T-shirts.

Blue jeans weren't boxers. My toe wouldn't have been able to pull them up. Without another thought, I dropped the ruined jeans to the ground. "You have to help me put them on." The last bit of my dignity coiled into a ball and shriveled up to die.

Tyler didn't say anything. I wouldn't ever tell him how much it meant to me that he didn't taunt me, but it was better that things went unsaid. When we talked about shit, that's when it got awkward.

It was a long, torturous journey down the stairs. I shuffled into Tyler's backseat. Sliding backwards across the cloth, I had to sit the length of it so my leg could stretch out. Tyler watched me with a muscle by his temple popping in and out. "Is this going to hurt you?"

he finally asked.

Now he was worried about that? After I'd ass-scooted down the last four steps and ninja'd my way into the backseat? *Yeah, great timing, Ty.* "Dude, I'm fine. Go."

He hesitated. Leaning just far enough back that my foot couldn't reach him. "I have something I have to tell you."

"Okay?"

"Last week, when you were in the accident..." he hesitated.

"Man, do not make me drag this out of you. Just say it."

He leaned back and rubbed over his face. "Okay, so you were in the accident. The only reason I knew was because Brittney called me. She was hysterical. Her family was at the hospital with your mom. I guess they'd made it to the hospital ahead of you in the ambulance, and she watched them drag you in on the stretcher."

The worst part of what he was saying was that I could imagine my sweet Brittney. I could picture her horrified face as she watched me. "Okay..."

"She called me, and I was pissed, okay? I was mad because she knew before me, and I was mad that she was even there. She had no right being there after she fucked you over."

"Why?"

"I don't know. She was freaking out, man. She wasn't making a lot of sense. Which is why, I guess, she didn't tell me your parents didn't actually call her about you. I had no clue she was already *there* when they brought you in. I thought whoever called her thought of her before me, and it just lit me on fire, dude. I practically flew to the hospital. I..."

"Wait. Why're you telling me this now?"

"Just wait, I'm getting there." He blew out a heavy breath before continuing. "Anyway, uh, you were out of it, and they wouldn't let anyone see you. She...oh God, you're gonna kill me. Look man, I just, I thought she abandoned you, okay? It wasn't like with Annie. You know what I mean?"

"I have no clue what you mean." But my knuckles curled because this was Tyler, and I knew him better than anyone. It had to be pretty bad if he couldn't even say it.

He breathed again. His lined face radiated a sliver of the agony I'd been in these past few weeks. "Annie found out I cheated on her, she basically walked in on me, and she still didn't believe it. That's how much she trusted me. Brittney...she...well, she didn't have any damn faith. She was supposed to stand by you and have your back and—"

"Ty?"

"And she turned against you. She didn't defend you. How hard would it have been to tell her brother to fuck off, you know?"

"Tyler!"

He tugged his hair back off his forehead with both hands. "I... it's..."

I leaned forward. Blood raced through my veins. "Fuck! Tyler! Tell me what you did!"

He met my gaze. His bloodshot eyes pulsed with agony. "I pulled her hair," he whispered.

"Huh?"

"Not a little. A lot. I, uh, I yanked her hair. I told her to stay the hell away from you. I didn't know Toby was going to come in and tell you all the stuff he did. I didn't know she believed you didn't do it. Of course you didn't, but I didn't know. Do you believe me, Bare? I really didn't know, and you were all banged up, and she was just there. Vulnerable and upset and I...I don't even know what came over me. I pulled her hair. I got in her face."

The image of Brittney's strawberry hair knotted around Tyler's knuckles made me see red. "Drive." I fell back against the door.

"Dude…"

"Drive," I snapped.

He walked around the car, hands in his pockets, shoulders hunched.

When he crawled into the driver's seat, I dove at him. Falling onto the floorboard, my leg instantly burned, but my hands tightened around his neck. "How could you?"

His forearm slid between his neck and the crook in my elbow, keeping me from killing him. "Chill," he choked.

I chilled, but not because he told me to. He wouldn't drive if I killed him, and I needed him to get me there. "I'm pulling Ann's hair."

"No! That's stupid. This is my fault; take it out on me."

"Nope, it's decided. I'm doing it." If ever there had been a question about my maturity, it was just answered. I deadlifted my ass back into the seat, pulling the heavy cast up with me.

After a second of letting Tyler suffer, thinking I'd actually be able to catch Ann with my leg bound up, I huffed. "Fine. I'm not, but you're fixing this."

"I know. I plan to. Honestly, I thought she'd come talk to you anyway. That's why I didn't say anything. I really thought she'd—"

"Ty, shut the fuck up and drive."

The east parking lot was almost full by the time we got there. Still, Tyler drove around twice. "What're you doing? Just park."

He caught my eye in the rearview. "I was trying to find something closer."

For me.

I shook my head. Staying mad at my brother-friend was impossible. "Park," I demanded.

"You're sure?"

"Yeah. You're late anyway."

He glanced at the dash. "Fuck," he hissed, and then pulled into the first available spot we came to. "Shit, shit, shit," he kept saying. "Coach is gonna kill me."

He walked twice around the vehicle, grabbing all his stuff, then he yanked open the driver's door and peeked his head in. "Dude, I gotta go. You got this?"

"I got this," I said, but I sat with my head leaned back against the glass of the backseat window.

The sun started to set, and there was a booming of the marching band before I began the awkward shuffle out of the car. By now, the team would have taken the field. I wouldn't have to deal with any actual sympathetic looks from my classmates or half-ass-sympathy from underclassmen.

That had been a vain hope.

Almost everyone in the bleachers stared at me as I crutched across the track, trying not to make any noise, which was impossible. The gossip hungry small towners all shifted in their seats to get a good look at the guy who'd survived the fatal accident. If I had a free middle finger, I'd have flipped it at them.

I wanted to climb all the way to the top of the bleachers to make it nearly impossible for them to watch me. My leg already ached though, and going any further than the small opening at the front bleacher was unrealistic.

My hands out behind me, I found the cool bleachers as I sat down. I scanned the sidelines.

My heart turned to melted butter inside my chest.

Standing with fifteen bouncing cheerleaders, Brittney wasn't moving at all. Her thin lips hung open as her hazel-golden eyes blinked rapidly. Whatever emotion she was trying to hide, it stayed hidden.

I rubbed my palm over my chest as I attempted to keep that stubborn beating organ in place. It amazed me that so much shit could happen inside my body that couldn't even be seen on the outside.

Someone tapped her arm, and she turned, going back to doing a half-hearted cheer.

I eyed my Converse. This would be easier if we didn't get into another one of those stare-offs. Kicking a rock back and forth with the dirty toe of my shoe, I listened to the game. Because there was so much crowd noise, I had no clue what was actually happening out there.

And I was too big of a coward to look up and see.

A pair of white cheer shoes stepped between my Converse and the cast.

"Hello, Barry."

Her voice trembled. Silky, white legs disappeared beneath the royal blue skirt that was made for her.

I looked back to the other cheerleaders. They sucked at pretending they weren't watching us. "Britt?" What I meant to ask was if she was going to get in trouble with the other girls. I wanted to know how she was doing. I wanted to know if she missed me or thought about me or if I had affected her at all.

Her name seemed so much more important than any of that. And I didn't have enough air in my lungs to say anything else.

Her fingers twisted up under her hair, under her pony tail. "I... oh, this is silly. I've been very worried about you, and I wanted to call."

"But Tyler asked you *nicely* not to."

Her eyes widened in surprise. "Yes, something like that."

"Yeah, don't worry. I'm getting him back for that. My plans are somewhere between Nairing his eyebrows and waxing his legs."

She smiled, almost convincingly. "That's not necessary. I'm fine. Besides, he had a right to be upset. Some of the things he said were true. I did abandon you—"

"No..."

"Barry," she sighed, warning that she wanted to finish. "I did. For no reason whatsoever, I let the smallest thing break my faith. You've got a past that makes you seem untrustworthy, but you've never been anything but good to me. I shouldn't..." Tears welled in her beautiful eyes. She hurried to blink them away. I struggled to stand. Dammit. Stupid fucking leg. She was crying, and I couldn't even get to her to wipe her pretty eyes.

A hand caught under my elbow, pulling me to my foot.

Toby smiled. Twisting, so he could whisper into my ear, he said, "I'm hoping you're going to make sure she never cries again. It's really annoying listening to your baby sister cry."

"It's your fault," I mumbled back.

He winced. "Yeah, no one's perfect. Just so you know, I still don't love the idea of this."

With full blown crocodile tears dripping down her cheeks Brittney shoved at him. He stumbled backward. As a result, I wobbled. Brittney threw her arms out, catching onto my shoulders. Then she scowled at her brother. "Oh, I'm sorry Barry. I am. Toby, you just go away!"

He put up his hands and took a step back. "Trying to help."

"You've done enough," she snapped.

Could she be any cuter? I caught her face in my hands, swiping my thumbs over her pink cheeks. Struggling to keep the crutches under my arms, I kissed tears on each cheek, moving slowly toward her lips. Our mouths hovered but didn't touch.

"Barry," she caught my wrists. "I have to apologize."

"Okay," I said, letting my body remember the familiarity of her. I needed this.

I *needed* Brittney. More than I'd ever needed any painer.

I was the kind of guy who needed to depend on something, and Brittney was the kind of girl who needed someone to depend on her.

Why else would she volunteer and teach Sunday School and do all that other good shit? We balanced each other.

"Barry, I'm serious. You can't just forgive me before I apologize. I need to grovel and beg."

"Get to it," I said, letting my lips find the corner of her mouth. Maybe my favorite corner. Nope, the other one tasted just as good.

She giggled. "Barry!"

"What?"

Her lashes fluttered, landing on her cheeks. "I haven't begged."

"You don't have to. You had every right to think I was a scumbag. I do have a bad reputation, and you're wrong—you have been hurt by it before. I stood you up, remember? That boy who stood you up was the same one with Gwen that night. Britt, I can't swear to you what happened with her, I really can't. I can only tell you that I don't *think* I did anything like that, and I promise you I'd never do anything to hurt you. I'd die before hurting you."

Her arms twisted around my back. "I know."

"You know?"

"Yes," she nodded matter-of-factly. "My family is big on second chances, but third…not so much. My daddy probably will kill you if I cry myself to sleep again."

I swallowed the knot in my throat. "You've been crying that much?"

Her eyes rolled. "I'm sad without you, Prescott. I admit it. I kind of like you."

"Kind of?" I'm a jerk. I needed to hear her say it.

"Okay, I love you."

"I love you, too."

Her eyes widened. "I know you do. You've never said it, but I know."

"Oh yeah?"

"Yeah, the first time I was in the Charger, you said it wouldn't hurt *me*, and I know you loved your car, so you should have been telling me not to hurt *it*. It was the other way around. It's silly." She blushed. "I had a feeling you loved me then, or I hoped."

I kissed the end of her nose. "That makes no sense at all."

"I know." She laughed. The other cheerleaders were giving her hell because their formation was off and it was almost end of the first quarter. I watched her go before struggling to sit back on the bleachers.

There were men beside me who hadn't been there before.

Mitch chomped on his popcorn. I didn't know who had taught this guy how to torture people, but he was a master at it. "You kiss my daughter again like that in public, and I will have to do something about it." His voice was low, presumably so the world wouldn't know what a scary ass pastor he was.

I gulped. "Uh, technically—"

"Did you just *uh* me?"

Fear tickled my spine.

"Dad!" Toby laughed once. "Sorry about him, Barry." His arm wrapped around my shoulder. "But seriously, if you hurt her, I will kill you. I have a gun. I know how to use it. And I have a lot of friends who are screwed up enough to help me hide your body."

"You two are the worst Christians I've ever met."

"That's what I keep telling them." A soft feminine voice giggled.

"Gwen?"

"In the flesh."

I scooted to the edge of the bleacher, so my ass nearly fell off. "I'm sorry," I said. "I really don't remember what happened, but I don't think I hurt you. I'm not apologizing for that. If I apologize, it means it happened, and I don't think it did. I'm sorry I left you there like I did. I woke up and bailed, and if I'd just hung around and talked to you the next morning, none of this would have happened. It didn't occur to me until recently what could have been done to you while you were lying alone in that room."

She stared at me, not blinking. "Thank you, Barry."

Then she leaned back and wrapped her hand around Toby's fist. "Are you satisfied?" she asked him.

He shrugged. "I still don't like him." He stared out at the field like I wasn't even sitting there. "But Brittney doesn't care what I think."

Mitch's arm went around my shoulder, over the top of Toby's. They were holding me down. I caved under the weight of the appendages, though I tried not to let them see me shrink.

"We're clear?" Mitch said. "No hurting my little girl."

"Never."

Brittney turned and gave me a smile. Her palm flattened over her chest. A sign I instantly returned. *I love you.*

We all watched the game. It was one of many benched games that would rush together because the jersey-clad figures on the field were never where my eyes focused. She was the center of my world—my addiction.

THE END

ACKNOWLEDGEMENTS

Mom, because this book, like the one I wrote before, is the best book you've ever read, you are my very best friend.

I know I've never had a chance to tell them, but to the McCartys. There was a time when you invited me into your immaculate home and welcomed me like family. Though I didn't know it then, I know it now. You inspired the Wilson family. The kindness at their core to the love they show to others came from what I saw in your beautiful family.

My best friends are better than any other best friends. Amber, Diana, and Rachel. I know that being my friend is difficult sometimes because I never answer the phone, but you've stuck with me all these years. More than that, you've been there for me. You may not have understood why I locked myself in the basement to write out a story for the voices that spoke to me, but you never doubted me and you never questioned me (except about when I'm getting married and having babies, but I think that was a legit concern).

Mrs. Rennaker, thank you sooo much for looking over this and not judging me because my mouth is much fouler than it was when I was in high school. I learned a lot in those afternoons preparing for the plays you directed. Mostly, I learned to be myself and to never give up on something I wanted. In many ways this series is complete because a teacher saw a girl who hadn't ever acted a day in her life, and she gave her the lead. Dreams do come true. You taught me that.

Ellie at Move to the Write (www.movetothewrite.com) and Anita at RacePoint (ww w.race-point.com), you're both absolutely amazing. And finally, thank you to Scott Crawford for letting me use a photo of your amazing car!

ABOUT THE AUTHOR

A. C. Land has been a lover of stories since she first read about Peter Pan giving Wendy an acorn and teaching her to fly. She always dreamed of telling big stories about small towns.

Residing on a farm in the rural Midwest, A. C. loves playing with her rambunctious dogs, Charlie and Riley, making decorative cakes, taking pictures, and drinking flavored coffee.

A NOTE ON ADDICTION

January 16, 2005 1:45 PM. That's the day and time my father died. He died of a stroke at the age of 41. I was sixteen.

He did not have a bad heart, or cancer, or any disease that would deteriorate his body or organs. He had a monkey on his back. It's very real. And those who do not have it do not understand the draw of it. Never let someone tell you that addiction is not a disease because I have watched it deteriorate families and whittle away at those that I love.

Addiction doesn't just kill people. It steals, it robs you blind even though it wishes it could love you more. Addiction choses pills, needles, and pipes even though it does not want to. Addiction takes everything and it is not sorry.

Do you know what else addiction is?

It's not there.

My father never watched me star in my first high school play. Or graduate high school. He never held my nephews (his grandchildren). He never knew that I wrote a book, and published it, and then dedicated it in his memory.

We have a beautiful thing in this life and it's called choices. On July 7, 2007 my mom took a new last name and Jeff became my stepdad. If anyone ever wondered where the inspiration for Mitch came from it was this horribly traumatizing man right here. I still have nightmares about all of the boys he ran off. I was very young when he came into my life and chose my mom and me.

I think too often we dwell on what Addiction takes away and not what we're given back. So to the man that chose to sit through hours of my horrible high school acting, my graduation, adopting three little boys who weren't even his, and has waited all this time to see these books in print these are also for you dad.

www.ingramcontent.com/pod-product-compliance
Lightning Source LLC
Chambersburg PA
CBHW020244200626
46816CB00001BA/122